DREAM OF TIME

DREAM OF TIME

NANCY J. PRICE

SYNCHRONISTA LLC

GILBERT, ARIZONA

Access ebook versions, bonus content & more at DreamOfTime.com

Published by Synchronista LLC

P O Box 2586 | Gilbert AZ | 85299

Web: synchronista.com

This book is a work of fiction. Any references to historic events, real people or real locations are used fictitiously. Other names, characters, places and events are products of the author's imagination, and any resemblance to actual characters, places, events and/or people, living or dead, is entirely coincidental.

Dream of Time
Nancy J. Price
Synchronista LLC
© Copyright 2013 by Nancy J Price
ISBN-10 0989390918
ISBN-13 978-0-9893909-1-0

Contents

1: From darkness	1
2: Back in the now	2
3: Gone again	3
4: The Now – Dream or not?	4
5: The third day	7
6: The Now – A good day	11
7: Out and about	13
8: Discovering this world	17
9: The Now – To accept the impossible	24
10: Getting ready to go	27
11: My house	30
12: The Now: Sweet home Oakland	36
13: My first day alone	37
14: The new me	43
15: The Now – Holding on to the Now	45
16: Proving it to myself	47
17: Clothing differences	50
18: Going downtown	54
19: All turned around	60
20: The Now – Proof	68
21: Who's there?	69
22: Making my report	73
23: Golden	76
24: Hair today, mess tomorrow	79
25: January 23, 1900	82
26: Knock knock	86
27: The can-do girl	88
28: Superhero how-to	93
29: Doing it wrong	96

30: My new hobbies	98
31: Like peanut butter & jelly	106
32: The first half of February	114
33: The Now – Wrong number	119
34: Newsworthiness	122
35: Something old, something new	123
36: Good news or bad?	129
37: Gone	135
38: The test	136
39: The Now: Searching for the answer	141
40: The Now – Of questions and answers	145
41: Taking care of business	151
42: The Now – Wrinkles in time	153
43: Funny money	156
44: My so-called social life	162
45: Party on, Wayne	170
46: One step forward, two steps back	176
47: Past meets present	184
48: The waiting	191
49: The Now – Trip to SF	194
50: It's pure dynamite	199
51: Why ask why?	206
52: Can't touch this	211
53: Time Scene Investigation	215
54: On the inside	223
55: Gossip girl	229
56: The Now – Summer begins	237
57: Beside the seaside	240
58: Fairy godmothers	248
59: The Now & the Then – Of fairy tales	252
60: The view from here	260
61: A world of changes	267
62: The heart of the matter	273
63: The Now – Bad mommy	280
64: The chessboard	283

65: Pies and surprise	289
66: The Now: Pearl's legacy	295
67: Intent	302
68: Predictions	307
69: The Now – Being there	312
70: The letter	315
71: Reverse	320
72: Surveillance	325
73: A silver dollar	330
74: The Now – The new picture	337
75: The Now: No options	341
76: The Now: Live in the present	344
77: Rise and shine	351
78: Looking for a Pearl	354
79: Here there be dragons	359
80: Lost	371
81: Messages	376
82: Can you dig it?	382
83: Curiouser and curiouser	386
84: A is for answer	388
85: Behind the curtain	391
86: Messages from the past	397
87: The Long Goodbye	405
About the author	411
Notes & thanks	412

For my father, Gary Robinson
San Francisco born & bred
and who always knows the answers

1: *From darkness*

Gunshots. Shouts. The roar of an explosion. Those were the sounds that came out of nowhere, and made me open my eyes.

The moment I did, my entire world was filled with shimmering arcs of color, each bursting out of a backdrop of a velvety black. I couldn't tell what I was seeing, but my mind insisted on trying to decode the blurry images. Was I was witnessing a plane crash, or were those red, blue and yellow lights on some kind of crazy spinning Christmas tree? At that very moment, neither seemed impossible.

Teetering on the narrow edge of consciousness between being awake and not, I struggled to take in as many impressions as possible. There were occasional shouts, some whispers, and a variety of smells — mostly ammonia, alcohol... and maybe some iodine. Bright lights, some dimmer glows... and I could just make out a jumble of horns and whistles and shouts. And me — physically? That was easy to describe: I hurt absolutely *everywhere*.

As the colors popped and sizzled, I had to fight harder and harder to stay aware of my surroundings. But before I could make sense of what I was seeing, a silhouette of a man intruded on my Lite-Brite view, and, slightly panicked, my mind decided this would be a good time to surrender.

Before my heart could flutter even once more, I was awake. I opened my eyes to see tiny toes wearing Princess Pink nail polish pressing up against my ribs. My favorite five-year-old was sprawled sideways across the bed, snoring softly, deep in a sleep I hoped was more peaceful than mine.

2: Back in the now

I know most people think of sleep as a soothing respite from a busy day. They'd say it was calming. Restful. Refreshing. That wasn't the case for me. I got to put a big X in the "None of the above" box when it comes to describing my own experience of nighttime shut-eye.

For as long as I can remember, my dreams have been vivid — wild, strange and often stressful nighttime delusions. Those dreams always felt real when I was in them, but were totally surreal in retrospect.

But something got switched up recently, and I don't know why. My dreams have gone from being normal nighttime sleep fantasies to feeling like actual, factual experiences, even after I wake up. Most of my impressions, though, have been hazy at best. Realistic, yes, absolutely — but muffled and faint, like my head was stuffed in a paper bag while the party was going on around me.

In the gentle light of day, I could translate certain aspects of the past night's experience using common sense. The bright explosions were, in all likelihood, something like fireworks — and if that was correct, I was watching them through a window five or six stories high. And the overwhelming aromas? They reminded me of my high school chemistry class.

Of course I realized none of that was even remotely logical. Nobody had set off fireworks anywhere near here for months, I live on the second floor, and all the windows in this place look out over tall trees. The only kind of lab I'd visited during the past twenty years was to get blood drawn, and those places smelled more of bleach than anything else.

So far, though, nothing was ringing alarm bells, or making me think I should somehow take these sensations more seriously. These little bursts of fantasy were odd and notable even as just what anyone would have assumed them to be: dreams.

3: Gone again

The smell would always hit me first, but the ammonia, alcohol and urine aroma subsided more and more quickly with each visit, thankfully. At least it was helpful as a confirmation I had arrived... even if I didn't know where I was.

This day was hazy again, and although I was more alert to what was going on around me, I couldn't open my eyes. I was doped up on something so crazy, I imagined hearing little tiny fairies tying even tinier weights to each one of my eyelashes, which is why my eyes were stuck closed.

Even though I was loopy, I could still feel some other not-so-pleasant things. It took me a while to realize I had a killer headache, and my throat was really sore. To make it more interesting, every time I tried to talk, I felt like gagging, and no sound even came out. Most of the time, though, the pain kind of stood off to the side and didn't really get in the way of me dancing around la-la-land.

Somehow, I contentedly amused myself for hours on end — singing songs in my head and re-imagining various movie plots. I think I slept away most of the day, judging from the different intensities of light filtering through my eyelids catching my attention from time to time.

And then, blessedly, the dream was done, and I was back where I belonged.

4: The Now – Dream or not?

I've often had recurring dreams, but this was getting to be something entirely different. Now, I was having a serialized dream — I only needed to tune into the sleep channel for a new episode every night.

Twice a week, there were three things I particularly dreaded about the mornings: Getting out of bed, putting on clothes, and forcing myself to walk down to the gym. The silver lining of the angst derived from my weird dreams was that I got all of that accomplished without even cursing the workout gods.

Upon arriving at the gym, looked around for Vivian, an old friend who had turned out to be the perfect workout buddy. The girl loved exercising, never met a weight machine she didn't like, and wouldn't let me escape this smelly place until I put in at least a solid hour of huffing and puffing.

She was adjusting her heart rate monitor when I sidled up to her. She glanced at me briefly before saying, "You look like crap." Viv was never one to mince words.

"I haven't been sleeping well," I said, and she nodded knowingly. "I told you: Too much caffeine."

"No, no, no — that's not it. I've been having dreams…"

"How is this news?" she cut in. Stopping people mid-sentence is just one way she amuses herself. "Have you never had a dream before?"

"I didn't finish that sentence, Schmivian," I laughed as I laced up my right (way too expensive but supposedly fabulous) shoe. "I have been having really intense dreams. Wild dreams. Dreams that seem every bit as real as what we're doing right now, even when I wake up."

"Oh, *those* kind of dreams," she said, nodding. "You're single, Robin. Not surprising to have a little nighttime fantasy action."

"No, not that kind of dream. You have a one track mind, you know that?"

She put out her hands in a "What can you do?" gesture. Then she gave me her real answer. "Hey, well, yeah — you're an intense person, and I'm sure your dreams are intense most of the time. You just don't always remember them, that's all," she said, with a shrug and a wave of her hand. "I know what it's like! I've even fallen in love in a few of my dreams, and for a few days, I can't stop thinking about the girl." She downed the last of her water, then tossed the bottle into her bag. "Usually the girl is some beautiful soap star, so there's not any question about whether or not it's real."

I forced a smile. *She doesn't get it, and I sound like an idiot who can't stop talking about herself. And then talks to herself about herself.*

Fortunately, before I got too meta, Vivian interrupted my train of thought. "So what do you think it means?"

Maybe she does get it. A little.

I squeezed my foot into the left shoe and bent over to tie it. "I guess that depends on how I am going to think about this. Either I just have a wild imagination, or it's a message or something. Like there's something I'm supposed to learn."

"My money's on the first one," Viv snorted, then raised her eyebrows up and down a couple times. "Or maybe those little pills you're taking aren't just multivitamins. Hmm?"

For the next half hour, as I labored to jog nowhere on the treadmill, I also obsessed. Could it be something I was eating, or related to something in the environment? The whole Bay Area was often more smoggy than foggy. Maybe those days where I walked in the "fresh" air from place to place were hurting more than they helped.

So what about my food? I loved ethnic cuisine — the more authentic the better — and happily devoured everything from sushi to Tandoori to some lovely gooey Camembert. Therefore, ingredients from several different continents had made their way into my body, along with, erm, more than a couple extra pounds.

The more I thought about these possibilities, the more my intuition told me to dismiss them, because the most likely (though admittedly least exotic) culprit was probably my typical stress level.

Before I had kids, a colleague — himself a type A+ personality — said that on a scale of 1 to 10, I could be about a 12 in terms of intensity. It seemed true enough at the time, and I wore the label as a sort of badge of honor. Motherhood had tempered it a bit, and the divorce tweaked it some more. Still, there were days I got so wound up, it seemed like I was carrying around two fifty-pound weights on my shoulders.

Now was one of those times. The irony was that the whole exercise thing was supposed to help me manage my stress levels... but to be honest, it was a diversion at best. Today, nagging the crap out of me constantly was the need to decide if I was dreaming, or if something else was going on here.

Believe me: I wasn't trying to make this into something it wasn't. I was just trying to *understand*. Since I'd never been able to steer or otherwise control my dreams, I didn't particularly want them to become real. I just hoped they would gently fade away like usual, and, if anything, leave me with some lingering sense of happiness or purpose, or solve some problem. In my book, that's what dreams are for.

And if that wasn't the case... well, I'd cross that bridge when I had no other choice. Because right now, to consider there was something more to this situation might mean a panicky, overwhelming feeling would start to crawl into my chest... and that was something I'd do almost anything to avoid.

5: The third day

As usual, the first few minutes were really fuzzy — a lot like when you wake up slowly and you're not sure if a sound you heard was real or imagined. Then came this terrible strong whiff of ammonia, which snapped me awake in an instant. And there, not three inches away from my face, was one absolutely enormous eye. I gasped, shut my eyes, and everything faded to black.

Hardly a second later I was awake once more, overwhelmed again by the horrible ammonia smell. Though I didn't really want to look around, curiosity got the best of me, and my eyes cooperated by actually opening.

Asleep or awake, I didn't know, but I did see four people hovering over me. Three were young women, wearing white dresses and matching caps, and one was a short and paunchy man — probably about the age of all the girls put together — who had a white coat on over his clothes.

It felt like I was flat on my back and didn't have any strength to speak of. Without even moving my arms, I could feel the edges of a mattress, so I could tell I was on a really narrow bed. Was it a kids' cot? Military issue?

"The smelling salts worked that time, doctor."

"Indeed," the man grunted. Without looking up from the chart in his hands, he asked, "What do you remember?"

I couldn't tell if he was talking to me, so I didn't say anything.

The doctor glanced at me then yelled to the nurse standing two feet away, "Smelling salts!" The woman started to move her hand toward my face and my arms decided to start working. I grabbed her before she got the ammonia stuff near my head again, telling her in a tiny voice, "Please, no! I'm awake!" Unsaid: Stick that god-awful stuff in my face one more time, and I'll hurl it across the room.

Dismissing the nurse from that duty with a curt nod, he looked at me and asked me again, enunciating each word very clearly, as if deafness was the issue here. "*What... do... you... remember?*"

I had no idea what he was hoping I'd say. If it was about the last thing I remembered, well, did he honestly want to hear about my kids dropping a metric ton of glitter on the carpet last night?

I gave in and asked the stupid question. "About what?"

The dude actually rolled his eyes. "As to why you are here, of course." Just to underscore his impatience, he added a little huff at the end of the sentence.

In addition to the worst headache in the history of ever, I felt odd and floaty and had a hard time stringing two thoughts together. Whatever meds they had me on provided a nasty reminder of some surgery a few years back — especially the slow and incredibly queasy recovery period.

As if on cue, I felt my stomach lurch. More now than ever, I was in no mood to play twenty questions — especially in my own dream.

"I don't know," I croaked. "Get to the point." Every word I spoke felt like a spear tip was being sunk in my throat.

His eyes bugged out a little bit, and the nurses looked away... but I swear I saw one of them trying to hide a smile.

Given that there was no reply to my question, I realized I'd have to coax information out of these people.

"Please. What? Don't remember." Again, the truth. I looked around the poorly-lit room to see lots of beds, about half of them with people out like a light and tucked up tight. "Where?"

I was pretty sure I wasn't in Kansas anymore.

"The police brought you here. This is a hospital of sorts." Now *that* made sense, though this place was pure retroville. It had been designed in some throwback style that wasn't really half bad, if a little clinical. The bland white tile walls and gray floors were accented only by gauzy drapes hanging from bars suspended from the ceiling between the beds. The whole setup was probably cheap to build and maintain — cheap, of course, being the requirement for everything nowadays.

The doctor drew himself up as tall as his squat little form would let him, and gave me a chilly look from over the top of his wire-rimmed glasses. "You took a nasty fall, and suffered head injuries."

When the last of his words tumbled out, I was still processing the first statement. I *fell*? How? Where? Had my daughters been there? My thoughts were so muddled, I forgot it was just a dream, and started to feel a little panic attack coming on.

He just looked at me as I was starting to hyperventilate, and decided to ignore me. He handed the chart to one of the nurses and said, "The ladies will answer your other questions. I must tend to my other patients." With that, he chugged off.

The nurses looked nearly as happy to have the old guy gone as I did.

The three of them weren't wearing ID badges, but, too tired to bother asking their names — I would just forget them in about five seconds, anyhow — I decided to secretly dub them Sabrina, Jill and Kelly. The doctor could be Bosley, and I'd be Charlie.

"Fell?"

Jill answered. "That is correct, Miss. You were found at the foot of the stairs in your house."

"House?"

"That's right," she said. "Your home on Clayton Street, here in San Francisco."

With as much volume as I could muster, I told them all, "This is just a dream." The words came out loud and clear.

Kelly, who had been reading my chart, looked up and did the Nipper the dog head tilt.

"No stairs," I explained to the three angels, ripping my throat to shreds just to make my point. "No house. Live in Oakland. Apartment."

Then it was Kelly's turn to chime in. "Miss, it's understandable that you are confused. But you have been with us for two months now. You hit your head, and have been asleep for a very long time — what we call a 'comatose state.'"

As bizarre as it seems, my mind kept frantically searching for memories. It simply could not accept this was only a dream. It felt absolutely real. Over and over I reminded myself each thing I was seeing, hearing, smelling and feeling was imagined.

The three nurses looked at me expectantly, probably hoping I'd signal my acceptance and understanding. But I wasn't ready for that. I knew I'd regret using any more words, I had to say one last thing. "No coma. Dream."

Sabrina — apparently accustomed to crazies in her ward — was quick to dismiss me. "Be that as it may, dear," she said, "right now, it's time to change your napkin."

What a completely random thing to say.

"My what?" Was it lunchtime or something? It was then I realized the other two nurses had quietly ducked out.

Without a word, Sabrina closed the gauzy curtains around my bed, turned back around, then and folded down the bed sheets. Still without an explanation, she purposefully lifted my nig htgown all the way up up to my belly button. I started to get a little nervous, as I was not at all sure what kind of party she was planning. Before I had the chance to wonder too much more, I noticed that — wrapped neatly around my hips and between my legs — was the hugest cloth diaper anyone could possibly have the misfortune to see.

    Worst. Dream. *Ever.*

6: The Now – A good day

The next sound I heard was my phone alarm beeping and vibrating on my bedside table, and I was, once again, overjoyed to be back.

Now I knew everything I'd been through last night — the visit to the "hospital of sorts" — was pure fantasy. It was an annoying, gross and rather painful dream, but a dream nonetheless. I decided I was not going to give it any more power by dwelling on it. If I ignored it, the whole thing would just go away. Or so I hoped.

～～～

With no school for the rest of this week, I took advantage of the chance to stay in bed as long as possible... which meant I had an extra twenty minutes or so — just until my daughters woke up and started peppering me with a thousand questions and suggestions for our day.

The first order of business was to head down to the coffee shop. That was actually by request of the kiddos, but one I was absolutely delighted to accommodate. Most days, caffeine was my "mommy's little helper" of choice.

In queue amusement was provided by the kind of cute hipster dude standing in front of us, who was leaning all the way around me, trying desperately to flirt with the chick at the end of the line. The lady looked like someone's trophy wife, complete with recently-acquired golden globes and a rock to rival the Hope Diamond on her left ring finger.

Though I'd only been divorced for two years, already my experience showed guys definitely flirted less with me now I was single. I didn't mind so much, because as a mom, I got more than enough attention as part of a pretty awesome club. It helped that my kids were cute little attention hounds who could take the simple act of drinking hot chocolate and turn it into a performance. This was especially true of my youngest, Iris. With her big, expressive eyes and all the silly faces she liked to make, she was the queen bee in her kindergarten class.

Lily, three years older, was amused by her sister's antics about half the time, and spent the other half trying to widen the gap between herself — a terribly mature third grader — and her pesky little shadow.

But today, my goal was to make that gap disappear. We were going to park along the lake, then feed the ducks as we walked, skipped and jumped our way to Children's Fairyland, a retro little theme park that was reportedly the original inspiration for Disneyland. It had always been one of my favorite places to go when I was little. Our visit always started the same way: a ride on the train that circled around the storybook park, with ice cream cones to follow. Every time we all chose the same ice cream — mint chip — I was reminded that I really had created a couple of mini-mes.

‧ ‧ ‧

After play time, we went to a movie, had dinner out, then walked back home. We were all that good kind of exhausted that comes from a good solid break from the usual routine.

"It was a good day. A very excellent day," Iris told me as she put a line through the date on her calendar. "I think we should do that every time there's no school."

"Well, probably not every time you're out of school, but we will do it again. Soon."

She was so worn out, the poor little gal didn't even ask about a specific date for our next grand adventure.

The day had indeed been grand — doubly so for me, because I got a most welcome respite from sore throats, adult diapers, and the folly of falling down some stairs and landing in a coma.

Just before I went to sleep, I spoke some dream suggestions aloud. I'd read online about making those sort of positive affirmations before drifting off at night. The idea was that you were supposed to be able to create and steer your dreams any way you chose. "I am going to have happy dreams, about France. There will be wine, cheese and a handsome prince."

Pulling up the blanket tight to my chin, I turned on my side, and repeated those phrases until I was so tired, I could speak no more.

7: Out and about

So much for positive affirmations. I woke up in the same damn place. Again. Apparently the second — and third and fourth — verse was the same as the first, but each a little bit louder and a little bit worse.

Given that I was here once more, and it was as real as ever, I grudgingly accepted the conclusion that this was not all pretend. I had scarcely a clue as to precisely what it *was*, but it seemed that this strange new experience had simply been formatted to fit my dream. Viewer discretion was most definitely advised.

As I'd done over the past few days, I contemplated my oddball predicament while staring out the window, which was only a few yards from where I was tucked up tight in my bed. It wasn't much of a view: the side of a brick building which, from my vantage point, displayed an portion of an ad encouraging me and the others in my ward to RINK CA-C. Based on the stylized lettering, the message was presumably part of a retro-style Coca-Cola billboard, but I liked to imagine other possibilities.

With a start, I realized that I had been looking out of this same window when I first gained consciousness in this place. That was the night I saw fireworks. A lot of people had apparently been celebrating something big, and I hadn't been invited to the party. Counting back the days, I realized that all this must have happened within the past week. Why, then, in my head and in my heart, did it feel so much longer than that?

While I was zoning out — I mean, uh, pondering the meaning of life — Kelly rolled up to my bed so quietly, I jumped about three feet straight up in surprise. In front of her was a truly bizarre contraption. It looked like someone had pulled that old wicker chair (the one with pea-green velour upholstery) out of Great Aunt Irma's guest room, then slapped on some wooden wheels.

Try as I might to talk, my voice came out rough, raspy, and barely audible. Instead, I gestured with a head shake and my hands up in the air — the gesture known worldwide for being used in lieu of asking "What?"

"I thought we would go for a stroll," she said, gesturing to the device, which I decided looked like an elderly millionaire recluse's wheelchair. "It's an invalid chair," she added, as if answering the question I hadn't yet asked. (I didn't know if "invalid" was a politically-correct term, but I guessed it was better than "disabled" — or, going way back, "crippled.")

With help, I sat up, then slowly pulled my legs out from under the covers. It was the first time I'd seen them completely, and a sorry sight they were. Compared to the pins that kept me upright in the Now, these two were short on fat and muscle, and long on skin and bones. With an admirable degree of patience, Kelly helped me slip into a woolen bathrobe, then hooked her arm around me so I could stand. Never loosening her grip, we side-stepped together until I was able to clumsily collapse in the wheelchair.

She rolled me down the aisle in the center of the room, between the almost too-neat little rows of steel beds. Something definitely seemed fishy, but it wasn't until we went into the next ward that I figured out what it was. All of the patients in this room were women, and I noticed that, apart from Dr Grumpy, every other person I had seen in this place was female.

Hospital? Nic e try. This was the infirmary at a women's prison, and I was an inmate.

With disquieting clarity, so many of the things I'd seen and heard over the last several days clicked into place — including the plain-Jane accommodations, the archaic equipment, and the often lousy bedside manner.

A cold, damp chill writhed up my back to my neck, then settled in my throat, which was already hurt from speaking just a few words. This was no dream, honeybunch. It was, quite clearly, a nightmare.

As she wheeled me around, she told me the building was four stories tall, plus had a basement for laundry and maintenance. The floor I was on, the fourth, was divided lengthways into three strips. The middle strip housed my ward, which, if you were in a vegetative state, was apparently the local hotspot. I decided to dub the back half of the ward where my coma buddies and I were parked "the crisper."

In the front section — near the nurse's station — were people who were hooked up to some mean-looking breathing tubes and other kinds of scary medical devices, the likes of which I'd never seen. The women who needed the most care, I learned, were positioned closer to the central hallway, so they could be tended to without the need to traverse the thirty or so yards each time. The long-term patients, like I was (or had been), were stationed at the distant side of the room, as we weren't exactly making constant requests of the staff.

The room was long and narrow, and for some reason, they kept the lights down low. There was only one window letting natural light into the space, and that was at the end furthest from the entrance. Since my bed was positioned about ten feet from the back wall, I actually had the closest thing to a view that anyone in here could get.

The wards east and west of mine, however, both benefited from several windows dotting the otherwise austere white walls. I supposed it was only fair that the people who were able to actually sit up on their own could look outside.

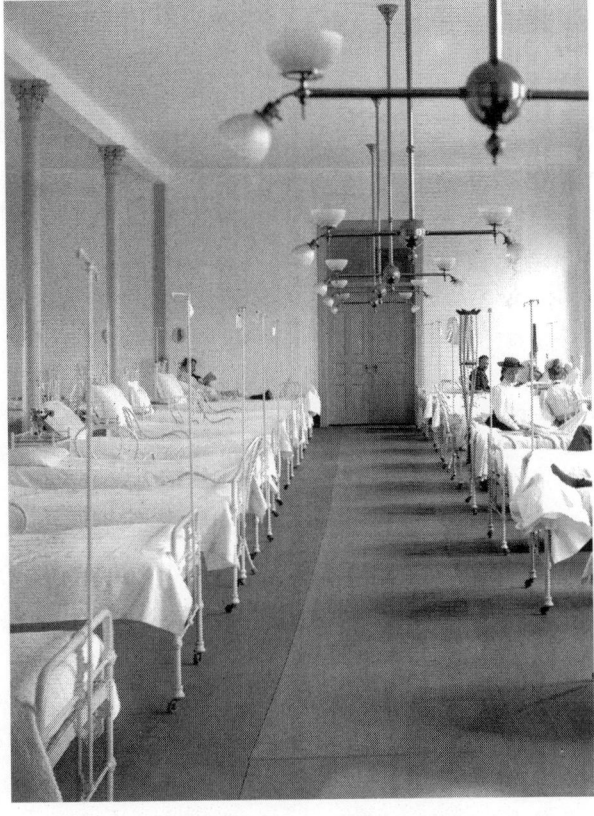

Nurse Kelly wheeled me to a spot in the west ward, where she parked me in a wonderful patch of late afternoon sun that was streaming in. Through the high windows, all I could see was a pristine blue sky, with puffy white clouds, and the vibrantly green top of an elm tree. I relished my time luxuriating in the sunbeams, a skill I'd learned from my once-upon-a-time kitty, Ruprecht. For a prison, this was about as beautiful and peaceful as you could probably get.

Soon, though, shadows were creeping across my face. With the sweetest "please" I could muster, I grit my teeth against the pain and quietly asked

Kelly if I could move to another spot — one closer to the beds that were all lined up in front of the windows.

"I'm sorry, but I can't. We mustn't get near the residents in this area."

Oh, that didn't sound good. "Why?" I rasped. I wondered — were they dangerous? I eyed the bedridden women suspiciously, looking for anyone who might have a shiv, or even a sizable fist.

"We need to keep you well back from these folks, because they are quite sick," she said. "They have what we call 'communicable diseases,' so we need to be sure you don't get too close."

Trust me: This is not what you want to hear after you have been breathing the same air as some highly contagious people for the past twenty minutes.

My headache, which had dwindled to nothing over the past half hour, came roaring back.

Why the hell had she brought me into a room with a bunch of sick people? At first, I couldn't fathom an appropriate reason — then considered that maybe, due to security issues, our options were severely limited.

"Bed please," I said, and my nurse nodded. This time, there was no sightseeing and no small talk, and we passed "Go" just because it was the only way to get back to my ward.

A couple nurses I didn't know fed me dinner — soup and jello — and, shall we say, "cleaned me up." To kill some time, I asked if they had a TV, and with some exasperation, they said no. Undaunted, I requested something to read, and that they could do. I expected a couple three-year-old copies of *People* magazine, but was instead handed the one and only book they had available: a fancy leather-bound edition of the Bible. Even though I had never been a regular church-goer, that night, I read about archangels.

Once the darkness had settled the room, I tried to doze off, knowing full well that entering a dream state was the surest and fastest way out of this place. But although I was tired and on some mind-bending medications, I simply could not relax. How poetic, I thought, that I was having such a vivid and disturbing dream, and I wasn't able to snap out of it because I couldn't stop thinking about how vivid and disturbing it truly was.

Curled on my side and with my cheek pressed into the pillow, I stared into the starry sky outside for hours, until, blessedly, sleep whisked me away.

8: Discovering this world

After an all too brief visit to the home of my birth, otherwise known as Not This Place, I was here once more... and again, it felt every bit as authentic as my waking world. This was no cheap knock-off universe — only the high-end genuine name-brand kind of dreamland was good enough for me.

The first and most important thing on today's to-do list: I wanted to regain my degree in using the bathroom like a normal person. Although yesterday I'd graduated to the use of a bedpan, there would be something pretty damn liberating about being able to use the facilities any time I wanted.

After a bit of a tussle with the sheets, I finally managed to prop myself up into a sitting position. The only people I could see were unconscious or sleeping, and my calls for help came out quiet and raspy. It was a little disconcerting there was no nurse call button... but then again, that only made sense. If this is where they stored the veggies, it was pretty much pointless to install all the bells and whistles.

I'd just have to go it alone. Tentatively, I pushed my bony white feet off the edge of the bed, and slowly let them meet the floor. The tile was icy cold, and a wave of goosebumps rose up to my knees. Undeterred, I tried to stand up. It took about two seconds to realize my legs were about as strong as toothpicks, and unless I got some actual help, this was going to end very badly. I sat back down with a lurch. The bed squeaked from the sudden movement, and the sound echoed conspicuously through the room.

With surprising speed, a middle-aged extra from "The Flying Nun" materialized from out of nowhere, and sharply scolded me for trying to get out of bed.

"Where do you think you're going, missy?" she said with an Irish brogue so thick, I had to replay her words in my head a couple times before I understood what she was trying to convey. "Lie yourself down now," she said, while using her hand to push my head all the way back to the pillow.

"You'd best not be forgettin' to get some help next time, now will ye?"

"I guess — sorry," I said, feeling not at all apologetic. "Have we met?"

"Not since you've been awake we haven't," she muttered as she tucked in the sheets around me so tightly, she practically fashioned a straitjacket. "I'm Sister Mary Reginald. I keep a close eye on the goings-on around here."

"I bet you're quite good at your job." This was the truth. I imagined this nun didn't miss a trick.

And she didn't. The very next moment, she called me out on my word choice. "You bet, do ye? Gambling is an evil thing, it is. Goes right against God."

"I didn't mean it like that. I —"

She cut me off. "Perhaps if you were a more cautious sort of girl, you wouldn't have landed in hospital in the first place! So you hush now, and someone will be by later with your bedpan."

With that, she walked away, her habit bobbing slightly from the quickness of her step.

It was for the best she left then — it really was. Had she lingered, I might have just given her a few thoughts on the wisdom of berating the injured, even if they did happen to be in jail.

∽ ∽ ∽

Once I was sure Nun Ratched had left the floor, I tried my bathroom adventure again. This time, one of the Angels caught me — quite literally — when my legs suffered from performance anxiety. She was far from angry, though, and actually congratulated me on my persistence. "But wait here for just a moment, and I'll be back."

Before I got bored enough to try to stand up again on my own, she returned with a fantastic FDR-esque wheelchair. She helped me to sit down, then speedily wheeled me out of the ward, away from other patients and various sharp objects to the empty hallway toward the rear of the building.

"We are going to start therapy to try to get your strength back. That way, if you decide to go walking, you won't end up crawling instead," she laughed.

The first order of business was to get me back on my feet. She held me by the elbow and guided my steps as I walked up and down the halls three times. By the end of those few runs, I was pleased to note I was no longer doing the Frankenstein's monster swagger, and actually looked nearly human. But progress had its price: I was worn out.

Phase two began when she wheeled me into a small, square room that looked like it was originally intended to be someone's office. It was empty, save for a table, two chairs, and some light barbells.

Keeping in with the theme of no rest for the wicked, my workout resumed immediately. She started me off with two 1-pound barbells, and I was seriously dismayed at how heavy those tiny weights seemed. Thirty reps with each arm was all I could manage.

I wiped away a trickle of sweat from my forehead. It was way too hot in here. Kelly must have agreed, because she pulled up the sash on the window as high as it would go to let in some wonderfully cool air. With both hands, I pulled my hair up into a ponytail, allowing the breeze to play on my neck. If I wanted to keep doing these workouts, I really would need some elastic bands for my hair.

Next up, I needed to try to use my legs to move from a sitting position to standing. When you haven't used your legs much for the past couple months, believe me — that's a significant challenge. This was going way beyond tiring, and encroaching on tearful exhaustion.

"A break, please?" I was surprised to find that getting the words out hardly hurt my throat at all.

Kelly agreed, and put helped me back into the chair. While I rested, she would go do something down the hall, so I would have a few peaceful minutes until her return.

"Awesome. Fantastic," I told her. "And take your time!"

She left, and I was thrilled to just stay where I was — thoroughly enjoying the peace, solitude, and freedom from exertion.

Five minutes ticked by, and, inevitably, I started to get bored. Still exhausted, yes, but bored. Since the window was open, I decided to check out what was going on outside. I'd been stuck in here for much too long, and I missed the real world.

With considerable skill, if I do say so myself, I brought this strange slender body to a standing position, then walked the few steps over to the window with nary a stumble. Poking my head out the window, I looked around, but could not figure out what I was seeing. I blinked a couple times, shook my head, and then my brain returned a "system error" warning.

Leaning back into the room, I peered around the indoor space to check whether or not my vision was on the fritz. Everything seemed perfectly normal in here. Strange. Peeking out once more, this time, I leaned out and craned my neck to get a better look at whatever was going on here.

When you were a kid, did you ever put your face right up to the glass on one of those huge snow globes? So close you could almost imagine the tiny world inside was real, and maybe — if you wished really hard — you could step right into it? Well, that's what I saw, except in this scene, everything was moving and fantastical and vibrant, and there were no huge chunks of fake snow.

It didn't look like any version of San Francisco I knew, but instead seemed as if I was peeking into a full-color picture ripped out of a book about the Wild West. I saw at least two dozen horse-drawn carriages of all different shapes and sizes, carrying hay and lumber, wooden crates and passengers. The streets the wagons were riding over weren't smooth concrete, but were unevenly tiled with cobblestones. Men and women, dressed to the nines, populated the sidewalks; and of all the buildings I could see, not one was more than five stories tall.

It was beautiful. It was quaint. So what was it doing in my dream? If I wasn't hallucinating, I must have missed a sign somewhere explaining the situation below. A parade? The circus? Maybe they were filming a movie?

Just as I wondered if I was witnessing the creation of a major motion picture event, a group of little kids spotted me, pointed, then started waving. So astonished by the attention, I forgot about everything else — including the hard work of standing. My legs started to crumple beneath me. To avoid falling, my hands flew to the only thing within reach: the windowsill. The next thing I knew, I was hanging halfway out the window, looking straight down at the pavement four stories below. Four very, very *tall* stories, those were.

Just as it was occurring to me my bladder may or may not have decided to maintain integrity, I felt firm hands grab me by the arm and the back of my robe, and haul me back inside.

I didn't need to turn around to see who had rescued me, because she got right in my face the moment I landed back in my chair. Kelly's expression was equal parts horrified and Grade A pissed off. "What are you doing?" she squawked. "Are you trying to kill yourself?" I looked back, and realized I'd been hanging out of a wide open window with a waist height sill. There was absolutely nothing to hold a clumsy, thrill-seeking (or even potentially suicidal) person back from splattering on the pavement about fifty feet below.

"So sorry. I just saw something really strange out there, and kind of forgot what I was doing," I said. And even though I'd nearly fallen to my death, I wanted to try again. "If I'm careful, can I take another quick peek?"

She glared at me, then stomped over to the window and slammed it shut with perhaps a little more vigor than the poor sash deserved. "You may look," she said, "but only through the glass! Do not open the window."

"Keep my arms and legs inside the building at all times — I get it." It came out as a whisper.

Kelly extended her arm, then helped me up to standing again.

"Before I do, um, do you think you can take a gander outside and tell me what you see?"

That sweet, dear soul decided to humor me, and peered out the window while I watched from a safe distance. "It looks like a usual sort of day," she reported. "Lots of people going about their business."

"So it looks... *normal*... to you?" I took some tiny, tentative steps toward her.

"As normal as apple pie. No monsters or scary dinosaurs or whatever you thought you saw."

I can admit that, despite the nurse's reassurance, I was a little afraid to look out there again. But the curious part of my soul apparently trumped the fearful one, and I opened my eyes to this world once more.

                                                                                ∽∽∽

The panorama below took my breath away. Again. Everything looked exactly as bizarrely old-fashioned as it had two minutes ago, except the carriages had moved further down the road, and new people had come into the picture. Everything was punctuated with marvelous bursts of color — red and green and orange in particular.

The only thing that might have surprised me more was if I had looked down and seen Santa's Workshop, complete with a bunch of elves making toys and dancing around candy canes.

"So, does everything look normal to you?" Kelly said as she peered over my shoulder.

"It looks... interesting." That is, of course, a polite word meaning "strange," such as might be used upon hearing your friend named her kid Banana.

It was so interesting, in fact, that my mind was just about to explode under the weight of a thousand questions. First and foremost on my mind was, at long last, the issue of when. Given that she would probably consider it an odd follow-up to our discussion of the normalcy of what apparently passed for everyday life here, I tried to phrase my question as casually as I could.

"Do you know today's date?"

"Today is Sunday, January the seventh," she said, with a matter-of-fact tone.

"The seventh. Right. And the year?"

There was an exasperated little sigh. "Are you playing wise with me, Miss?"

"Not at all." I tapped my noggin. "Memory problems, remember?"

"Well, that's what all the hubbub was about the other night — the fireworks and the cheers. Do you remember? We were ringing in the new year... a new century, even." She paused, waiting for me to signal that I understood. But I didn't. Not yet. Not really. My mind was all a jumble, and even though I heard the words she was saying, none of them were registering.

With a surprisingly gentle tone, she finally finished answering my question. "It is now the year of our Lord 1900."

༄ ༄ ༄

Nineteen hundred? I would normally never believe a word of something so outlandish. The problem was the concept actually made some sense, based on what I had seen outside... even though that was just about the *only* way it made sense.

My world's axis completely tilted with this revelation. It's lucky I was already sitting down, because a wave of dizziness forced me to fight against the urge to revisit my breakfast. I took some slow breaths and tried not to think about anything until the worst of the sickness passed.

While intellectually I realized this was a dream, that didn't keep my mind from trying to constantly put everything I was thinking and seeing and hearing into a logical framework. The difficulty I was facing reminded me of being hyper-sensitive while in the throes of PMS: Despite being painfully aware that my mental state was completely distorted, the tide of emotions were still nearly impossible to rein in.

If I could get just a little more information, maybe this would start to feel more comprehensible. I asked Kelly, "So this is January 1900. That means the President is...?" Before the twenties, which guy was in the Oval Office when got sort of fuzzy for me.

"William McKinley, dear. Same as it was before your fall."

"Okay, good to know." What else would be helpful? "Has there been any big news recently — like any major world events?"

She had to think for a moment. "Well, I'm not sure if it's what you mean, but I read this morning that the booers attacked Caesar's Camp yesterday."

I had absolutely no clue what any of that meant. Caesar — the dude — lived in the BC years. And as for people booing him, well, that made no sense either. But I thanked her, and didn't ask any more questions. Kelly had already gone above and beyond the call of duty just putting up with me today, and I did not want to press my luck... plus, I really did not know how much more weirdness I could handle at the moment.

There was just one more thing I needed to know.

"And this place is a..."

"Hospital."

"Not a prison?"

"A prison?" she scoffed. "Surely not! Why ever would you think such a terrible thing?"

I had supposed the austere, minimalist accommodations were just part and parcel of being behind bars. Apparently, however, all of this was simply standard hospital issue in this era.

Consequently, then, that meant the lack of common medical equipment in the place — defibrillators, blood pressure monitors, IV drips — wasn't due to lack of funding or because peeps in the clink didn't deserve such care, but simply because such things hasn't been invented or weren't in wide use yet. That, in particular, was nearly impossible to wrap my head around. How many other things I considered commonplace had yet to be invented in this time?

As stunned as I was by the truth of the here and now, it was just another day on the job for the nurse pushing my wheelchair.

"Do you want to do a little more work on your arms and legs, or would you rather head back?" she asked. I chose option B. Even more than I needed the opportunity to rest, I needed time to *think*.

9: The Now – To accept the impossible

You know the day has at least even odds of being pretty lousy when you wake up to shrieks of, "The toilet won't stop! It's not *stopping*!" Therefore, the first order of business had nothing to do with dreams or history or any the wild things I'd seen and heard, but instead involved a plunger, a mop and a copious quantity of bleach.

After I regained control of the bathroom situation, and issued a firm reminder that flushing four times in quick succession is less likely to fix a problem, and more likely to create one, it was quiet time for everyone. I bought the girls' relative silence with what we called "rainy day packs." These were little kits I made up every now and then, and only used on rare occasions, in an attempt to keep the experience special. Today's selection: Shrinky-Dinks, one of my own childhood favorites.

Once the kidlets were settled in with their plastic sheets and a set of colored markers, I went into the other room, took a deep — supposedly cleansing — breath, and considered my situation.

I was a girl who had been born in the 1970s, attended college in the nineties, and started a family in the twenty-first century. But this week, somehow, I witnessed the clock ticking over from the year 1899 to 1900, and was now returning to the same year every night in my dreams.

Ridiculous. In fact, I felt stupid even saying that last sentence in my own head.

The good news about the nurse having told me about Caesar and the booing thing was I now had something definitive I could research. Fortunately, I didn't have to look far. The front page of the Sunday paper — from January 7, 1900 — trumpeted the news:

GENERAL WHITE REPORTS THE REPULSE OF THE BOERS
The following telegram was received from General White January 6, 9 a.m.: "The enemy attacked Caesar's Camp at 2:45 a.m. in considerable force, The enemy was everywhere repulsed, but the fighting still continues..."

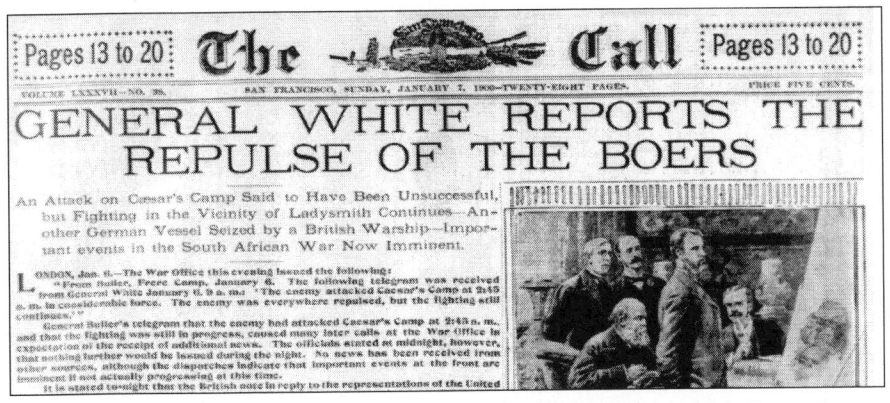

Cue the tingles up and down my spine.

While I had my proof, I must have been doodling on my binder that day in history class, because I didn't remember learning about any of this. The web provided some enlightenment, informing me that the Second Boer War was fought between 1899 and 1902, and the warring parties were the British Empire and the Afrikaans-speaking Dutch settlers of the South African Republic and the Orange Free State.

Okay, so it was "Boer" not "booer," but ultimately, the subject matter itself was moot. Everything she had told me was spot-on. If I took this to mean I was indeed visiting the San Francisco of more than a century ago, what did it all mean? Was I time traveling or... something else that didn't even have a name?

The problem: Time travel was not possible.

Arthur Conan Doyle famously wrote: "Once you eliminate the impossible, whatever remains, no matter how improbable, must be the truth." But this situation here? If I discarded the impossible, I was left with nada. If, however, I elevated time travel to merely "improbable" status... well, that actually made more sense than any other scenario I could imagine.

I did my research, checking out various reputable websites for scientific opinions about time travel. While there are mountains of fiction and plenty of personal testimonials, according to the scientific community, there has never been a single verified case of someone traveling forward or backward in time. The consensus seemed to be that visits to the future *might* one day be possible — but the idea of going back to the past is a lot more problematic. Most such journeys seemed to require the use of a time machine, wormhole, portal or some other physical facilitator. In any case, all the experts agreed:

Humans are not anywhere close to having the ability to travel through time.

Maybe whoever (or whatever) was responsible for my trips to the past avoided the problems posed by annoying physical barriers by sending only my psyche back to the golden olden days. Perhaps it was sort of like of email versus snail-mail. "Oh, please," I could tell people who questioned my veracity because I didn't disappear, then rematerialize dressed in vintage attire. "I'm *virtually* time traveling, darling. It's the only way to go."

∽ ∽ ∽

So, for the sake of argument, let's say I was actually spending my nights in the late Victorian era. That made my brain seethe with questions. I didn't want to just know about my strange new world — I wanted a cheat sheet.

For that, I needed only the internet. Easily enough, I found several different online archives featuring things like newspapers, photos, books, magazines and more from 1900. There was a veritable treasure trove of turn-of-the-century information online, because everything from that period was out of copyright and in the public domain.

I started my past life exploration by punching terms like "news stories 1900" into a search engine. There were some interesting events that year — such as the annexation of Hawaii and the launch of Kodak's Brownie camera. Then there was sad stuff, such as the hurricane hitting Galveston, Texas, which killed eight thousand people. William McKinley was indeed President, and would win a second term later in the year… only to be assassinated in 1901 — a horrible death by gangrene, more than a week after being shot.

There was so much information out there, I couldn't decide what was going to be helpful. The only timely, relevant intelligence I found was in the year 1900, Hershey's introduced their milk chocolate bar.

Still, what I had learned gave me purpose: My mission, which I chose to accept, was to pay close attention to the world in my dream, so I could figure out the best way to put my encyclopedic knowledge of the future to good use.

10: Getting ready to go

The day had finally come: Tomorrow, I would be leaving the hospital. The sudden end to my stay was kind of a surprise to everyone — including me. Apparently a last-minute decision handed down from on high, my suspicious mind immediately assumed it probably had to do with money — or lack thereof. It was all so very "Little Princess."

While I was incredibly grateful to be moving out from behind these bland and supposedly-but-not-really sterile hospital walls, I wasn't exactly excited about my prospects. I was already starting my new life with a weak, tired and sore body — and sometimes the effort to make it through the day was so intense, the entire world tasted bitter.

One thing that was really emblematic of my whole situation was the fact that nobody was coming to take me home. When I had asked about my family, the staff sidestepped the question a bit, saying only that we "weren't close." Um, yeah. Given that not a single relative had visited me in the hospital certainly supported that idea. By the same token, no friends had visited, either.

I was apparently flying solo in this life.

With a sad and sudden clarity, I finally understood that seemingly strange phenomenon of people in jail for whom escape is the furthest thing from their minds — they would prefer to stay behind bars. Even just two weeks ago, that concept would have had no sense to me whatsoever. Why would anyone choose to be confined when they could be free?

But I get it now. It actually was crystal clear. It's all because being on the outside, without knowing what to do or where to go — and how to get there even if you managed it — is incredibly daunting.

In my case, I was lucky, because this girl here (thumbs pointing to myself) had a house. Alas, I didn't know where it was, and had not the least idea how I would find my way there. Did they even have the equivalent of taxicabs in this era? Was it safe for a woman to walk on the streets? Where was I going to get food, medicine, clothing, toiletries?

There were, too, much larger questions I'd have to deal with in the near future. For one, how would I possibly earn a living? I didn't know a lot about this time zone, but was pretty damn sure that web design was not a viable career option here.

There were undoubtedly a thousand other brand new challenges I'd be facing in the days ahead, and I wasn't sure if I was up for all that. But, in the words of Helen Keller — a woman who knew a thing or two about adversity — "Life is either a daring adventure or nothing at all."

∽ ∽ ∽

I called it my exit interview; they called it the discharge procedure.

So many people came to say goodbye to me that it seemed almost uncomfortable — and their numbers were not at all in line with the sum total of medical professionals involved in my care. I remarked on this disparity, and the clerk laughed. "Well, goodness gracious, of course! You're as fascinating to these folk as the Bearded Lady or the Armless Wonder."

Just lovely. I was right on par with a circus sideshow attraction. I was The Girl Who Lived.

And this girl was named Jennie — they had told me that much in everyday conversation. But when I scanned my hospital discharge papers — which, amazingly, consisted of only three pages — I found a problem: *Genevieve Vecchiarelli diMedici*.

That alphabet soup was my *name*. I had no clue how to pronounce two out of the three words there, let alone spell them. Evidently, I was of Italian heritage — that much I could gather. Sadly, my grasp of the Italian language was pretty much limited to brand names and pasta dishes. Luckily, I hadn't been dumped in Italy, because, given my vocabulary, I'd be fat from eating cannelloni and gelato, and broke from wearing Armani and Prada while driving a Ferrari.

To inflame matters more, I couldn't yet remember how to spell my middle or last names well enough to come back to the Now to figure out how they were pronounced. Until I figured that out, I'd just keep my medical paperwork handy.

∽ ∽ ∽

Despite my newfound celebrity status, for my first foray into the outside world, I would be in secondhand clothes. Apparently the dress I was wearing when I was brought in had been thrown away. ("It was ruined, dear," was all they would say.)

Indeed, when I came back from what was hopefully my last bathroom break in this joint, I saw that someone had left a box at the end of my bed. Inside was pair of black boots and a simple dress — cream-colored with a tiny pink rose pattern stamped on the cotton. That was it. No bra or underwear or socks or anything else.

When I put on my new getup, I stole a clean pair of the little knicker things I'd been wearing under my gown, deciding that the amount of comfort that cheap bit of cotton would give me would more than outweigh any possible negative karma I might face for the theft.

Shortly thereafter, Nurse O'Neill offered to accompany me back home, and I said yes so quickly, I think I made her head spin. Really, I was perfectly cool with accepting charity. I didn't worry that she had probably only asked to be polite. To me, this was a brave new world, and I wasn't too proud to admit that I needed a little help.

11: My house

Stepping out from the small hospital lobby and into the outdoors nearly knocked me flat, because I was completely unprepared for the barrage of sights and sounds and smells (a stench, really — let's be honest). Imagine the lovely aromas of sewage and coal smoke combined with the odor of manure, which was being delivered fresh each minute by the horses powering every vehicle. As if that somehow wasn't enough of a welcome to the outside world, the next moment a group of men walked by, and it was immediately obvious they worked hard, liked their beer, and bathed on a very irregular basis.

It truly was such an assault to my senses that I didn't move from the step outside the doorway until Nurse Martha O'Neill took gently led me over to the carriage that had pulled up during the minute or so of my daze. I stepped up and sat down, still pretty much in la-la-land.

Once I was seated, I stopped paying attention to the mechanics of getting from point A to point B, because I was so captivated by the scenery. Mind: Blown. I absolutely felt as if I'd dropped in on some quaint movie set just after the director had yelled "action." (I half expected to see a telltale Hallmark logo in the bottom right hand corner of my view.) Everything looked so bright and crisp and *new*.

The journey itself offered another kind of eye-opening experience thanks to the painfully rough ride. My skinny behind did not fare well because I was sitting on an unpadded seat, riding over rough cobblestone roads, on wheels that looked like they were made of wood with a thin band of metal as a sort of tire. If I didn't already have a headache, the jarring jaunt would have given me a nice one.

After several minutes, we slowed to cross a street. There weren't any stop signs or red light/green light systems yet, so you had to really pay attention to what was going on around you. It was a kind of scary free-for-all that reminded me a lot of riding in a cab in modern-day Manhattan.

"We're almost there," Martha told me with a matronly pat on the knee. One street sign caught my eye: Haight Street. I had to laugh. "I live near here?" She smiled and nodded.

That was so groovy. I knew that sixty-odd years from now, this place would represent the paisley-patterned heart of the hippie movement, and brilliant talents like Janis Joplin, Jimi Hendrix and Hunter S Thompson would all call this area home for a time. Alas, I was born too late to be there then, and now I was way too early... and either way, this tidbit wasn't going to impress Nurse Martha.

We turned the corner, and then the carriage/buggy/wagon stopped alongside the sidewalk. I gathered my few belongings, and the driver was kind enough to help me down so I didn't face-plant. Getting out of that thing was like trying to get out of a lifted SUV — you just sort of go and hope you make it in one piece... and it didn't help I was still a little wobbly in general. In contrast, Martha stepped down with great finesse, taking the drivers' proffered hand, but scarcely needing it.

Once we were both on terra firma, I started looking at the houses to try to figure out which one might be mine. All the homes on the block were stunning — ornamental in a classic style, featuring elegant moldings and bay windows. I had no idea which I owned, but every one of them was a winner.

"It's number 333, over here," Martha said, leading me to a home with a beige and dusky plum-colored exterior. It was perfect, except...

"If this is my house, why is there a 'For Sale' sign in the window?"

"I would imagine it is currently for sale," she answered, just as calmly as could be. She took her time before looking over and giving me a sly wink. "It is probably because they didn't expect you to be such a wonderful miracle, dear." Martha took my arm and led me up the walkway to the front door. "As I told you before, I was there when they brought you in, and there really was little hope you would survive. Nine times out of ten, when someone comes in with an injury so severe, they pass on within a couple days."

"I guess I am stubborn."

"Stubborn, and with purpose," she told me as she patted my hand. "I believe the angels kept you here because you have something to do. They let you sleep for two long months so you could be ready to face your challenge. Now here you are. Home, and all ready to begin."

She produced the house key — a big steel skeleton key with an ornate top — and handed it to me.

"Now here I am," I said as I fumbled with the key, turning it every which way until at last the bolt was freed.

The door creaked slightly as I opened it, and I stepped over the threshold. My house had given me anything but a warm welcome — there were no glowing lights to greet me, no friendly hellos, and the temperature in was exactly the same as out.

So much for my "home." The tears that had been threatening to fall all day started to actually well up. I knew if one managed to slip down my cheek, the floodgates would open, so needed an immediate diversion. I took a deep breath and forced myself to focus on the details of the house itself to keep my mind from veering into sad and lonelyville.

Strangely enough, as soon as I walked ten feet inside, it felt like I was in a more modern era. The house was utterly Victorian, featuring lots of wood moldings and heavily-patterned wallpaper. But it didn't feel as much like a blast from the past as it seemed like I'd stepped into a museum exhibit. That idea, at least, was a lot easier for my mind to process.

From my vantage point in the foyer, looking into the living room, it very much looked like someone was in the process of moving in or out. Most of the rugs were rolled up, and sheets has been thrown over several pieces of furniture. There were conspicuous gaps where end tables and chairs had perhaps once been, leaving the room looking like an unfinished puzzle. It was clear a lot of Jennie's stuff had been sold off or taken elsewhere to get the place ready for the real estate market.

And on that note, there was something I needed to do. I turned on my heel and made a beeline for the front bay window, then pulled the "For Sale" sign out from where it was tucked against the glass.

"Won't need this," I announced to the shrouded furnishings, as if reassuring them they would be allowed to stay. Nurse Martha peeked out of the kitchen and gave me a kind smile that instantly reminded me of how my grandmother looked in my dad's baby pictures.

Then she looked past me, to the horse and buggy still waiting outside. I felt like the schlub who "forgot" her wallet when it came time to pay the bar tab. "Is the driver waiting for payment? I can try to find my purse."

"No, dear," she assured me. "He will be taking me to my house next, and I will sort it all out then. Don't you worry." Her voice was so gentle and reassuring, I thought she would make an amazing grandmother one day.

She gestured to the kitchen, and said, "I'll leave you with a few muffins, Jennie. I made them myself. And two apples. This will get you through tomorrow, I'd expect."

I hadn't come close to figuring out what I would do about food, and now I didn't have to worry about it tonight at all. "Thank you — thanks so much." I was fighting to hold back the waterworks now.

"There there, dearie," she murmured. "You've had a hard time of things lately, and I'm just glad I could help."

Before she left, she gave me a few last instructions. "Walk, walk, walk," she told me. "You need to get out and walk, every day. Start with a mile or two, and try to get up to eight or ten miles each day. The fresh air will do you good and cast out disease, but be absolutely sure to bundle yourself up, and always wear a scarf over your neck — even indoors."

With a big smile, I assured her I most definitely would... and felt a little bit bad I actually had no intention of doing the "cast out disease" and bundling up portions of the plan. There were so many crazy superstitions in this time — folk remedies that would supposedly ward off illness and banish mysterious contagions. Still, it was so kind of her to care. It warmed the cockles of my heart — no scarf required.

A minute later, I waved goodbye to Nurse Martha, then carefully closed the front door behind her. As the lock slid home, I could finally take a long, deep breath without anyone evaluating the quality of my respiration or asking how I felt.

And so it begins.

For a second or so there, I actually felt a glimmer of a can-do attitude. But then it was gone.

At last alone in a foreign place and time, now I just felt helpless and hopeless. It was impossible to forget I'd been unceremoniously dumped here. My cries had not been heard by whoever or whatever had parked me in this primitive place... or if they had been, they were being ignored.

All I wanted to do was go to sleep, so I could go home — to my *real* home. I yelled something to this effect and waited. And waited. The only response I got was a twinge on my forehead where my scar itched. If that was some sort of sign, it couldn't mean anything good.

With a heavy heart, I tried to think practically. I was stuck here for now, so what next? It was time to start preparing for a long winter's night, and I needed to see what I had available. In the waning afternoon light, I checked out the two stories under this roof.

The house was deceptively large — much bigger than I'd expected based on how it looked from the front. As it was neither humble or opulent, I guessed it would probably fall somewhere right near the center of the upper middle class home strata.

Downstairs, there was a living room, a dining room, a kitchen, what would probably called a parlor, and something like a den or library. I'd venture upstairs soon enough, but from what I could see from the stairwell, the second level had a few bedrooms and a bathroom.

As pretty as this place undoubtedly was, and classic and graceful and alluring and all the other words a real estate agent would probably use in a sales brochure, to me, the whole thing could be summed up in two words: cold and dark. And over the next several hours, I knew it was only going to get colder and darker.

Apart from the obvious lack of practicality, quite frankly, the thought of being in a pitch-black Victorian house creeped me out. It didn't matter this place was still so new I could practically still smell the paint and plaster. Unfortunately, I had seen too many horror films over the years that had been set in homes that looked a lot like mine. ("Pacific Heights," anyone?)

I tried to get the lights, stove and fire going, but had no luck at all. Everything ran on gas — there was no electricity in this house yet, and probably not even in this part of the city. I suspected there must be a gas main valve somewhere, but I hadn't the foggiest idea where that might be, or how I'd turn it on even if I found it. Grudgingly, I realized I would need to get some assistance to get it all going, especially given my (lack of) mechanical aptitude. I didn't want to be the stupid lady who blew up her house and set the block on fire.

The two clocks I could see both said different times, and didn't appear to be working, despite each being correct twice a day. I could tell from looking at the sky, though, that it was already very late in the afternoon, which meant soon, I'd have no light. For a flickering moment, I considered heading to a hotel... but realized I didn't have any way to find such an establishment. If my kids had been here, there would be no question — we would figure out an alternative. But since it was just me? I could rough it.

With the issue of light out of my control, I decided to start preparations for a long night. I started up the stairs and was struck by how the chilly echo of my heels against the hardwood was such a loud and lonely sound.

I slid down to sit on the second step of the wooden staircase to take off these annoying shoes. I pulled the bow at the top of my boots and skipped the step of loosening the black cord that zig-zagged all the way from my ankle to mid-calf. Of course, as soon as I started to pull the shoe off, I found my foot completely stuck in the style of a Chinese finger trap.

I may have said a naughty word at this point.

Grudgingly, I loosened the laces, all the while sending up a little prayer of thanks to the people who would eventually invent zippers and velcro.

Finally, clad in quiet bare feet, upstairs I went to go play Goldilocks. (I'd been reading the book out loud three times a week for the past month, so had every word of the story memorized.)

On the house's second story, I discovered a wide landing leading to four bedrooms and one small bathroom. Only three of the bedrooms actually earned that title, while the fourth had no bed — just an empty dresser. The room in the front had rumpled sheets and the pillows were at odd angles, looking like the bed hadn't been tended to since my sudden departure a few months before. That was a little odd, given the state of the remainder of the house, but I supposed whoever had been working here had used it to rest in between packing everything up.

But not knowing who had been sleeping, sweating and drooling on those sheets, I decided to pronounce that bed Too Dirty.

The next bedroom had a full-size bed, where apparently the entire contents of the linen closet had been dumped onto it, making a mountain probably three feet high. That bed, therefore, I dubbed Too Soft.

The last room had only a narrow twin-size day bed, which, though it probably would be comfortable enough, was decidedly Too Small.

I went back to Soft room and removed all the blankets and comforters and pillows and sheet and towels, and started to rebuild the bed to make a warm nest. There were down duvets and pillows, cotton and woolen blankets, and a couple pale yellow throws that felt as if they were made out of cashmere. In addition, there was one stunning patchwork quilt, the entire middle section of which had been carefully crafted from hexagonal pieces of patterned fabric in richly-colored jewel tones.

By the time I was finished, only the towels and a few extra sheets remained, stacked in neat little piles on the floor. I was going to sleep in Princess and the Pea style, because I had now made this bed Just Right.

12: The Now: Sweet home Oakland

After the exhausting, overwhelming experience of January 17th, I was beyond thrilled to wake up and find myself in my own cozy bed — the one with super-soft bamboo sheets and two memory foam pillows, one of which had my cell phone tucked underneath. I was so delighted, in fact, that I scooted over to the center of the bed and made sheet angels. After a minute of that, both girls jumped on the bed to join me. We ended up on the floor, giggling like crazy and twisted up in a mass of sheets.

Minus the extreme fatigue and the effect of hospital-grade drugs, I had fallen asleep with the clearest head I'd had since this whole thing started. This meant that for the first time, when I woke up here in the Now, my other life seemed less like a dream and more like another reality. Plainly put, my mind started to go along with what my heart had been telling it for a week already.

Certainly, yesterday's carriage ride and subsequent arrival at "home" offered a lot of clarity, too. No longer was I having a recurring semi-nightmare wherein I was stuck in a hospital for days on end. Simply having been out and about a bit had helped me to accept what seemed to be.

೧೯೧

Once my ex picked up the kids for school, I finally went outside. It was mid-morning, and the sunlight was bright and warm and wonderful. I was suddenly overwhelmed with this feeling of gratitude — just for being lucky enough to be back here. In fact, I almost wanted to get down on the ground and kiss it... but it was covered in blackened bits of gum and other stuff of dubious origin, and probably smelled of pee. So I blew it a kiss with my hand, and savored every step of my quarter mile walk to the little place with the coolest cappuccino foam art this side of the Bay.

13: My first day alone

Although I had tried to stay up as late as possible the night before, when I woke up more than a hundred years earlier, my impression was that I had slept surprisingly well.

The thoroughly foreign soundscape is what actually got me out of bed. Single pane windows kept out the rain and the wind, sure, but not much of the noise. The loudest part of the morning was the traffic. Even with the windows closed, I could clearly hear the sound of hoofbeats and drivers yelling 'yah' and 'woah' to their horses. I half expected to see one a ghostly little prairie schooner go disappearing into the wall, just like in the old Chuck Wagon dog food commercials.

To get a better look at my new 'hood, I opened the bay window in the front bedroom. The window groaned in protest at me for manhandling the sash. Of course there were no window guards or other safety devices — a clear reminder that the era of the frivolous lawsuit had not yet begun. Between what I'd seen at the hospital and this house, it seemed like everything in this era was an OSHA nightmare.

I looked out at horses clip-clopping down the streets, pulling along carts laden with fruit, bricks, bales of hay and wooden crates containing treasures unknown. The breeze that swirled about the room was nippy, and I could make out the slightest hint of fresh ocean spray, which took a little bite out of the ever-present fragrance of manure.

All this made me consider one truism: No matter when or where a person is, one should always be grateful to have indoor plumbing. And I most definitely was. I was lucky, because I really don't think I would have coped with having to use an outhouse... or worse. Dropped into a situation where the weather was freezing and the crapper was a hole in the ground, I may well have resorted to diapers (which, as I'd recently learned, weren't really as horrible as they sounded). The bathroom in this place was absolutely freezing, but at least it was *inside* the house.

After I'd finished chilling myself in the loo, I decided to find out what kind of person Jennie was by… well, snooping through her house. I couldn't explain why, but I had the distinct impression that she wasn't ever coming back, so how could she mind?

"My" residence on Clayton Street featured a lot of dark wood — way more than I was used to. I knew in later years, much of the woodwork in homes of this age would be painted over, which worked nicely since it left the sculpted form without contributing to a gloomy overall appearance.

Every part of the place that wasn't wood or white-painted paneling and molding was covered with the most wonderfully ostentatious types of wallpaper. It was so very Victorian. All the décor featured bold color combinations and splashy designs, and featured lots of flowers and damask patterns. One of my favorite papers adorned the entry hallway, and had a design that looked like a paisley and a fleur-de-lis had a love child, then an ivy plant grew over it.

Tucked into a dark corner of the foyer was a telephone on a little tiny desk. The placement seemed strange, but I supposed it had to do with wiring restrictions or something. The thing didn't have a dial, and actually looked like it might electrocute me. I did pick up the earpiece once, and heard people talking, so quickly hung up. With party lines and operators and such things, I felt so far out of my element, I wanted to avoid using it if at all possible.

At the far end of the central hallway, opposite the front door, stood a huge grandfather clock. I opened the glass door on the bottom portion of the tall piece, and gave the pendulum a push. I couldn't imagine that was all it needed to start it up again, and would be just one more thing that I had to figure out when I got back to my original reality.

Though the living room setup really gave the impression that nobody lived here, it had the essentials: two love seats, a chair, a coffee table and some mostly-empty bookshelves. Pushed into a corner and hidden under a dust cover, I found a piano and a thick stack of sheet music. I didn't know any of the songs, but they included these gems:

The Absent-Minded Beggar
When Dewey Comes Sailing Home
There's Room For One More Star
My Hannah Lady, Whose Black Baby Is You
I'd Like To Have a Photograph of That

I thought the titles sounded pretty awful... but then again, when you consider modern music like "Call Me Maybe" and "Gangnam Style" — well, I guess the nineteenth century didn't have the exclusive on strange song names.

Moving toward the back of the house from the living room was — based on the appearance of a table and chairs — apparently the dining room. Below a brass six-armed chandelier stood a subtly-carved cherry wood dining table with eight chairs. Nearby was a matching sideboard, on top of which was an ornate and incredibly ugly candelabra that splayed its candle-less tentacles over half the surface. That was the only thing in the house that didn't seem to fit, but looked like it instead belonged in a dungeon somewhere.

Through an open doorway was a basic but functional kitchen. The core of the room was tiny by today's standards, and offered just two freestanding cabinets on the floor, two attached to the wall, a sink and stove. Prep space was minimal, and I imagined the nearby table was likely pressed into service as the need arose... but it wasn't likely to be me who needed it. I realized there was no McDonald's or Wendy's equivalent in this era, but as long as I could, I would be trying to figure out ways to avoid cooking.

It's not like I had a lot of choice at the moment. The icebox — habit made me call it a fridge — wasn't cold, and the stove wouldn't heat. I'm sure there was something I needed to do to make them work, but since they weren't appliances I could just plug in, I didn't want to deal with it just now.

I knew enough history to be aware that guys actually came around periodically and delivered big blocks of ice, which you would arrange your food around to keep cool. But simply knowing what needed to be done didn't make it happen. To make it work meant finding out how to make the ice man cometh, and dealing with that on an ongoing basis. That was honestly more than I wanted to think about right now.

I told myself it would be different if I were running a household — but for just one person, it seemed dumb call in help to start up the stove and icebox.

For the time being, I could fend off starvation with the help of the red apples and spicy-sweet-smelling muffins Nurse O'Neill had left for me.

෴ ෴ ෴

With the main part of the house surveyed, it was time to get nosy. I absolutely felt like I was prying into someone else's life. Reminding myself I wasn't here by choice, I decided I had to make the best of my situation... and therefore, snooping was entirely acceptable. Besides, as far as anyone else could tell, I was merely looking through my own belongings.

I started my hunt in the dining room, because that's where I was already standing, eating an apple.

In one of the top drawers of the sideboard, I found a few things I had wished for the night before: four candles, a box of matches, and one of those quaint little candlestick holders with a loop for your thumb. (I later discovered this thingie had a name: chamberstick.) It would be helpful to have a little light in case I woke up in the middle of the night, especially because the high ceilings in this house seemed to hold a whole lot of darkness.

Other finds included a hardwood cheese board, two crystal wine coasters, a small cloisonné salt cellar and its tiny mother-of-pearl spoon, a box containing silverware for eight, four egg cups, and, inexplicably, a gray wind-up mouse toy with a key.

Moving on to the sideboard's double doors, I hit the textile motherlode. Nestled within the cedar-lined cabinet were ten tablecloths, twenty-odd place mats, about about a hundred identical hemstitched linen napkins, and probably at least twice that many lace doilies of all different shapes and sizes. I couldn't fathom a use for so many doilies, but the year was still young. Perhaps I could start a doily appreciation club, or simply distribute them to the poor in lieu of cash.

I moved on to the secretary — a tall piece of wood furniture, with bookshelves covered by glass doors on the top, a fold-top desk just below, and three drawers at the bottom. For a piece with so many nooks and crannies, there were surprisingly few treasures. Mostly, it held a lot of nineteenth-century air.

In a desk drawer, I found the most helpful thing: a small leather coin purse — black with a little silver closure. I dumped out all the money inside onto the table. The money looked a little different, but I could make sense of it. I tallied it up, and counted seven dollars and thirty two cents.

Despite it sounding like just enough to buy a couple lattes, I guesstimated the seven bucks and change would have the buying power of at least ten times that in my time. So I was looking at the equivalent of roughly seventy bucks in the currency I knew, which was certainly plenty to buy some food... at least enough to get me through the next few days while I tried to figure out this odd, crazy, and, yes — downright disheartening — situation.

రా రా రా

Plopping myself down into one of the formal dining chairs, I realized that, as my mom used to say, I was all dressed up with no place to go. What should I be doing? What *could* I do?

I needed to think, but I couldn't just sit still and ponder all that was on my mind. For the best results, I had to view my problems obliquely, not head on.

Holding a nickel on edge, I flicked it with my finger and started it spinning.

It had taken me more than two weeks to even get to this point in Jennie's life, and you can bet that I wasn't going to be happy sitting around the house, just waiting to figure out what I was doing here. In my other existence, fine — life didn't have to reveal a purpose. I had my kids, and had to do my best for them. But here? When such deliberate care had been taken to drop me into this person? What was I supposed to do?

The nickel spun for a good fifteen seconds before petering out. For me, that was almost a record. Next challenge: Get two pennies spinning simultaneously.

If a friend had explained a situation like this one — minus the woo-woo sci-fi elements — what would I tell her to do? I'd probably channel my zen-mama self and offer her my cosmic perspective. Think positive. Imagine there is a goal, and it will make itself known soon enough. (Granted, it felt a little less silly to offer this kind of counsel after a couple glasses of wine, but the message remained the same: Consider this an opportunity.)

The pennies chased each other over the tabletop until one zigged when it should have zagged, and the two coins collided with a sad thunk sound. I lined up a dime, then gave it one solid flick. It spun so fast, it looked like a tiny metal globe was floating over the surface.

I needed to believe there was a purpose — even if I didn't have evidence. I needed to convince myself that, somehow, everything I felt inspired to do was ultimately bringing me closer to fulfilling my destiny in this place. And despite it hardly being my strong suit, I needed to be patient.

The dime and it twirled and twirled for longer than any of the other coins. Suddenly, it made a beeline for the edge of the table, jumped off and continued spinning on the ground. There it stayed *en pointe* for another ten seconds until it lost steam and slowly teetered to a stop, heads side up.

Sometimes, I'd see little metaphors in life that helped me make sense of my strange little universe. So, if my little ten cent piece could make a huge leap, keep on truckin' and end up right side up... well, maybe I could, too.

One of my favorite quotes elbowed its way into my mind — words famously spoken by the man who would become president next year, Teddy Roosevelt: "Do what you can, with what you have, where you are."

On that note, I decided to make a list of my assets.

Who I knew: Nurse Martha. Um — that's it. (I didn't count the other hospital peeps.)

What I had: $7.32. Three muffins. One apple. A chamberstick. A million napkins and doilies.

Ah, yes. The world was my oyster.

14: The new me

Now that I didn't have 24/7 supervision, I finally had a chance to check out my new self in the full-length oval mirror on a stand in the master bedroom. This was the first time I had been able to take something other than a quick glance at this body, because the hospital had offered me no privacy at all. Even the bathrooms were communal, and the "looking glasses" had been no bigger than my head.

In my view, she was pretty, if somewhat plain. The girl didn't have anything particularly remarkable about her — no marks or moles or birthmarks or other unusual features. Jennie had a pretty face, despite the scar on her forehead, but otherwise... well, let's just say that she was never going to be a contender on *America's Next Top Model*.

But since she was a girl, this body was so *young*, and so petite and lithe. Especially after being fed through a tube for the past few months, "my" muscle tone was pretty much nil, and there was very little extra fat. There was just a bit in the right places — enough to keep Jennie from looking anorexic.

I had no experience being a really skinny person. My 21st century body was stocky by heritage, and, let's face it, never exactly bounced back after having babies. In a fist fight of me then versus me now, I'd wipe the floor with my Victorian self. But if the two of us went head-to-head in a dating pool? Undoubtedly, the tiny and pretty Jennie would win all the hearts.

As Robin, I never had hips that stuck out further than my stomach, so the fact that this girl had super-flat abs was a total novelty. I didn't miss my belly pooch and the full hips that had so disappointed me by emerging in high school — but I could hardly fault them, because they had served me admirably, helping to create and deliver two of the finest persons on the planet. Stretch marks had been my constant companions since about the fourth month of my first pregnancy, and it was strange to see no such lines on this skin.

True to this girl's Mediterranean roots, her silky smooth skin had a light olive tone. I bet it would tan very well — something I'd never been able to do with my overly-fair skin in the Now, because the sun would quickly turn me bright red with a freckle fiesta.

In my teens, the same growth spurt that pushed me up to 5'8" had delivered D-cup boobs, and things had only expanded in that department through pregnancy and nursing, so it was a new revelation to discover breasts that were small and perky and tipped with rosy nipples the size of nickels. On the topic of what separates the girls from the women, the hair "down there" was considerably fuller than I was used to, but not so bad that I would need a garden rake to help me tame it. For the legs and underarms, though, I would definitely be needing a razor or miniature machete.

Which brings me to the embarrassing reality: Looking at this new body was truly, madly, deeply and completely strange. I was standing there looking at a naked girl who wasn't really me, which was uncomfortably awkward and voyeuristic. Don't get me wrong — it would have been just as bizarre to have suddenly discovered that I was equipped with a twig and berries. Given that the previous owner of this form was 16 years younger than I was only enhanced the creepy factor.

My hair was short — it had been cut to accommodate the lovely holes they bored in my skull to take off some of the pressure while my brain recovered from its trip to the bounce house. Even the finest hat money could buy would only partially cover the Frankenstein-like scars on my forehead from what was clearly a major knock on the noggin. (The other marks — from where they had drilled my head open — were, fortunately, now obscured.)

But when they prepped me for surgery, by the grace of the gods, they didn't shave my entire scalp. It looked as if they had drawn a line over the top of my head from ear to ear, and shaved only what was in front of that line. Over the last few months, the chopped hair had grown back about an inch and a half. On the flip side, my locks were as long as they had been before, and went about halfway down my back.

If you have been reading carefully, you will know exactly what I'm describing — business in the front, party in the back. That is correct: In the year 1900, I invented the mullet. If that crappy hairstyle somehow gets popularized decades too early just because of me, I might never forgive myself.

15: The Now – Holding on to the Now

You know you're not sleeping well when you consistently wake up five times as tired as you had been the night before. Normally, I'd try to get to bed earlier, sleep in more, maybe take a few naps... but not only did my mom duties preclude most of these options, I knew that the moment I would lay my weary head, I'd wind up back in My Own Private Idaho.

Some part of me insisted that if I stayed busy enough, consumed enough caffeine, and played my music at slightly below ear-piercing levels, I'd be able to postpone my departure until I was ready to accept and handle the whole past scenario. My hope was that this jaunting to the past stuff was sort of like a plane trip — if I missed my flight, I would end up on the ground until the next available departure. I wasn't holding my breath the strategy would work.

Despite the odds, I started the day by downing one of those nasty-tasting energy elixirs. Then throughout the day, I filled my belly with more than three (but fewer than ten) homemade iced coffees. By the time I was utterly overcome with exhaustion, I was trying every trick in the book to stay awake. I had the windows open to let the brisk air in, had music blasting my headphones, and tried to stay on my feet, walking around with even the occasional groovy dance move.

Up until last month, I would have wondered why the hell someone like me — relatively intelligent, fairly well-traveled and somewhat adventuresome — would balk at the opportunity to get so up close and personal with the past. Yes, it was probably a once-in-a-lifetime opportunity. A lot of experiences are unique and rare — like being jolted awake by a big earthquake — but that doesn't necessarily mean that they're pleasant, or you're hopeful for a repeat.

It made me think about all those failed Hollywood marriages — where Mr Gorgeous marries his Mrs Perfect — and three years later, they're kaput, usually because a bird in hand is never better than two in the bush.

All my years on this earth have taught me that joy is relative. It all depends on where you are in life, what you're used to, and what you strive for. Visiting another time and place certainly illuminated how much I appreciated (and took for granted) every day, and all the wonderful things in this modern world.

Here, I was warm. I was in my element. My babies were here with me, and most of my family and friends were nearby, or just a couple mouse clicks away. I could lounge around in comfy clothes, work on my own schedule, and eat whatever I fancied. If I got bored, there were about a thousand different things to do within a ten-mile radius.

But there? There, it was cold. It smelled bad. I had very little strength. I had a perpetual headache. I couldn't figure out how to work their stupid lights. The clothes were uncomfortable. I had no idea what to do with myself. And I didn't know a soul.

By half past one in the morning, the yawns were coming non-stop, and I'd long past the point of diminishing returns and was twenty steps into Crazy Town. I could scarcely form an intelligible sentence, let alone a cohesive thought. Ironically, so much of the day had been spent stressing about having to go back to 1900, I'd made myself even more tired than usual. After splashing some water on my face, I turned on the TV, grabbed a book, and sat down on the least comfortable chair I owned. The last time I looked at the clock, it was creeping up on 2 am, and I knew I would not be able to hold out much longer.

I was right. A moment later I was shivering, and opened my eyes to the beams of light that were making a halfhearted attempt to warm the skies and the streets of old San Francisco.

16: Proving it to myself

Time traveler or delusional? Now that I had some freedom, and was pretty certain that I was revisiting a page in history, it was time to prove to myself that I was not insane... or, as the case may be, determining if I actually *was*.

To that end, I wandered aimlessly around this house that was supposedly mine, trying to find some inspiration. When the floor creaked, I thought about hiding something under a loose floorboard. Then, slipping into the role of the potential future homeowner, I imagined my response to someone knocking on my door who said they wanted to mess with my hardwood flooring and then take whatever they found there. That would be a hearty *helllll no*.

My eyes fell on my coin purse. I opened it up and retrieved a bright copper penny. Maybe, if I could wedge that penny deep into a crack between bricks in a wall, maybe it would escape detection for a hundred-odd years, and I could find it again in the future.

I'd already started to tell myself that the chance that nobody would extract it from a hiding place was minuscule, when I remembered the terrible 1906 earthquake. A huge portion of the city fell or burned — or both — and that would likely render even the most clever concealment tactic useless.

When I got back to my time zone, I would check the old newspaper archive that was online and see how this neighborhood fared during that disaster, but I didn't want to waste any effort on the penny concept until then. It would be too depressing to dream up a scheme that might never answer my question definitively. That would only serve to make me feel that much more in limbo.

I'd searched the Library of Congress web archive before, back when I was trying to track down some of my family that moved into the Bay Area in the early 1920s. There were thousands of newspapers archived — the complete editions, not just the front pages. I remember marveling at the politically-incorrect headlines, while finding the vintage advertisements and fashion spreads to be simultaneously fascinating and amusing.

And now here I was, apparently living in that fascinating yet amusing era.

It was right then that a thought — so simple, so logical, so obvious — popped into my head with such strength that it actually made me twitch: I could place a classified ad in the newspaper for my future self. Such a method wouldn't inconvenience anyone else, nor would it get lost during the in-between years.

I just needed to decide on something unique to write.

It was incredibly tempting to create a message something that, if someone interpreted it correctly (and at the right time), they could be rich beyond the dreams of avarice. I wanted something with words that had *definitions* in the past, but had true *meaning* in the present. I could combine them all in a short message that read like something in English had been translated to Chinese, then into Japanese, and then back into English, like "Target apple text web tweets. Yahoo!"

As soon as I started thinking about that concept, though, something felt off. Nothing major — just a sort of intuition, pushing toward something less prescient and more personal.

After mulling it over all evening, a plan emerged. I decided to use my daughters' initials, along with the description of a crazy colorful creature they had invented for story time the night before. Scribbling the words on paper, I moved them all around until I had a version that was as good as it was going to get:

Love to LJH IMH from a purple orange dotted feathered lizard

After reading that no classified ads could be placed by phone, I was left with either mailing in my ad and money, or taking it in myself.

The fastest and most efficient way to place the ad would be to trundle down to *The Call* newspaper office in person. But I'd have to do it tomorrow — Friday — or else wait until their business office reopened on Monday. There was no way I was going to put it off any longer than I had to. I was way too eager to get this question answered.

I knew from my random bits of research that the paper was headquartered in what was, by far, the tallest building in the city. Because of its height, I decided that I didn't need a map — I could use the building itself as a beacon.

It wouldn't be quite as handy as using my cell phone's GPS app, but I should manage to navigate my way downtown easily enough.

Now, of course, I can't help but wonder: If I hadn't been so confident — *overconfident* — in my ability to get from Point A to Point B and back again, would my entire life in 1900 have gone another direction entirely? Or, perhaps, would fate have just figured out another way to get the job done?

To this day, I can't tell how much of my lifetime as Jennie had depended the play, and how much on the player.

17: Clothing differences

If I planned to go out in this world, I might as well look the part... but it wasn't going to be easy. See, I can tell you right now that anyone who says, "Everything was so much simpler years ago," never had to get dressed back then.

Putting on proper attire was a job and a half. In fact, it was so complicated that when I was back in the Now, I had to look up directions. I kept looking for a simple version outlining the way to put on the clothes the proper way. Apparently I didn't miss the guide — there just wasn't one. I found several articles that went into exhaustive detail about each item of clothing, but the specific how-to was still pretty vague. I was left with the impression that, at best, only two or three people on the planet actually knew, step-by-step, how women dressed in 1900. (I also learned that they called their outfits *toilettes* — which finally shed some light on why some perfume was often called "toilet water"... but did nothing to explain why the thing you peed in was called a toilet.)

With the information I was able to find, by observing other women, and by trial and error in front of a mirror with the actual items of clothing that Jennie had purchased during her time behind the wheel, I figured it out. Mostly.

The top half:

First, there were huge cotton undergarments. They were amusingly full and puffy, but at least the material was thin. Over that, most women would don a corset — one that, if laced up correctly, would curve my torso into the favored "bust-and-butt" out fashion of the time. Forget that. I laced up that puppy as loose as I could while still making sure it didn't slip down or fall off. Even so, the whalebone frame supports made it incredibly uncomfortable. How uncomfy? If you've ever had an annoying experience with an underwire in a bra, you get the drift — but just multiply that by about twenty.

Next, I had to wriggle into a corset cover — made of a fabric similar to the underwear — then a petticoat slip that went from my waist to the floor.

(I was supposed to wear two for proper fullness, but decided to simplify the process and only put on one.)

The bottom half:

I have been a bikini underwear girl since I swapped out my granny-panty briefs when I was about ten years old. But here, sadly, the concept of snug-fitting underwear hasn't caught on yet.

Instead, I need to wear what they call "drawers." These are sort of like floppy white cotton capris (they go from the waist to slightly below the knee) that have an opening in the crotch, along the lines of the flap you would find on mens' boxer shorts. Some were quite plain, others had lace and ruffles around the leg openings.

Having so much air "down there" has been disconcerting, and I'm still not used to it. It feels like I've gone commando in a dress. The whole point is to give you the ability to use the toilet without having to get half undressed.

Next up I had a garter belt, necessary to wear the requisite stockings. The stockings were made of silk, and weren't like today's tights or pantyhose, but almost reminded me more of a second skin. They didn't have elastic to expand and hug your legs, and therefore were sort of loose-fitting and prone to wrinkling at the ankles and knees... and just sagging all over the place. Not attractive.

There was one bustle available, but since I'd read that they were in or out of fashion depending on the week — plus looked uncomfortable and unnecessary — I skipped adding one to my ensemble.

Finally I got to the fun part: the dress itself. I had about twenty different options available, the majority made with cotton of varying weights, but a few others made of crepe, satin and woolen fabrics.

Jennie had clearly been a fan of bold colors, because apart from one gray dress, the gowns I found ranged from those in Easter egg shades to jewel tones. After some hesitation, I decided to take a walk on the wild side, and selected a purple cotton dress with of navy blue horizontal lines on the top half. The sleeves were long, fitted all the way down the arm, with a slight flare near the wrist.

Slipping into the gown, I noticed it had been constructed with exemplary attention to detail. Not only were the stitches tiny and neat, they were doubled at all stress points. I couldn't find even a single loose thread. After some concern that I wouldn't be able to fasten all of the tiny hook and eye clasps that ran up the back of the dress, I found that really, it was just like putting on a bra with a foot-long closure panel.

It fit so exquisitely, so effortlessly, and I realized that none of her clothes had come off the rack at any store — they had all been either custom-made or finely tailored to fit every contour of Jennie's body perfectly. (If anything, the dress was a little looser than it had probably been before, but the fabric accommodated the weight loss admirably.)

The most popular footwear was apparently the boot, of which I found an impressive range. (I read online that you could also get what are termed slippers and sandals, which are a far cry from what we know by those names, but are more like typical everyday women's shoes.) The shiniest boots in the cabinet looked impossibly small. Then I looked down at my feet and was surprised to see that they looked pretty tiny, too.

As there were no socks to be found — were they not yet invented? — I pulled a stocking up my calf, then slowly worked one of the boots over my right foot and ankle. To my surprise, the thing fit perfectly. After I stepped into the left boot, I laced them both, then stood up and wiggled my toes. Though fairly new, the black leather had been worn just to the perfect degree to be comfortable but still supportive.

Now all dressed, two more little things were required since I was going to be seen in public: covering for my hands and my head.

She had three pairs of white cotton gloves, and one pair of black. I chose white, and they went on easily enough — only giving me hassle when it came time to button them at the wrist. (It was much easier to fasten the left with my ungloved hand than to try to button the one on the right with slippery fingers.)

Finally, I needed to choose a hat. There were five headpieces on three wire dummy heads. They all had faux flowers, feathers, beads or other accoutrements that I normally wouldn't be caught dead wearing on top of my head.

Right off the bat, the hat that looked like a pheasant died on it got a no vote. Ditto the chapeau that seemed like it would be right at home in Princess Beatrice's closet. I chose the simplest hat there — one made of dark blue felt, which had but one feather and a comparatively tasteful pearl brooch — and plonked it on my head.

And *voilà*! The result: Stiff, compressed, weighed down, and thoroughly uncomfortable... but absolutely ravishing. Looking in the mirror, I decided that I would totally be at home on *Masterpiece Theatre*. I wished more than anything that my girls could see me now. Iris was always harping on me to wear dresses more often, so it was a shame she couldn't get a load of me now.

I turned from side to side, and was amazed at how much space this slight little body now required. The bottom edge of the skirt spanned about four feet, which meant I took up sixteen square feet of surface area just standing still.

Walking around dressed in twenty pounds of clothing that felt like fifty was another thing entirely, and the corset conspired with the other items to shift my chest forward somewhat awkwardly. I learned in a hurry that slouching would be painful — if not impossible — in this getup, and couldn't decide if that was a good thing or a bad one.

In all, it reminded me of being pregnant, when you had to get used to your new and unimproved center of balance — but with the addition of so many skirts that you have to rely totally on feel to figure out where your feet stop and the ground begins.

To get the hang of it, I took a few steps. As I walked, the skirt of my dress and all the petticoats combined to make a soothing swish-swish-swish sound. When I stopped, the momentum would carry everything back one swish and forward halfway again. I enjoyed the sound, so I paraded around the room, taking a few paces at a time, then stopping suddenly to see how many times I could get the skirts to rebound. (This had been repeated far more often than any sane person would admit, but the movement somehow soothed me.)

If the mirror could whisper its secrets, it would tell you that, for a moment there, I was ridiculously captivated with my reflection. While I'd normally shy away from being in such a narcissist... well, this I allowed for one simple reason: I simply couldn't believe that the person being admired was actually *me*.

18: Going downtown

By the time I had eaten, taken care of some other important tasks (like nodding off while sitting on the sofa — you know, to gather my strength), then made myself presentable, it was already well after 2 o'clock.

The gloves on my hands made locking up the house a bit slippery, but the third time was the charm. Carefully, I took each step from my porch to the street level, and didn't stumble. I was so proud of myself. Turning down the street, I walked as quickly as I could without feeling like I was going to tip over. These shoes were nice, but there was something about their angle or maybe the heel that felt a little awkward. I was sure that, in time, things would smooth out — and until then, I decided that I would just be very, very careful.

A young woman walked by me in the opposite direction, and offered me a pleasant, "Good day." I returned the compliment, and smiled and smiled and smiled because that she hadn't even looked at me twice. I had blended in. I had actually put on all these ridiculous pieces of clothing in a correct enough sequence to pass muster with the locals. *Muahahahaha.*

Where was I going? I knew I needed to head northeast, and should take a cable car or streetcar... but I was sketchy on the how exactly to do that. It's funny: None of the old papers offered a primer on how to use public transportation. Fair enough. In my day, I doubt there was too much call for a step-by-step tutorial on how to ride the bus.

I needed to find out where to catch the cable car. In this era, they didn't have bus-type shelters, and rarely were the stops even marked. I'm sure if I had just waited another day so I could look into where the various streetcar lines stopped, I would have found a more efficient way to do this... but impatience got the best of me, as per usual. The nurse had encouraged me to get on my feet, so it was all for the best, anyhow.

In need of assistance, I decided it was time to initiate an encounter with the citizens of this brave new world. I looked around, considered my options, and chose to approach an older couple who were out walking hand-in-hand. I asked them if they knew where I should wait for a trolley or streetcar going downtown. The man deferred to his wife, who pointed me in the right direction. "See that carriage with the blue? Just past there, dear, go right a few blocks. You'll see people waiting on the side of the road."

She was right, and at the intersection of a small crowd and the cable car tracks, I found the stop. I stood with a few other nattily-dressed gentlepersons waiting for the trolley who nodded their hellos. There were also some kids hanging around — ragamuffins who, in my day, could have easily auditioned for a community theater production of *Oliver!* I was pretty sure they were only interested in grabbing the moving trolley cars and jumping aboard just for kicks — and probably to avoid paying the fare in the process.

Though I'd never have admitted it to anyone there, the idea of sneakily catching a car actually sounded deliciously fun (and wonderfully unladylike). Alas, I well knew that even in my real, well-fitting, twenty-first century body, such an endeavor would be a dangerous trial of my eye-hand-foot coordination. Given my experience thus far in this skin — yeah, that would not be something wise to attempt.

Fifteen minutes later, I was being whisked downtown at a slick twenty miles per hour on the Market Street Cable Railway.

When we finally hit Market, the chaos level ramped up a few notches. People were getting on and off, milling around, and I could hardly see through the throng enough to read the street names. Worried about missing my stop, I ended up getting off the car a little too early. But hey, at least that meant I could do a little sightseeing... because I had to walk about four long blocks to get to *The Call* offices.

And the sights I did certainly see.

If my carriage ride from the hospital two days ago had been like looking at a movie set, the process of actually tromping along the boulevards and avenues was like being an actor in a scene.

The streets were variously made of dirt, something like asphalt, layers of gravel, cobblestones, and even wood — and all were definitely more bumpy than I was used to. They were especially tough to navigate in my narrow, high-heeled boots. I came perilously close to twisting my ankle at one point, and gave a guy a thrill when I instinctively reached out to brace a fall. I grabbed hold of his coat, which helped me manage not to topple completely over. I think he thought I was trying to lift his wallet, because he eyed me suspiciously as he helped me stand up, then not-so-subtly patted his pockets to ensure everything was still in place before dismissing me with a curt, "Good day."

The roads were also covered with something we didn't have to deal with in the modern day — horse manure. It was everywhere, and nobody seemed to notice or care. I could smell it from inside my house, but once I got outside? It was overwhelming, quite disgusting, and so pungent in spots it made my eyes water... and I smiled to think that my girls would have been laughing about the smell as loudly as they complained.

Calling out to me and demanding attention was the fashion of the day. Maybe I didn't watch enough period dramas, but I was astonished by so much of what I saw.

For one thing, I hadn't expected the women to be wearing such a huge range of colors and patterns. In fact, their dresses, hats and accessories were, in some cases, downright gaudy. I had thought Jennie's wardrobe probably represented the extreme end of the splashy scale, and expected most people would be wearing peach, olive and other muted shades. Oh no. Clearly, many of these women were not shy about wearing bold tones and patterns. (If this was daytime wear, I couldn't wait to see how they dressed up.)

And as fascinating as the people were, the buildings were the stars of this city.

Although San Francisco was hardly pristine and perfect, pretty much nothing was more than 50 years old — and most business addresses were a lot newer than that. Very few places had been around long enough to be derelict, and with so much hustle and bustle going on, you could feel what history books would confirm: this city was growing every year.

Just a couple years back, I had a very needy client who worked downtown. By paying me at more than double the market rate, he bought the opportunity to micro-manage my web design work, which meant weekly visits to the City's financial district.

At the time, the commute had been an annoyance. But when I was walking those same streets in the year 1900, I was grateful — actually jump-and-click-my-heels delighted — to be one of the only people in the world (if not the only one) to bear witness to that juxtaposition.

Even though I wasn't a huge fan of modernism — the look that's so prevalent now on the city's many skyscrapers, with elements like flat facades and lots of steel and glass — I could appreciate it for what it was. But what made my heart sing? The fancy styles of the past. I could spend all day admiring the buildings that featured intricately carved stone, decorative moldings, columns, arches, and all kinds of other architectural embellishments. It was truly art.

The buildings also weren't nearly so gigantic and imposing in 1900. You could walk around and still see more than tiny patches of blue sky and sunlight. The closest the city got to having a skyscraper was the tower I was going to go see. It had fifteen floors, and, with great pride, was proclaimed the tallest building west of the Mississippi.

After I turned one more corner, I was relieved to see the Call Building just in front of me. Called the Central Tower in the Now, it had only been open for two years and was absolutely picture-perfect. It was clad with some kind of pale stone, and featured a very ornate — borderline garish — Baroque dome that looked a lot like the top half of a Faberge egg. I got that goosebumpy feeling when I remembered how this structure, so new and vital now, would be pretty much toast (literally) in about six years.

After risking my life to cross the street, and nearly getting run over this time by a hay wagon that appeared out of nowhere, I was hugely relieved to finally arrive at Market Street at Third. The doorman smiled, nodded, and let me into the bright and shiny world where this world of information lived in luxury.

If the top of the structure was fancy, its lobby was downright posh. It was shaped in a semicircle, and the walls and pillars were clad in marble. The gorgeous tile mosaic floor had a big CS fashioned into it. The initials were for the publisher and industrialist Claus Spreckels, who was perhaps best known for founding the Spreckels Sugar Company. His son owned the building, as well as the newspaper itself.

Three huge, shining bronze doors led to more elegance. Door Number One: The Call offices, Door Number Three was the Columbian Bank. And if you picked Door Number Two, in the center, that opened to a trio of fancy bright copper elevators and a marble staircase. (I also noticed that every doorknob I saw carried the CS monogram. Clearly Mr Spreckels had a very healthy ego, along with the bucks to back it up.)

Utterly exhausted after my journey, my fresh-from-the-hospital body cried out all the more when I found out that only the Call's business office and press room was in this building. I had read that the office I needed was located on the thirteenth floor, but clearly something had been changed along the line. Now, all of the editorial and art staff were housed in The Stevenson Annex — another building down the street. "These aren't the droids you're looking for," I said out loud, but nobody seemed to care. Lots of foreigners in this town I guess.

Somehow, I was able to persuade myself to keep walking just a little bit more. I literally had to encourage myself to take it step-by-step. This constant pain reminded me way too much of labor to be any fun, and I wasn't going to get a cute little kid out of it either.

When, at long last, I arrived in the Classifieds office, I was so happy to be able to sit down that I think my eyes teared up a bit. I didn't mind one bit that I'd have to wait at least twenty minutes — besides, this way, I'd have a chance to eavesdrop on the process. I overheard someone offering a reward for their bicycle, a middle-aged woman looking for a housekeeping gig, one man who had two chickens for sale, and two people who needed tenants for rental properties.

By the time it was my turn, my heart rate had returned to normal, and I could speak without taking ragged gasps of air between each sentence.

"Miss... um, Demi..."

"Yeah — don't worry about it. Just call me Jennie."

"All right, Miss Jennie."

Overall, the process of placing the ad was simple. I asked for it to be posted under the personals section, and the young guy who carefully transcribed my message didn't ask any of the questions I had somehow been dreading. His affect was very much like a man who had seen perhaps not *everything*, but more than enough to know to just take the money, and don't ask any questions.

At a penny per word, my ad cost eleven cents for a one-day insertion. After handing over a nickel and six copper coins, he handed me a receipt, and I was on my way.

19: All turned around

Like a creaky old grandmother, I walked along the cobbled streets, back to where I'd exited the cable car. My corset had begun to feel extremely cumbersome, I itched in places I could not scratch with any dignity, my stockings were getting baggier and droopier with every step, and I constantly had to hold up the ruffly bottom half of my dress to avoid dragging it through all sorts of muck.

Now that I had real-world experience looking like a proper turn-of-the-century lady, I tell you: the idea of wearing a bikini briefs, a comfy bra, a simple cotton T-shirt, yoga pants and some super-comfortable sneakers never sounded so wonderful. Furthermore, I hereby swear that I will never again complain about any item of clothing that contains elastic.

Despite not knowing the comfort and convenience that awaited them in the years ahead, all the other women I saw waiting for a ride downtown looked so poised and serene. If things were pinching, slipping and itching under those pretty skirts and dresses, they sure didn't show it. I wished I had half as much grace.

Finally the cable car rolled up to the stop, and every able-bodied man, woman and child hustled on board. It filled to capacity quickly, but I wasn't going to wait for another one to come by. Already rush hour — such as it was — unless I wanted to hang out downtown for another hour or three, it was time to skedaddle. I planed both feet on a step near the back of the car, and held on for dear life as the conductor started to roll us up the street. The instant he rang the bell, I knew that for the rest of the night, I would have Judy Garland stuck in my head, singing the words, *"Clang clang clang went the trolley."*

Once a few people cleared out of the standing-room-only area, I moved to a nearby seat. In a display of chivalry that's never out of place, a peppy-looking young businessman offered me his seat. I took it calmly and graciously, but was so thrilled to be able to sit down, I nearly hugged him first.

Being seated also meant I could look out the window, and I finally had a view of something other than one guy's overcoat and another man's elbow. I almost wished I couldn't see out so well. That cable car ride will be forever seared in my mind as one of the most harrowing experiences in either of my lives. At several times, it felt way too much like we were taking an open-air trolley through Pamplona's running of the bulls. Although none of my fellow passengers blinked an eye, it seemed to me like the streets were full of people who were either completely oblivious to traffic, or every one of them had a death wish. People would randomly wander on the tracks directly in our path, several boys played chicken, a few carriages made terrifyingly close dashes around the tram, or tried to be the first across an intersection.

Ultimately, to avoid wetting my cute little drawers, I had to turn and focus on the road we'd already safely traversed. Constantly in awe of the newness of this town, I know that I appreciated details the other people here wouldn't think twice about. I loved to look at the buildings, and reveled in the intricacy of the detail on the moldings, the perfect stonework, and how the crisp edges of the bricks and blocks had no weathering and wear.

Then, outside of downtown proper, everything calmed down, and I could lean my head against the glass, and daydream while I watched the city go by. The roads and houses were so clean and uncluttered, it seemed like a Disney version of San Francisco. There were many lots, occupied only by some scrubby grass, and even entire blocks without a single home.

So captivated by the scenery, twenty minutes went by before I realized I'd been watching the world whoosh past for a little too long. My neighborhood had slipped by without me noticing, and I was now a couple miles away from home. It took more than half an hour to figure out how to get back to where I needed to be. After I finally backtracked, took a different cable car, and then disembarked at my stop, dusk had fully arrived.

I pushed myself to keep putting one foot in front of the other by repeating that I only had to go about four blocks before I could finally take off these horrible boots and get something to drink.

Those four blocks turned to five, six, seven... and by the time I had counted to twelve, I found I'd circled right back around to the damn streetcar stop again. I was seriously, head-smackingly pissed off at myself. How could I have possibly gotten so turned around that I couldn't even figure out what general direction I should be heading? The last time something like this happened to me, I was traipsing around with my girls in a double stroller, so I made a valiant — but ultimately vain — attempt to remind myself that

I'd been through worse.

Hungry, exhausted and aching everywhere from forcing my muscles to work so hard, my very last nerve started to show major signs of fraying. Screwing up my trip home was just the cherry on top. Even before that, with the anxiety that was apparently part and parcel of living in a time that was not truly my own, I was way closer to the verge of tears than I'd like to admit.

Even knowing I was lost, I persisted and kept walking. Certainly there was some landmark I'd noticed as I walked by that could help me identify where I'd been. But I could think of nothing except how there had been a closed carriage with blue curtains — which now, naturally, was nowhere to be seen.

I had been out wandering aimlessly for so long, night had fully fallen, and it was cold. I was shivering from my nose to my toes, and could hardly hold my hands still. This svelte bod didn't have as many insulating layers of fat as I was used to, and a stiff breeze would chill me to the bone (especially when the wind managed to shoot up my dress).

Nearly frozen, irritated and humiliated, I was ready to cry uncle, aunt, second cousin — whatever needed doing to get out of this mess. So when I saw the welcoming lights of a brick-faced building with brass letters that spelled out POLICE, I was drawn to the double doors like a moth to a bug zapper.

I stepped into the station house, and tried not to say a bliss-filled "aaahh-hhh" too ridiculously loudly. It was so lovely and warm in there, I only wanted to go curl up on the floor next to their heater and sleep until morning. It wasn't a half-bad idea, because by tomorrow's light of day, I would definitely be able to find my way home.

"How may we assist you?" asked the man at the desk. He looked like Santa, and that somehow made me a little more comfortable.

"I'm sorry," I started to say, "I'm a little bit lost."

"This is the Stanyan Street police station. Where do you need to be?"

"Well, um, actually, I'm trying to get home. I know it's near here, but — well, see, I just got out of the hospital, and I can't quite remember where I live, or how to get there."

"And your name?"

This was a moment I had been dreading. "It's Jennie," I said. Taking a deep breath, I attempted to guess my last name. "Genevieve... Demedeecy."

As soon as I answered, he looked over his glasses and appraised me with fresh eyes. "Oh, Miss Demedeecy, very well," he said with a smile. "I must apologize — I think I have been saying your name wrong all this time."

Even though my cheeks were already flushed from my walk, my pronunciation gaffe made my face even redder. "Oh, well, no problem. Everyone says it differently. Even I switch it up now and then."

He laughed, naturally assuming I'd made a joke. Joke was on me.

"Allow me to find someone to assist you. Just a moment."

Sadly, my legs didn't have the strength to hold me up for another moment. Once Santa walked back to find an elf or whatever he was going to do to help, I shuffled over to the closest seat in a row of wooden chairs. I hoped he wasn't rushing, because I was so delighted to be out of the nippy night air and off my feet for a bit.

As I was reveling in the joy of my fingers and toes and ears and nose beginning to thaw, Kris Kringle came over to me. With a fittingly jolly smile he said, "Officer Donovan here will see you home," and pointed vaguely somewhere over my right shoulder.

I looked to the right to see who was going to help me... and I swear that the moment I caught a glimpse of the officer, time seemed to almost stop. I was still turning around, and suddenly it was like being in one of those shampoo commercials when everything is in slow motion, and you see the chick's hair fan out before she faces the camera and smiles knowingly.

I'm pretty sure I was smiling, but it was anything but a self-assured, knowing smile. When I think back, I am pretty sure it was the happy face of a three-year-old being handed a lollipop the size of a dinner plate.

This uniformed policeman walked toward me, and my brain practically exploded with synonyms for gorgeous. See, in any time — and probably in almost any place — Officer Donovan would be considered staggeringly handsome. The guy seriously looked like he would make a fine living in my day as a dancer... the kind that goes onstage, rips off his uniform and takes dollar bills from the gleeful audience.

Wincing slightly as I stood up, I straightened my voluminous skirts and tried my best to look like a supermodel. With my limp, the rumpled dress, and hair that was going every which way, I *so* totally nailed it.

He stopped about three feet away from me, and gave me a slight bow. "Hello, Miss diMedici," he said, putting yet another spin on my last name.

Abruptly I realized how young and, um, vibrant this new body was. The cop simply gave me a little grin, and — boom! — I was feeling a happy little tingle. His eyes — they were amazing. A cool crystal blue.

I took a deep breath and reminded myself that he was about half my real age, and that helped tone things down. (Well, a tiny bit, anyway.) It was all but impossible to look away. I actually moved my hand up in front of my eyes to interrupt the connection. *Come on, Robin. This is a cop, and it's time to act like a normal human being.* "Act" was indeed the operative word here.

I extended my hand and uttered the best line ever: "It's nice to meet you."

A look of something like indecision or mild concern flashed across his face, and after an uncomfortable pause, he shook my hand. "We have met before, but I'm sure you don't recall that — a consequence of your unfortunate accident, I imagine." I could sense a hint of a British accent there.

I nodded, "Yeah — yes," quickly correcting myself to a more proper affirmative. "I guess you know where I live then?"

"Yes, Miss," he smiled. "I just looked it up in the Crocker-Langley city directory. It's not far."

Now *that's* service.

He scrawled something in the ledger on the desk, put on his hat, then held the door for me as we exited the building. So proper.

A wisp of wind hit me squarely in the face the moment I stepped outside, and I hurried to button up my jacket. I wished I hadn't brought one that was so lightweight... but, then again, I never expected to be out after dark. As if on cue, Officer Donovan took off his coat and put it over my shoulders. I should have objected — it was my own stupid fault for not being dressed properly, not to mention dragging this guy out at night to walk a bumbling idiot home. But the coat was so warm, and he was so sweet, and I really was so grateful.

We took a route south along Golden Gate Park, then went east on Fell Street when we hit the park's panhandle. At every turn, the cop explained to me where we were, pointed out landmarks, and explained how I could always use those as future breadcrumbs.

As we walked, I tried not to stare. Since my eyes were going on autopilot again, I stayed slightly behind, and hopefully out of his view. He was tall, had strong shoulders and a slightly muscular build. His face — with the perfect Cupid's bow on his lips — reminded me a tiny bit of a young Johnny Depp, but less broody and exotic, and more English and adorable.

"Just about half a block until you're home," he said. Therefore, "not far" was about half a mile... meaning I had gotten myself turned around even more than I thought. My legs should have been protesting loudly by now, but instead, I didn't hear them make a peep. I think anything they were complaining about was completely drowned out by my joy at going home at last, and going there with such an escort at my side.

Some of the houses we passed were starting to look a little familiar, probably because they were the same style as mine. Most had the glow of lamplight coming from inside, which looked so warm and welcoming since it was so dark outside. With a start, I realized that without any lights at my home, the place would be like a tomb. I hadn't made any preparations for dealing with the raw night.

So, I decided, I would just have to forget about food and focus only on sleep. If I took things slowly, I could probably feel my way over to the staircase. Then once I got to the second floor, I was pretty sure I could find the room I'd slept in last night again, and the bathroom, where I could at least get a drink of water.

That's when another option occurred to me, delivered to me in a voice that reminded me a lot of my high school basketball coach. *Suck it up.* In this case, that would mean shrugging off any embarrassment, and actually request some help. It made sense, I decided, because that's exactly the advice I'd give to anyone else in my position. So why not take it?

Although I felt stupid asking Mr Hottie McHotterson for assistance, my options were limited. My best bet: Just *act* like I had the chutzpah required.

"There is one thing I wonder if you can help me with," I said, stumbling slightly over the words, which, in turn, made me even more nervous. To add insult to injury, my subconscious interpreted my stress as the cue to launch into verbal diarrhea mode: talk that was fast, messy and annoying.

"I don't know anybody here yet — not that I remember anyhow, and so I have no one else to ask. I just got home from the hospital, as you know, so there's a lot I haven't figured out. I will eventually, of course, but need some more time to kind of get myself set up here again and so forth. It won't be too long before I'll get back on my feet, so to speak, but they say sometimes you just have to ask for help, so..."

As I spoke, I saw his brow begin to furrow — slightly at first, and becoming more pronounced as I rushed through my monologue. A somewhat concerned expression from the receiving party was par for the course when I was blathering, so I was merely marginally embarrassed, not concerned.

His look made me lose my train of thought for a moment, but with effort, I was able to finish my sentence. "So, do you think you could help me turn on the gas in the house? I don't have any light, and it's really cold, but I have no idea where to look or what to do."

Considering it was not a particularly amusing request, I was bewildered to see Officer Donovan start to roar with laughter. It was quite a sight: a handsome man in a proper police uniform who was so far beyond a mere chuckle that he was nearly out of breath. Like an idiot, I began to giggle — even though I wasn't in on the joke, the amusement was infectious.

Finally he was able to talk again. "Is that all?" he said. "I thought you were going to ask me for money!"

"What? No! Nothing like that," I sputtered as a beet-red flush crawled across my face.

"Don't worry," the officer said. "I would be happy to help as much as I can."

When we got to the house, my favorite policeman went around the back, where, I assume, he turned on the gas main. Then he came back to the front yard, where I was waiting by the garden gate. With extreme formality, he asked if it would be acceptable for him to come inside to light the lamps and start the stove, adding, "If you'd like, Miss, we can wait for a chaperone."

Was this some Victorian etiquette thing?

"Don't be ridiculous. We don't need a chaperone. I promise that I won't bite," I told him. Then my mouth continued on its own, and added, "Well, not unless you want me to." Now we could both blush.

I must hand it to the man — he handled my horrendously cheesy remarks with aplomb. After missing only a single beat, he asked, "Shall I also take a look around inside, Miss? Check the property?"

"That would be fantastic — thank you. And please call me Jennie. 'Miss' makes me feel like I'm six years old."

❧ ❧ ❧

It took him only minutes to hit the lights. I don't know what sort of magic he used, but the place looked completely different — elegant, romantic and inviting — in the glow of the gas lamps. I waited in the foyer and savored the ambiance (and the slowly-building warmth) while he took a quick sweep through the house — ground floor first, then upstairs. I heard his footfalls going up and down the hall, and doors opening and closing.

"All clear," he announced as he at last descended the stairs and came into the foyer.

"Well, that's good," I said, showing my gift for stating the obvious. "And thank you so much for your help. I really appreciate you taking the time." I really was grateful — probably much more than he could ever imagine. This day had been a disaster, but he was the payoff that made it all worthwhile.

The words inviting him to stay for cup of coffee or something were on my lips when I realized that I could hardly offer java — or even half-decent hospitality. The house was still as cold as a morgue — I'd need to light the fireplaces for any real heat, apparently — and the only edibles I had on hand were one and a half slightly-stale muffins. Not exactly party time. Out of options, I instead launched into a clumsy goodbye.

"Well, goodnight, Officer, and I hope I will see you again soon," I said. "For good reasons, I mean. You know — not because I'm lost again, or you're arresting me. Not that I'd do anything that you'd have to arrest me for, of course, but..." Oh, mouth. You so enjoy foot.

"My pleasure, Miss," he said. "I look forward to seeing you again, too, and hope sincerely I will not need to arrest you." He was trying to keep a straight face, but failing miserably... and that just made the boy all the more endearing.

20: The Now – Proof

One benefit to the time travel was that even though the paper wouldn't publish my ad for another two days, it didn't matter. From the vantage point of Now, it was all in the past, and whether that little classified notice appeared in Monday's edition or Wednesday's was of no consequence. I had only to go to sleep in order to prove myself.

And prove myself I did.

My oddly-worded announcement showed up in the personals section on page 29 of the Sunday paper, sandwiched between a request from "a gentleman of good character" who sought a brunette to marry, and an ad touting "Your bust enlarged 6 inches; failure impossible; harmless." It was like my little message through the decades was purposely cocooned in with the ever-present desires of humankind.

It came out exactly the way I'd written it, too, albeit in the clunky handset type common to the presses of a century ago: *Love to LJH IMH from a purple orange dotted feathered lizard.*

While the end result was only the size of a postage stamp, its meaning was huge: I finally had evidence I was actually traveling back and forth in through the years. Equally important, I finally had evidence I wasn't buckets-of-crazy.

As a bonus — and for the bargain-basement price of just eleven cents — I had changed history in one small but indelible way.

21: Who's there?

I woke to find the sun fighting its way through the fog, shining thin ribbons of light into the bedroom. For the first time in this place, I didn't feel like this day was going to be a nightmare. I had a plan. I had some purpose. I even — sort of — had a friend.

That happy vibe only revved up a couple notches when went downstairs and discovered the morning newspaper had been slipped through the letterbox. Fresh reading material (boring though it may be) was particularly welcome in a house mostly devoid of books.

I adjourned to what my grandfather had always called "the reading room" and checked out all the news fit to print during my morning constitutional.

Murphy's law proved itself to be alive and well, even in the year 1900, because after not even two minutes, the doorbell rang. And rang. And rang again. Then someone knocked.

I wasn't going to answer it. I debated getting up, and decided there was no point to answering the door, because who did I know here? In all likelihood, from what I'd seen, it was a nosy neighbor — which was the *last* thing I wanted to deal with right now. When the rings and knocks persisted, I decided it was more likely a door-to-door salesman, and I needed neither a set of encyclopedias nor some Fuller brushes.

Besides all that, I was wearing only a sleeveless, short-legged cotton bodysuit thingy that would have been considered pretty revealing even in my day. I wasn't in the mood to give anyone that kind of thrill this morning.

So I sat back, flipped the page, and waited for them to go away.

The next sounds would have made me pee if I hadn't just a moment ago emptied my bladder: a heavy key turning in a lock, and the front door opening.

No no no no no no no, I thought. *Please don't have sent me back to all this way just to have someone go all Jack the Ripper on me.*

"Hello, there — anyone home?" a man called out.

I was frozen with fear and couldn't answer (even if that had somehow been advisable).

Another voice — a woman's — said, "See? She's not here. Let's get this over and done with."

Then there were footsteps going up the stairs. Keep in mind, I'm upstairs — admittedly, at the far end of the hall — but I was sitting on the toilet, terrified, one-piece underwear around my ankles. I was immensely grateful that I had closed the bathroom door almost all the way.

Because of how the bathroom was laid out, hiding behind the door was about my only option. I rushed to wipe, and discovered then that there was, of course, no toilet paper to be found. Trying to ignore the feeling of grossed out in favor of feeling a general panic, I pulled up my clothes and tiptoed the five feet across the room after grabbing the plunger — the only thing in there that could possibly be used as a weapon of sorts. I aligned myself with the hinge side of the door and peered out.

I couldn't see too well, but was able to tell that the two of them were in the front bedroom, where they bickered as they tossed things into a couple of suitcases. With all of the smooth, hard surfaces in the house — the wood floors and paneling — and most of the rugs rolled up, their voices were perfectly audible.

She started, "There's nobody here, so now can you tell me why the rush?"

"Just shut your mouth and pack it up."

"Not until you tell me what it is that we're doing here."

While shoving stuff into a bag, he answered, "I got wind that Jennie woke up, and she's going to be coming back here. So we have to get these things out now, because I don't know when she will be coming home."

"Oh, yeah. We can't let her find this stuff."

"Which is *why* we are *here*," he answered, like he was reprimanding a dog. "Load up those satchels, and use the pillowcases for anything that doesn't fit."

I couldn't see exactly what they were jamming into the bags, but it looked like mostly random knickknacks and a few bound stacks of paperwork. Then the guy pulled out the bottom dresser drawer, tossed what looked like some clothing (probably mine) on the floor, and yanked out a panel at the bottom of the drawer. Neat stacks of cash from the bureau were quickly slid into a black satchel, with the excess slipped into his pockets.

"I'm done," she told him just before he snapped the last bag closed.

"A couple more things and then we can get out of here," he answered, and stepped out into the hall. On the wall were four small framed oil paintings that had I'd glanced at before, which seemed notable only for looking pretty nondescript. He took them off the wall one at a time, folding them up in a sheet.

"What are those?"

"They're paintings — she got them from her father," he said, hoisting the load under his left arm. "I know a pantywaist who's going to plunk down a hundred bucks for them. Each."

"Don't you think she'll notice those missing?"

"Nah — she didn't know what she had."

I moved my head down a little to get a better look at what they were carrying. A moment later, the chick dropped her bags, looked straight at me, and started walking in my direction. I think my heart actually stopped.

"What are you doing?" he yelled at her.

"I have to *go!*"

"Damn it, Mags, you can hold it."

She stopped in her tracks. Then, just like a modern-day teen might, she huffed, rolled her eyes, and trudged back down the hall to pick up her bags.

My heart started beating again, and I realized I'd been holding my breath, too.

He went down the stairs first, and she traipsed a few steps behind.

"So," she said, "this is where it happened?"

"Certainly is."

They disappeared below my field of view, but I could still hear every word.

"Holy mackerel! How did she survive that?" Her voice was squeaky. Annoying.

"I don't know," he said, and I could imagine him shrugging. With a laugh, he added, "I suppose I didn't push her hard enough."

It took about ten seconds for me to process what he said. Could I have heard him correctly? There really wasn't another way to interpret that statement.

If my body hadn't been programmed to stay stock still, I might have bounded out of that little bathroom, leaped over the railing, and gone kamikaze on his ass.

But no. My little waif-like new self stood there, shivering on the cold tile floor, for probably five minutes after they left. It wasn't until the shakes got so bad that I actually bit the side of my tongue, which snapped me out of my reverie.

Seriously — had I truly just seen a man who wanted me dead... one who had been bold enough to do something about it? I think the answer was yes. And as such, this day's dream had now been officially elevated to nightmare status after all.

22: Making my report

The police station looked a lot less imposing in the light of day. I felt stupid and scared and confused, and hoped I was doing the right thing by coming here. Would they believe me? Would they care? And even if they did, what could they really do to help?

I asked at the desk to see Officer Donovan. Two ticks later, he came up to the counter.

"Oh, yes — I remember you. You're the girl who didn't want money," he said with a big smile.

Was he flirting? I hoped he'd be up for exploring that concept another day.

"I need some help. Again. And don't worry — I'm not asking you for money." I sputtered out a little nervous laugh, then reminded myself to take a slow breath. "Someone broke into my house this morning. Well, I think they had a key, but I didn't let them in."

He smoothly shifted into a professional mode, and gently asked if I'd been hurt. After I assured him that I was fine, he questioned me further.

"When was this?"

"I guess about an hour ago." Time seems more fluid when you don't have a cell phone clock in your pocket.

"Did you confront them?"

"No. I hid in the bathroom."

"Did you see the person, or people?"

"Yes, I got a little glimpse. Mostly I listened. There were two of them — a man and a woman. I'm pretty sure he called her Maggie," I said, and saw him stiffen. "But I didn't hear his name. I think they knew me, but they definitely weren't acting like friends of mine. They were taking stuff out of my house, including what looked like a lot of money, and some other stuff."

I started fiddling with a pencil on the desk, nervously rolling it back and forth in tiny motions with one finger.

"Other stuff, meaning... ?"

"Some paintings, some silver maybe. I'm not totally sure. I was, you know, hiding."

"Well, of course I will help you. We will write up a report right now."

"Thank you. I really appreciate it." My hands were actually trembling now. "But there's something else," I said. "I overheard the man say something that really freaked me out." At the moment, I couldn't care less that I used a completely anachronistic turn of phrase.

"What was that?" he asked, his eyes showing genuine concern.

"You remember how there was that accident a few months back, and I only woke up a couple weeks back." He nodded. "Well, the guy told the girl that he had been there when I fell down the stairs."

The officer inhaled sharply. He reached out as if he was going to put his hand on mine, but stopped short and instead rested it on the desktop just a few inches away.

"He said that he hadn't pushed me hard enough."

∽ ∽ ∽

This time when I walked home, I had *two* cops to accompany me. If my neighbors liked to spy out their windows, they would definitely I was some kind of delinquent for having cops at the house twice in the space of just a few days.

After unbolting the door, I let the two men go in ahead of me. Following quietly behind, I pointed out where the baddies had been. The officer I didn't know stayed with me in the foyer, while the one I knew checked the ground floor.

"Nobody down here," he said, then asked me to stay downstairs while they searched the place more thoroughly. I parked myself at the dining table to wait while they worked. My fingers beat a constant rhythm on the table as I heard furniture being moved and both windows and doors opened and closed.

After ten or fifteen minutes, the two officers came downstairs and talked in the hallway, too quietly for me to hear. With a tip of his hat, a smile and a "Miss," the other guy left, and Officer Donovan came into the dining room.

"The house is secure for now, but the first thing to do now is to change the locks. Front and back," he said. "We also checked all the windows. There were two that were open just a bit, so we latched those up, but you might want to buy window locks as well."

"Definitely. Absolutely. Will do that today."

"Would you like to give me your report here, or come back to the station?"

"Here, please, if we could." He nodded and then looked at one of the chairs. "Oh, please," I said, "have a seat."

He walked around the table and pulled out a chair opposite me. Victorian propriety strikes again... but that was okay. The guy was still super hot, but I was not at all in the mood to play drool at the cop. In fact, I'd been on the verge of tears all morning, and almost couldn't wait for him to go so I could cry for about an hour.

"All right, Miss diMedici," he said.

"Please, no 'Miss' stuff — remember? Call me Jennie."

"I will try," he said. "But it's not..."

"Proper?"

He nodded and shrugged.

"Let's forget about the cult of propriety here. You're in my house, sitting at my table, helping me out. Again. I think you've earned the right to use my first name."

This obviously wasn't as easy a decision for him as it had been for me. After a few beats, he offered a compromise. "How about this: When it's just you and me, we will use our given names. In public, we won't. Will that work?"

There was something so conspiratorial about the idea that it almost made me want to giggle. "Yes, that will definitely work. There's just one problem."

"What's that?"

"You haven't told me your first name yet."

With a big smile, he stuck out his hand. "Travis Donovan, at your service."

"Charmed, I'm sure," I said, and completed the handshake.

The Q and A session took about half an hour, and it turned out to be a helpful diversion. When *Travis* asked me the questions for his report, his demeanor was professional and strong, but also calm and soothing. *Travis* offered so many encouraging little words here and there that I felt better with every tick of the clock.

Even now, looking back, I can't remember what exactly he told me... but I do know that when all was said and done, I didn't feel like I needed to cry anymore.

23: Golden

Just when I was finally starting to feel okay with these back-and-forth shenanigans — getting slightly comfortable with life in the year 1900 — the break-in happened and made me feel uneasy all over again.

If I never went back again, I wouldn't miss the place. But I *would* miss getting to know Travis.

I felt ridiculous for even thinking such a thing, because in reality, I was closer to age 40 than to 30, and here this guy probably hadn't even hit the quarter century mark. But let's face facts: He was absolutely beautiful, and I was absolutely smitten.

See, there's a certain security that comes with lusting over a movie star or TV actor: It ain't ever gonna happen, so go ahead and think up the craziest fantasies you want. I felt that same brand of safety with the cop. Not only was he way, *way* out of my league, I was a person living in a borrowed body and on borrowed time. But, hey — just because I wasn't buying didn't mean I couldn't enjoy window shopping.

The kids were at their dad's until tomorrow, so I decided to take a break. Until I fell asleep tonight, I was not going to ponder my role in the grand scheme of things. I wasn't going to play right into the hands of whoever or whatever was sending me back. Today, I was going to put the script aside, relax, and maybe daydream a little about the guy I had met.

It didn't occur to me until much later how Fate aced the game with her own brand of reverse psychology.

∽ ∽ ∽

Right after he and I first met, I had run a newspaper archive search for "Officer Donovan" in the San Francisco newspaper, but didn't come up with much. Now that I knew his first name, though, it occurred to me that I should try again, just for fun. Kind of like Google-stalking through history.

There was only one result — a tiny two-column-inch story. While it wasn't the kind of gossipy piece I wanted to find, it was exactly what I needed to see.

STABBED IN PERFORMANCE OF DUTY
Police officer Travis Donovan was stabbed once in the knee yesterday in an alleyway off Fulton Avenue near Masonic. The incident occurred shortly after one o'clock in the afternoon, during an attempt to question city resident Walter Houlihan in connection to a recent burglary. As Donovan turned down the alley, Houlihan buried a six-inch dagger in his leg, to the hilt. Donovan removed the knife and held the prisoner, who attempted to escape. Surgery is to be scheduled, and it is thought that the officer has a very good chance of recovery.

While the boy's injury hadn't been life-threatening, I felt in my bones that this needed to be stopped.

The incident had occurred in the early afternoon of January 23, 1900, which was was tomorrow in my Then timeline. I had been looking for a reason to go see Travis, so how perfect was it that I now had a legitimate one? With such foreknowledge, I was uniquely equipped to save him from that attack.

So it was settled: Bright and early tomorrow morning, I would go down to the police station in person to warn him. Somehow.

The more I thought about it, the more I realized there was no good way to phrase such a warning. For example, three possibilities I considered:

From the top, I deemed those options dumb, dumber and dumbest.

But what was the best way to convince him that he was in danger? All that came to mind were variants of the above three ideas.

To think get out of my useless thought loop, I concluded that I had to get out of the house for a little bit. A change of scene meant a change of mental state.

In every session on the elliptical machine at the gym, moving to the rhythm of my music, I usually had at least one random revelation. But since the girls weren't home, I didn't feel like spending an hour of my alone day exercising. (Besides — half the reason I worked out was to set a healthy example for the kids. If they weren't around to witness my tremendous discipline and increasingly firm abs, why bother?)

Since I needed to think, I would take a walk... to my favorite thinking chair, which just happened to be at the coffee shop a few blocks away. I even instituted a personal reward system: If I came up with a workable idea, I could order a mocha. If I didn't, I was stuck with plain water.

Twenty paces from the door, my lightbulb moment arrived — and of course, I instantly realized I'd been overthinking it.

I didn't need to *tell* Travis that he wasn't safe — all I had to do was steer him clear of the situation by whatever means necessary. I could divert him with questions about my case, ask for advice on securing my house, get lost again, or maybe even invite him over to my place for tea and crumpets. The worst case scenario (which wasn't really all that bad) would have me tailing him so I could help out in case he ended up in some hairy situation.

There was a lot I didn't know much about — such as standard police procedure in that era, what kind of weapons an officer would carry, how men of this time generally felt about dating eccentric young women who had recently emerged from a vegetative state — so I was not going to worry about details. I would just figure it out as I went along. And as long as he didn't end up meeting a certain burglary suspect around lunchtime, we'd be golden.

24: Hair today, mess tomorrow

I read that even in the not-too-distant past, women seldom washed their hair. In this era, they only went through the routine every two to four weeks or so — and when they did, it was a separate, long and drawn-out affair. And since you couldn't really buy prepared shampoos here, you had to cobble them together yourself by mixing together things like eggs and soap and ammonia. (From what I had observed so far, these people delighted in over-complicating even the most basic things.)

Forget *that*.

I decided I would make the process easy-peasy by simply washing my hair during my bath. Great idea, right?

So many things went wrong in this process, I almost don't know where to begin. I suppose I'll go in sequence:

Started bath. Soon realized water was frigid, so added more hot water while using the toilet facilities. When done, put one foot in to check current temperature; scalded said foot in seemingly boiling water. Resumed adjusting water temperature. Got into bathtub, but due to excessive fiddling with the hot and cold taps, the moment I was seated, water started to flow over the side of tub. Pulled out plug, then quickly exited bath in attempt to minimize waterfall.

Ran naked into hallway to find towels. Nearly slipped and fell to my death (again). Discovered there were no towels in the linen cabinet. In heat of the moment, forgot where any other towels might be. Eventually decided to use the only absorbent material available: a sheet. Returned to tub area and draped sheet on floor to sop up some water. Looked up when I heard the end of the water circling the drain.

Repeated process of filling the bath. Got the temperature and water level more or less correct this time. Stepped into bath. Enjoyed few moments of bliss.

Began to bathe. Soap smelled bleh, but seemed to clean well enough. No shampoo available, so started washing hair with the soap. (Not the wisest choice.) Soapy water dribbled into eyes, and eyeballs felt like they had been stung by hornets. Ran fresh water to clean them out, which helped, but froze remainder of body in the process.

Went to rinse hair, and could not get fingers through the mop on my head. Had I lathered up with a cup of glue? Strands were not just tangled, but seemed completely knotted and very sticky. Rinsed ten more times; planned to brush it through later.

Decided to cut losses and get out of tub. Leaned over to get towel, which had been neatly placed on the towel rack pre-bath, but lost my grip. Dropped towel into the still-pooled (and now very cold) water. Used small unsoaked portion to get most of water off my face, then dried off my feet so I wouldn't slip again in the hallway. Just after crossing threshold to the bedroom, slipped anyway.

Very, very carefully regained upright posture and walked over to the bed without further incident. Spread-eagled self on bed to air dry until it was too cold to continue, then snuggled up under blanket. Was so nice and cozy, ended up falling asleep, and napped for an hour. (Did not return to modern era during this time.)

Finally got out of bed. Looked in mirror. Discovered matted bird's nest on head.

Got dressed and tried to comb through my hair, but it was impenetrable. In the Now, would just dump in some conditioner and be a much happier camper. Here, conditioning rinse not yet invented, so decided to substitute something that was available: olive oil.

Carefully, massaged drops of oil (plus water) into hair, and brushed it through piece by piece. It worked well enough, but made my hair very greasy — exactly what I was trying to avoid in the first place.

Felt like I was being taught a lesson here. I didn't understand what was being said, but I definitely heard the tone.

At least I was finally clean and dry. Bright side and all that, right?

෴ ෴ ෴

Back in the Now, one of the first things I did (after taking a long shower where I relished every moment spent with my real shampoo) was to try to figure out where my hair washing endeavor had gone so terribly, horribly wrong. It didn't take too long to find this mention in an article from 1902:

Never rub soap directly upon the hair, for it sticks and cannot be removed with ever so many washings...

"It sticks." Understatement. Next time — assuming I could build up enough courage for a second attempt — I decided I would try a proper shampoo recipe I discovered in a Sacramento newspaper from March of 1899:

Make a shampoo of the following ingredients: One ounce of green soap (an article resembling soft soap and smelling like melon seeds), 1 tablespoon of powdered borax, the white of an egg, and a pint of very warm water. Dissolve the borax to the egg, beating slightly. Put the soap into a bottle, and add the hot water, and shake well; then add the egg and borax, and shake until all is well blended.

Before I go to bed tonight here in the Now, I think I will wash my hair once more. In some sort of cosmic way, maybe it will slightly offset the annoyance of the greasy mop I'll be wearing when I wake up.

25: January 23, 1900

The moment I stepped onto the sidewalk in front of my house, I was greeted (more like accosted) by two effusive and chatty women who apparently knew me. I said one word — *Hello* — and that was apparently the signal they needed to launch into two solid minutes of babbling and bragging.

After they peppered me with opinions on my health and neighborhood gossip — all without even stopping for half a second for me to slip in a word or two — I stopped listening and started plotting my escape.

The moment they started to speculate about my police officer escorts the day before, I seized the opportunity. I muscled my way into their ramblings and told them I was, at that very moment, headed back to the station with another clue in the case. That news got them both to perk up.

"Oh, goodness gracious — a clue! What is it?"

"It's a piece of information used to solve a mystery," I said with a smile, "but that's not important right now. "

After a nod to each lady, I politely excused myself and marched down the street in double-time.

❧ ❧ ❧

Given how often I'd been visiting the police station recently, I deserved a punch-card to earn a free donut or something.

When I arrived there this morning, I peered around the area behind the front desk until I spotted a friendly face. Travis was so occupied by the paperwork sitting on the table in front of him, he didn't even notice me until I slid up alongside him and offered a quiet, "*Hola, amigo.*"

While not startled, he did look surprised. "Miss diMedici," he said, and stood up. "I was just thinking about you — your case, that is."

He pulled out a chair for me, and said he had been planning to visit me to discuss some of his findings.

"I used the resources at my disposal, and discovered the two people who entered your house were likely Walter Houlihan and Maggie Gallagher."

The moment I heard that first name, I gasped, but not for the reason Travis assumed. "*Houlihan*? Are you sure?"

Now the events of my last day in the Now all made sense. Smart-ass little brat Fate had played me like a harpsichord. I had triggered Travis's investigation into my case, which was going to lead to his attack. This was something new — not just history playing itself out.

"Do you remember him?" Travis asked. "Several of your neighbors stated you and that, uh, gentleman were seen together on a number of occasions, and he had been in your house several times."

"Well, he certainly did seem to be making himself right at home," I said. "And how lovely everyone noticed I'd been entertaining some guy in my house."

That's when he told me nosy neighbors, had, in fact, been my salvation. I had been found by the lady next door, who came by to share some hot apple strudel. She had grown concerned when Jennie didn't respond to the doorbell.

As the story goes, nosy local baking legend Karoline Werner had gone all around the outside of my house, peeking into each of the ground floor windows. Finally, her wildest dream came true when she saw someone lying on the floor in a dark pool of drying blood. While her actions may have been of the somewhat creepy variety, if the lady hadn't, I probably wouldn't be here.

"On October thirty first, Halloween night, a neighbor found you lying face down at the bottom of the staircase in your home," Travis said, watching me carefully, probably to make sure I wasn't going to flip out. "The ambulance attendants initially thought you were, uh, not alive — you didn't seem to be breathing — but then they found a weak pulse."

"So does this guy — Walter, I guess — have a criminal record?"

"Well, Houlihan has had several arrests for theft, and one for battery, but no formal charges were ever filed due to lack of evidence."

"Was the chick ever arrested?"

"'*Chick*'? Uh, Miss Gallagher, no — she has no record at all," he said, "but it should be noted that Miss Gallagher and Mr Houlihan are now a couple."

My mouth automatically volunteered, "Sucks to be her."

"Excuse me?" He didn't look offended, only confused, probably because ladies don't say 'sucked.'

"I said, 'Shucks... to be her' — like, uh, it would be really disappointing to have your friend arrested." It was a lame explanation, but would have to do.

Travis nodded like that somehow made sense, and continued to tell me about the case. "Another officer in the department did get statements from the both of them, along with those from three women who live nearby," he told me. "Ultimately, no witnesses to the incident itself came forward. Without anyone to say otherwise, it wasn't considered to be anything but an accidental tumble down the a set of stairs, and termed 'misadventure,'" he said. "As you can imagine, events such as this are unfortunate, but not uncommon."

I mentally paged through court cases I knew — from the strange-but-true OJ Simpson-type stuff to the hundreds of complaints I'd seen presented by district attorneys, who prosecute the offenders, on *Law & Order*.

"And as for trying to make a case now? What kind of proof do we have? Do we even have any?"

"I checked with the hospital this afternoon," he said. "Unfortunately, the clothes you were wearing at the time of the accident were incinerated months ago, and you had nothing else in your possession. The rug in your home was disposed of, and the blood cleaned up, so we really don't have anything to use as circumstantial evidence."

"Nothing to use except my head, that is," I said, tapping my scar.

That got a laugh, and then he read me a couple excerpts from my medical record. Along with a break in my left distal humerus, I suffered a depressed skull fracture to the left side of my frontal bone. They operated to lift off the bone fragments, and to relieve the increased pressure on the brain due to the injury.

"What about witness testimony — meaning me?" I asked. "I could mention what they said when they broke in."

"If we tried to present what you overheard to the court, it would likely — and at best — be considered hearsay, because doctors have gone on record to say you have no actual memory of the event."

"Their word against mine."

"Even if that was allowed, in my experience, Mr Houlihan could simply say it was an accident. He was not legally required to report such an incident, nor does he have a duty to rescue."

"Argh! Son of... " I remembered to censor myself, and smoothly changed the way I was going to end that sentence. "A gun." I had a feeling that even the relatively benign word 'bitch' would not be appropriate in this place.

"So to bottom line it," I said, "the courts can't help us and there's nothing we can do."

"Actually, I was planning to stop by Mr Houlihan's workplace later today, to ask him a few more questions. Perhaps you would be so kind as to help me determine what specifically went missing from your home."

I started interrupting him with a barrage of "no no no" before he'd even finished talking. "Please — let's not. I don't think talking to him would be the best course of action at this particular juncture." I sounded like I was reading from the script of a courtroom drama.

Travis sat up very tall in his chair and asked, "Has the man threatened you?"

"Nothing like that, don't worry," I said, all the while trying to coax a smile to my lips. "We can still work on the case against him, but I don't want to directly involve him with it in any way right now. I think it's better for everyone — and probably safer for me — if he doesn't know he's a suspect."

Slowly, my favorite police officer's posture relaxed. "In that case, I don't think there is any legal recourse at the moment," he said, a resigned look on his face. "I'm so very sorry."

Though he was disheartened by this lack of progress, I couldn't be happier. The only thing I'd hated more than the idea of him getting hurt was the knowledge I was the one who put him at risk in the first place. And the only thing I loved more than believing I was keeping him out of harms' way was the realization that I had been able to do so wholly because of actions I'd taken in my other life.

With the ad I'd placed last week, I had done something in the past to change the future... and just today, I had seen it worked the other way around, too.

So even while I was thanking Travis for his help, I was plotting and planning.

Now that I knew the player, I had options. Walter was bound to do something to get his name in print. Therefore, in my time, there should already be clues I could use to catch the creep in the act.

So what if the crime that would eventually get him a jail sentence didn't have anything to do with Jennie? If I could keep him at arms' length while helping secure some sort of justice, that was good enough for me.

26: Knock knock

Given how I'd successfully saved Travis from his appointment with a knife blade, I tromped along the city roads back to my house filled with a sense of purpose and possibility. Things were just about to begin. Finally, I could let myself get excited about the opportunities afforded by my access to the future.

After I figured a few things out, I would have the chance to help people in this time zone. I fancied myself a sort of superhero (minus the tights and cape and codpiece). I would be unstoppable.

Unstoppable, that was, until it came to the women who lived near me. As I turned down my street, I realized that the hardest part of the whole deal was going to be dodging my neighbors. Unfortunately, the degree to which Victorian culture required personal participation was truly staggering to me, a product of the introvert-friendly internet age. I already had a little taste of society, 1900s-style, and wasn't fond of the flavor.

While my release from the hospital hadn't attracted much attention, the morning after I arrived home wearing a policeman's coat, the women on my street started to actively take notice. They hadn't yet demanded an audience, but I kept finding all these mini business cards scattered on the foyer floor, each of which apparently had been pushed through the mail slot in the door.

After the whole debacle with the break-in, I was completely in no-go mode for visitors — which was made worse because there was a decided uptick in the number of people dropping by. It was all about the gossip quotient: If *one* police escort had piqued their interest, *two* such chaperones had made them practically rabid. If I thought I could somehow avoid the attention, I was fooling only myself.

By mid-afternoon, it was clear: The ladies I had run into that morning en route to the police station had been just the first wave. By the time I got back home a couple hours later, strangers started "calling." I don't mean telephoning — they felt welcome to show up at your front door any time between about nine in the morning to six in the evening for a nice little hi howdy. The expectation seemed to be that I would not only let them in and keep 'em company, but my place would be clean and I'd have refreshments at the ready.

I didn't know these people, was still getting my bearings, and felt about as sociable as the latest contestant to be kicked off a reality TV show. When they inevitably asked about the police presence, I channeled the grace and calm of an experienced first grade teacher and explained I had simply gotten lost a couple times. The nice officers had showed me home, and that was all I was willing to share. (I refused to even mention anything about the Walter and Maggie fiasco.)

Caught completely off-guard, I let a few of these folks in before I figured out how to manage them. Soon thereafter, started playing up my exhaustion, pain and need for healing. (Hey, it was mostly true. Coma girl here!)

A remarkably perceptive older woman noticed my discomfort at having to address this issue and offered me a tip to help minimize the visitor count. Upon her suggestion, I posted a little handwritten note by the doorbell, essentially excusing myself from hostess duties, but thanking my dear friends and neighbors for kindly for dropping by.

I spent the rest of the day indoors, making plans and writing lists. Finally, when the moon was high, I went to the other place — the land where history had already been made, and the only ones who cared about my comings and goings were the people I had created.

27: The can-do girl

The fog that January morning was eerie — kind of like the London mists you see in Jack the Ripper movies. Every time a wagon rolled by, it seemed like a little bit of the haze would cling to it, and the mist would be pulled along a bit, like a wisp of taffy. Inside and out, it felt chilly and damp, which only added to the dreary feel of the whole place.

But for right now, it didn't matter. Regardless of the weather, today was going to be a good day. That's because I had looked into the future, and figured out how to save three lives by tonight.

That made it sound so simple, when in fact, finding the right people to help had taken up my entire day in the Now. The media outlets of old had only limited space in which to print the most interesting and important stories. Unfortunately, the things editors in the Then considered to be newsworthy seldom matched up with the kind of things I could fix.

At the outset, I decided I was going to avoid any heroics that involved putting myself truly at risk — like trying to pull someone our of a burning building or getting in the middle of a gunfight. That concept led me to spend an hour coming up with guidelines to put into play while I scoured two different San Francisco newspapers.

I was on the lookout for incidents or accidents with the following in common:

- *Preventable*: I had to have enough information — and advance notice — to stop something as early as practical in the process.
- *Identifiable*: Needed to be able to figure out who my subject was, and to clearly ID the issue/danger.
- *Accessible*: Should not require me to be somewhere or break in someplace I would not normally (legally) be able to enter.
- *Reasonable*: Must be something I could accomplish on my own — without reliance on another party, or the need for any weapons.

With those tenets in mind, I found two definite saves, one pretty likely opportunity, and a dozen other mishaps that were close but not quite workable. For my first day on the new job, though, I was pretty sure that three tasks would be plenty.

༄ ༄ ༄

Rescue number one involved a newborn baby girl who had been abandoned. In the original timeline, the poor little thing would be found dead from hypothermia late this afternoon.

When getting dressed, I skipped the corset and the other constrictive undergarments, threw on a simple blue frock, standard-issue boots, then cozied up in a thick winter jacket I had found in the downstairs coat closet. I didn't know what it was made of, but a couple dozen soft and furry animals had apparently given their lives for its creation, and I wasn't going to make their sacrifice for naught.

Next came the most difficult part of my plan: Getting out my own front door and down the street without being stopped by the busybody brigade. I peeked out the window, searching for a moment when the street was nearly empty. For a while, it looked like I was going to have a long wait. Then someone must have baked a batch of cookies or started handing out free booze, because everyone suddenly descended on the home about ten doors down. The timing was great, and I didn't care what was going on over there. The moment the coast was clear, I hurried out the door, down the street and around the corner without once looking back.

After a frustratingly slow cable car ride, I arrived at the intersection the article had mentioned. I got there a full twelve hours before the baby had been discovered in the previous timeline... yet the alley was quiet. *Too* quiet. I stood completely still, but couldn't hear even the faintest whimper. I remembered that there had been no estimated time of death reported in the news. Could I already be too late? With a light hand but all possible speed, I checked each of the boxes and crates scattered on either side of the grubby alleyway. I found nothing, nothing and more nada.

Near the back door of a bakery, a box full of wadded newsprint stood on its own. Something about it — the placement, perhaps — looked unusually deliberate. I stepped over to it and carefully lifted the papers scattered on top. Contained within was one beautiful tiny newborn. Her eyes were shut, and the little fists clutched to her face were closed tight. It took a moment to find a pulse, but finally it was there — steady but slow. She was wearing only a petite nightgown made of some thin material, and from her color and weak breaths, I could tell she was chilled to the core.

"Hey there, sweetheart," I cooed. "We're going to get you all warmed up, okay?"

After I unbuttoned the top half of my jacket, I removed the rest of the crumpled newspapers covering the baby. In one smooth movement, I tucked the little girl against my chest, then buttoned the coat closed around us both. The heat my body offered was the surest and safest way to keep the baby warm for now. With my arms crossed over my chest, I made sure she had space to breathe, and hurried off to the nearest hospital. It was at least fifteen minutes away by foot, and while the streetcar would probably be faster, its schedule was too fickle to rely on today. When her ice-cold hands and feet were nestled against my dress, I realized the baby was so much colder than I expected.

Little one started to wake up about five minutes into the journey, and by the time I pushed open one of the hospital's front doors, she was starting to wriggle and mew like a hungry kitten. "It's going to be okay, little love," I sang to her. "Hang in there."

As soon as I was in the building (which appeared to be just as primitive as my former residence), I demanded immediate assistance. "Baby here — nearly frozen to death!" I called out to anyone who would listen. A nurse rushed over to me as I opened the top of my coat. I looked down at her wee bald head, and for the first time, felt a stab of fear. *Did I find her in time? Is this just like what happened before?*

Another nurse hustled over with a gurney and formed a little nest with a few blankets. I gently lifted the baby up and out, gave her a quick kiss on the noggin, and handed her over. "She has a weak pulse and slow, shallow breathing, but she's a lot better than she was twenty minutes ago. She wasn't even conscious when I found her." As the words spun out of my mouth, I quickly considered each to make sure I wasn't using any futuristic terms they wouldn't understand.

As the women nodded and rushed off with the little girl, yet another nurse walked over to me. She looked older, sterner, and definitely in charge. There were no pleasantries, but simply, "Tell me what happened."

Fueled by adrenaline, my story tumbled out: "I was in an alley about a mile from here and found the little girl, and I was worried she was dead, so held her close to get her warmed up, and brought her here as quickly as I could," I paused for a breath. "She woke up a few minutes ago, but of course she still needs help."

"Why were you in the alleyway?"

"Pardon me?" At that moment, her question seemed about as relevant as asking me my favorite color.

"How did you happen to be in the alleyway where the baby was found?"

"I was just... looking for something."

"Looking for what?"

What, indeed. It was a scuzzy back street with garbage cans and rats and other things that would probably make me sick to my stomach. I offered the first remotely plausible idea that bounced into my mind. "Newspapers. I was looking for a paper from the other day — there was a story I wanted to cut out. For my scrapbook."

"A story. I see. *Which* story?"

A little alarm bell went off in my head. *What was with the third degree, lady?*

"It doesn't matter. I was just here to bring the baby, and now I have, so I'm gonna go," I said, then added a snarky, "You're welcome." As I turned to leave, I saw her nod to one of the burly security guards. In an instant, he was by my side and had clamped my wrist in his sizable hand.

"What are you doing? Let go of me!"

The nurse answered for him. "We need you to wait here until the police arrive. It's quite contrary to the law to abandon an infant."

"You have this all wrong! I didn't abandon her — I *rescued* her. I found her and brought her to you!" I heard my voice's pitch rising, and strained to stay calm. "I'm the good guy here."

"If it's not your child, Miss, how did you know she was a girl?"

Ouch — nice catch. "Well, I guess she looked like a girl..." I knew that I sounded less than convincing.

"And you just *happened* to find her in a deserted alleyway. At dawn."

"Just to be clear: She is not my baby."

The moment I said that, she pressed her lips together so tightly, it looked like her mouth had been erased. After making me stew for an agonizingly long thirty seconds, she finally answered, "We will just have to let the police decide."

I did not like that idea one bit. For multiple reasons, I was trying to do these rescues on the down-low. In particular, I couldn't have Travis catching wind of anything that would make him question my sanity... well, not any more than he already did.

"Lady — nurse — ma'am," I said as an idea winked and flirted with me. "If Mr Muscles here," gesturing to the dude who had yet to release his grip on my arm, "would give us a little privacy, I can prove it to you. Beyond the shadow of a doubt."

In stony silence, the woman walked over to an empty bed a few yards away. She motioned for me to come over, and my wrist was released. Once I reached the bed, she pulled the drapes closed around us, then waited with her arms crossed for me to take the next step. She clearly thought I was either going to bolt for the exit, or launch into a teary explanation of why I had to leave my baby. I was glad I could offer her a little more of a surprise.

Without offering a word in my defense, I slipped off the big, warm, furry minky thing and set it on the mattress. Before the nurse could even begin to process what was going on, I bent forward, grabbed my dress around the knee level, and pulled it up to the bottom of my ribs. All I had on under the gown were my bloomers, the top of which I pulled down to a little below my navel.

"See this?" I said to the woman, whose eyes were now as wide as dinner plates. "Is this the body of a woman who has recently given birth — or *ever* given birth?" It was awesome to show off this flat belly... all firm abs and smooth skin.

With a barely audible voice, she replied, "I don't think so, no."

Not good enough. I turned from side to side like a runway model. "I can show you more if you want."

Sadly, I think I was grossing her out. "That is quite all right. I believe you," she immediately answered while trying to avert her eyes from my relative nakedness. "My apologies."

While I wrestled my clothes back into place, I saw the nurse peek. She looked visibly relieved to note that I wasn't stripping down any further. When I was once again properly attired, she opened the curtain and said to the security guard, "This lady may leave. I am confident she is not the child's mother." Next, she turned to me, straightened her perky white cap, then nodded her head. "Thank you for bringing the infant to us. I expect you saved her life."

Now *that's* what a superhero likes to hear.

28: Superhero how-to

On the streetcar ride back home, what I'd been too scattered to consider while at the hospital hit me like a ton of bricks: I was putting myself in real danger. How had it not occurred to me before?

My mortality wasn't the issue. This body had already defied death, and whoever put me here probably could make me survive anything... and that was exactly the problem: I didn't need to worry about dying. I needed to be concerned with a fate even worse.

If someone caught on to my little parlor tricks, I could now envision a couple scenarios. In the first, people would assume I was completely bonkers, and I'd find myself with an all-expense paid trip to the land of straitjackets and lobotomies. In the second, someone would discover (and believe) I was from the twenty first century... and that could bring about so many different problems, not the least of which was torture and ET-style experimentation.

The other rescues I had planned didn't happen until this afternoon, and I was not going to call them off. There were lives at stake, and I'd made a commitment. But how could I play it safe? Over and over again, I came to the same conclusion: I didn't have enough data. There were no case studies, no legal precedents, and — to my constant dismay — no instruction manuals for any of this stuff.

By the time I exited the trolley, I was so worked up, I almost looked forward to the distraction my nosy neighbors would offer.

The ladies did not disappoint. My dress, skin tone and apparent health all got rave reviews. I felt my ego breeze up to the sky, and gratefully offered my own compliments in return. Then one woman went on to say she thought my hair looked "lovely," and that's when I realized they were all completely full of it. Nice, well-intentioned and adept at boosting a girl's confidence... but their pants were fully on fire.

Strangely enough, even after all the praise, my head wasn't too big to fit through the front door. But although its physical size hadn't changed, its emotional status had. I was now ready to stop wallowing and to start thinking.

I honestly hadn't considered about how the actions of a Good Samaritan might be considered suspicious. Given what I knew now, what did I need to change about my plans for today so I didn't find myself behind bars — or worse?

It all boiled down to having an alibi. I needed to have a reason and supporting evidence for being at the rescue locations. I couldn't just show up, swoop in, make an impressive save, then dash off without arousing suspicion. While I'd make every attempt to fly under the radar, if I was ever questioned — even as just an innocent bystander — I would need a simple story that made sense.

Turned out, all I needed to do was to re-imagine the scenario as if it had taken place in the modern day. *What would Robin do?* Boom... I had my shallow-but-practical answer: Shopping always made sense. Consumerism was a universal constant, offering the perfect cover for spies and criminals, the rich and the bored, heroines and time travelers.

↬ ↬ ↬

I got to the scene of the next rescue an hour early. I had plenty of time to could scope out the site, of course, but also so I could pump a little cash into the local economy — my pretext for showing up at the right time and the right place.

Fifty-five minutes later, I had a bag with three hard-to-find "alligator pears" (what they called avocados) and was stationed at the scene, about twenty feet from the corner of Post and Montgomery.

Then I saw my subject — around forty years old, long pea-green coat, and a book held so close to her face she could hardly see where she was walking. Her entrance was perfectly on cue, and I felt the surreal "I'm on a movie set" daze try to root my feet to the ground. But there was no time waste. I had to keep Irma here from focusing so much on her reading that she would step right off the curb. That's how she fell down and broke her crown, and history went tumbling after.

"Excuse me, ma'am?" It took several seconds to actually get her attention, but once she realized I was talking to her, she stopped so suddenly the women walking behind her nearly plowed her down.

"Are you speaking to me, Miss?" The words took a slow roll off her tongue. She seemed a little bit stoned.

"Yes I am, thank you," I said, and gestured her over to the inner portion of the sidewalk and away from the flow of traffic. "Pardon the interruption, but I saw how much you're enjoying you're reading, and had to ask: What is the title?" It was an arbitrary question — I hadn't seen the name of the book, the newspaper hadn't mentioned it, and it really didn't matter. All I wanted to do was to keep her safe until we moved beyond the location of her slip and fall.

"This?" she said. "It's just a silly British book, by this man Wells. It's called 'The Time Machine.'"

She had me at "time." Instantly, the rhythm of my heart started booming in my ears.

"Are you serious?" I had to ask. She angled the cover toward me, and there were those very words, neatly printed in gold above a winged sphinx design. Now I knew for sure that the party responsible for sending me back to this place fancied him or herself quite the comedian.

"Sounds like a fascinating premise," I said, and opened my mouth to say more. I wanted to tell her to be careful, or to suggest that she pay attention to where she was walking, but I didn't. My task was done — the dangerous moment had past — and now it was time for me to get out while the going was good. So instead of issuing instructions, I offered her thanks, waved goodbye, and hurried down the street with my bag of avocados.

As I walked, I recapped the event in my head, and decided I'd earned a good solid B grade. I had kept it simple, and got the job done with no muss, no fuss and no threat of arrest. My line of questioning could have used a little work, but it had been serviceable. Next time, though, I'd do a little more scout work and prep to smooth out the rough spots.

Screams erupted behind me, jarring me out of my self-congratulatory review. I spun around, and took in a chaotic roadway scene, complete with wounded animals, injured people, spilled barrels of beer, and an overturned carriage. The accident had not occurred on the road where Irma had been destined to perish, but around the corner on Post Street.

Beyond the crying women and arguing men, I could see one person, lifeless and broken on the cobblestones. Moving closer to the body, I saw red stains seeping through pea green wool in a half dozen places where the horses' hooves had crushed the bones beneath.

The novel we had discussed only a minute before was loosely clasped in one hand, though some of the gilded lettering on the red leather spine was now hidden under a thick smear of fresh blood. Only two words were still visible: *The Time.*

29: Doing it wrong

Instead of heading straight home after this kick in the teeth, I had to play a hunch. I took a roundabout route and stopped by the hospital where I'd brought the cold, sweet baby this morning.

The nurse who I'd impressed with my washboard abs was still on duty, and dropped what she was doing to head me off at the pass. She looked pained. I think she thought I might be planning to drop trou on this visit.

"Don't worry — not here to disrupt anything. I just wanted to check on the little girl I brought in this morning."

Her expression scarcely changed, except for her eyes widening slightly. We shared a very long silent moment before she finally spoke.

"The baby... she had apparently been ill. It wasn't just the hypothermia. We think she had a blood infection."

I couldn't believe what I was hearing. "Is she going to be okay?" I knew even before I said it that I was begging for bad news.

"She..." the nurse sighed. "She is already gone. I'm terribly sorry."

I don't remember what I said in reply, or even if I said anything at all. The next memory I had was of looking down, watching my tears making dark splatters on the pavement outside.

❦ ❦ ❦

"Defeated" wasn't even remotely strong enough to describe the acidic, gassy pit of despair that was my mood.

I did the only sensible thing: I went straight home. There, I grabbed a bottle of wine and climbed into bed. Forget my commitment to the other person who I was supposed to help — the trolley would take off his leg and he'd bleed out, just as history had dictated. *Pffft*. I wasn't like I could change it anyhow.

This sucked.

I wasn't used to playing the helpless victim or the girl who can't accomplish anything on her own, because in my real life, I was the opposite.

As a single mom, I was used to flying solo, and with no net. I had battled the moldy demons from the darkest recesses of the fridge, banished spiders and other creepy crawlies, performed exorcisms on the monsters in the hall closet, and many times attempted to invoke the spirit of cooperation. I even once conjured an ridiculously clever cloud costume from thin air when a very cute someone who shall remain nameless remembered her role in the Earth Day pageant at school a mere two hours before the event.

In my work life, too, I routinely went the extra mile. As half-assed as I might be about the things I didn't really care about, I had been able to accomplish near-miracles when something inspired me.

Across the board, I could be good at solving problems and making things happen. I could actually be great at it. And as evidenced by the fact I was here in the goddamn nineteen hundreds, some entity had drafted me for my particular talents, and for a particular purpose. But if they weren't going to fill in the details, I was going to be left to my own devices to figure out this puzzle... and that's what I had been doing.

So why was everything turning bad? So soul-crushingly, mind-numbingly awful?

A little later — a bottle of wine later, as it happened — I finally fell asleep. Just before I drifted off, I crossed my fingers and hoped my dream state would give me answers... or, at least, pony up enough hope to keep me going.

30: My new hobbies

It took me a few days to get my head on straight — I can admit that.

When I woke up in my real body and real time, feeling a thousand times better than I had during my last few moments of awareness in the Then. Most of my calm came from the fact that history — and all its ups and downs — had been restored to its proper place: the past.

As such, it was a lot easier to make the decision to just *let things go*. I even recited my own little version of the Serenity Prayer: *Timelords, please grant me the serenity to accept the things I cannot change, the courage to change the things I can, and wisdom to know the difference.*

It was all about knowing the difference. Despite having the ability to time travel, I was not psychic. There would be no more hit-or-miss shots in the dark based on what I thought I should be doing.

For now, I would force myself to be content taking the hints provided to me, because, clearly, whoever sent me back in time enjoyed making a point. I was going to lead with my heart and not my head, and wasn't going to worry about planning and strategizing until I needed to.

As long as I maintained full control (such as it was) over my own "real" life, I could afford to be generous with the second life that — I needed to remind myself — was a gift. Like the pink footed pajamas my great aunt would leave under the Christmas tree every year, this probably wasn't what I would have chosen for myself, but it was a gift nonetheless.

Well... maybe if I repeated the sentiment often enough, I'd come to believe it.

At the very least, it felt like I now had permission to spend my time in 1900 exploring, appreciating and trying to understand the people and their city.

⌁ ⌁ ⌁

What better way to see the city, I decided, than to take a public transit route from end to end? There were seven or so separate cable car lines available, plus some electric streetcars, so it was a great way to cover a lot of ground without compromising my own safety or shoe leather. (I still got plenty of walking in every day... partly out of necessity, but also because if I didn't, I'd feel guilty about not living up to Nurse Martha's expectations.)

The world I had grown up in smelled more *processed*, for lack of a better word. When I was back in the Now, I was noticing car exhaust, air fresheners, cleaning solvents and the smell of paint and carpet more than I ever had before.

But that wasn't the only thing about the air that was decidedly different in this time. Instead of being mostly full of car and bus exhaust, it instead smelled of dirt and grime and coal and sweat and sewage and other things I couldn't yet define... all with a thick overtone of horse crap.

Truly remarkable about the city blocks were all the things that *weren't* there. You know, those ordinary things you just walk by and don't even notice anymore... well, not until they're gone. It was strange to be able to travel along long expanses of sidewalk without being hindered by newspaper boxes, bus shelters, posts for stoplights and parking meters, no parking or street cleaning signs. There were lampposts, but they were so quaint-looking, they rather enhanced the landscape.

There was no painting on the streets either — no crosswalks or colored curbs letting you know where you could and couldn't park. No BUS ONLY and SCHOOL ZONE painted in narrow letters on the ground, and no warnings about the dire consequences of blocking intersections. There also weren't any street reflectors or raised pavement marker dots, and a complete absence of any double yellow lines, white dashed lines, and bike lanes.

All that was missing did, however, create a scene of total chaos. The only traffic rule seemed to be for drivers to stay to the right. Otherwise, it was a total free-for-all. Pedestrians and wheeled vehicles of all sorts crossed paths at every conceivable angle, and I found myself holding my breath over and over, expecting at any moment for someone to get run over, a carriage to plow into a streetcar, or for some little kid to get smooshed by one of those newfangled automobile things.

Once I saw that, as impossible as it seemed, these people managed not to get killed by the dozen, I could chill a little and focus on the more interesting stuff.

It was so amazing to be even slightly up on one of San Francisco's many hills, because the water views from there were absolutely remarkable. With fewer tall structures in the way, almost every elevation offered a sight line that would cause grown real estate agents to cry with joy as they tacked on an extra zero to a home's asking price. The bay and the land were in harmony.

In the Now, people often talk about gratitude — and I totally agree: We take way too much for granted. But we're hardly the first generation not to fully appreciate all we have. The people in the Then seemed quite blasé hustling about their days, paying no attention to the stellar views and the beauty of the city as a whole.

I think I was the luckiest of all, because in both timelines, I could see San Francisco with fresh eyes — appreciating both what it had been, and what it would be.

∽ ∽ ∽

Now *and* Then, Travis Donovan was constantly on my mind. It was ridiculous. For one thing, I wasn't even myself — truly. Lusting after a guy from within someone else's body? That was just creepy and probably bad karma or something.

Yet even as I told myself that over and over, I kept finding reasons to see him. Excuses, really. For instance, during the course of my many neighborhood explorations, I just happened, *somehow*, to stroll by the station house five or six times a day.

I was actually seeing the sights and getting things done, but I was also fervently hoping I'd catch a glimpse of a certain someone. I even had cover stories prepared:

- I was trying to get to know the area better.
- I was enjoying the park (Golden Gate Park was just across the street).
- The streetcar route I used the most was near the police station.

The first time I saw Travis on one particular Tuesday, he waved at me from across the street just before going into the station. I cursed my bad luck for being on the wrong side of the road — a wasted opportunity. Now I'd have to go do something else, because it wouldn't do to be seen walking the exact same stretch of road an hour later. (See, I was okay being a stalker, but I didn't want to be too stupidly obvious about it.)

Finally, I succeeded in painting myself into the corner. Two days later, and after about the fourth "Fancy meeting you here!" incident, he took the hint and invited me to join him for lunch.

"Lunch" in this case meant sharing his sandwich and apple in the park across the street, but that was fine by me. I didn't need fancy.

I followed his lead, and walked to the middle of the park, where the Spreckels Temple of Music was being built. I wanted to tell Mr Donovan how beautiful the bandshell and concourse would eventually be, but promised myself I would utter not a word about any future beyond today.

We settled ourselves on a steel bench away from the shade of trees so we could enjoy the bit of sunshine the day had deigned to offer. Unfortunately, the moment I sat down, my appetite completely vanished. My stomach had been colonized by butterflies.

Simply having food in hand, though, would offer a perfect excuse to sit and make small talk. Or so I figured.

He unwrapped the sandwich, which had been already sliced in half diagonally and then carefully wrapped in waxed paper. He let me choose my own half, explaining that today's luncheon feast was ham, cheese and butter on whole wheat — what my lunch date called granary bread. The "sarnie" was very simple and small compared to what you might get at a New York deli nowadays, but I was grateful not to have to worry about smearing mustard on my face or having an errant bit of pork fall into my lap.

Despite my mind going a mile a minute, I couldn't think of any words worth sharing. I was totally freezing up. I nibbled at the sandwich and tried desperately to try to think of something intelligent to say.

It didn't work.

Fortunately, Officer Donovan was an expert at putting people at ease, and I was no exception. Soon enough, he had helped me crack through my silence, and I was providing enough chatter for two.

I told him about one of my recent grocery store finds: bottled Coca-Cola. It was in a glass container unlike any you'd see today — tall with straight sides, and a little cork stopper at the top. It looked like an exotic brown potion. Along with the Coke logo, the bottle said "Chattanooga, Tenn," so that baby had come a long way.

When I bought the two they had in stock, the cashier — like Travis — was completely baffled by my excitement. It was a product I actually remembered, I said, which seemed to be explanation enough. (The tasting experience wasn't much of a thrill. The stuff was remarkably similar to the Coke of the Now, though a little heavy on the syrup and light on the fizz.)

The talk of memories segued into him telling me a little about growing up in Great Britain, which, in turn, led to the story of how he came to live in America.

"My father is an orthopedic surgeon back in England. About twelve years ago now, he moved the whole family here so he could teach techniques to some doctors stateside," he said. "We ended up staying for nearly five years."

Travis, already well into his school career at that point, stayed behind at a boarding school to finish out high school... but never returned to Europe. His dad was annoyed his eldest son had not only stayed in America, but hadn't even gone back for a visit.

"Father, you see, always hoped I would follow in his footsteps. It was just bad luck I was born the type of person who felt sick seeing large amounts of blood."

"I'm sorry — did that totally derail your career hopes?"

"Not at all," he laughed. "It derailed my father's hopes, but not mine. I never wanted to go into medicine. But to add insult to injury, I chose a 'peasant' job with the police."

"Wow — he actually said peasant job?" (Every time I used the word "wow" I cringed, but it just kept slipping out.)

"Among other things. That's probably one of the least offensive terms he used," he said, and finished his sandwich. "So what incentive do I have to make the journey back to Blighty? Father still hates that I'm a copper, and there will never be anything I can do to change his mind. I could become chief of police for the entire state, and he'd still think I shortchanged my future."

"For what it's worth, I think you have a very bright future."

He shrugged and said, "What about your own future?"

"My future? I have no idea. I'm just trying to get the past off my tail first."

Since I'd been away from home for two and a half months — and considering the nature of my injuries — it seemed like everyone had expected me to end up dead. "So people now stare at me with these somber expressions, or quickly look away from my wounded head, as if it had sprouted snakes."

"Well, of course, lest you turn them to stone," he laughed, looking straight into my eyes, then taking in my jagged scar. His smile — a *real* smile that touched every part of his face — never wavered.

As I talked, I noticed he looked at me more than a few times with a slightly confused expression. Finally, I asked why he was looking at me "like that."

"Like what?"

I squinted my eyes a little, tilted my head and smiled slightly. "Like this."

He laughed. "Ah, yes. That would be a slightly surprised face. A face wondering at how someone so young can already be so wise."

"Well," I said, happy that he noticed, and happier still that he said something, "I've been told I have an old soul."

෴෴෴

The next day, we met again for lunch — same Bat-time, same Bat-channel.

I learned he had recently been promoted to working foot patrol in the neighborhoods to the east of the Park and north of the Panhandle.

Up until last month, in fact, Travis had spent most of his working hours as a mounted officer — riding around on horseback, patrolling Golden Gate Park. The way he told it, the job consisted largely of rousting vagrants, catching pickpockets, and trying to stop public indecency… which was mainly people who were happy to pee in public, and "idiots" who were hooking up for a two-buck romp in the grass.

Dull, right? Then he mentioned the most unpredictable part of that assignment was being on the constant lookout for runaway horses — which were often harnessed to carriages when they bolted. As Travis said, "When you put two brains in charge of one wagon, and one of those brains has the instincts of a wild animal, sometimes unfortunate incidents occur." Unfortunate, indeed.

He let slip that he had recently helped stop a runaway carriage, and that save earned him some serious points. He didn't want to say much more — "I was just doing my job," and so on — but when I got back to the Now, I looked it up.

It turns out that during the second week of January, Mr Horse Whisperer did something so notably heroic, he merited his very own story in the newspaper, which began as so: "Park Policeman T. J. Donovan distinguished himself yesterday afternoon in Golden Gate Park by a very clever display of nerve and good horsemanship in stopping a runaway team of horses, preventing what certainly would have been a serious accident."

It went on to describe the scary adventure, and ended with: "Those who witnessed the clever capture of the runaway team were loud in their praise of the officer's brave act, and declared it to be a display of cool judgment and great horsemanship."

This action was, in fact, what triggered his promotion — and he was very thankful to have a new beat.

I was thankful, too. How couldn't I be? If he had been on patrol in the park the night I wandered into the police station all dazed and confused, I probably wouldn't have met him at all.

෴෴෴

I suppose it was part of his charm, but Travis seemed pretty much oblivious to the fact he was a gorgeous creature. It wasn't that he wasn't observant — he seemed exceptionally so — but more that such things seemed to be of no concern to him. I fervently hoped it wasn't because he was completely disinterested in a relationship, but only that such things weren't on his mind right now.

When lunch was over and we started out of the park, I happened to ask a question — one that l ed to a conversation that would only muddy the waters.

"How far away do you live?"

"I share a flat with a roommate up, oh, about eight blocks from here," he said, gesturing northward with a nod of his head.

"A roommate, huh?" I said. "What's her name?" There was simply no way for me to resist the opportunity to find out if the boy had a girlfriend.

"Ha, very funny. *His* name is Jack, and *he* is a firefighter."

"Oh," was all I could say, with a smile frozen on my face. That's because until that very instant, it hadn't occurred to me that Travis might be gay. The idea so scrambled my thoughts, I couldn't even speak for at least twenty steps.

After jumping on the hamster wheel of useless thought for a few rounds, I decided I was going to ignore the whole issue entirely. If he was, he was, but there was no polite way to ask a relative stranger — a late nineteenth century stranger, no less — his sexual preference. It just reminded me how much I hated the entire process of dating. It was awkward and annoying and altogether uncomfortable. This "is he or isn't he" kind of thing? Part of the reason why.

Despite my current physical form being slightly more than twenty years old, the me inside really had another decade and a half more experience under her belt. In short: I felt way too old for this silliness.

Before the frustration had time to froth and bubble and cloud my day, clarity descended. I was sure now that I wanted more than just a friendship with Travis, and didn't want to patiently wait to see if anything developed. I needed to try to make this happen. I didn't think fate would mind, given that I wasn't using future knowledge to tip the odds in my favor.

The reward was worth the risk, so I was going to do what people had done since the dawn of humanity: put myself out there, face embarrassment, suffer some uncomfortable silences, and face the very real possibility of rejection... all in the name of love.

31: Like peanut butter & jelly

My heart went all a-flutter every time Travis flashed me a look with those bright blue eyes. His gaze could be so intense, it was actually to the point where I had to look away after about half a second. If I were to maintain eye contact any longer than that, I'd blush fifty shades of red. Over the past few days, I had spent a lot of time stealing little glimpses to avoid going on overload.

Part of my problem was that I was genuinely torn about my feelings for him. He was adorable and sweet and charming and handsome and hot. But as soon as I thought about the fact that he was a little more than ten years younger than (the real) me, I felt like I was a cougar on the prowl.

I had the classic devil and angel on my shoulders. The little pitchfork holder was saying, "He likes you! Go for it!" while the sweet little haloed one told me in a snotty tone that I was almost old enough to be his mother... you know, if I lived in one of those ancient societies where girls gave birth at age 13.

Yeah, I sent the angel packing. At the end of our next lunch date, I decided to take a big step: inviting Travis over to my place for a noontime meal.

"You've been so great — sharing your lunch with me so many times," I said. "Maybe I could return the favor tomorrow?"

"I'm not working tomorrow," he said, and I felt my smile start to falter.

"Sorry — I didn't even think. Of course, you have plans for your day off. Maybe when..."

He cut me off. "I was going to say, I would be charmed."

Oh boy. Now what? I thought for sure that he'd politely decline. My mind rushed ahead to think about what I should serve. Should I go fancy? Simple? And since he was British, should I serve tea or something? Did I even *have* any tea?

I got the distinct impression I should have spent a little more time preparing for this kind of best-case scenario. One of my schoolmates had been particularly fond of telling me, "Your mouth is writing checks that your ass can't cash." Ahhh, once again, old friend, I am proving you right.

"That's great! Fantastic. Excellent." And it was. But now that I'd committed, I was feeling the pressure. *I better not screw this up.*

Though he agreed, Travis had seemed slightly hesitant when I suggested we eat not at the park, but inside my house.

"Oh that's right," I said, before he had to explain. "Being unchaperoned is contrary to the social customs of this era." I rolled my eyes.

"'Social customs of this era' you say?" he laughed. "You have forgotten more than I realized."

"Ah, you have no idea."

He thought for a minute, with his hand stroking his chin. "I suppose," he said, drawing out his response as long as possible, "that, perhaps..." he paused and could no longer stifle a grin, "perhaps it would be acceptable."

෴෴෴

So I could start my luncheon prep, I decided to stop by the shops on the way home to pick up a few ingredients. In the grocery store, I walked around in circles, trying to decide what I could serve that would be appealing and tasty, yet not beyond my culinary skills. My cooking ability was hindered greatly because ovens and stove tops didn't come with temperature guides. (Recipes of this time simply say to "bake" something — usually there's no length of time or heat level indicated.)

After wasting most of an hour hemming and hawing about what to buy, I decided to shoot for the moon, and make him a futuristic delicacy: peanut butter and jelly sandwiches.

Seriously — peanut butter hadn't really been invented yet (or at least not commercialized), so I was going to make my own. I wasn't sure how much time that would take, so to simplify, I bought pre-made bread and strawberry preserves.

I started shelling and grinding the nuts that night. I mashed and stirred and crushed those suckers, but the peanuts stubbornly retained their sand-like consistency.

Turns out, I didn't know how to make peanut butter. I thought it was going to be simply a matter of pureeing the legumes. Maybe that's all I needed to do, but a hand-crank grinder was a far cry from a food processor.

It was dark when I gave up for the night. I had an angry red blister forming on my right palm from rotating the handle for a couple hours. Instead of throwing away the whole mess, I decided to do some research online in the Now. Perhaps my peanut butter could be salvaged... and maybe even my lunch date could be, too.

෴ ෴ ෴

When I awoke back in the Then, I had only three things on my mind: Peanut oil, salt and honey. Those ingredients were all I needed to make my peanut meal into something more resembling peanut butter.

It helped a lot — though it wasn't perfect, having a texture halfway between chunky and creamy, but with the benefits of neither style. But the taste? I figured when it was put on bread and smoooshed together with the jam, it would be pretty close to the bag lunch favorite.

Eleven o'clock arrived so quickly, I didn't even have time to finish setting up as much as I planned. Maybe it was better this way — less of a chance to over-think it.

At 11:03 the doorbell rang. The boy was right on time. I took a moment to breathe and get a little zen, then opened the door.

How I wish I had a picture of what I saw that morning. For the first time, Travis was in his civvies instead of his police uniform. Of course, casual wear in the Victorian age was the equivalent of dressing to the nines in our day: chocolate-brown pinstripe suit, silver-grey tie and a brown felt bowler hat.

He looked snazzy. Or natty. Dapper. Dashing. Rakish. So many old-timey adjectives to describe an amazing-looking guy, but didn't know if any were appropriate for this decade.

"Hi — and wow. You look... fantastic."

"Thank you," he said, looking only slightly uncomfortable under the weight of the compliment.

"Please, come in." I stood back and opened the door wide. As Travis walked over the threshold, he brought out a beautiful bouquet of roses — *red roses* — from behind his back and handed them to me. I brought them up to my nose to take in their fragrance, and tried to hide the fact that I couldn't stop smiling.

Then there was an awkward moment of indecision where neither one of us knew whether to give the other a hug, a kiss on the cheek, a handshake or just wave. We settled on a semi-hug with a near-cheek kiss.

For no good reason, I was so much more nervous than I'd been on any of our previous lunch dates. That feeling was only amplified because he was out of uniform. To me, that meant I was no longer just part of the job — I was taking up this man's personal time.

Just as I was thinking how I'd better make it worth his while, I realized how stupid my plan was to offer him a PB&J sandwich. What was this — playgroup? It was too late to come up with another menu now, so maybe I could try to sell it as something exotic and wondrous, like "gourmet peanut purée."

After escorting him to the living room, I invited him to have a seat on the sofa. I had artfully arranged the cushions to make the seating area look welcoming... plus to make sure that if I eventually sat down with him, there wouldn't be a huge gap between us.

"Would you like some tea?" See? I knew how to entertain.

"Certainly, thank you, Jennie," he replied, that English accent sounding rather posh, perhaps due to his proximity to tea.

Exiting to the kitchen, I put the blossoms in a small vase, then got out two teacups with saucers. (The only mug-like containers people had were beer steins.) The teapot was already hot on the stove, so I pulled down the tin of tea I'd seen in the cupboard. Upon opening it, my heart sank when I saw the container was full of loose leaves. As I hadn't given the tea topic much thought, I expected to see little tea bags. My inventory of the cabinets and drawers the day before had not revealed a tea strainer, so I had to improvise. I decided to go with tea, Chinese-style, and dumped two teaspoons of leaves into the teapot.

After making sure the teapot and cups were safely balanced on a tray, I set it down on the coffee table in front of Travis. With no sugar or cream in the house, I couldn't offer the usual add-ons, and, mercifully, Travis didn't ask.

To continue the fiasco, I poured the tea, which came out only straw-colored. Pretty sure it was supposed to be more of a nut brown shade, I told him, "Maybe it needs to steep a little bit more." He took a sip, smiled, and pronounced it "wonderful." That's when I decided there was only one wonderful thing in this room, and it sure as hell wasn't my tea.

While we partook of the slightly-tinted hot water, we made small talk. I was so preoccupied by thinking about how and when to serve the food, and trying not to stare at his eyes and nose and dimples and neck and wrists and hands, that I have absolutely no recollection of what we said. (Presumably,

I didn't come up with anything too freakish, because he didn't run away.)

Finally, it was time for me to serve the *pièce de résistance*. After clearing the tea, I went into the kitchen and took out two small plates. On each, I carefully placed a PB&J, along with five apple slices in a cute little half sunburst pattern.

As I walked back into the living room, I flailed in my attempt to explanation these wacky sandwiches. "My mom used to make me these when I was little. They were my favorite," I mumbled. *Please, brain: Stop funneling me the most inane thoughts for a few minutes here. My first grade lunch choices aren't exactly newsworthy right now.*

I set the plates down on the table, and he nodded his approval. He didn't know what he was getting himself into. Peanut butter wasn't a thing, and for all I knew, to the Victorian palate, this might be as strange as chocolate-covered pickles.

He took a bite, started to chew, and for a few agonizing seconds, I couldn't tell if he was enjoying it or trying to keep from vomiting. Every moment that passed, I became more and more sure it was the latter. Handing him a napkin, I told him, "I am so sorry — it's the first thing I've tried to make since the hospital. You can spit it out — I won't be offended."

"Spit it out?" he said after swallowing. "Why would I spit it out? It's marvelous — very unique. Never tasted anything quite like it." He took another nibble, then asked, "How did you learn of it?"

"Well, I guess I have some memories of my childhood, and this is one."

"You were raised in Italy, is that correct?"

"Apparently," I laughed. "I don't really remember too much about that, but have certain random memories... and this is one." Not quite a lie.

"What do you call it?"

"Peanut butter."

I watched him take yet another bite and chew it slowly. I imagined him savoring the sandwich flavors like he was tasting a fine wine. I could almost picture him describing the fancy futuristic condiment as being "velvety and toasty, with a buttery mouth feel." And why not? Back in the Now, I'd read that in a few short years from now, peanut butter would be considered a delicacy — something served in only the finest city tearooms.

Finally, though, I could calm down about having presented him with a lunch menu so mundane in my timeline, it wouldn't have impressed anyone since peanut butter and jelly sandwiches first became a thing during WW2.

While we ate, he asked about of my other memories of Italy — which, I told him, were quite vague and distant. Fortunately, I could speak somewhat knowledgeably about Florence, Rome and Venice, figuring the cities couldn't have changed too much between my visit during college and a hundred years prior.

Then he told me about how, shortly before moving stateside, he spent one long lazy summer on Lake Como. I *oohed* and *aahed* appropriately. That led to us discovering we were both members of the seaside appreciation society. And that, well... that led to talk of the future: a visit "one day" to the Golden Gate — a patch of land where a red bridge would eventually stand, and where the Bay opened its mouth ever so slightly to the chilly expanse of the Pacific.

We chatted for I don't know how long — way past the point of us both having clean plates and empty water glasses. To me, it seemed like our rapport was growing stronger and more lush with every word shared. Then, during a rare lull in conversation, all of that feelgood fizzled when Travis pulled out a gold watch from his vest pocket and checked the time.

"Sadly," he said, and looked me in the eyes so I could see that he meant it, "I will have to take my leave in about thirty minutes."

Well, of course — it only made sense he had more planned for his day off than lunch with the local needy chick. But somehow the fact that he had to say it caused me to start tripping over my tongue in all sorts of ways. I started blathering. Trying to talk while trying to think while trying to clear the plates was not a good mix for me.

"Okay, let me just go get the cookies now so we can finish up. Sorry for the delay," is what I meant to say, but it came out with some random emphasis, sounding more like *okaymumble blahblah GOblahNOWblah sorryblah*.

"Pardon me? I couldn't quite make out what you said," Travis called out, but I'd already reached the kitchen.

I grabbed the cookies, slipped them on a plate (after nearly dropping half of them on the floor), then hurriedly headed back into the room.

"Oh, nothing," I said, answering his question about ten seconds late. "Just... babbling about cookies."

"Ah, I see," he said, but instead of looking at me like I was an idiot, this little concerned look spread across his face that made me want to just kiss him right then and there. "I thought you were saying I should just go now."

I shocked myself — and probably him — with the squawk of semi-laughter that popped out of my mouth. "Oh my God, no!" I said, a little too quickly. "I don't want you to go at all! You can stay — stay all day if you want." And then I felt myself blushing from my toenails to the very ends of my hacked-off hair. In my head, I was hitting myself with one of those cartoon sledgehammers for chittering like a 12-year-old girl meeting some teenybopper rock star in person.

The only way to get this over with was to actually get this over with, so I took several hurried steps across the room, holding the store-bought cookies on the little plate out in front of me. Step, step, step, almost there... and then I did something that made every other stupid thing I'd done that day look like rocket science. I stared at him as I walked — looking not where I was stepping, but only at my destination.

The next part I remember as if it was in slow motion, even though it probably only lasted ten seconds in reality. Just a short distance away from Travis, as I passed the goldenrod velvet armchair, I tripped over my own shoes. The cookies and I went airborne while my arms cartwheeled wildly, desperately trying to catch my fall.

For a moment, I thought I was going to crush the spindly-legged coffee table, but then I realized I was angled a little more to the right. A fraction of a second after I realized I was going to fall right on top of this sweet guy on my sofa, I saw myself getting closer, closer... then plunging face-first into his shoulder.

And you know what he did? Even though it happened in a flash, he didn't throw up an arm to stop me and the cookies, didn't lean to the side, didn't flinch away. That boy put his arms right out and did what I couldn't do for myself: He caught me. I think the look of amazement was still on my face as it smashed into his collarbone.

It was the most painless fall *ever*.

↬ ↬ ↬

As I pulled my face off his shirt, I found myself looking right into his eyes, and watched his pupils dilate as he processed what had just happened. Then it was my turn to realize I was completely lying across him and he had his arms around me — my feet weren't even on the ground.

"Are you all right?" he asked me, and after a beat, I saw his eyes wander down at my chest. I followed his gaze to realize that my (admittedly minimal) cleavage was now augmented with crumbled and squashed cookies.

"Oh — I am so sorry," I said, my face flushing even more deeply as I frantically tried to think of how to extricate myself without making more of a mess.

"No apology needed," he smiled. "It was a rather graceful fall."

My stomach did a little jump.

"I have been rehearsing this, actually," I somehow managed to say. "Tell you what: It's a lot more fun with someone to catch you."

He pulled me a little tighter, and I didn't mind one bit that the cookies were littering even more crumbs into my dress.

"I'd think that I'm the one having the most fun," he said, and with every word, his breath pulsed softly on my cheek. I could smell a hint of his soap or shaving foam — a clean, warm scent — maybe sandalwood? It suited him.

Travis had always been so sweet to me. Helpful. Kind. Plus he was funny and smart and every other quality that would be in the "plus" column on a personality questionnaire.

So why was I hesitating? I think it was mostly because I couldn't forget that wasn't really myself. What if this body's rightful owner came back and found itself in a compromising position? I ran through about another dozen what ifs, and with each, my resolve evaporated a bit more.

All I needed to do was lean a tiny bit forward. As I did, he slowly tilted his head toward me, and I could feel the warmth of his skin as he moved closer. Then my eyes closed and mouth opened slightly, and I lost track of anything else, because I was delivered the Greatest Kiss Ever In The History Of The Universe.

And that is how, on a blustery February day in the year 1900, I stopped worrying about where this life was going to take me, and finally started living in the moment.

32: The first half of February

The day of our first kiss had been a turning point in more ways than one. Once our relationship had finally been launched into the stratosphere, I started to feel I had a future here. I could finally let myself make plans for the weeks and months ahead.

It had been exhausting to spend so much of each day waiting to be plucked out of this era. If I was here on borrowed time, so be it — but I was no longer going to hesitate about every choice.

To date, I had been acting like I was merely wearing Jennie's body (but more in the *Freaky Friday* way than in the "It places the lotion in the basket" sense, from *Silence of the Lambs*). But now I was sure: Jennie was not here. I really felt like the girl was gone... and wasn't coming back. I didn't know if that was one hundred and ten percent true, but I needed to make a decision one way or the other. The only way I would get anything done here was to jump in with both feet. If it was going to be sink or swim, I was going to be a mermaid.

◦◦◦

So now that Travis and I were more than "just friends," what did that mean? I wasn't entirely sure.

See, from the first smile across a crowded room, the customs were markedly different here. You didn't take your "boyfriend" or "girlfriend" out "on a date" here — none of those terms meant anything. Instead, there was a totally different vocabulary for the entire process. You "call on" a girl you like, and if that works out, you start to "woo" her. Wooing possibly leads to a "courtship," when you get to do crazy stuff like hold hands. A few months later, if you were still going strong, he would become a "beau." Further along the line, you'd get engaged — betrothed — and, boom! Before you know it, that guy is your husband.

If you weren't necessarily on the marriage path, well, in the year 1900, believe me: that was a very fine line to walk.

Realize that when one was out and about, one needed need to keep any coloring outside these lines on the down-low, lest a girl's reputation be "ruined." The hysteria with which people here concerned themselves with such things called to mind the reaction a middle-aged man should expect today if he was seen walking down an alley, hand-in-hand with a neighbor's 12-year-old son... while both were wearing only swimsuits.

It was also pretty near impossible to have anything like a private moment outside of your own home. People will look — people will stare — and they won't look away just because you give 'em the evil eye. Screw subtlety. Ladies in particular will gawk at you like you're a four-headed alien with googly eyes for doing little more than talking loudly or laughing in public. (From what I've seen, what passes as an acceptable laugh here would be a demure smile or — if something is especially hilarious — a gentle titter behind a hand.)

This I knew from experience. Although I'd been here for about a month and a half, there were apparently still things I did that people thought were surprising — if not downright shocking.

One crime against etiquette that I kept committing involved me opening doors for myself, and even (heaven forbid) holding them for other people, including those of the male persuasion. Now, it was fine to open doors for myself when there wasn't a man in the immediate proximity. But if there was a guy even ten feet away, walking in the opposite direction, he was supposed to make sure that no woman or girl had to dirty her glove on a door handle. Stupider still, I was supposed to hover around the door until some dude opened it for me.

To this issue at least, I had a new solution. Whenever I was out with Travis — who was chivalry personified — he would constantly be opening doors for other people, often stopping me mid-sentence with an, "Excuse me a moment," while he had to leave me standing there so he could assist some fair maiden (or old biddy) with her ingress and egress needs.

By the same token, b eing in law enforcement in the Then meant doing a lot more than just enforcing the legal code. There was a whole social/good Samaritan side of things that you just don't see in the Now. For example, it was considered an officer's duty to help women cross over the railroad or streetcar tracks, and to help elderly ladies with their groceries.

But I was not jealous. Honestly, I wasn't. I got past the whole possessive thing by the end of my twenties... but I'm not denying it was kind of annoying to have chivalry demand so many interruptions.

Still, none of that could cast even the slightest shadow on my little sunburst of happy. Getting cozy with a cop offered fringe benefits above and beyond companionship, safety and security.

I hated to sound like a badge bunny, but when Travis was in his uniform... well, to borrow a phrase from my youth — 85 years hence — he was, like, *so* totally fine.

The uniforms of the Then were very different from today's — more formal and with fewer accoutrements. To start, the shirt and jacket sleeves were long, never short, no matter the season. The coat itself was long, too — going down to the mid-thigh — and was made of plain blue wool. I heard several people call police officers here "bluecoats."

There was a neat row of brass buttons that went down from neck to waist. Then, the back of the coat featured four decorative buttons below the belt, so he looked very smart from the front and from behind. (I asked him the point of the buttons in the rear, which didn't have buttonhole counterparts. He said that they seemed to exist only to make the experience of sitting and leaning back uncomfortable.) The pants were of a darker blue, and had a pleat in the front and a narrow band of gold trim down the outer edges. To hold those up, he wore a black leather belt with a brass buckle.

Travis, like all police officers, had a nightstick attached to a loop over the wrist on his right hand (because he was right-handed). Under the coat was a pair of handcuffs, and, yes, a gun. His was a shiny Colt .32 revolver, and while he was licensed to carry a service weapon, all police officers were required to keep their revolvers concealed.

The rank insignia appeared on both sleeves — in his case, a single stripe that encircled the cuff. On the left side of the chest, there was a seven-pointed star that said SAN FRANCISCO POLICE and his badge number.

Finally, when he was on duty, he had to park a bucket-style hat on his head. These were not attractive things. In fact, they reminded me of the hats the bumbling Keystone Kops would wear. The only nice thing about it was the silver insignia, again, with his badge number.

When Travis was dressed like a cop, he was on duty — even if not technically on the clock. But when he was in street clothes? He was funny, relaxed, charming and wonderfully romantic. Having already had the opportunity to get to understand his work persona, every day now, I looked forward to getting to know the man himself.

The downside of spending a lot of time with Travis was that he ended up getting an ever-clearer picture of my seemingly schizophrenic self.

Attempting to be one person, while simultaneously remaining mindful of another life experience, often required a high level of mental agility. When I was tired or had a glass of two of wine in me, it became harder than usual to keep my feet firmly planted in a specific era.

After Travis and I sat on the sofa and enjoyed a half bottle of some anonymous, unbranded red wine, I got a craving for broccoli beef and pork fried rice.

One thing so fantastic about the Then was that within just a couple miles, I could get completely authentic ethnic food — Italian, Chinese, Russian, German, Swedish, French — from fresh-off-the-boat immigrants. (This stuff is not to be confused with the Americanized versions of Now that have evolved over decades — especially true in the case of treats from Italy and China.)

Just because they had a wealth of exotic cuisines at the ready doesn't mean that everyone understood them, or was ready to embrace something new... as I found out that evening.

"I don't want to cook tonight," I said to Travis. "Is there anywhere here we can pick up Chinese food? Last night I found a ten dollar bill taped to the back of my glove drawer, so I'm buying."

"*Chinese* food?" He sat up straight on the sofa. "Are you serious?"

"Yes, totally! I love Chinese. Doesn't everyone?"

"No, everyone most decidedly does *not*," he said. "I, for one, have no desire to eat any dog or rat, thank you very much."

"Eww — I don't want to, either," I told him. "What on earth makes you think that's what Chinese people eat?"

"Experience," he said. "I've been to Chinatown, and assure you it is a bizarre place. Very strange food. Very few women, and almost no Caucasians. High crime rate, too."

"Oh, please. It can't really be like that — or at least, it's cannot *all* be like that."

"How can you be so sure?"

Without being able to make use of future knowledge, he was right. How could an amnesiac be certain of any such thing?

"I guess... memories?"

Travis looked at me, and I saw something in his eyes that reminded me of how my mom would sometimes contemplate our dog. Little Indiana would get so excited by the sight of her leash, she'd go all *Scooby Doo* on the slippery floors, and start sliding into the walls and furniture and any people who happened to be in the way. Mom would look at the pup with this expression that seemed to say, "You're so stupid... but so cute."

"Out of all the things in the world," she said, "you remember getting food from a Chinaman." It wasn't a question. It was a statement of disbelief, and I wasn't going to belabor the point.

"Okay, then how about Italian?"

"Now *that* is something we can do."

Like sands through the hourglass, so were the days of our lives... at least during those first few weeks. Life was delicious and everything was blissfully uncomplicated.

There were two gorillas in the room, though, and their significance depended entirely upon my mood. The first was the question of how far we could go in an era where the relationship I wanted didn't need to end with a marriage proposal. The second big issue on my mind was if and when and how to tell Travis that I was, in truth, a 21st century woman in a 19th century body.

But those? Those were matters to deal with later. For the time being, I was just enjoying the exhilarating, electrifying process of falling in love.

33: The Now – Wrong number

One Saturday night in the Then, which joined up to a Thursday in the Now, I didn't say goodnight to Travis until we'd whiled away hours cooking dinner at my house and playing on the piano. I had been able to introduce him to some classic music — classic from my point of view, anyhow.

He was beyond impressed with some of the old songs I knew... tunes with titles like "Can't Help Falling in Love" and "Have You Ever Seen The Rain?" I told him I couldn't exactly remember where I learned them, but, gosh, it felt like I'd known them all my life.

When I finally did get to sleep in 1900, I woke up about ten seconds later to find Iris standing over me, lightly slapping my face, which was apparently a move she'd seen used on TV to rouse women who had fainted. I had slept right through my alarm, and we were late late *late* for school. Only the other day, I'd promised myself that no matter what went on in the past, it wasn't going to interfere with my life in the now. Nice try.

The morning rush turned me and the girls into three headless chickens, but we managed to get everyone dressed and in the car in about five minutes, whereupon the girls dug out a couple granola bars — breakfast! — from my purse to gobble down on the drive. (Parenting always is about trying your best for your kids... but sometimes, it just boils down to choosing the least crappy option.)

For once, I was happy that the drop-off line at school was moving slowly — enough so that I had time to find a few bucks worth of change in the ashtray to pay for the kids' lunches.

Only when my kiddos were walking away from the car did I notice that that Iris was dressed head to toe in denim, while Lily had slipped on a plaid shirt and red stretch pants... and then a blue tutu and leopard-print rain boots. Ahh, my girls were style icons — one wearing a Canadian tuxedo, the other seemingly a future Betsey Johnson.

I told myself that at least my eldest wasn't likely to get in trouble for being under-dressed, and then hoped they didn't have to run in PE today. I wasn't sure how those galoshes would fare racing around the football field.

༄ ༄ ༄

Knowing I'd lose all momentum if I went back home, I grudgingly went straight to the fitness center. I got started 45 minutes early — something completely unheard of for me. I was so early, in fact, Vivian the infamous gym rat hadn't even arrived yet.

After my half hour of cardio, I started a circuit through the weight machines. When I finally checked the time again, it was 9:30, and Viv was fifteen minutes late. As strange as it may have been for me to start exercising early, it was twice as odd for my workout buddy to be anything other than absolutely punctual.

I sent her a quick text to make sure she was okay, and to find out when she'd be here. Two seconds after I pressed "send," I got an automated reply, telling me that the number I was trying to reach was not text-enabled, and if I wanted to send an audio message to the line, I could do so for only a dollar. Yeah, no thanks.

So I dialed her number... and got a deli. Twice.

My phone was clearly being stupid today, so I finished up my workout solo. In the locker room afterward, I scribbled out a little note and stuck it through the vent into her locker.

After hoisting my purse and gym bag over my shoulder, I turned to leave. Twice as I was walking away, I heard some lady say, "Excuse me," but it wasn't until the third time she repeated it that I looked to see who she was talking to. I turned to find she was staring right at me, my note in hand.

"I think you put this in the wrong locker," she said, holding out the little scrap of paper for me.

I smacked my forehead. "I'm so sorry! I meant to put it in locker 254."

There was no hesitation. "You did," she said. "254. That's my number."

Closing my eyes, I double-checked the number in my memory. Vivian's was definitely 254, and the locker's position seemed correct, too. "Did they just assign it to you today?"

"Uh, no," she said, her tone already growing impatient. "I've had it for, like, eight months."

"Sorry. I guess I got confused." There was more I wanted to say, but she had already given me a sour face and turned away.

When I got home, I manually dialed Vivian's number from my land line, and the same guy answered. That time around, I didn't even ask for my friend, but covered by requesting their business hours.

So strange.

After keeping this conundrum in the back of my mind for a few hours as I plowed through work, I finally came to the conclusion that all the time travel must be screwing with my memory.

It was a logical assumption, given how much effort went into keeping my two lives moving forward — even though going back and forth between worlds was becoming pretty commonplace for me.

But as I switched back and forth between locations every day (at least that's how it seemed), I was starting to feel some overlap. The place I'd just been didn't fade as quickly anymore. In fact, I was realizing more and more that moods, cravings, energy and fatigue were more frequently slipping through time with me, sometimes making it tough to differentiate one world from the other when I had my eyes closed or let my thoughts wander.

Looking back, the smudging of the lines made me surprisingly successful at ignoring the possibility that one of my best friends had disappeared. But the simple fact that I had to *convince* myself that everything was truckin' along just fine in Vivianville should have been my first clue that everything, in fact, was not.

34: Newsworthiness

Lest my intentions were not obvious, I want to make something clear: Time travel was a secret I didn't enjoy hiding. I had wanted to tell Travis all about it when we first started meeting for lunch... but worried our budding relationship couldn't handle so much disclosure. Once we became a couple, the urge to spill the temporal beans became more intense, but I was now waiting for the right moment to let him in on the nature of my reality.

Because my claim sounded so bizarre, I concluded the timing of the announcement was everything. The best thing I could do was to wait until just before some act of God or other kind of newsworthy event, so I could immediately back up my revelation with evidence. To that end, I started looking in the newspapers specifically for stuff I could predict to prove my case.

There were all kind of stories coming up over the next week — but were they unusual enough and timely enough to do the job? I didn't think so.

Still, though, I learned a lot about what was going on in this fair city by simply turning to the society columns. These news briefs served as the Facebook and Twitter of the Victorian age, allowing zealous oversharers their place in the sun. By checking those news pages regularly, I soon became extremely well-apprised of the comings and goings of my fellow citizens, thanks to the nosy little reports published each day. A few examples:

Miss Louise Blythe has gone to Phoenix, Arizona, where she will visit friends for the remainder of the winter.

J Alexander, a wealthy merchant and land owner of Susanville, is at the Grand for a short stay.

H W Frank has returned from a business trip to New York City.

Miss Alice Doncaster was given a very enjoyable surprise party Saturday evening, February 11. The evening was very pleasantly spent in dancing and games. A delightful repast was served at 11 o'clock.

(And you thought today's social media offered TMI.)

I knew I'd get around to it sooner or later, though — it wasn't a question of *if*, only of *when*.

35: Something old, something new

Travis stopped by on his way to work the next morning (requiring a circuitous route that probably tripled his commute) just so I could walk up to the station with him. From there, I headed east a few blocks to a cute little cluster of shops offering everything a person could need, and a little bit more.

For my part, it wasn't early-morning retail therapy, but more like self-preservation. See, just as I was got used to the fact the stores were tiny and selection minuscule, I found out *nothing* — apart from church — was open on Sundays. It had been hard for me to find enough to keep me occupied in this era, and then fell the bombshell that this world was pretty much closed between midday Saturday and Monday morning. As a result, I made damn sure to get out while the gettin' was good, and aimed to do my shopping at the least-crowded times of day.

That's because Sundays weren't the only problem. Over and over, it was demonstrated how much I become used to a fast-paced society. The people in the Then had comparatively so little urgency, making waiting in line behind more than a couple slowpokes feel like a form of torture.

It seemed like everyone was moving in slow motion. Now, I understood a basic relaxed mode — I'd spent a few summers working in "hang loose" Hawaii — but this was different. They were precise and polite, but seemed not to remotely understand the concept of hurry... which was actually something I probably knew too well.

People here were very slow and I was unusually fast, and that juxtaposition was a little painful.

It's not just the way they moved, but it's the way they talked and walked and spoke. I realize I'm probably one of a million adults with borderline (and undiagnosed) ADHD, so the gap was even wider than it might otherwise have been, but more often than not, I caught myself wondering how people here got *anything* accomplished.

Even a lot of the cops (Travis excluded, of course) were, for lack of a kinder w ord, rotund. The chances of those guys passing the modern-day police physicals? Somewhere between slim and none — pun intended.

It wasn't just that they moved slowly, they had very patterns they needed to complete, and seemed very resistant to change... especially changes I suggested. Like to put a little hustle in that muscle.

"While she is figuring out what she needs, perhaps you could help me, sir?" I asked the butcher when the fussy matron ahead of me was taking her own sweet time choosing between beef tongue or lamb bladder or some such thing. In return, I got a glare and a terse, "I will be with you in a few minutes, young lady."

I was so incredibly close to walking out of there, just to show Mister Meat Man where he could shove his few minutes. But in lieu of cutting off my nose to spite my face, I did a couple deep breathing exercises and told myself to pretend I was just acting. If I could just play the part of a patient young lady, I'd be fulfilling my current role in this life... plus I'd be able to get my damn bacon without having to walk another ten blocks to the next butcher shop.

Once I had my pig strips (Travis's term) in hand, along with a couple links of sausage, I visited the nearby dry goods store — one of my favorite haunts. The little toys and trinkets, in particular, were fun to see — things like mini railroad toys, doll house furniture, magic lanterns and lantern slides, "harmless rapid fire" toy guns, and even sets of Tiedler's Winks (which would later be cleverly renamed Tiddlywinks). They also carried almost every non-food item you could imagine, many accompanied by sales literature making ludicrously untenable claims. (One tagline that made me snort out loud was on an ad for a Gramophone: "It will give no end of pleasure.")

When I entered the shop today, a twinkling crystal illuminated a small basket with postcards, the backs of which were decorated with beautiful marbled and combed designs. I picked one up that featured loops and whorls made with paints of a rich reddish brown, violet, peach and olive green, with scattered bits of a yellow so pale it was nearly white. As I ran my finger over the slight texture the patterns made, a little bell went off in the back of my mind, suggesting they seemed very familiar. Not just the type of work, but specifically a piece with this range of colors and marbling effect. I couldn't quite place where I'd seen it before, but since they were so pretty and the memory so notable (if vague), I decided to buy the postcard.

As I wandered around the shop and collected various other little treasures, including a circular brooch set with a rainbow of colored stones, which I chose mainly because it looked like a little CD. For Travis, I picked up a newly-published volume of Sherlock Holmes stories I thought we could read to each other over the next few nights, in lieu of watching the myriad twenty-first century TV versions via the web. It's almost the same thing, right?

When I set everything down in front of the cashier to pay for today's finds, I felt that little fragment of memory tugging at me again. No specifics still, but with each extra second of thought, the more intense was the feeling there was something essential that should not be forgotten.

∽ ∽ ∽

I tried to remember the connection during the whole walk back home, which only made me more and more frustrated. Not until I attempted to cross the street and was nearly mowed down by a teenage boy on a bicycle (ah, some things never change) did I make a hint of progress. I established one concrete memory: *when* I'd seen the paper before. Despite this particular card pattern being unique to the late nineteenth century, I felt sure my memory of it had been created during my lifetime as Robin, not Jennie. And that was weird.

More thoughts trickled in over the next hours — though, as before, the less I focused on the questions, the more quickly the answers came to light.

I tried to distract myself with stuff around the house. I whipped up a batch of a killer spaghetti sauce, washed some sheets and pillowcases and then hung them out in back to dry, swept off the front porch and even polished the dining table. I had all kinds of interesting ideas pop into my mind — alas, nothing more on the note paper.

Nothing more in the idea department until I took a bath, that was.

After enjoying about twenty minutes of a blissful water experience — one scented with lavender and soothed by Epsom salts — my epiphany finally arrived.

I had seen that design on mail delivered to myself, with handwriting that looked almost exactly like my own. I couldn't remember exactly what the note said, but something along the lines of there having been a robbery... possibly at some hotel. A few people died, and this led to more violence.

I hopped out of the tub and started to roughly towel myself off as I tried to recall anything else from the message. Still dripping a little, I tiptoed down the hallway to get the blank journal I kept on my bedside table, where, I scrawled down what I remembered of the message.

Once the memory had been recorded, I finally let myself ponder the most obvious, nagging question: Why hadn't I remembered any of this before?

But, really, I knew the answer. I didn't need to be told or to figure it out.

I didn't remember it before, because it hadn't been so before . In some version of this timeline, I had used the card I bought today to write myself a note, and somehow managed to get it delivered to my home address more than a hundred and ten years from now.

This was crazy, crazy stuff, and my body knew it, too — every hair on my neck and arms was standing on end.

Simply put, I had altered history. Stranger still, short of having purchased the paper, I hadn't actually done anything to change it. Yet.

↪ ↪ ↪

When I woke up — this time, to the swooshing sound of a text message — I only glanced at the phone long enough to keep it from making any more noise. I got up from bed, asked myself, "If I got a letter right now and wanted to store it safely, where would I put it?" and the answer came to me: my little fireproof safe.

My safe... well, really a little lockbox I kept in the kitchen behind the canned goods, contained only stuff an someone who enjoyed kids' immunization records and first report cards could love. There was no cash, no jewelry... but as I flipped through the papers within, lo and behold, there it was: the postcard I was looking for.

Creepy chills time came again when I realized that in an alternate universe (or something along those lines — who knows?) my own hands had placed the envelope containing the card in my own safe.

Did. Not. Compute. My mind just couldn't reconcile whatever must have occurred to make such a thing happen, and for some reason, that filled me with despair. It was kind of like thinking about how infinitesimal humans were in the scheme of the whole universe.

But I was here now, and might as well play along. It was certainly a lot less depressing, at least.

"Mom? What are you doing?"

Those five simple words made me nearly jump out of my skin. I hadn't realized anyone had come in the room, but now Iris was right behind me behind me, standing on her tiptoes and trying to see over my shoulder.

Shoving all the rest of the papers back into the safe, I answered, "Nothing — just work stuff." Somehow, I felt guilty about lying to a five-year-old. "I was getting an old letter out," I added, and felt a little better.

"Can I see?"

Ten different ways to say "no" entered my mind, but I decided to ignore them all. Let the kid take a look. She could barely read, so where was the harm?

After shaking the envelope, the card fell out into my hand. It had the exact same design, but the paper stock was yellowed and there were tiny brown flecks scattered across the surface, possibly scars from by centuries-old raindrops. My handwriting was immediately recognizable, and once I read the words, I could also tell I had written this missive. I was exactly like one of my many lists, and contained every detail my I'd normally single out.

> KEEP THIS NOTE! Robin - Please hold on to this card until it makes sense.
> Feb 25, 1900 at about 11am, Walt & Maggie try to rob $ guests of a pink diamond necklace @ Palace Hotel. Found them via society page. Goes wrong and 2 shots kill couple (wife preg with twins). Look for newspaper headline: "Two bullets kills four."
> Never caught/not suspected/no leads until Maggie makes a deathbed confession in 1949. Says shots were accidental when man grabbed for gun BUT after they killed once people, started a years-long spree leaving 20+ dead until Walt dies from flu in 1918. Theory: By stopping the first, those dominoes won't fall. BTW: These people might be Vivian's relatives.
> I found out too late to fix this the first time, so hoping this note leads to a second chance!

It ended with my signature.

"I want to read it," Iris said, and put her hand out. "Please?"

With great reluctance, I passed it to her, hoping she wouldn't fixate on the multiple instances of "kill" in the note.

All the while she was wearing a very stern expression, I watched her eyes alight on every word. Finally, she handed it back to me. "That says Robin," she announced as she pointed to the salutation — probably one of the few words she recognized on sight. "So it's for you."

I nodded. She nodded. And with that, my youngest wandered off to find something more interesting, and I went into my bathroom and shut the door so I could ponder for a few minutes in relative peace.

Maybe it was because how badly things had gone last time I tried to fix the past, but every time I thought about changing history, I felt like tossing my cookies. Yes, of course, every action of every day alters the future... but this was different, because I saw the effects nobody else would ever know. It was way too much — too much responsibility, too much stress, too much strangeness — for a nobody like me.

Right now, though, that hardly compared to the despair that crept into my heart upon realizing I needed Travis's help sooner rather than later... but had only a handful petty crimes, wedding announcements and sports scores available to substantiate my wild claims.

But once Travis had been initiated into my league of interdimensional transference (one of the many names I called this thing I do), I was confident he'd be thrilled to help me figure out how to keep those people safe, and to stop things from snowballing with Walt and Maggie.

One thing he probably couldn't ever help me with was one more big question on my mind. See, finding this postcard in 1900 allowed me to set into motion a chain of events I would soon return to deal with. But now, since the goal of informing myself had been achieved... did I still have to send myself the note? If so, when?

Oh, time travel. Just when I think that maybe we could be friends, you go and kick me in the teeth.

36: Good news or bad?

After we finished dinner, we stayed at the table and chatted. After some small talk, and a couple glasses of wine, I finally worked up enough courage to broach the one subject I'd been avoiding.

I had only roughly sketched out the angles I needed to cover so it didn't sound too rehearsed. While there were no guidelines available for how to break news of this nature, when I was back in the Then, I looked up a few tips online. Specifically, I read things like "How to tell your parents you're gay," and "Explaining your cancer diagnosis to your loved ones," figuring those two topics were roughly on par with the gravity of the news I had to share.

After taking what I learned from the web, I tweaked the concepts to make the delivery a lot more upbeat and a little more me.

I thought I'd try to hit it from an oblique angle, rather than just announcing while we cleared away the dishes that hey, guess what! I am a visitor from the future.

"If you could know three things — just three things — about future events, what would they be?"

"Like what?" he said, and I could sense a little wariness in his voice.

"Almost anything. Final score of a baseball game, when another earthquake would hit, who will win the next presidential election... well, not that one, because that's not for several months."

I would have just answered with something random, but he thought about it for a moment.

"I suppose information about an earthquake would be helpful."

"Okay — I came prepared for that one. Ready? Alaska. Magnitude 7.7 quake in October."

He snorted. "You are a fortuneteller? You want to wait for nine months to prove you got it right?"

"Okay, bad example."

He mulled for a moment more, then said, "Perhaps advance notice of a great whale swimming into the Bay, or something of that nature."

"Good one! Can't remember if there was anything along those lines, but I'll check."

"You don't remember something that hasn't happened yet. Interesting."

"Isn't it?" I gave him a little wink. He blushed, but it was a happy blush, not my kind of I-am-so-stupid blush. "How about I make this easy on you. I took the liberty of finding out about a something happening soon. Tomorrow, Kentucky will name their new governor... but before the announcement, the guy gets shot. He dies four days later."

"That is an awful story!"

"Don't shoot the messenger. So to speak."

"So," he said, clearly If you know this is going to happen, why don't you stop it."

"Yeah, I don't think anyone would believe me. They would probably think I was in on it," I said. "Also, I can't remember the bad guy's name for some reason."

"Also, the American Association of baseball clubs gets its start tomorrow in Philadelphia."

"A league to rival the National? I guess that's not entirely unexpected." I looked over at him, and there was a definite twinkle in his eye. "And if your guesses come true — what then? Do we get you a job with a traveling carnival? 'Madame Jennie tells your future.'"

"No thanks," I said. "I'm allergic to elephants."

I know he was kidding around, but I was pretty sure the humor was an attempt to veil the fact that he now believed I was more than a few fries short of a Happy Meal. I took a break to give him a long, luscious kiss in the hope he'd be assured I was worth the trouble.

After a few memorable minutes, he was finally able to use his mouth for talking again. "I have to ask," he said. "Where is all this coming from?"

"Well... I have a confession to make," I told him.

He sat up straight then leaned forward a little, as if girding himself for some bad news. "I can't decide if I'm more concerned or intrigued."

"Go with intrigued," I said. "The simple version is I am not quite who you think I am."

"You are not the very beautiful girl with the very long Italian last name I'm loathe to pronounce any more often than I must?"

"Not exactly. Let me explain. And yes, I know this is going to sound completely off-the-chart strange. So please hear me out before telling me

I'm one serious whackadoodle."

He smiled and agreed, and I felt so bad, because I knew there was no way he was prepared for what I had to say. I just hoped if I sort of eased into it, it would somehow make sense to him. Looking back, I don't think I really comprehended how much of a toll a reveal like this could take.

As is my way, I came up with a rough plan, then winged it.

"When I woke up from the coma, I was so confused about everything because I had no memory of ever being this person," I said, gesturing to my current self.

"Yes, I understand that," he said.

"But I do have memories of another life — and I'm still living that other life, too."

There was a whole lot of silence before he finally admitted, "Apologies, but I'm not following along here at all."

"Yeah, I'm sorry. Let me just cut to the chase. The mind inside this body — the real me — is from more than a hundred years from now. I'm a time traveler." I closed my eyes. "Yes, I know it sounds completely insane, but it's true."

"A time traveler." He paused, then asked, "Is there a punchline?"

"If there is, I haven't found it yet."

"I see." His eyes lost their usual sparkle and he didn't say anything more. I started to get the feeling he was close to dismissing my claims completely.

"Just... just... just let me prove it to you," I stammered. "Ask me anything." Deep breath. "I don't know everything, of course, but will answer your questions to the best of my ability."

"Okay, well, why are you telling me about this now?" It was beyond obvious he wasn't buying one word of this. I consoled myself with the fact that, at least, his tone wasn't snarky.

I straightened my dress and sat up straight. As calmly as I could manage, I replied, "Because I need your help. Something is going to happen next week we need to stop."

His hand started massaging the back of his neck.

"I have wanted to tell you for a long time, but was just waiting for the right way to do it."

He nodded as if thinking all of this over. "I guess I'd like to know how you go from here to there? I suppose you have a time machine?"

"No, I'm not H.G. Wells, Travis. I am being serious. When I go to sleep here, I wake up in the future... and when I go to sleep in the future, I wake up here. I suppose there's no physical switch, but just a kind of consciousness exchange."

"How do you make it work?"

"I have no control over it. It's not something I signed up for or planned. It just started to happen."

"Is the real Jennie then living in your time?"

"No. I don't know where she is, but I get the impression she's just... gone. Maybe she died in the coma."

"Ah."

"You don't believe me," I said. It wasn't even a question.

I watched him struggle with his answer for a full minute before he finally could spit it out. "I don't *disbelieve* you."

I puffed out an exasperated sigh before I could stop myself.

"That's okay — I understand. I sure as hell wouldn't believe it if you told me something like that," I said. "You're not from the middle ages or something. Or the year 2400, right?"

"Not as far as I am aware, no," he laughed. "But you can't truly expect me to immediately believe something so..."

"Outlandish?"

"Yes!"

"Far-fetched?

"Yes."

"Crazy? Impossible? Insane?"

"Now I didn't say that," he said, taking my hand and kissing it. "But what would you think if I told you the same thing: I was a traveler from the year, say, 2100?"

"Well, knowing what I know now, I'd probably be inclined to believe you."

"Then what if I told you I was from the planet Mars?"

Yes, I got the point... at least in terms of how nonsensical it all sounded.

"... I'd probably think you were either a lunatic or you were joking."

He nodded with this irritating little "I told you so," shrug.

"But," I said. "If I was inclined to believe you — thought you were being earnest — I'd ask you to prove it to me."

"I agree. So prove it to me. Perhaps prove it to yourself."

"I *have* proven it to myself," I told him.

"How did you do that? How do you know it's real and you're not just —

well, dreaming it?"

"With this," I told him, and slid a small envelope across the table. "Inside."

"What is this?"

The puzzlement apparent on his face was adorably amusing. I gave him an extremely brief overview of this amazing thing we had in the future called the internet, comparing it to an enormous, searchable library everyone had at home.

"So, I sent myself a message. Posted it in the newspaper here, and looked it up in the internet newspaper archives in the future."

I showed him the note: *Love to LJH IMH from a purple orange dotted feathered lizard*

He angled it toward the light so he could read it. After a moment, he handed it back. "I don't understand. What does it mean?"

"It's not supposed to make sense to anyone but me. It's the girls' initials, and then how they described the main character in a bedtime story we made up before bed one night. I took the main character's description and put that in there, too." I laughed, "Figured it would be the only newspaper notice in the history of ever to use that exact combination."

Proudly I looked down at my little scrap of paper, and it gave me a boost of confidence. Every time I thought I was dreaming or hallucinating or worse, I just had to look back at this notice. It was all the proof I needed.

But evidently I was the only one swayed.

"I think this is fascinating," said Travis. "I do. And there's much food for thought..."

With a heavy heart, I watched him stand up and straighten his coat. I could guess what was coming.

"...but I also feel I need a little time to think about all of this."

In a bit of a panic, I started to scramble. "I could find some baseball game scores for you, or tell you something that's going to happen tomorrow or next week."

"Yes, that's a possibility, but I feel it might be a bit too..."

"Easy to cheat?"

"I'd never put it in those terms, no, but such a thing would only go so far."

For several moments, we just stood there. The thickness of the silence was choking me, but I wasn't going to beg him to believe me.

Finally, hat in hand, he leaned over and kissed my cheek. "I will see you later."

I wasn't counting on it.

"Goodbye, Travis," I said, on the verge of tears. Then I used both hands to softly close the door on what had been the best part of this life.

37: Gone

When I woke up, it was rainy and foggy and gray and miserable... and it so completely fit my mood.

After leaving me at about 11 in the morning, Travis hadn't come back at all yesterday. That was probably for the best, because by mid-afternoon, a bottle of vodka and I had become close friends, and were having the most awesome pity party.

Way too much of the day back in the Now had been wasted moping and trying to find something immediate and impressive I could use to sway Travis. Sadly, the timing of my announcement coincided with some of the most uneventful and utterly predictable days in world history. The only benefit of was that I could openly cry, drink, yell and otherwise bemoan my fate in the Then.

When I crossed back over to my real time zone, it had taken nearly every ounce of energy I had to hold it together in front of the girls for fourteen long, long hours... but at least that wore me out enough to make it easy to fall asleep at the end of the day.

When I landed back in this time, my energy was all but zapped. Yesterday's anger was gone, and all I had coursing through my veins was heartbreak.

Stepping slowly, I made my way down the stairs to make a cup of coffee. Right as I walked by the front door, the bell rang. It was so shrill, it scared the crap out of me, and pushed me right to the brink of tears again.

Realize, though, that I thought I'd given up on Travis already. I decided he was stick-a-fork-in-it done with me. Still, the moment I heard that chime, a tiny bit of optimism popped up out of the woodwork. Before I could talk myself out of any expectations, my hand had already started to open the door.

And there stood Travis, little rivulets of rainwater dribbling down his face, looking like a drowned rat wearing a policeman's hat.

Before I could say a word, he spoke.

"I know how I can believe."

38: The test

When I saw him standing there, words completely failed me. I just stood there and gaped at him.

"I will come back later and tell you about it — I have to get to work now," he said. "But I have a plan, and I didn't want you to think I had given up on you."

Of course that made me cry.

Travis gave me a quick kiss — on the lips this time — and then disappeared off into the morning mist.

I was left alone to wonder what he could possibly have in mind... but at least I could now allow myself a little bit of hope.

∽ ∽ ∽

His shift ended at six, and it usually took him about twenty minutes to get here after he clocked out.

Every second that ticked by after 6:20 got me more and more wound up. At 6:45, startling to fume, I told myself that if he wasn't here by seven, I was leaving and going somewhere -- anywhere but here. I was especially annoyed I couldn't even call to leave irritating voicemail messages asking where he was.

At 6:53, the bell finally rang. I turned the lock, and couldn't help but pre-load a glare for whomever was on the other side of the door. I hoped it was Travis, but I was done with expectations for the day.

Pulling on the handle, I swung the heavy door wide open.

I think the smell hit me even before I realized Travis was holding a wooden crate in front of him.

He looked at me and held the box down a little lower. With his right hand, he pointed to the individual containers within, naming each one: "Chow Mein. Mou Goo Gai Pan. Chop Suey. Char Shu. Goy Chee. And, uh, that's some rice, and some tea called Oolong."

I was so stunned, I couldn't speak — couldn't move — just stared at his hands wrapped around the crate.

"Can I come in? I've been carrying this food for almost an hour, and I'd really like to put it down."

The sparkle had returned to his eyes — and when I noticed that, it helped knock me out of my reverie. "Oh yeah, of course, please do," I said. "I can't believe you got us Chinese food. That is just... wow. Thank you."

He set the individual little containers on the dining table while I got out plates, silverware and a few napkins from my vast collection.

"I'm terribly, terribly sorry to be so late," he said at last. "I was relieved of duty early, but it still took a long time to get the food, and then to get the streetcar back up here. Did you know what it's more than *four miles* from here to Chinatown?"

"It's fine," I said. "I'm just happy you're here. Really, really happy."

The food was fantastic and flavorful — the best meal I'd had in this lifetime. And the fact that Travis had gone to all this effort for me made it all that much better. (He even made a point of telling me he even got shark fin soup... and although it sounded awful to him, he was going to try it.)

"I'm wondering, though," I asked — because I had to ask, "How come you believe me enough to still talk to me?"

Between bites of Char Shu (the rich and smoky barbecued pork) he replied, "For one, I have never met anyone who talks like you. Your syntax and word choices, your speed."

"Youmeantalkinglikethisallthetime ?"

"Precisely," he said, and gave my nose a little affectionate tweak. "And you say 'wow' and 'yeah' a lot."

"Yeah." Big smile.

"There is also the depth of knowledge you have — the likes of which I have never seen from another soul. It's as if you have an entire library on tap. It's rather remarkable," he said. "Quite honestly, I look forward to bringing you to parties — show you off."

Although we'd eaten an incredible amount, we still had enough left for at least another meal. I re-packaged the food, and placed it in the newly-iced refrigerator. It could be dinner tomorrow.

After we cleaned up, Travis started to explain his plan.

"I placed notices in two different newspapers on the east coast — they will be published in the morning," he said. "They are both for you. In the future."

"I see — it's a test."

"It is a bit of a puzzle. I'd like you to figure out the answer and tell me in the morning."

Travis had posted two ads. He gave me a search term to find the first one — his initials and then mine — and once I found that notice, it would give me the key to the second. Then, with both in hand, I would alternate words from each. From there, I needed to take the first letters or numerals of each word or number, and that would, at last, tell me something I needed to research. There were 15 characters I needed in total.

Once I understood the process, the plan seemed pretty workable, given the resources I had in the Now. I was completely confident I could figure it out.

"Very crafty! How do you know I'll be able to work out the solution?"

He smirked. "From what you have told me about the information available in your age, I doubt you will have any problem."

I told him I'd report back in the morning... but all the time was hoping I hadn't oversold the expansiveness of the internet, and hadn't unduly inflated my own search engine expertise.

Travis pulled out a piece of paper with something that looked strangely like a flow chart.

"I've diagrammed the process here, although I realize you won't be able to refer to this on the other end, so to speak."

"Cool. This is... impressively complex," I said.

"I used to want to be an engineer," he explained. "But my grandfather was a police officer, and his father, and his father."

"Yeah — I've heard that song before."

The self-satisfied grin stayed on his face, leading me to ask if there was anything else I needed to know.

He laughed. "Yes, there's something more. You will need to know the cipher."

"Cipher? As in a code?"

He nodded.

"And how am I supposed to figure it out?"

He promised he'd give me the key I needed later that night — just before we fell asleep.

For some reason, that turned on the tear faucet again. "Thank you, Travis," I said between sobs. "I thought you'd given up on me."

"Not at all," he said, resting his hand on my face and caressing my cheek with his thumb. "I just needed some time to come to grips with all of it."

"I realize my claim sounds... extraordinary."

"I would have to agree. But, I'd say that's quite fitting, as you are quite an extraordinary lady yourself," he said, looking deep into my eyes. "Please know I do feel bad for even asking. But I'd really like something that will prove beyond the slightest shadow of a doubt."

"Don't apologize. I understand. I'm sure I'd want to do the same thing."

Now he took my hands into both of his wide, warm hands, and said, "I believe, though, that you believe. And I want to believe."

"All right, Mulder. And until then..."

"Until then," he said, pulling me close, "I will offer you the benefit of the doubt."

With his arms still around me and a smug little grin on his lips, he added, "Besides — I suspect taking you at your word will have its benefits."

Immediately, I proved to him that his latest theory, at least, was the absolute truth.

∽∽∽

The evening had been spent enjoying various fun and games — quite literally — and we even played on the piano for the first time in this house. It was nearly midnight when we finally "retired," as Travis would say.

But instead of leaving like he usually did, he was going to stay... simply to sleep beside me. He didn't say as much, but I knew why he was sticking around tonight: He wanted to feel fully confident his test methods had worked, so he needed to be sure I didn't leave in the middle of the night to break into telegraph office records, or to buy up early morning newspapers, or anything that could possible constitute cheating. I couldn't blame him one bit. He was giving me a great chance to prove myself, and I wanted him to know in his heart the results were utterly real.

I went to lie down while he did whatever guys do in the bathroom for fifteen minutes at a time. (I didn't want to know. Really.) By the time he climbed into bed and told me the cipher I needed, I was so fuzzy and close to dreamland, I'd nearly forgotten my quest.

"I must give you the key," he whispered. "From did to night."

"Pardon me?" I said, trying to drag myself out of my stupor.

"*From did to night .*"

"I don't know what that means. Did tonight what?"

"No, no — the word 'did' to the word 'night.' That's just to help you find something specific."

I had no idea how that fit into the scheme, but I silently repeated "did to night, did to night," over and over again, until I was gone from that place and time and in another.

39: The Now: Searching for the answer

As soon as I woke up in the now, there was no waiting. Still mumbling "did to night," I grabbed my laptop from my bedside table and ran a search for GVD TJD in the papers from February 1900.

Now my head was clearer in the here and now, I was starting to feel pretty sure this wasn't going to work. One way or another — whether it was going to be due to a printing error or faulty page scan, or simply a result of history acting like a stubborn child who must do things his way — I had exceedingly low expectations.

A few seconds later, the newspaper archive site returned an error — their data was currently unavailable. Out of habit, I pressed reload to try again.

Well, paint me blue and call me Nellie. Or something. There on my screen was a single wonderful, amazing matching result. It was from the New York *Tribune*, and the date was spot-on. I could feel my heart beating in my throat.

The notice was under the column heading "Domestic situations wanted." Ha ha.

Re: GVD TJD. Respectable Man of Useful Intelligent Textiles. Also Stenographer. See also DVG DJT

That was perhaps one of the strangest sets of words I had ever read, and I couldn't figure out any significance to them apart from their prescribed use to outline a code. At the end of the blurb was the second search term I needed to use.

No waiting around this time. In a separate browser window, I ran a new search, and nothing hindered me this time — although two results popped up. The first was for a newspaper in Kentucky, and when I read the actual scanned page, saw the match was only the result of poor text recognition. Scratch that.

The second notice was in the newspaper out of Washington DC. I knew it was correct the moment I read the strange ad copy, even though the notice had been published a full day after the first:

Re: DVG DJT. Overseeing Engineer Job. Lengthy Employment. 111 55th.

As I looked around my house for a piece of paper and a pen that actually worked, I giggled, imagining people of the era reading these notices and assuming they'd been written by some absolute idiot. (I also checked: 111 55th was a real address, at least in the here and now. I wondered if there had been inquiries made about the job notice.)

Blank paper and pens were nowhere to be found, because if one has children, it's apparently a rule that they must abscond with all adult writing implements.

With an old bank statement and a broken green crayon, I started to solve my little puzzle.

First, I took the words from each ad and placed them on separate lines.

Respectable
Man
Ohio
Useful
Intelligent
Texan
Also
Stenographer.
See also DVG DJT

Overseeing
Engineer
Job
Lengthy
Employment
1111
55th

Here were the first letters of each word in the New York notice:

R
M
O
U
I
T
A
S

And the letters from the DC notice:

O
E
J
L
E
1
5

Trade off those letters, starting with the first, and I got this:

R O M E O J U L I E T A 1 S 5

The name of the Shakespearean play jumped out at me right away, and then I stared at what was left for about twenty seconds before realizing it could only mean one thing: Romeo and Juliet — Act 1, Scene 5. I knew but a few of the most popular lines from that work — and most of those because I'd helped a friend rehearse for her part as a Capulet in the high school play — but had no clue which part this was. From what I understood, I was looking for a question I needed to answer.

Enter Mr Google. As I typed in the query, I realized my hands were shaking a little. Then, with a jolt, it occurred to me I wasn't just playing a game or deciphering a little message from a friend — I was going to prove (to myself, at least) this time travel was no trick, and really and truly did have lives in two different centuries.

Was I ready to know for sure? Could I handle it if what I found made no sense, or if I got back to the Then and my answer was wrong?

Only one way to find out. With a flourish, I hit enter.

Two clicks later, the full text of the scene was up on my screen. Into my browser search box, I entered the word "did," and only one instance was highlighted on the page.

I followed with my finger to "night" — 17 words along. There were three little sentences:

"*Did my heart love till now? Forswear it, sight! For I ne'er saw true beauty till this night.*"

That wasn't a question. That was a *statement*. Goosebumps rolled up my arms, and I felt a happy little shiver.

So here it was, 7:16 on Saturday morning, and I was half wishing this day was already done, just so I could go back to see that amazing, amazing man.

40: The Now – Of questions and answers

I had started telling the girls about my dream travel soon after it began, weaving the characters and situations into a story... because to them, that's just what it was.

At first there had been the three nurses, one very kind, one nice enough, and one meanie. The kind nurse had ended up being given the ability to fly, the middle one got nothing, and the grumpy one had her nose turn green. (I may have embellished the story slightly.)

They had been enthralled by the introduction of Mr Lucky, the policeman, who helped the Rainbow Princess (my character's name, per Iris) when she got lost in the village — and the two of them really were excited when Mr Lucky helped protect Rainbow from the bad wolves.... let's call them Wally and Maggie. More recently, the princess had met a motley cast of characters — her neighbors — who we named the Village People. They brought her highness a variety of baked goods, and kept her well-apprised on the status of the other commoners.

But even more than the stories themselves, the girls loved how, for once in their lives, I could invent new tales to tell them night after night after night. In the past, it had always been their dad who was the master at creating stories on the fly. Now, as far as they were concerned, I had the magic touch, too.

I couldn't wait to tell them the latest — about how Mr Lucky sent Rainbow a secret message, and she was the only one who could break the code.

There would be no stories tonight, though. It was Saturday, so my girls weren't home.

Without anything other than work to occupy my time, and no stories to tell, time passed slowly. I found myself repeatedly drifting by the fridge — in search of snacks, yes, but mostly to look at and touch my kids' art and photos posted there. My littlest had mastered drawing people who had no necks and arms splayed out, while her big sister was on a flower kick. Daisies, tulips and multi-colored lilies — of course — were Lily's favorites.

Weekends in the Now were tougher for me since I started traveling, because I really missed seeing my kiddos. During the week, it was bad enough. Since I was spending a day in the Then for every day in the Now, it felt like I only got to see them every other day. But when I accounted for them being at their dad's house on Saturday and Sunday? I had five days in a row where I didn't get to see my girls. I had never been away from them for so long before, and I didn't like it one bit.

Ever since I'd gotten settled in the year 1900 — reached a little equilibrium — I'd streamlined my life. Instead of letting it sprawl across the day and night, I did what I needed to do in the most efficient manner possible, and as much as possible, work was now confined to the girls' school hours. Between eight in the morning and three in the afternoon, I was a powerhouse, sketching logos, creating icons, tweaking photos and all the other creative fun that let me bring home the bacon, and fry it up in a pan.

❦ ❦ ❦

At around three in the afternoon, halfway through cleaning out the kitchen cupboards, a stray thought entered my mind. With all the hoopla about telling Travis, I'd completely put aside all thought of the purpose behind it all: to save that family in 1900, and hopefully to get my friend Vivian back.

It seemed fair to assume something I had done in the past had tweaked events enough so Vivian and I hadn't become friends, or she didn't live in the area anymore. (Those were the only options I could really handle at this point. If someone would have suggested to me that maybe she didn't exist, I'd close my eyes and plug my ears and hum to myself.)

❦ ❦ ❦

A little over-the-counter sleeping pill helped ease me off to sleep that night. Without it, I was sure I would have tossed and turned for hours — insomnia from excitement.

As soon as I felt the room temperature drop about ten degrees, I opened my eyes... and jumped when I realized there was another pair of eyes looking right back at me.

"Sorry — didn't mean to startle."

I just laughed. "'Did my heart love till now?'" I said as I pulled him close for a kiss. "'Forswear it, sight!'"

Travis held me close and whispered the last line into my ear: "'For I ne'er saw true beauty till this night.'"

Before I said anything else, I had to stop and give him ten more kisses.

"Here's a question," Travis said when I finally let him up for air. "What should I call you?"

"'Sweetheart' would be good, or perhaps 'Dearest Darling.' If you want something really different, try 'Googly Bear.'" I batted my eyelashes. At this point, I was downright giddy.

"That wasn't quite what I meant," he said, knowing full well I wasn't being serious. "I was thinking more of choosing between Robin or Jennie, or even Genevieve."

"Yes, I know," I laughed. "Well, I've guess I have gotten used to Jennie, and that might be easier. I can only imagine some busybody inquiring why you're calling me Robin."

"So right now, you're home asleep."

"Yeah. So weird, isn't it?" I sighed in the comfort of his arms. "Who says you can't be in two places at once?"

"I suppose any gentleman should ask this one: Are you married?"

"Not anymore."

"Widowed?"

"Divorced." (Slight gasp.) "But don't worry — there's not much of a stigma there anymore."

"Truly?" (Eyes wide.)

"Really truly. I'd say about half the adult population is divorced, so if it was still a big taboo, we'd all be in trouble."

"My goodness." (Sad look. Head shake.) "That is somewhat disheartening." (Pause. Crooked smile.) "Then, if I may ask: Are you being courted by anyone?"

"Yes — yes I am," I said with no hesitation. "He's handsome and intelligent and charming. Name's Travis."

(Big grin.) "Very good. What I hoped to hear," he said.

"I don't know what I should ask. How about you tell me what I ought to know?"

That was another easy one to answer. "I'd have to say the most important thing about my other life is that I have two amazing little girls."

"You're a mum?" (Jaw drops. Eyes bulge.) "That, uh, is a surprise." I believed it. In fact, I hadn't known someone's eyes could pop out so much without requiring corrective surgery.

"How old are your children?" (Eyeballs start to return to sockets.)

"Lily is almost eight years old, and Iris is five."

"Dear Lord Almighty — how old *are* you?" (Voice raised an octave, eyes bug out again.) He looked so much like an incredulous little boy, finding out for the first time how babies were made, I nearly asphyxiated on giggles.

When I finally regained my composure, I responded in the annoyingly enigmatic manner women have (presumably) used for millennia. "Older than I look, but younger than I feel."

∽ ∽ ∽

The questions resumed over breakfast of eggs and toast, courtesy of Travis's mad stove skills.

"So what was it like when you... arrived in this time?"

I told him the first thing I remembered (somewhat clearly, anyhow) was the sound of people ringing in the new year. "Before that — not too much. I mean, if I think really hard about it, sometimes I can get a vague sense of the earlier days in the hospital. No sights or specific sounds, but just the light on my eyelids and sounds and smells in a big blur."

I explained how there had been something really strange about these dreams I couldn't quite put my finger on. They had a very distinctly different quality from any other I could remember.

"Granted, this body was just coming out of a coma, but still — I didn't realize what was happening. I just thought it was a vivid recurring dream."

"When did you first realize you really were in a different year?"

"Not until about a week later. That's when I finally got a look outside. I pretty much knew right then, just because of the way it looked and the how it all felt. Plus the detail — the whole scene — seemed way beyond anything I could imagine."

He buttered his toast as he thought this over, then asked, "Have you traveled through time before?"

"In retrospect — maybe. Not anything nearly as clear as this 'adventure' or whatever you want to call it. But, looking back... it might be possible."

Then it was my turn to ask the questions.

"So how did you put my puzzle all together?"

"First I figured out the message I wanted to send," he said, "then worked backwards from there. How to identify the passage, then created the code, then wrote up the advertisements." He pronounced *advertisements* in the properly British way.

"Very clever," I said, "and very quick thinking!" He blushed.

"Once that was all ready, I sent telegrams to the newspapers on the east coast. From two separate telegraph offices at different times of the day." He explained how wanted to be sure everything about his experiment was beyond reproach, for his own peace of mind.

"Not that I didn't trust you," he said, growing redder. "Just... it was..."

"Shhh — I get it. Don't worry."

That's when Travis sheepishly admitted he had come by yesterday morning not only to ease my mind... but to make sure I was home, and had not seen what he was up to. He also secretly checked on me mid-day by peeking through a window. "I didn't look at what you were doing," he assured me, even though I wasn't mad at all. "I just saw movement somewhere in the room, and that's all I needed."

I gave him a hug. "Honestly, I understand. And I think your plan was perfect. It worked, right?"

He smiled, but I could tell there was something more on his mind. I thought he was still feeling guilty. Turns out, the sweet guy was just feeling mortal.

"I have to ask, and it sounds so terribly ghoulish..."

And then I knew. I knew exactly what he was fishing for. "Do I know when you die? Or when I do?"

Travis nodded sheepishly.

"Spoilers!"

That just confused him, and I felt bad. "It means it would spoil the surprise — of life — if we knew. Well, that's how I choose to think of it, anyway." Then I told him the sad truth: There had never been an obituary or anything whatsoever I could find regarding Jennie's death, or that of Travis.

I didn't know why. Had history not been written yet, was it just too much in flux... or was information being kept from me for some reason? I knew I could wonder every day and night for the next two decades, and I'd still never have an answer... because that was apparently not how this worked, and that annoyed me no end.

"It's like a stupid game," I explained with a huff, "but I don't know the rules, don't know the other players, and can only see a corner of the board.

I keep walking into walls and falling of the edge because I can't figure out what I'm supposed to do."

Travis took my hand. "I think when one considers the way you and I met, and how we got along so well from the very start... well, not to be too presumptuous, but I think I may well be one of the other players in your game." He kissed my palm. "Together, we should be able to work this out, yes?"

41: Taking care of business

The next day, I finally went into detail about about what my note from the future — or the past... or both? — had foretold.

Travis said he had a plan, and I let him run with it. Having a cop at your beck and call was pretty awesome, especially since I was tired of coming up with a seemingly endless stream of ideas and explanations.

Besides, the main event wasn't for a few days yet. If one thing didn't work, there would be time to try something else.

∽∽∽

"It's taken care of." Travis made this pronouncement that evening when he was scarcely though my front door.

I didn't know what he was talking about, but still did not like the sound of it. I closed the newspaper I'd been reading and folded it in half.

"'Taken care of'? What do you mean?"

"Walter and Maggie met with a bit of foul play. They were apparently robbed... and beaten up some."

I don't know what I had been expecting, but it wasn't this.

"Oh my god — seriously? You shouldn't have done that. It could be traced back to you — to us, and..."

"Shhh, shhh," he soothed me. "I was not there, Jen. All evening, I was at the station. Around four o'clock, I heard a report come in." He caressed my hair. "They will be fine — they're patching him up at the hospital now. It seems the pursuers broke Wally's fingers. Maggie was not hurt, but very scared." There was a pause. "So I hear."

"Vigilante justice is alive and well, I see."

He shrugged. "I know there were a few gentlemen who work security at the Palace Hotel who were concerned, justifiably, that their jobs — and, of course — their patrons, were at risk. Coupled with the criminals' past offenses, apparently some people felt a little retribution was only fair." This just made me groan.

"I thought you would be happy, Jen," he said. "We certainly stopped this hotel robbery, and have, as you said, kept the dominoes from falling."

I took a deep breath. "That's the point, I guess."

"So why do you seem upset?"

"Because I'm torn," I said. "On one hand, I think, 'Yeah, kick his ass!' But another part of me just hates the thought of sinking to that level."

I could tell Travis was struggling to understand. After a moment, he said, "I won't pretend to know what the police are like in your time, but here and now, we do what we can ourselves. It's part and parcel of the job."

He tried to soothe me by kissing my cheek and lightly pinching my nose. "Besides, there's no need to dwell on it now. What's done is done, and have no doubt: The world is better for it."

I had no response to that.

"May I?" he asked, gesturing to today's *Call*, and I handed it to him.

"I guess I'll see when I go back tonight if the hotel robbery story is gone, and, I guess, if there's a new one in its place."

Travis opened the paper. "The hotel robbery won't be happening, don't worry," he said and smiled. Then he started reading, "And the other thing won't be in there, either."

"How do you know?"

He looked up at me. "If they reported every time a low-life thug got what he deserved, this," he waved the paper, "would be forty pages long every day."

"Walt and Maggie — they'll live," he said, with a half smile before turning back to his reading. "They will live, which is a lot more than could have been said for that man and his wife."

42: The Now – Wrinkles in time

As soon as I rolled out of bed, I made sure the girls were getting ready for school, and then I went online.

My stomach clenched when I saw the same horrible newspaper story was still in existence, and hadn't changed one bit as far as I could tell. Travis's plan hadn't worked, and we hadn't fixed history. Not yet, anyhow.

Before I plunged into obsessing over a new plan, I needed to take a little me time. After closing my laptop, I tiptoed over to the bedroom door and closed it. Shuffling quietly over to my bed, I grabbed a pillow and screamed into it for a few long and satisfying moments until I felt better. With that out of the way, I opened my door, made the kids' lunches, and took them off to school.

Around nine in the morning, just as I'd started really rolling with work — a text popped up on my phone.

Where r u? Mama waits!

The message was from none other than Vivian.

Fourteen and a half minutes later, I was at the gym, holding a very confused friend in a bear hug.

"I missed you!"

"Missed me?" she laughed. "You mean since yesterday?"

"It feels like I haven't seen you for a week!"

"If you missed me — sure, I missed you too!" she said, hugging me back and still laughing. "But you know we better be careful, or my wife's going to get jealous."

I gasped — I'd almost forgotten. "How is Samantha? Still pregnant, right?" One of my worries had been that my messing with time had somehow changed the fact they were going to be moms in just a few months.

Now Vivian was looking at me a little strangely. "She was an hour ago, unless you know something I don't."

"Nope — just checking."

"Um, did something happen to you?"

"Yes, but no. You remember meeting yesterday? Here?"

"Yeah," she said, and I could see her eyes narrowing in concern. "Sure I do. You don't?"

"What do you most remember about yesterday?"

"Well, I we did our usual rounds, and then I got you to spin with me for half an hour. Not that you didn't bitch the whole time."

The moment she said it, I remembered it. I could still recall her not being around, but had memories of the spinning class, too. They both existed in my mind, almost like they'd happened on different days.

"Right — yeah!"

"And the guy with the split in his pants. You *have* to remember that, because you nearly bust a gut trying not to laugh."

Suddenly, that (slightly obscene) image was my memory banks, too. "Yes," I said. "I do, actually! Awesome." Feeling these quasi-new memories being born was such a strange and wonderful sensation.

"You're crazy. You know it's true, right?"

"Of course, Viv. That's what you and I have in common."

I thought for a moment and something else popped into my head — this one not a memory, but an idea. "How about this — we blow this joint and go get coffee instead. Relax for one day."

"Really? I'm supposed to keep you on the straight and narrow with your workouts. You sure you want to?"

"Positive," I said, leading her to the glass double doors opening to the rest of the world. "I can afford a day off, because I worked out extra yesterday, right?"

༄ ༄ ༄

An hour and a half later, I was back at home, and back at work. The heartbreaking hotel murder story was still on my screen, sandwiched between news of an east coast blizzard and details about a recent stagecoach robbery. On a whim, I hit F5 to refresh the page.

When the image reloaded, there was no mention of the Palace Hotel at all. I scanned through all the pages of the original newspaper edition and all of those through the next seven days. And hallelujah! The story was indeed was gone, gone, gone.

So not only was Vivian back (and had never known she was gone), there was no robbery and shooting to worry about anymore. Double win!

Sure, the 1900s vehicular semantics still confused me. (I was always trying to figure out the difference between buggies, carriages, coaches, wagons and carts.) And it was true that I continued to wrestle with tasks any six-year-old in the Victorian era could easily manage.

But it seemed that when I let fate be my guide, apparently I *could* make minor repairs to history.

Maybe I could put that on my résumé.

43: Funny money

"You know how the first time we met, you thought I was asking you for money? Well, now I'm asking you for money," I said to Travis. "But don't worry — I only want my own loot."

He hadn't even blinked. Clever boy was getting wise to me already. I continued, "There must be a bank account or safe or something, somewhere around here... but I can't find anything. I'm down to about two bucks, so think I better deal with this situation sooner rather than later."

"More than happy to help you on your treasure hunt," he said. "I presume you have already looked for a big black X marking the spot?"

"Strangely enough, I didn't," I answered. "Now, I *did* find a huge X that said 'money here' underneath, but since it was red instead of black, I knew that wasn't it."

I told him how I had searched through the whole house, upstairs and down, but focused on the desk on the lower level. I had ransacked all the drawers and shelves at least ten times, and scavenged very little of value. The entire bounty: Papers, envelopes, sealing wax, pen nibs (but no ink), some random lengths of wire, one postage stamp, two keys that didn't seem to fit anything in this house, a few coins and a compass.

"May I show you some magic?" Travis asked, then showed me a little trick. With one of those pieces of wire in hand, he slipped the pointed end into a tiny hole drilled on the side of one of the cubbyholes. That pushed in a little spring, which allowed a small hidden compartment to slide out. To my untrained eye, it had just seemed like a decorative piece of carved wood... but to a cop in this era, it looked like a place where secrets were stashed.

Tucked inside the narrow cubby was exactly what I had been looking for: a blue leatherette passbook. The gold-stamped logo on the front told me that I had been banking with the Mutual Savings Bank of San Francisco. Upon flipping through the pages within, I discovered three things I needed to know: there was an account in my name, there appeared to be nearly $400 in it, and I needed to head downtown to their office on Post Street in order to get any of it.

Even with passbook in hand, the idea of going to the bank to take out some money made me ludicrously nervous. I knew was a fake, how wouldn't they know it, too? What if they asked me some question I couldn't answer? As far as I knew, the only people here who carried identification were police officers. Even passports weren't required yet for international travel.

"Would you possibly consider coming with me?" I asked Travis. "This whole thing just seems really daunting to me." I didn't tell him that I was working myself into such a panic that I might throw up any second now.

He sweetly assured me that they would know me at the bank, and I'd have no problem accessing my money. And yes, he would come with me.

"Whatever they ask, whatever they say, be calm, be confident. If we need to, we can tell them about how you had a head injury," he said. "But don't borrow trouble."

"Don't tell me that you don't still have banks. No, wait — let me suppose — you don't use money anymore."

"Oh, we have money. We just don't touch it very often." As we journeyed downtown, I told him about a world full of credit cards and ATMs, electronic bills and online payments... all of which left him to deeply question our generation's sanity.

◡ ◡ ◡

From the outside, Mutual Savings Bank looked like most other financial institutions — ornate, grand, and somewhat forbidding. But inside? The moment I walked in the front door, I got a bad case of the giggles, because the place totally reminded me of Gringott's. There was the ornate wood paneling, the design in the mosaic floor, and even enormous chandeliers. (I kind of doubted, though, that Harry Potter had a vault deep in the tunnels below.)

A man at the front curtly asked me to state my business, then directed us to a cashier on the right.

The brass plaque on the cashier's desk told me that his name was George Story... but if he had a story to tell, it was a somber tale with no poetry in those words. His hair was oiled to the extreme — just like his mustache — and the man's lips were locked in a perpetual sneer.

Mr Story took my passbook, examined the front page, then flipped through to see the most recent entries. After a few moments, he glanced at me, and over the top of his eyeglasses, appeared to size me up, then did the same for Travis. I looked right in Mr Banker Guy's frighteningly-deep-set eyes and smiled as best as I could.

Like everyone in this decade, the man took his own sweet time. Finally he spoke, but said only, "Miss diMedici." I struggled — hard — against my urge to blather, to deliver answers to questions that had not actually been asked. I sat still, and was eventually rewarded with, "How nice... to have you visit us again."

"Thank you," I said while I tried to shake off his oogy gaze. "I would like to get some cash, please."

"Do you wish to withdraw such funds... from this account... or another?"

That was not a question I'd been expecting.

I fumbled for a response.

Travis jumped in to help. "How many does she have here again?"

"Miss diMedici has two accounts with us."

I looked at Travis, who shrugged.

If I were at home, what would I ask? And in a snap, the obvious question came to me. "What are the balances?"

George adjusted his glasses and peered at the tiny writing in the ledger. "Your passbook... is... correct. The first of the two contains... three hundred... seventy two dollars... and... eighteen cents."

That kind of sucked. Travis, however, raised his eyebrows and nodded. Apparently he thought that was okay, even though it reminded me of my finances during my college days.

"The second account... contains..." he said, then paused, looked up at me, and down at the desk again. "A moment, please." He picked up the ledger and walked off, taking it over to a rotund bald man seated at a fancy-schmancy carved wooden desk inside one of the offices situated around the periphery of the bank. The two men consulted the figures, looked over at me, discussed something in hushed tones, nodded, looked at me again... and then the cashier returned.

Mr Story finished his earlier sentence as if he'd never even stepped away. "...twenty three... thousand, six hundred thirty seven... dollars... and eighty-two cents."

That number would have been impressive to me even without accounting for inflation.

"Twenty three thousand you say?" Travis said, and I could see that he was trying (and kind of failing) to appear nonchalant.

"Twenty three, yes... and six hundred... thirty seven dollars. And eighty-two... cents."

From the corner of my eye, I could see Travis's hand slip up to rub the back of his neck. His eyes were huge, and his face was starting to pale.

I leaned over and whispered, "Are you okay?"

"Yes, fine," he said, and gave me a weak smile, nodded too many times, and kept massaging his neck.

Mr Story folded his hands primly in front of him and asked, "How much do you care to withdraw today?"

For some reason, all the questions, the strange situation, and even Travis's stress kind of overwhelmed me. Without thinking, I just defaulted to asking for my usual cash withdrawal — three hundred bucks. That sounded like more than enough to get me through the next couple months in this place... and maybe even some new shoes.

"*Three... hundred...* dollars. Are you," he paused for a the length of ten ellipses here, "certain?"

"I think," Travis started to say, then looked at me. I gave him a "go for it" gesture. "I think fifty dollars will be plenty for today."

"Fifty, then," I told George, "out of the second account, please."

෴ ෴ ෴

After I got my dinero — three ten dollar bills, two fives and ten ones — and escaped the banker's clutches, I checked on Travis. "How are you feeling? Your color's a little better, but you looked like you were going to pass out for a second."

"Oh, don't worry! I'm fine." He straightened his jacket. In a hushed tone, he added, "Surprised, I suppose. I have never known someone — especially a lady, which I say with no ill intent, of course — but for dignified, refined gentlewoman such as yourself to try to take out such a large amount of cash at once."

"Really?"

"You do know that $300 is a year's wage for a lot of people, right?"

"I hadn't really thought about it — sorry. Thank you for helping me out."

It was kind of hard to imagine three hundred dollars seeming like a mind-blowing amount of money... even though I supposed that in the Now, it might seem like a windfall to the grossly underpaid toy-assembly workers in rural China.

"Quite honestly," he said as he offered me his arm, "I've never known anyone as young as yourself to have that much money in the bank."

"Eh — whatever," I finally said. "Having a little money or a lot, it doesn't matter. I've had both. What it's really helpful for is to avoid stress and the need for debt collectors. As long as you can pay all your bills and have enough left over for some fun stuff, it's all good."

෴෴෴

The doorman did his job with a flourish, and we stepped out into a day that seemed even sunnier now than it had been fifteen minutes ago. There were a bunch of people standing off to the right, so we veered left. We walked at a pretty good trot, arm-in-arm, down the street... even though I had absolutely no idea where we were going. I think we were both just happy to be out of that bank.

"So," I said. "May I take you to lunch?"

"No — I couldn't possibly," he said, then must have noticed my confusion. He quickly added, "We can have lunch, most certainly, but it will be my treat."

"You came with me on this boring errand to the bank. And apparently I have money. The least I can do is to take you out. Please?" I felt his arm pull slightly as he stood up straighter.

"From my upbringing, I have learned that the only women who can pay for a gentleman's lunch are his mother, his grandmother, and the Queen," he said. "And, even then, it's not always permissible."

Oy — not this again. I now solemnly swear that I will never again insist on going Dutch when a friend tells me that she or he wants to treat. I will graciously accept, and return the favor when it makes sense to do so.

"If I ask you a question, do you swear to tell the truth, the whole truth, and nothing but the truth?" He nodded. "Is this some etiquette thing, or would you prefer not to have lunch with me today."

"If those are my options, it's the former, and decidedly not the latter. "

"How about this: If, before we went into the restaurant, I secretly slipped you a ten dollar bill to pay for lunch — "

"Five would be more than enough."

"A five-dollar-bill, then, so you could pay the restaurant tab. Would that adequately appease the gods of social graces?"

He didn't answer right away. This concept had to be going against something deeply ingrained in men of this day and age.

"Travis, please — I can afford it. If it helps, it was almost certainly family money, but now it's mine. I'd like to spend a little of it on a nice meal with you," I said. I read his tight lips and squinty eyes as dubiousness. "Think of it as a little thank you for helping me with so many things. I'm happy to sneak around the social customs of this era, but I want you to be okay with it, too." I squeezed his hand.

"I am okay with it."

"Good. I would hope so," I said, and added with a wink, "Because if you and I are going to be an item, you're going to have to get used to things being a little non-traditional more often than not."

⇆ ⇆ ⇆

The next time I visited the Internet era, I came up with a rough method of mentally converting currency amounts in the Then to the Now. I would basically multiply every 1900 dollar by 25 to give me a ballpark idea of how much something was worth in the money I knew. Conversely, every dollar from the future was worth about four cents here. That somehow seemed really sad.

Using this math, I worked out that the $300 I had originally planned to withdraw equaled more than $7,500 in modern dollars. And the fifty bucks that Travis suggested was a better amount? Like getting out $1,260 or so from my local ATM.

As for the amount in the larger of my two accounts, well, I have never been great at doing math in my head, so I really didn't think ahead about what to expect from multiplying Y times X.

After I calculated it once, though, I did it again to make sure I had figured it correctly. I still couldn't believe the answer.

By my conservative estimate, I had the equivalent of $590,000 worth of money — in Now dollars, that was — at my disposal. That would most certainly buy a lot of lunches, shoes, wine, dresses, Chinese food, gas lamps and almost anything else I could think of.

Well, anything except love, health, happiness… and the ever-elusive time traveler's instruction manual.

44: My so-called social life

After Travis found out who I really was, and understood the nature of my reluctance to socialize, he started a campaign to help me out of my shell. Apparently my people skills were a little rusty.

Part One of his plan included me being a gracious hostess, actually inviting people inside my house. So far, I had only done this when he was around. He was sort of like my coach and a translator, all in one.

Part Two was an offshoot of Part One, and had me playing the part of welcomed guest. This scenario consisted mostly of me making lots of extra food, and delivering it to neighbors. This I actually enjoyed a little bit, particularly because I had more control. (In other words, it was a lot easier to leave someone else's house than it was to kick someone out of yours.)

Why would I be in a rush to leave someone's home? Because of conversations like this:

(After this lady was all blah blah blah about her worn out sheets...)

"The Emporium is having a sale today on bed linens," I said.

"How wonderful! And how do you know about such a thing?"

"I read it in the paper this morning."

"Oh, the newspaper. How nice." She spoke those words like I'd offered to show her some earwax.

Undeterred, I continued. "You don't read the newspaper?"

"Of course not, dear," she answered, thoroughly dismissively. "Why would I?"

Two could play at that game. "Well, maybe to find out about what's going on in the world?"

She put down her cup of tea and looked at me. "My husband Clancy will tell me everything I ought to know," she said with a tight smile. "He always does."

I gave her the same smile right back. "You don't ever feel compelled to find out for yourself?"

"There's no need, really, now is there?" Then she leaned forward toward me, conspiratorially. "Though I will admit to reading the Society page on Sundays," she whispered, as if this were terribly vulgar.

"I actually look forward to reading the newspaper each day," I said.

"Well, Clancy looks to it for the politics and the stock reports, and of course the notices of lodge meetings," she answered as she smoothed on her gloves, "but I think it is awfully dull, and quite often find it terribly unpleasant. I feel it's best not to concern my mind with such things. Besides, reading the newsprint always leaves dark smears on my hands, and that is such a bear to wash off."

~ ~ ~

"Keep trying," Travis counseled when I vented to him later. "It will get better. Not everyone is that shallow."

I smiled and nodded... but made a quiet bet to myself that I wouldn't find another soul in this place who made me feel at home the way my boy did.

And then I met Peter, who lived nearby. He was gorgeous, with big brown eyes and a laugh that could melt even the hardest of hearts.

A couple times a week, when the lady of the house was napping or otherwise occupied, Peter and I would sit on the sofa and cuddle. I'd whisper all my secrets to him while caressing his mostly bald head.

Our relationship was almost ideal — except when it came to diapers. His mom, Priscilla, showed me how to change the floppy cotton things, and how to safely fasten the pins so they wouldn't poke the little guy or come undone. (The sheer volume of diapers a baby needed in this era seemed amazing to someone used to the super-absorbent disposables.)

Peter had recently celebrated his first birthday, and was so adorable, a follow-up was already in the works. Prissy, as she was called, was visibly pregnant again, but with her constant "morning" sickness, needed a little reprieve every now and then to get through the day.

The mommy's helpers were being coordinated by another neighbor, Mrs Fletcher, who — to my great surprise — asked if I'd be interested in joining in.

"You used to care for young Peter before your accident, you see, and we hoped you might want to help again."

I felt a little like I'd finally been accepted into this quirky little society... and I have to admit, it felt pretty good.

Apart from the diapers and the bottles, baby care was pretty much the same as in the Now. Those timeless little nuggets of life here and there were somehow very reassuring to me.

∽ ∽ ∽

The next item on Travis's agenda was getting me outside on a regular basis, where I would have no choice but to repeatedly meet and greet the folks on my street.

When it came to quantity over quality, Part Three was a winner, since taking an evening stroll was *de rigeur* in this age — especially for the couples and families in my area. It was very much a social thing, but in my case in particular, it even had physically therapeutic benefits... at least as long as I didn't follow the latest fashion trend.

See, many of the ladies of this time had a really odd gait. When a woman was walking in such a way, it looked like she was going to fall flat on her face at any moment.

I looked it up online, and this uncomfortable lope was apparently called the "kangaroo walk," and had just started to come into style. (Blessedly, it started to fall out of favor about three years later.) Here is how it was described in a newspaper article from this era:

Have you learned the kangaroo walk? It's the real thing in pedestrianism this season. It's a blending of the two-step waltz and the forward skate stroke. The head is held upright and slightly bent forward, the body is stiff with a backward slope. The walk itself is a chain of sliding strides that fetches you up at your destination all right, but is a continuous suggestion of accidents. The kangaroo is good exercise — and that is about all that can be said in its favor, although it is quite the mode.

There were walking rules I *did* follow, because they made a little more sense. For example, I could abide by these guidelines:

Hold the head proudly, which, of course, means high; this gives more fresh air to the lungs, helping them to cast off disease... Always be careful to carry the skirts gracefully; nothing looks quite so untidy as to drag the skirts through the dirt of the streets. It is not only untidy, but it is tempting disease.

So many articles about putting one foot in front of the other? I guess when your modes of transport are limited, the few you have become a big deal.

When you walked along the street or promenade, people always acknowledged each other. Some might actually say "hello" or "good evening," but mostly people nodded — this slight little downward tilt of the head I thought of as a reverse "yo" nod. If, perhaps, it was someone you knew well or you were a person who accorded great respect, you might get a hat tip, a bow, or both.

Occasionally, people would exchange a few words, after first moving to the edge of the sidewalk, so as to not create a traffic jam. Even so, such chats rarely went on very long, because it was understood that if there was anything to discuss, the parties would merely chat long enough for one party to invite the other party to drop by — "pay a call" — later.

Of course, every rule has its exceptions.

"Well, hello, Jennie," some man offered by way of greeting, including the little nod thing. To me, he looked pretty much like every other guy with dark hair and a mustache. His hands were in his pockets, and there was a woman by his side wearing a dark blue dress, paired with an enormous cream-colored hat that had pine cones on it. She had been walking in the preferred style, which made her look like she had a stick up her ass.

I had no clue who either of these two were. But it didn't matter. Whereas before I might have looked to Travis guidance, I decided to use the techniques I'd learned over the past week, and jumped right in.

"Hi, there," I said, and then added, "I'm sorry to say that I've had some memory loss, and, unfortunately, don't recall your name."

The man opened his mouth as if to speak, but nothing came out. His mouth opened and closed a couple times, as if what I'd said had completely thrown him. All I could think of was that line from *Mary Poppins*: "Close your mouth, please, Michael. We are not a codfish."

I felt Travis slip his hand out from my elbow, and instead put it protectively around my waist. "Jennie," Travis said, "This is Mr Walter Houlihan, and Miss Maggie Gallagher."

Now it was my chance to play cod. I couldn't help it. These two looked only vaguely like I remembered from when I peered at them from behind the bathroom door. In fact, they looked almost *normal*, and not really very malevolent at all. Way more lame than evil, I guess because they were wearing fancy clothes, and not carrying bags full of my stuff.

The silence was so long, and so awkward. I finally broke it by admitting I didn't remember meeting either of them before... which was the truth. Upon hearing that, though, Walt looked relieved. I knew why, but tried to keep that from showing on my face.

"Oh, well, we were friends once," he said, staring directly into my eyes, projecting waves of creepy smugness. The long, chilly silence was broken by him rummaging around for his a pocketwatch. When he brought it into the light, I saw his hands for the first time. The left one looked pretty banged up, but the right was still heavily bandaged. I quickly looked away.

Maggie hadn't yet said a word, but instead had spent the entire time making minute adjustments to her hair, hat and dress.

"Nothing to say, Mags?" Travis said, obviously trying to rile her. But why not? She was every inch a girl who knew that her number one asset was her looks. With her big eyes, rosebud-shaped lips and great skin, she was actually way prettier than I expected — especially since Travis had once described her as "not tremendously homely."

"Hello, Jennie," she finally said to me, then looked at my guy. "And of course, you, Travis, I already know."

Travis just looked at me and rolled his eyes a little. Then Walter caught my eye by waggling his tongue at me from just the right angle so nobody else could see it. He was so oogy, I actually felt a little bile rise in my throat.

"So you and Mr Donovan here..."

"*Officer* Donovan," I corrected.

"Right. Guess you and him have a thing now. Seen you around town a few times."

"Good for you," I said, and gave him a slight smile, just so he didn't get the pleasure of knowing he'd pissed me off.

With the slightest tip of the hat, Travis said, "Have a nice evening," and, with a nod, took my arm and we started walking.

When I was sure nobody was in earshot, I let loose with my impression of the terrible twosome. "What a monumental bitch! And him? Total asshole."

And with that, Travis joined in on the codfish game. "I — I have never heard you swear before."

"Eh, well, because of the kids, I try not to. But they're not here, and that's not really swearing anyhow," I said, resuming my rant. "Those two are creepy. They deserve each other."

"I agree," said Travis. "Walter *was* quite the smarmy bastard. She was even worse. I apologize."

"Hey — you have nothing to be sorry for."

Silence. Silence so deep, crickets wept.

"Wait a minute," I said. "Did you call her 'Mags'?"

He blushed furiously. I'd never seen him so red.

"Oh my god — wai t. You know Maggie, like, as more than just a suspect?"

"Yes... or I did, at any rate."

"You were buddies with good ol' Mags and didn't tell me?"

His eyes were squinty and his face looked pained. "It didn't come up, so I was waiting for the right time."

"You knew her *and* you ended up on my case, before they even broke into my house? That has to be one of the biggest coincidences ever."

"Not a coincidence, really," he said. "They knew who you were, and assigned me to you on purpose."

That made no sense to me, no matter how I twisted and turned it. I gave up and just asked him why.

He took his time to respond — instead checking the time, cracking his knuckles, examining something apparently fascinating in the distance over my shoulder.

I wasn't going to let this one go unanswered. I got in the way of his view out the window and asked, "How come they did that, Travis?"

With a heavy sigh, he looked at me, and finally answered, "Because you and Walter were 'dating', as you say, and now he and Maggie are together." He shifted uncomfortably in his chair. "And, well... quite a while ago — long before you came into the station that day — Maggie was my fiancée."

Um, *what*? I could not have heard him correctly. "Say again?"

"My fiancée. We were engaged."

"Yeah, I know what 'fiancée' means." I caught myself before I added a "Duh," and actually felt a little bit bad for him when he looked down and studied the cracks in the pavement.

Why was I annoyed? I didn't even know. As a divorcée with two kids, I was hardly one to complain about previous relationships. The more I thought about it, the more I realized what I was feeling wasn't jealousy. What was getting to me was that he hadn't told me this before — and I had to ask him in order to get this news. To add insult to injury, he'd been with *that* bitch? Of all the girls, in all the towns, in all the world... Maggie?

"As I said, I was waiting for the right time to tell you," he said. "When we first talked about her in relation to your case, you and I didn't know each other very well. It wouldn't have been professional to mention it then. Besides..." He let out another deep sigh — one of those 'I really don't want to say this' sighs. "I didn't want you to think I was somehow biased in her favor. Because, I can guarantee you: If anything, it was completely the opposite."

We kept walking as I considered all of this.

"So they assigned you to my case for what — to continue the investigation?"

"No, nothing like that," he said. "I'm not a detective, anyhow. I think Joseph — the gent you first spoke to when you came into the station — just thought it would be poetic for me to help you."

It was so hard to stay irritated at this man.

I scooped up Travis's face in both my hands and gave him a kiss. "You made the right call." I know myself well enough to realize that if he had told me about her then, I wouldn't have reacted well. And while I am already being brutally honest with myself, I'd have to admit it might have even kept me from trying to get to know him better.

෧෧෧

Alas, much like a kid with a stick, I couldn't help but poke at the beehive, and brought up the topic again at dinner.

"So how did you meet her?"

"Who?"

I gave him The Look. "Mags? Your best gal?"

"Pffft — she's not the best at anything." Travis took a bite of my latest *Iron Chef*-esque challenge: macaroni and cheese, 1900s-style.

"Met her the usual way," he said.

"What's that mean?" I asked. "At a brothel?" To my mind, that suited her.

Despite clearly not wanting to have this conversation, that got him to laugh. "No, of course not," he said. "Years ago, our parents knew each other, and since we were both now living in San Francisco, they thought we would make a logical match."

"And were you? A match, that is."

"Superficially, I suppose. She was the appropriate age, from a good family, had a bit of money, and was in the process of becoming a fine upstanding citizen," he said. Travis leaned back and looked at me, "I suppose that last opportunity is now past the point of no return, is it not?"

"I'd say so, yeah."

"More wine?" he said, leaning to reach for the bottle.

"No, thanks — I'd like to stay on this topic for now."

"Whatever you say, dear," he said, and leaned the opposite direction to give me a long, lingering kiss.

"Mmm — wonderful, Travis," I said when our lips finally parted, "but that's not going to sidetrack me either."

Another sigh — this one, at least, followed by a smile and a wink. "What else do you want to know?"

"How did you end up engaged?"

"Refer to the first answer."

"Your parents?"

"It was their expectation... and back then — you know, a year and a half ago — I had a much smaller view of the world. I figured I could do much worse, so why not? I'm sure we would have become fond of each other eventually — even if it was never true love."

I told him that seemed so incredibly depressing. Limiting. Frustrating.

"I agree, at least in retrospect," he said. "At the time, though, it was simply a 'typical' life. Get born, go to school, get a job, get married, have kids, retire, have grandchildren... and then they plant you in the ground and stick a rock on top so they don't forget who you were. Your whole life is summed up by a name and a date carved into stone."

I had no words.

He stood up, took my hand to pull me up next to him, then wrapped both arms so tightly around me that he was probably halfway hugging himself.

"It's all utter rubbish. I know that now." He nuzzled my neck and my hair. After a few breaths, I heard him say in a voice just above a whisper, "Nothing could ever approach what I have right here."

45: Party on, Wayne

Standing on some stranger's freezing cold front porch, I shifted back and forth uncomfortably. For the first time in this era, I was dressed divinely. This — yet another course in my social development — was to be my first proper dinner party, given by a man named Mr Wayne, who Travis somehow knew from work, and his lovely wife... whose name I had already forgotten.

In honor of the occasion, I was wearing a new taffeta dress, which shimmered blue or aqua, depending on the light. In my hair was a barrette with blue faux jewels and pearls, which matched the double-strand pearl choker around my neck. Finally, my shoes and shrug matched the pearls' creamy color.

Travis had told me — with his eyes and with his mouth — that I looked beautiful, and held my hand when he took my arm as we walked along the street.

I hoped he didn't notice that whenever he glanced away, I shimmied from side to side. The movement wasn't because I was nervous (though I was)... it was all about trying to fix a maddening bloomer wedgie without doing something unladylike to my dress.

As I heard the doorknob rattle, I threw caution to the wind and made a last ditch effort, tugging down by my knee, thereby instantly bringing new meaning to the word relief.

A portly man, who looked eerily like Mr Spacely from *The Jetsons*, opened the door and heartily welcomed us in. I remembered the whole routine, from offering my hand in greeting — like a lady, not a man — to giving Travis my coat for him to hang up, and then waiting for my boy to introduce me around.

I expected that last bit to be the most painful part, because I was exceptionally bad at remembering names. Fortunately, shortly after getting both of us a glass of champagne, Travis got pulled into a police-themed conversation, effectively putting our lesson on hold. The diversion was welcome, because I wanted the chance to look around.

Foot-tappingly upbeat ragtime piano music provided the soundtrack to the evening. It was a pleasant surprise, since I had somehow been expecting a maudlin pump organ to be playing instead. Still, nobody was dancing — just eating and drinking, jabbering away in various groups, and monopolizing the space in front of the grand fireplace, where a fire roared and warmed the whole room.

Sipping my champagne, I reeled around the perimeter of the conversational cogs in time with the music, taking the opportunity to study the men and women who looked like they'd just stepped out of an antique painting. While the men were clothed in suits of neutral shades, the women were wearing gowns of all different cuts and colors — nut brown satin with a lace-embellished bodice, a pale pinky-orange silk dress with frilled tiers from top to bottom, and a light blue lace-up dress with a plunging V-neck over a chantilly lace scarf beneath — but all had one thing in common: each was so beautiful, any one would make a museum curator's heart sing.

Just when my glass was nearly empty, I rounded the corner and fell in love. The source of the music was not a trained musician whose fingers danced over the keys, but a beautiful player piano. It looked like had come straight out of a western movie, except instead of being worn and dusty, it was pristine and polished.

There was a bench in front, so I sat down and watched the machine work, a couple times allowing myself to softly lay my fingers on the keys as they moved of their own accord.

Probably ten minutes went by before I was startled by a deep voice over my shoulder. "You like her?" I turned around and Mr Spacely — erm, Mr Wayne — smiling at me, Travis by his side.

"It's absolutely wonderful," I gushed as I stood up. "I've never known anyone to have such an instrument in their own home. It's even tuned perfectly!"

Wayne lovingly caressed the top of the cabinet. "I found this beauty in a little town called Jerome in Arizona. Small town, but wonderful copper mines. I bought it from the saloon owner for a hundred dollars, then had to pay another thirty to get it shipped up here," he told me proudly.

"What a deal," I said. "That's amazing!" From behind the man, Travis caught my eye and nodded no. "I mean, to own such a fantastic piece of history — can't put a price on that," I added, and gave him my best smile. After little small talk, our host went to greet other guests.

Travis was doing a poor job of suppressing a grin. He took my arm and leaned down to my ear to speak quietly. "You know, the man was telling you how much it cost in order to impress you. Leave it to my girl to tell him he got a bargain!"

"I'm sorry — was that bad? It's just the first thing that came to mind."

"No, not bad at all. Rather amusing, in fact."

After just seconds of standing on the sidelines, an incredibly tall man came over to talk to Travis about the city police budget or some such thing. Not wanting to stick around for perhaps one of the dullest topics in the room, I wandered off to get refills on our drinks. While he gestured that he was up for another glass of champagne, I thought I'd switch over to the punch, since I didn't know how this body would handle any more alcohol.

Just to be sure, when I got to the drinks table, I pointed to the pinky-red beverage and asked the man in the suit who was filling the cups, "Is this spiked?"

"No, Miss," he said. "It's just punch."

"Alrighty, then. A champagne, and one of those, too, please." With some magically smooth moves, he poured the champagne into a wide-mouthed glass, and the punch into a pressed glass teacup, then set them down on the table in front of me. I had seen other people slipping him tips, so I gave him a dime and crossed my fingers that was enough. (I was actually proud of myself for remembering this time, especially since I had missed handing out several gratuities during the past weeks.)

I delivered Travis's bubbly, and then, with his encouragement, wandered from group to group. I hovered around the periphery so I could hear what was being said, but didn't have to participate unless I was good and ready.

I was hoping I'd find an intriguing conversation to listen in on, but wasn't holding out much hope. The men were talking about politics and industry, and the women seemed to all be gabbing about sewing and their husbands. I made a few circles around the room, stocking up on food and drink as I strolled by. The hors d'oeuvres were strange but kind of tasty, and I deliberately did not ask what was in them. I was pretty sure they would tell me I was chowing down horse brains on toast and fermented goose eggs, or something that sounded equally vile.

Eventually, I heard a loud male voice that seemed to cut through much of the other chatter.

"The era of the horseless carriage is coming — mark my words," said this supremely confident older man as he lit up his cigar. "The champions of the horse may pooh-pooh the idea, and assert that pleasure-loving man will never surrender the steed of flesh and blood to a mere piece of twentieth century mechanism. They may, in fact, claim that there is a lack of enjoyment, and absence of thrill of the delightful sort, and no end of danger in riding on a machine run by electricity and gasoline -- but they can only rank as special pleaders on one side of the controversy."

A crowd had formed around him by now, and the speaker was loving every second of it. Travis leaned toward me and whispered, "Pompous ass. He's been rehearsing this oratory all week, I'd wager." I did my best to stifle a giggle.

"As you all know, the steam car was once just as much of a curiosity, and was viewed with eyes as skeptical as the horseless carriage is today," the old guy continued, punctuating his remarks with his cigar. "Not a hundred years has gone by since steam was first harnessed to the paddle-wheels of boats and the flywheels of trains, and yet steam is being replaced here and there by electricity, and doubting Thomases are soon made firm believers in the beneficial results of new discoveries. Indeed — it has hardly been more than a dozen years since people declared that the electric streetcar would never be a success. Now, you see, it is in universal use. But of course! Electricity is indeed the wave of the future."

His little crowd of sheeple applauded.

"Electricity is definitely the wave of the future, but not to fuel automobiles," I heard someone say, and then realized that someone was me. *Oh.* But since I was making sense, I decided to hear what else I had to say. "I think gasoline will be what is used to power these 'horseless carriages' for the next hundred years. You betcha!" I watched with amusement as my fingers did the little rabbit ears when I said "horseless carriages." That was awesome.

"Dear lady, I don't believe we have met," said Travis's pompous ass, who seemed quite friendly, and up for a little bit of a debate. "But I respectfully disagree. I believe electricity will prevail over steam and your gasoline. Not to say the others don't have their merits, but anyone can see electricity is the most sensible option, and the most affordable. I am rather sure that, soon, we shall be able to buy an electric motor-buggy for about the cost of an ordinary roadhorse."

"Well, I can't say about how the cost compares, because how much does a horse cost? I haven't the foggiest idea!" I laughed. "But you can be absolutely sure my money will be on gasoline-powered cars. Automobiles. Whatever. Not that gas engines are necessarily a good thing — in fact, they're bad in a lot of ways, like in terms of pollution and fuel cost — but just because *that is how it is going to be.*" With that, I raised my punch glass in a cheery salute to the ass.

While I was on the topic, I threw a few other thoughts out there. "And let me tell you: in twenty years, the horse and carriage will be all but gone. And twenty or thirty years after that, we'll be cruising down the highways in our cars at fifty or sixty or more miles an hour." Now a little crowd had assembled around me. "Mark my words, people! I am the Oracle." Then I laughed, and they all laughed with me. (Or perhaps *at* me. I was totally beyond caring which.)

For the first time in public, Travis put his arm around me. He was so super sweet. "Aww. Hello, love," I said, but didn't give him a kiss, because I knew that kind of PDA would create too much of a public spectacle here. I felt my man steering me away from the crowd and over toward the kitchen. Maybe he did want some alone time with me.

"Hey, Jen," he said, and smiled. He gestured to my cute little punch glass and asked, "Out of curiosity, how many of those have you had?"

"I don't know. Why? It's just punch."

"It's punch, yes — but with vodka."

"No, no, no," I laughed. "This is just regular punch. I asked."

He reached out for my glass. "May I?" I handed it to him. He took a sip, then gave it back.

"There is definitely vodka in there, my dear."

I tried it again. It didn't taste at all boozy to me. I sniffed it, too, to double-check. "Are you sure? See, there are cherries in it, and lemons and oranges and limes. Plus, I asked him spick... *spicksivically*... if it was spiked, and he said it was *not.*"

"You asked him if it was spiked?"

"I totally did. I swear." I gave him the "Scout's honor" sign as further support.

Travis smiled and looked down, then covered his mouth and laughed just a little. "Ah, Jennie, I think we're having one of those language problems," he said, gently taking my cup and setting it on the nearest table. "What do you call that again, when what you say and what we say here are not the same?"

"'What we've got here is *failure* to *communicate*,'" I said in a stilted Southern drawl. Dear God — I *was* drunk.

"That wasn't the term I was thinking of, but it will do."

"Seriously — the guy lied to me?" I couldn't believe it.

"He didn't lie. He misunderstood. 'Spiked' doesn't mean anything outside the railroad industry, at least as far as I've heard — but I'll be sure to keep an ear out for it in the coming years," he said. "In the meantime, sweetheart, I think we had best get you home."

∽ ∽ ∽

The walk back to my place made me bitterly cold, and took too long. But Travis was right — the fresh night air did clear my head a bit.

When we got inside, he said, "Let me get you some headache powder. That will help you feel better when you wake up."

"And water. To avoid a hangover, I need to drink a lot of water. Like a whole gallon. Or more."

Travis tilted his head and looked at me, just like my old dog used to do. "A gallon of water? You think?" he asked. "How much *did* you have to drink tonight?"

"Well, I had one glass of champagne with you, and then like four — maybe six? — cups of that punch," I said. "But you stopped me on the last one, so that only counts as, like, half."

His head was still tilted.

"What?" I said. "That's not so much. They were teeny tiny little cups."

In response, Travis totally did the "not impressed" face. I had to laugh. How could I not?

"Right, then," he said. "I think I'll get you *two* sachets of the headache powder. You start on the water."

"Okee dokee, artichokey." And while it turned out I couldn't guzzle a gallon, I did manage to choke down two tall glasses of the stuff. That was apparently good enough for him.

"I'll tuck you up in bed now, and you can sleep it off," he said as we climbed the stairs.

"Pffft. I'm not even tired."

About eighteen seconds later, I woke up — fresh as a daisy and feeling frisky — back in the Now. I guess zipping forward through time was one way to beat a hangover.

46: One step forward, two steps back

It didn't take long for my little bit of happy went skidding out the door.

The papers still showed we changed history. As I said, the whole hotel robbery thing never happened — there was never a headline anything like "Four killed with two shots." But in its place, like a nasty game of whack-a-mole, something else popped up in its place — an even more tragic story than before.

I tried to get as many of the specifics as possible committed to memory before I went to sleep that night. As soon as morning hit, I knew I'd have someone to talk to, because shortly after he learned about my other life, and a little bit after we went public with our relationship, Travis pretty much moved in.

I'm not one to kiss and tell, but suffice it to say, we had fantastic chemistry. I didn't have to think or force or wonder or worry about anything. It all just worked, and worked perfectly.

Okay, I will say *one* thing: Over the past hundred years, technology may have changed, advances made in science, tastes in art and music may have changed, and society itself may bear little resemblance to the past... but I can tell you one thing for sure — the human body? It's timeless.

܀ ܀ ܀

The moment the bright sun in the year 1900 bit into my eyes, as I righted myself and grabbed for the paper and pencil at my bedside. Once as I had the highlights written down, I woke up Travis by walking my hand in a spider-like crawl up his back.

"It can't be morning yet," he groaned, and with his eyes barely open, grabbed my pillow and put it over his head.

"Sorry, but a new day has dawned, and we have much to do. Because although we fixed one thing, we seem to have broken something else," I said. "From looking at the paper for a week and a half from now, there's good news, and there's really, really bad news. Which do you want first?"

With a sigh, he pulled off the top pillow. "Good news."

"Well... it seems Walt and Maggie are not long for this world. They get killed — by their own hands, no less."

Now he opened his eyes. "And the bad?"

"They set off an explosion, and take thirty-four people with them, leaving another two dozen suffering from burns and smoke inhalation. It's messy."

He took back my pillow. "Keep going," he said, his voice slightly muffled by the goose down now covering his face.

"I read about it in my time, and I'm still getting memories of it now. Really weird," I told him. "Anyhow, it's one of those tragedies they teach you about in school — it was that big, that memorable, and that stupid."

To that, he gave a little snort in reply.

"They used dynamite to blow open a bank vault... and, well, it didn't work out so well."

I had learned that in 1900, many banks were still using large safes to protect their money. Newer and more prominent banking establishments, however, started to build reinforced areas — often called strong rooms — which served the same function, only could accommodate many more valuables. Some of these were really no more than reinforced closets, while others were larger purpose-built structures. These were typically installed in the basement level. But even though their existence might not be obvious to the casual visitor, these giant safes were no secret. When a bank had a huge vault installed, it was a big selling point, and they usually told the world about it.

But some banks... well, they were more about smoke and mirrors than spending money to protect their customer's assets.

"Walt totally miscalculated the yield. Well, I imagine he calculated it right for a typical strong room, but this one was mostly fake. It was a real steel door, but the front, back and sides of the vault were just plain old lath and plaster walls. It was all just for show," I said, trying to explain the ridiculously destructive scenario.

"They put enough explosive in there to take out reinforced concrete and steel — just assuming the bank's claims were true. But when that wasn't there, the blast just demolished the place. It collapsed the basement and four floors above. Then that building and the one next door caught fire."

The disaster was turned into even more of a goat rodeo because some of the contents of the vault — cash and bonds — were launched into the air and had rained down on the surrounding area. When there are hundreds of people grabbing frantically for pieces of paper littered in the street, it makes it hard for emergency vehicles to get in to do their jobs. The fire engines rang their bells and yelled and waved, but still at least one lady was killed when she was run over by a horse and carriage there to do a rescue.

I took back my pillow and slid over next to him. "The perps — the perpetrators, that is — were found, but they were burnt to a crisp, so they were never positively identified. They say it was a man and a woman, and I think it was Walt and Maggie. It all fits."

"It's definitely a possibility, he said, but sounded unconvinced. "Though we can't really be sure."

"Neither one of them was ever heard from again. I checked records going up into the 1970s, meaning census records — from June 1900 onward — along with social security data, draft registrations, city directories, death certificates, cemetery listings. Nothing."

"Maybe they moved on under aliases."

"I considered that, but found nothing that matched their descriptions or methods at any point during the next thirty years."

Travis nodded, and I could see he was starting to come around.

"There's more, though."

After many hours of searching, I managed to find a tiny legal notice tucked in one of the back pages of an issue of *The Chronicle* from October of 1900. It stated that a certain Mr Walter Houlihan and Miss Maggie Gallagher had abandoned their property more than six months earlier, and those items, along with various other peoples' unclaimed belongings, were to be put up for public auction during the first week of November.

"And, get this: The ad specifically mentioned tools, silver housewares, artwork, and some jewelry," I told him. "Now, they might have abandoned their identities and their families, but those two would *never* leave behind valuables."

I definitely had his attention now. I flipped to the last page of my notes.

"Just one more thing," I said, and he laughed. "What's so funny?"

"Are you sure you're not a police detective?" He kissed my free hand. "It's rare to hear a case presented so thoroughly — and never have I heard one from someone so pretty."

"Oh wow — really, Travis?" Now I was laughing, and he was the one confused. "Let's just remember that *female* and *intelligent* are rarely mutually exclusive."

He cleared his throat. "Yes, sorry. Apologies."

"No worries, mate," I said, and kissed his hand in exchange. "But I do have a theory on the explosive itself." He nodded.

"After I found the bank story, I did some more hunting, and a tiny little newspaper article noted that a couple days ago, an unspecified amount of dynamite was stolen from a quarry near Glen Park." Then I told him the part that, intuitively, I considered to be most damning of all. "It was stolen the same night we ran into Walt and Maggie. Maybe five, six hours later. Now while I don't really know either of them well, from what I've seen... well, seems like a plausible knee-jerk response..."

"Quite. Sounds exactly like what I know of Walter," he said. "So when is this supposed to happen?" he asked.

"This Friday. That gives us three days to stop it," I said. "You do believe me, don't you?"

"Doubt the woman who went forward and time and found clues leading to a certain passage from Shakespeare?" He slid his arms around me, and put his forehead against mine. "How could I not have faith in her?"

〜〜〜

By the time the morning church bell tolled nine, Travis had to be at work. As it was already a few minutes after 8am, and with all he needed to do to get ready for his day, we didn't have time to work up a plan just yet. We decided that we would meet by our favorite tree in the panhandle for lunch at one o'clock to strategize.

I showed up early and set out a little picnic, featuring one of his favorite sandwiches — and one I had introduced to him: crispy bacon, lettuce and tomato with homemade mayo. (The jarred stuff wouldn't be available until 1907, and then only in Philly.)

"I think the best course of action is to tell my Captain I received a tip. A very plausible bit of inside information about something that is supposed to happen this week."

"That won't work. You can't tell them like that."

"Why not?"

"Even if they never met her, when they're caught, it's almost definitely going to come out about the connection between you and Maggie!" I said.

"How are you going to explain you being given a 'secret tip' without making it sound like you're involved?"

"That's easy enough to justify — I was told because they knew me, through Maggie. It's flimsy, but so are half the reports we get in. It will be fine." He polished off the end of his sandwich and crumpled the wrapper. "If we catch these two red-handed, any former relationship with one of the suspects will be moot. I will simply not involve myself in the investigation after their capture and should have no problem being above reproach."

While such a sudden and thorough disclosure seemed overly simplistic, Travis assured me it would be convincing enough. He said tips like this were often used to start up an investigation, and the disgruntled former partner angle was as popular now as it had been in the days of the wild west... which, come to think of it, wasn't that long ago at all.

We agreed he would talk to his boss after work that evening.

༄ ༄ ༄

As I had done on several occasions over the past couple weeks, I arrived at the station house about twenty minutes before the end of Travis's shift at six. Sunset wasn't until around 6:30, but I didn't want to walk up there alone when it was starting to get dark. I felt too tiny to be able to seriously defend myself, even just against a drunken idiot.

Sitting quietly in the waiting area, I slipped through the pages of *Harper's New Monthly Magazine*, which offered the usual variety of excessively-wordy stories and articles, and more than a few ads for lovely things like Mrs Winslow's soothing syrup, a medicine that was said to help with infant teething pain. I knew its active ingredient was morphine, so, yeah, I'm sure it did keep babies from crying.

Another officer I didn't recognize came over to me and asked if I needed any assistance.

"Oh, no, but thank you," I answered. "I'm just waiting."

"Waiting?"

"For Travis — I mean, you know, Officer Donovan."

"Ah yes," he said, and gave me a knowing look. "I don't know if you remember me," he started. I nodded no. "I'm Officer Thomas, and we met you shortly before your accident," he said. "I was there to take a report of a burglary. Of course, you said that turned out to be a misunderstanding. You had misplaced some silver candlesticks, I believe you said."

"Unfortunately, I have no memory of that. But thank you for your help that day, and I'm sorry to have wasted your time."

"Oh, no problem, Miss. That's the job," he said, tipped his hat, and walked back to his post behind the long wooden desk.

Ever prompt, Travis arrived at the station a little after six. He took off his hat as he came in the door, and walked over to me. He looked nervous, and said he needed a few minutes to talk to his captain. I know it killed him to lie, but that was the only way we could think of to get the message across on such short notice.

After watching him walk back to the back offices, I returned to my magazine. Now, though, was just a prop, because I was doing my best to eavesdrop.

Once he got permission to speak to a superior officer, he slipped into Captain Thompson's glass-windowed office, half-closed the door, and started to explain the situation.

"Captain, we received a tip from an anonymous citizen that the First City Savings and Loan has been targeted for a hold up on Friday afternoon," Travis began.

After a long pause, he got a reply. "Indeed. How exactly did you receive this information?"

"Tonight, I was patrolling Waller Street, between Stanyan and Shrader, and a man spoke to me as I passed by him on a side street. He was wearing a hat and cape, and it was dark, so I could not see his face, and he did not wish to be identified."

"Go on."

Travis made a little bit of a show consulting his notebook, which really only contained the details he and I had decided on earlier. "Well, he was apparently a former partner in crime, but alluded to the fact that the other two had planned this heist and then cut him out of the deal."

"The thieves — a man and a woman — are reportedly armed with revolvers, and plan to use explosives to blow open the vault. They apparently stole the dynamite from a quarry company in the city, somewhere south of here."

"You don't say."

"Yes, sir. I just wanted to let you know, sir."

"Very well, Donovan," the Captain said, turning back to his paperwork and dismissing Travis with a nod. "I'll take it from here, and let you know what we find."

My first impression was that Travis looked defeated as he closed the door to Thompson's office. But as soon as he started moving in my direction, he pulled a smile out of his bag of tricks.

He offered me his arm, and the two of us left the station. We walked along the edge of the park in silence.

Once the station house was more than two blocks behind us, Travis finally felt comfortable enough to start theorizing aloud about this commanding officer's most likely plan of action.

First things first, they would have to get corroboration on the dynamite robbery. Then he figured that they'd do some sort of risk assessment on the bank and vault. But whether there would be an order to intervene? He didn't even want to speculate. "Captain Thompson is a hard man to read. He's smart and he's cautious, but I really have no idea what he will decide to do about this threat."

～ ～ ～

"I met Officer Thomas today — seems like a nice guy," I said.

"He is," Travis said. "Still pretty green, but nice enough."

"I know the fact I don't remember anyone sometimes confuses people. Even you!" I said. "When I came to the police station that one day, you looked kind of stressed out when you had to tell me we'd actually met before."

He paused to think, and I imagined him watching a rerun of the event in his head. "Well, I was a bit baffled, but that's not why," he said. "I expected that you would not recognize me. What I didn't expect was you trying to shake my hand."

"Well, I totally wanted to give you a hug and a kiss, but I didn't think it was quite appropriate at the time."

Travis laughed. "No, that's not what I mean — though that would have been memorable. It's just that women don't generally shake hands like that."

"What is 'that'?"

"You know — firmly, with the whole hand. That's a man's handshake, which is why I have been trying to help you with a more delicate touch, shall we say."

"If you're calling it that, I'd rather not. Sounds like a tampon."

"I don't know what that is."

"It's okay — it's probably better anyway."

As we rounded the corner to my street, he told me, "You and I had met before, but you couldn't have been expected to remember. Not after... the accident."

I tried to keep my exasperation under wraps. "You know, that's what Officer Thomas just called it, too. I didn't say as much to him, but it was no accident. More like attempted murder."

"So, don't you wonder what I thought of you the first time we met?"

The man was nothing if not brilliantly adept at changing the subject. I'd bite. "Sure — I would love to know."

"I thought you were pretty. Beautiful, in fact..."

"And?"

"And, well... you seemed thick as a brick."

"What does that mean?" I laughed, but was pretty sure he wasn't thinking of the Jethro Tull album.

"You know — not the brightest penny in the purse. One pickle short of a barrel."

"Okay, okay — I get it." I slipped my key into the lock and opened the front door.

He was determined to continue. "Bright as a coal bin at midnight. As useless as a bucket without a bottom."

"Oh yeah?" After shutting the door behind us, I started to tickle him. "Any more?"

"Had the intellect of a young pea," he said, in a very proper British accent. "Deprived a village somewhere of its idiot."

He was tickling me back now, so I threw in my two cents while gasping between bursts of laughter. "Not the sharpest tool in the shed. Dumber than a box of rocks. The lights are on, but nobody's home..."

Before long, the whole thing devolved into a tickle-fest, which, in turn, led to other sorts of fun.

Regardless of what the person in this body had been like before, she certainly wasn't a pickle short of a barrel for long.

47: Past meets present

The morning of the big event — later to be known as the "Sansome Street Fire of 1900" — Travis was pacing, talking quickly, worrying about everything. Stressed out to the nth degree. I felt terrible that I hadn't been able to find anything in the Now that could offer any more insight.

We knew were were on the right track, though. The day before, a couple other officers had confirmed that some dynamite had indeed been stolen last week at the exact quarry I mentioned. The thieves took two-thirds of a box, which was an incredible 33 pounds of unstable explosive — plenty to do the kind of damage I had read about about, given the structure of the vault.

"They first thought the stuff had been nicked by some bad seeds in the area — kids, really — but when pressed for any other possible witnesses, they said that a lady with long blonde hair was spotted around the time the sticks disappeared," Travis said. "None of them would admit to it, but it sounds like she provided the distraction while the gent made off with the stuff. "

But as for how the police would stop the disaster itself? That was still up in the air. They couldn't wait long, though, as the whole thing was going down later today. The next few hours would tell. And once there was news, he said, he would drop by to let me know or send a messenger with an update.

༄ ༄ ༄

Travis finally stopped by just before two in the afternoon, which was lucky, because by then the floor had started to glow from the heat generated by my nonstop pacing.

They finally had a strategy, he said, and he was raring to go. I'm not exaggerating — I don't think I'd ever seen him looking so energized and excited.

To Travis, the best news of all was that the powers that be had agreed to a stakeout at the bank. They would go in at closing time, and stay until... well, until the thieves were caught.

"They assigned a detective to the case — bloke named Charlie Cody —

and he is coordinating the plan. One of my men will wait with me in the basement. If they can spare the personnel, two more will be waiting outside, but it's down to me, really." To minimize risk, they would pull the nightwatchman off duty, then doing covert surveillance until someone makes a move into the vault.

"Since our break was based on an anonymous tip," he cleared his throat, "to make any case against them, we have to catch them with the explosive, inside the bank — but, of course, before they set any of the charges. If we catch them in the act, their gooses are cooked, according to Cody," he said. "Do you say that in your time? 'His goose is cooked.'"

"I've heard it, yeah. I know what he means."

The blast in the original timeline occurred at 10:03 at night — seven hours after the bank closed. Since the fire started when so many people were home asleep was much of what made the incident was so deadly. Men, women and children were overcome by smoke before they ever awoke, and the remains of 25 of the 34 victims were found near their charred beds.

We had taken a walk by the building the morning before, and the place looked so serene. It was an average four-story brick building with a couple dozen windows — each one, I imagined, representing a person. Puffs of light-colored smoke wafted gently from the chimneys, aiming for the clouds above. Less than two days later, the entire scene would be unrecognizable if we failed.

As soon as he left me, Travis was going to report to duty at the bank. The whole thing was going to start around three o'clock, and last until morning or 'til there was a huge explosion — whichever came first.

⌒ ⌒ ⌒

Roughly an hour after Travis left, the doorbell rang. I was slowly getting used to people regularly showing up on my doorstep, but at least I'd stopped thinking I had a next-day package delivery every time the chime sounded.

Yet another unfamiliar face greeted me when I opened the front door, belonging to a woman who looked to be in her mid- to late- twenties. She might have been pretty if she smiled, but she looked almost annoyed to see me.

"Genevieve!"

"May I help you?"

She threw her hands in the air, yelled, "*Perché stai facendo questo?!*" Then she pushed her way past me into the house.

"Hello?" I chased after her as she strode with purpose toward the kitchen, vainly trying to get her to stop, or to at least tell me what was going on. "Hi, there. Um — what are you doing? Who are you?"

With a thud, she dropped the bag she'd been carrying onto the kitchen table. Now she had both hands free to gesticulate wildly. "*Sono tua sorella!*" she said, hitting her chest, then waved grabbed me and pulled me close. I was too stunned to pull away. Fortunately, she apparently wasn't trying to kill me — instead, she kissed me on both cheeks.

"*Sì ?*" she said next, and her gestures suggested I should now be cool with the situation.

"See? See what?" I said, more frustrated than bewildered at this point. All I could glean was that she knew me. "I'm sorry, but I don't know what you're saying. I can't even tell if you're speaking Spanish or Italian or Portuguese or something else." My high school French was not helping me right now. "Do you speak English? *Anglais*?"

That got her attention. She stopped conducting her invisible orchestra and just looked at me for a long moment.

"Have you forgotten *everything*, Genevieve?" Now an Italian accent was obvious, though her English was well-practiced.

"I understand that you know me, and so hello — welcome. I don't know who you are, though. I had an accident and have forgotten a lot of things," I told her. "I can't remember much of anything, actually."

"No!" she said, then circled me like a vulture, her eyes narrowing as she examined me closely from all angles.

When she was finished, she clasped her hands and held them against her chest, and asked with a broken-hearted expression on her face, "You don't know *Italiano*?"

"No, I don't."

Before I knew it, she'd embraced me in a full bear hug, and started weeping into my shoulder. She eventually regained her composure, tried her best to smile, then patted my cheek. "*Bella Genevieve*," she said. "I am your big sister, Giovanna."

"A sister?" I said, amazed and stupefied and so happy. "I've never had a sister before!"

Giovanna ignored the idiocy of that statement and answered, "Yes, *bella*

— you are the baby of our *famiglia*, and it's only you and me left now." She took my hand. "I am sorry you don't remember me, but perhaps it is for the best. We can start fresh, yes?"

Over the next two hours, she used the food she had brought with her to prepare me a feast, the likes of which I had never seen in this place. There was crusty bread and several aromatic cheeses, fresh tomatoes and basil and spinach, and what she told me was pappardelle pasta — native to Tuscany, "our" region of Italy. She had also brought along a nice Chianti (and, fortunately, there were no fava beans on the menu).

The entire time, she talked, with both her mouth and her hands. She told me how our family had emigrated to America nearly ten years before, in 1890. Our father was a well-known art restorer, and after our mother died of some sort of illness Giovanna couldn't bring herself to detail, he had brought his two daughters to San Francisco. Here, he worked for one of the filthy rich railroad barons who lived on Nob Hill, and freelanced a little bit on the side for other art collectors and museums.

Re-gilding frames and fixing damaged paintings weren't the only things that our father did on the side, apparently. After a suitable period of mourning, he apparently became quite a Casanova — particularly to many of the wealthy and "mature" women of the area.

After living for several years in a guesthouse on someone's estate, Papa apparently bought a home across the bay, up in the Berkeley hills. This area, he said, reminded him more of Tuscany, but still made it possible for him to travel to the city as needed. And if he had to stay in San Francisco for days at a time — whether working or entertaining — he would stay at a nice (comparatively) little house he bought in the upper Haight.

In effect, the pretty kitchen in which we were standing had been part of his love nest. Two and half years ago, though, when their father got sick with some sort of cancer, Jennie moved in. Then, after dad died, the house was deeded to her — erm, me. Giovanna, as the eldest by about five years — and the one with a family of her own — was given the Berkeley home.

What I still didn't understand is why she had been so pissed off at me when she first arrived. I decided to be blunt and to come right out and ask. Hey — the girl was Italian. She could take it.

"Ha!" she replied as she wiped bits of tomato off her fingers before tossing the towel into the sink. I think she needed to have both hands available to communicate properly.

"You have been home, I hear from others, and you don't write me to say anything!" She spoke so loudly, I had to take two steps back. "I did not know that you had been so injured that you had lost your memory. Nobody told me this. Then I get a call from the bank, saying you wanted to take out some money, and I got very angry."

Ah, money. The universal tool used to screw up relationships since the beginning of time.

"I'm sorry this made you angry. I wish I'd known to let you know," I said. "But why did the thing with the bank aggravate you so much?"

"I understand — now — that you could not remember, but that was the money I told you must be set aside until you had children. That was Papa's rule: You get this house and an allowance, and anything more you must earn. But once you have children, you can have more of what he promised you, as long as it benefits the family. This is what we argued about the last time we saw each other. This was the day you fell down."

"Okay, I hear you," I said. "So did I agree with the thing about saving the money for a future family?"

"Eh... Yes but a little bit no. You said you were getting — how you say? — difficult words from that *bastardo* to get everything from Papa at once. But you agreed that our plan was for the best. Then," she said, putting one hand to her forehead, "you were going to talk to the *bastardo* that night."

"You mean Walter?"

"That is him, but I will not say his name! He does not deserve even that much."

This was an entirely new wrinkle in the case against Walt. Though it probably wasn't anything we could take to court, it at least had significance with regard to how Travis and I were studying the man.

I was eager to find out more. "What happened after that?"

"A message, saying that you were very much hurt, and nearly dying," she said. "So I came right away, and saw you once at the hospital, right after your surgery. They said there was no hope — you were gone, and only your body was there. I was told to let you die. 'Let her go in peace,' they said. You know what that means? They don't give you food anymore. You starve to death," she said, her voice trembling with equal parts anger and sadness. "No Italian girl, and no sister of mine, should ever die of hunger!"

"So I paid. Paid for them to take care of you and keep you alive until God called you."

Or, I guess, until God or whatever inserted another soul into that body. "Did you visit me again?"

"No. They told me, 'Don't come back — there's no reason. She can't hear you.' And then they said, 'We will let you know when she dies.'"

"How depressing. I'm sure that was hard to hear."

"But harder for you, yes?" she smiled, and pinched my cheek. "So I was very surprised to find out that you were at last awake and at home! And perhaps a little *arrabbiato* you did not write me or telephone me. I have a telephone now, did you know?" Then, answering her own question, "Of course you didn't. But now you know. So you can get one, too, and talk to me from time to time. *Bene*?"

"*Bene*, yes, sure." I hated the phone, but I wasn't going to tell her that. It was a novelty and a luxury here, and she'd just think I was even crazier than she already knew me to be. And speaking of crazy... "But you believe me, right? That I don't remember you?"

"Of course I do, *bella*. As soon as we started talking, I knew you were different."

"How?"

"Your *linguaggio*. No accent. I don't hear anything other than America in your voice now."

If she thought all she heard in my voice was 1900s America — well, it was a good thing that English was her second language. Still, her response prompted me to ask her the one question that had been eating away at me for a few weeks now: How was our last name pronounced?

"*DiMedici*," she said, emphasizing the second syllable, and ending it with a "chee" sound. She had this fantastic Italian intonation that I would try to practice... after she left. "It means 'of the Medici family' — *Famiglia de' Medici* — the great patrons of the Renaissance. One of our ancestors married a daughter from the family, and so we are not true Medici, but diMedici," Giovanna explained. "Normally, it would be a name like Di Giovanni, such as 'of Giovanni,' our father's name. But the Medici name carries influence, so long ago, that was chosen." She shrugged and gestured upwards with her hands. "This is all I know."

I knew only a little about the Italy's Medici clan, but did recall they had been powerful bankers and major patrons of the arts — most notably helping a young artist named Michelangelo Buonarroti get his start.

"Speaking of family, and before I forget, something for you!" After digging deep into her jacket pocket, her hand emerged wrapped in multiple strands of shiny metals and gems. Jennie's sister had brought over — or brought back — some family jewelry. There were gold necklaces with delicate pendants, cocktail rings with large semi-precious stones of amethyst and opal, gilded stick pins, bracelets and other adornments the elder Mrs diMedici had worn.

Giovanna explained in halting English that these baubles were all things she had taken from Jennie's house after the accident for safekeeping.

"That was probably a good idea," I said. A really good idea, actually, given who had been staying in my home while I was in the poppies.

With that, she stood up, having well completed her big sister duties for the day. "Now, I am tired, and when I am tired, my *Inglese* is *molto difficile*. Difficult," she sighed. "So I shall take my leave, give you kisses and good luck."

She gave me another kiss on each cheek, and this time I was in the right frame of mind to return the gesture. "Thank you, Giovanna. *Grazie*." I was pleased to have remembered that little bit of Italian, but that was nothing compared to her reaction. She positively beamed, and I saw a little glimmer in her eye.

"Grazie, Genevieve. To you, my thanks." After brushing away the hint of a tear, she took my hands in hers. "So very grateful that you are well once again. It is a miracle, truly."

From my little porch, I waved goodbye then as she walked down the dark street, each step with purpose and pride. The lady was opinionated. Abrupt. Strong-willed. Determined. And I hoped I would see her again soon.

48: The waiting

If you think waiting for news nowadays was discouraging, just try going from this land of instant communication to the Victorian age. That'll peg your frustration meter in thirty seconds flat, and give you a whole new love and appreciation for cell phones, text messages, email.

I was left to cool my heels at home until it was all over — and had to wait that long to find out how it went down... or went up.

Finally, he trudged into the house at a little past eleven in the morning.

Travis was healthy and whole, so I didn't even wait until he was inside before I started peppering him with questions.

He answered just one before holding up his hands and asking me to wait a minute. "Nothing blew up," he said, and then headed into the kitchen and grabbed a beer off the ice. I heard the hiss as he cracked the top, and then the came into the living room, sat down, and took a few swigs

"Okay," he finally burped. "Fire when ready."

I repeated my other questions — *Did you see them, Did you catch them, Did anyone get hurt,* and, finally, *What took so damn long?*

He told me everything I needed to know with a story.

"Just before the bank closed its doors to customers for the day, Detective Cody called me in to answer a few last-minute questions the manager had. So we're standing there in the lobby, in uniform, reassuring this bloke that yes, the bank should be able to open on time the next morning, and no, he really didn't need to hang around after closing," Travis laughed as he swirled the beer around in the bottle.

"The next minute, this dead posh blonde-haired woman comes walking in the door. She's all decked out in fur and diamonds, looking like she took the wrong turn going to the theater. I looked at her for a few seconds, and suddenly I realized — it's not a lady at all." He sighed. "It was only Maggie, trying to dress up like an heiress — part of their scam."

From the sound of it, the instant she locked eyes with Travis, Blondie knew the cops weren't on scene to discuss their pension funds or to try to raise donations for the Policeman's Ball.

Proving that it doesn't take a con artist long to realize when a situation is about to go sour, she just as quickly went into improvisation mode. She made a big show of looking in her purse, putting her hand over her mouth in mock despair that she'd forgotten something vital... then turned and walked right back out the bank's front door.

"I didn't see Walt, and don't know why she was there. It dawned on me much later that perhaps the plan had been for her to use the executive privy. Hide in there until dark so she could unlock the door."

Alas, as Travis said, it was moot at that point. Without a doubt, Maggie realized they had been made, which meant the heist was almost certainly off.

What then? He couldn't tell the detective or his commanding officer about any of this, because that could blow any credibility his tip — and, in Travis's mind, his worth as a cop — had in the first place.

So, in the damp, dark basement level of that building, Travis and the other officer waited... and waited and waited. Not until a quarter past eight did they finally shut down the operation, in preparation for the bank opening at nine.

Once all the people and gear had been returned to the station, he had to sit through an hour and a half of uncomfortable debriefings.

So there was no explosion... but there was also no arrest. That was good in the grand scheme of things, but lousy for his reputation.

After he told most of the tale, he got another beer and sat in silence. His eyes were steely and his mouth made a straight line as he lamented the day's trials. After about the thirtieth time he ran his hands over his head, I finally had to say something.

"I'm sorry."

"It's not your fault."

"Of course it is!" Tears were ready and loaded, and I didn't know how long I could hold them back. "There's no way you would have been in this situation if not for me and my stupid theories."

"It's my problem, Jen — not yours. I should have been more careful. Should have anticipated..."

"But, Trav — you have to think of the big picture here. You saved some lives tonight, and spared a lot of people pain. This was a win!"

He shrugged that off. "I know it's for the best. I know we stopped them — for now, anyhow. But because I can't *prove* to anyone that this was a legitimate situation, and that we kept something terrible happening... well, somehow it doesn't feel like a win at all."

I squeezed his hand. "So what did Cody say about all of this?"

Travis snorted then mimicked the detective's drawl, "Son, if every tip we got led to an arrest, every person in this fair city would be more nervous than a whore in church."

A little later, he told me about how, while he and another officer were waiting down under, they killed time by proving Travis's "hunch." For some crazy reason, he had the idea that the walls outside the vault weren't any more solid than the walls you'd find in your average home.

"We used a prisebar — you know, a crowbar — and just threaded it through a chip in the plaster. Twisting and pushing is all we did. No hammering. And eight inches later," he held up a small silver coin, "we found this. It's a brand-new dime."

He handed it to me and continued. "Actually pulled two of them out of there, but I gave the other one to the bank president when we met after. Took him aside and told him there was a hole in his vault, and suggested that the improper construction was probably what made his business the target."

"How did he take that?"

"The gent went red, and the vein in his forehead popped out. Said he knew of no such ridiculous thing, but he'd put his man on it to make sure."

"You gave him the other dime, so why did you keep this one?"

He rubbed the coin between his fingers, and looked at it awhile before answering.

"I think just because it's proof — for you and for me — that you were right. You knew the vault was not strong enough to withstand the explosion, or else I wouldn't have this dime," he said, then took another swig of beer. "With all the ribbing I'm going to get from the other lads this next week, only this ten cent piece will remind me that I wasn't so wrong."

I sat down next to him. "Even if you can't tell them."

"*Especially* since I can't tell them," he said, then curled his arm around my waist and softly kissed my cheek.

49: The Now – Trip to SF

Back in the Now, things were looking good. The horrific story of the bank explosion in 1900 was no longer history. Every search I ran returned the deeply satisfying "No results found." Now, the bank — like so much of the city — crashed and burned after the 1906 earthquake.

I wanted to see where it had been. Check out where, in one version of events, Walt and Maggie had brought the whole world down on themselves. I'd been to the city just once since I started visiting yesteryear, but today, I wanted to see something I had changed.

Since the girls had just a half day at school, it was time for a family adventure — this time, across the Bay. Even though we lived just across the bridge from San Francisco, unless I had a work meeting, I only made the journey into the city three or four times a year. (Dream travel notwithstanding, of course.)

I picked them up just before noon, and we caught BART to the city. It was a quick ride, and before we knew it, the escalator was delivering us into the sights, the sound and the chaos of this modern metropolis.

With Lily on my right and Iris on my left, the three of us walked hand-in-hand up the sunny street. Using only a paper map, I guided our journey. I didn't know what we would find there today, but I wanted to locate it the old-fashioned way.

It only took a few minutes to find. Standing on the sidewalk of Sansome Street, I oriented myself to the north and confirmed my location. This was it. After a deep breath, I looked up and took in my surroundings.

Twelve decades ago, this street corner had been home to a simple but quaint brick structure. Now, though, I was pained to find the same space was occupied by an unimpressive multi-story glass office building. To some, I'm sure it was a great piece of modernist architecture... but to me, the best thing about the design was how the mirror-like surfaces reflected the more elegant buildings all around.

"Are we going inside?" Lily asked.

"No — we're just looking, from right here."

Iris was more to the point. "Boring! I'm hungry." Her big sister nodded in agreement.

"If you can give me one solid minute with no interruptions at all, we can go get lunch. No talking, no wiggling, no silly faces. Think you can do that?"

"Yeah, but what if we don't?" said the ever-pragmatic Lily.

"We'll just stay here until you do."

I got my sixty seconds of silence. During those moments, I thought about how, the last time I'd stood in this spot and surveyed the scene, the weight of many lives were on my shoulders. I imagined that some of that gravity would have traveled with me.

Instead, I felt a whole lot of nothing. In truth, for all that resonated at that moment, I might as well have been gazing at a cement mixer.

But just as I'd told Travis, this was still a win — even if there was nothing to shout about from the rooftops. In a case like this, we had to appreciate that no news really was better than bad news.

܅ ܅ ܅

I let the kids choose the restaurant for lunch, with one caveat: it couldn't be a restaurant we had on our side of the bay, too. That successfully eliminated all fast food joints without making me Mean Mom, while significantly upping the odds that we'd end up with some relatively decent chow.

Without any prompting from me, we ended up at The Old Ship Saloon. After skimming the restaurant's history, I explained to the girls why this spot was unique. "Can you believe that the place we're sitting right now used to be a beach about 150 years ago? We would have been all wet, because this was right on the edge of the water."

Both of the girls looked up to hear the tale.

"See, when thousands of people came to California for the Gold Rush, they left behind a hundred or more of their sailing ships when they raced inland to search for gold. Right here is where they parked one of those big boats. They brought it up to the edge of the land and later turned it into a hotel. Then they put a brick building right on top of it. Even right this minute, deep below us, there's still part of that old wooden ship."

Lily set down her crayons and asked what nearly any third grader would probably consider to be the obvious question: "Is it haunted?"

I should have seen that coming.

"Well, I don't think so. Pretty sure everyone was off the boat before they buried it."

What wasn't said was how other things had happened here that would make a ghost of a miner 49er seem like no big deal.

In the Now, this place had a cool and interesting little bit of history. In the Then, though, it was a different story.

At the Turn of the Century, the same area was part of something called the Barbary Coast — a red light district so dark, it may as well have been burgundy. Of the area, Benjamin Estelle Lloyd wrote in 1876, "The Barbary Coast is the haunt of the low and the vile of every kind. The petty thief, the house burglar, the tramp, the whoremonger, lewd women, cutthroats, murderers, all are found here."

For sure, I wouldn't be visiting this same location in 1900. I'd already gotten a tiny taste of San Francisco at its worst, and it could be bitter indeed.

How foul? Let's just say that if you are a woman, loitering on the sidewalk is very much frowned upon. I am used to propping myself against a building while waiting for someone to arrive. But in the past? It's just asking for the wrong kind of attention, either in terms of the cops presuming you're a hooker, the glares from other women, and — the point of it all — indecent proposals from some men.

And when I say *indecent*, I don't mean things of just the "hey baby" variety — especially not when you're down by the docks. Those guys could be lewd and crude on par (if not beyond) with any from my original century.

In the safety of the now, sitting at a table with my girls who were busily coloring on their paper place mats, the danger seemed amusingly distant. It wasn't long before the humor segued into something even better: gratitude. Thankfulness for what I had right here at this table, and that when I did go to another time, I at least got to hang out in the nice part of town.

༄ ༄ ༄

When our bellies were full and the kids' supply of spooky stories exhausted, we started walking up from street to street, with no particular place to go. We passed countless restaurants, phone stores, clothing shops, and more chain drugstores than I could imagine anyone would ever need.

Then as we passed one wide alley (or narrow street — not sure which),

Ships anchored in the harbor - San Francisco, 1850

Lily caught sight of a sign that always piqued her curiosity: "Open 24 hours." She was fascinated by the concept of a store being always open, and wondered aloud who would possibly want to go grocery shopping at three in the morning.

But this 24-hour shop was the best kind: a bookstore... and didn't have any neon signs in the window to suggest that it was of the adult variety.

Keeping the girls behind me, I peeked in the door to confirm it was kid-friendly. A little bell rang, and the warm, welcoming smell of old books wafted through the air.

Inside, the floor space was minimal, but the stacks were tall — a good twenty feet high, I guessed. Thousands of secondhand books of every age and topic were jammed onto skinny wooden shelves. It was a beautiful thing to behold.

After Iris and Lily gravitated toward the children's section, a clerk directed me to the San Francisco history section. The collection of volumes there was sizable, and separated into every subcategory I could imagine. Running my hand over the volumes, my fingertips lit on a topic I didn't know I was looking for until I found it: True Crime.

I flipped through every title that even touched on the late 1800s and early 1900s, skimming indexes and chapter titles. Just one stood out, and not because it mentioned Walt or Maggie, but since it referenced someone better. Chapter 18 of "Greatest Grifters" recounted a story from 1905, part of which read as follows:

San Francisco Police Detective T. J. Donovan caused the arrest of Thomas, alias "Red" Dugan, who, as J. H. Hogan, on August 30, 1905, with a worthless check, obtained $500.00 from the People's National Bank (member). Joseph Decker, a confederate, in the guise of an Episcopal clergyman, accompanied Hogan to the bank and vouched for him as a member of his parish who had migrated from Bridgeport, Conn., and was desirous of transferring his bank account from that city to a local bank.

The officials became suspicious, then found a security bulletin containing a photograph, description and general information concerning Dugan. They contacted the police, and in the perpetrator's rooms, Detective Donovan found complete forgery paraphernalia, a certification stamp, perforator, etc. To the Detective, Dugan admitted the swindles committed by him.

On June 20, 1905, Dugan pleaded guilty to the crime charged against him, and was sentenced to not less than eight and not more than ten years in the State Prison.

Be still my heart! Not only did it say that Travis had been alive and thriving in 1905, he had even made detective.

There was something more about the book that appealed to me, but I couldn't quite identify what it was. The work itself, published in the late thirties, closely resembled its pulp fiction brethren, and certainly didn't look like anything more than a basic potboiler from the outside. Inside, though, I could there were enough details to make me believe that what had been represented as truth really *was*. They had Travis's name right, in any case, which was reason enough to spend ten bucks.

The girls found books they wanted, too. Lily had pulled a hardbound version of *The Little Princess* from the mid 1970s off the shelf, while Iris — still figuring out how to read — had spotted her favorite word on the cover of a slasher novel. "Just because one of the words in the title is 'candy' doesn't mean it's a good book for kids, sweetheart. How about we try something else?"

Ten minutes later, we were out the door. Each one of us had a treasure in hand to read and to remind us of our little adventure across the Bay.

50: *It's pure dynamite*

Travis always kept an unusual variety of trinkets in his pockets. He called them his "treasures," a name he told me dated back to his childhood. He would pick up items here and there, some bought and some found — things like five for a penny toys, bird feathers, an odd cufflink, a tiny bell, a couple colorful glass marbles, and little wrapped candies.

He'd show me each day's catch when he got home, and pick one or two items to keep. I was sure that yesterday's dime would end up in the "keep" pile. The rest he'd slip back into his pockets so he could hand them out to kids he met. Most of the time, he offered these treats just as a goodwill gesture to kids who were living on the street, but sometimes they were given as incentives to provide information or to run a quick errand.

Tricks like that last one helped him keep his ear to the ground. The more street-savvy ones required cash, just like their elder peers, but they were still little children inside. Though they'd never admit it outright — loved the bright, shiny, fun and tasty treats, too.

෴෴෴

"Here's the thing — what I read keeps changing. Each time I look, the papers are reporting something different, or nothing at all."

As we were preparing dinner, I was trying to explain how, just because I had a futuristic vantage point, it didn't mean that I could see everything I wanted.

"Could that be because their actions — or their plans — aren't set in stone?"

"That's the only thing I can think of. Sometimes, the changes happen quickly. Like I was reading one story that carried over to another page, and when I went to the next page, it was already different. When I went back to the first page, and the story had changed again," I said. "It was really disconcerting. Must be a little bit of what schizophrenia feels like."

"Guessing that is a form of dementia."

"Bingo, you clever boy."

I finished peeling the potatoes, and started to cube them. Travis was already hard at work chopping carrots and onion for our shepherd's pie.

"What is it like to experience a new future? You clearly remember the way things were before."

I thought for a few seconds — maybe a moment too long for Mr Impatient Pants, because he broke into my thought process with, "It's probably terribly hard to describe. Apologies."

"Actually," I said, "it is really *easy* to describe, I just needed to run it through my head a couple times." I took a deep breath. "You know what it's like when someone reminds you about something that happened years and years ago? You almost don't remember it until the moment they say it — sort of like you forgot it ever happened — but once they say it, you have this little memory that shows back up and then grows and becomes clearer and clearer?"

He nodded. "Like my brothers talking about things that happened when I was a lad."

"Right! Well, it's just like that. Not sort of — but *exactly*. To such a degree that I'm seriously wondering if many of the time that happens, we're actually witnessing a change occurring in time," I said, putting the potatoes on the stove to boil. "Wouldn't that be wild?"

"Wild? Indeed. But as for the future helping us any more right now..."

"Not so much. Yeah, I know." I stood back and crossed my arms to think. " How can we get ahead of this when we don't even know what their play is going to be?"

"It may not be fancy, but in my world, one way is to remove the weapon from the equation," said Travis as he started to brown the ground lamb in my new cast iron frying pan. "In this case, that should work well as a preventative, since dynamite is not easy to come by."

"Would he keep it in his possession? At home?"

"Oh, I would think not. Dynamite can be very touchy. Just ask my Uncle Martin."

"I didn't even know you had an Uncle Martin."

"I don't anymore, due to an unfortunate dynamite mishap."

The entire time the pie was in the oven, we were also cooking up a plan. Travis was adamant that we solve this problem now, because he could not — would not — let this go on for even another couple of days. "The longer the explosives are out there, the greater chance they will figure out some a way to put them to use."

At the tiny kitchen table, between bites of casserole, we came to the conclusion that Walt needed to be nudged into taking some sort of action that would lead us right to his treasure.

As soon as dinner was done, Travis asked me to write a note in my handwriting, and dictated the exact message he wanted to send:

We found your dynamite and have moved it. To get it back, wrap $100 cash in brown paper, and put where the sticks were. Must do before 10 am to-day.

It was a very simplistic approach, even for this day, but we decided that Walt would be just paranoid enough to bite. Even if he chose not to pay the ransom, Walt would probably at least check on the stash, or decide to move it. What we did know was that the terrible twosome couldn't just ignore a note like that.

After sealing the letter in an envelope, I wrote Walt's name on it, and then scrawled URGENT across the top.

Offering his usual dollar fee (ten cents up front, and another dime after delivery) Travis hired one of his helpers — this time, a 12-year-old boy named Jonny — to drop the letter through Walt's mail slot just after sunrise.

☙ ☙ ☙

Waking up before dawn and getting dressed in the dark was hardly the nicest way to start a day, but now I was very much on Team Travis, and wanted to get this over and done with as soon as possible.

The plan was incredibly straightforward: Follow Walt. I worried that things would get dicey if he took public transit. "What if he takes a streetcar? Then how can we follow him without being spotted?"

"Have faith, my girl," Travis said with a wink. "Walter is lazy, and Maggie even lazier. They wouldn't store the goods too far from home. A safe distance, but likely not more than ten minutes away."

"I defer to your expertise, sir," I said, because when it came to covertly tracking, the madness to the method was all mine.

I decided that we'd use a couple of simple disguises to pursue Walt without becoming obvious. Color, I decided, was one of the most memorable things we could use to our advantage. As long as the guy didn't repeatedly see someone with something particularly noticeable — a certain bold color of shirt or hat, for instance — it would be a lot harder to track a tail.

With this in mind, we created a few basic strategies. For instance, Travis would duck into an alleyway and swap out a light-colored coat with a blue scarf for a dark jacket and a red scarf. I'd do the same with a bright knit shawl, and take my hat off. We would each take a different side of the street, and stay as far away from Walt as possible.

It worked well until I switched off my colors the first time and emerged from a side street to discover Walter had turned back, and was now walking toward me. I darted off back down the street and hid behind a carriage, and watched breathlessly as he swapped a street vendor a nickel for an apple.

So because Walter wanted breakfast, I nearly peed my bloomers.

After I guesstimated he'd traveled back another block, I slowly emerged from my hiding spot, peering around the corner. I could just make him out amongst the sailors and workers as we entered the waterfront. Travis had been looking back between Walt's position and mine, and I swear he let out a sigh of relief when he saw I was safe.

The tandem tracking continued for just a couple minutes more, until Walter stopped and pulled out a key. He was standing in front of a metal hut — a small building that looked so poorly-built, I'm not sure how it remained standing. Apparently one of a series along with nine others in the immediate vicinity, the only thing notable about the place was the rusty chains and double padlocks on the door, and the number 6 painted in white on the front.

After a quick check of his surroundings, he unlocked the front padlock, opened the door, and slipped inside.

Travis gestured to stay put, and I did. We only needed to wait a minute for Walt to re-emerge, a satisfied little grin on his face. Someone looked happy to find out he had only been the victim of a prankster... or so he thought.

"Just you wait," I said under my breath, and worked hard — very hard — to resist the urge to give him a one-finger salute.

Once our target had hurried off down the road, Travis put his arms around me to warm us both up. "I thought he'd seen you — I was sure of it," he said as he held me close against his chest. "I was on my way over to knock him around when I saw he was just getting something to eat."

"I know, right? Who does that?"

"In any case, the building is locked up tight again. I can't see the locks too clearly from here, but based on the key he had, each one will take me at least a minute to pick. Probably more."

"That's a long time to be out in the open."

"Aye — too long."

The solution came to me courtesy of one of my favorite spy shows: We needed to think outside the box — or outside the lock, as the case may be.

But first, I had to make sure it would be feasible. I asked Travis, "What is that building made of? It looks like metal."

After carefully appraising the building, he said, "It's appears to be corrugated iron or steel."

"How thick is it?"

"It's just sheet metal — so about an eighth of an inch or so, I'd expect," he said.

Perfect. I nudged him with my elbow. "You thinkin' what I'm thinkin'?"

I could see him trying to follow my train of thought, but he didn't make it out of the station. "I... I don't believe I am, no."

"Forget the lock — forget the door. We cut through the *wall* instead."

In three seconds flat, that locomotive was going full speed ahead.

"Oh, my goodness — that is a tremendous idea!" he said. "We won't even have to move the dynamite ourselves if we do this right. Once we confirm it's there, I'll work out a way to report it."

He breathed a huge sigh of relief. "So much simpler. I was concerned about how we could move it safely. Such an unstable explosive, really." Unstable was an understatement — I learned the sticks would actually sweat nitroglycerin, so had to be handled with care if you wanted to still have hands when you were finished.

Before we went back home, Travis wanted to be sure we had all the information we needed from the site. "We will need some tin snips, then, a screwdriver and some gloves."

"It's going to be dark inside there, so you will want a flashlight or something, too," I added. "But obviously nothing with a flame."

"Flashlight? Yes, I can do that," he said. "Those were only just invented, but it figures you'd know about those. The company who made them donated a few to the department. I'm sure I could spirit one away for a short time, provided I slip it back before anyone noticed."

∽ ∽ ∽

The next few hours were spent assembling everything we needed. Getting the flashlight hadn't been a problem at all, he said — everyone at the station house thought they were far inferior to the typical (and more flammable) lighting options. When I questioned that logic, Travis explained that a lot of the reason was that the batteries were notoriously unreliable, and the device often only made short flashes... thus the name.

Instead of going under full cover of night, we decided to use the tall late afternoon shadows as our camouflage. Apart from the sunlight making it simpler to see what he was getting into, it was a hundred times easier to explain a woman's solo presence *before* evening fell, rather than after.

The walk toward the docks this time was, believe it or not, cozy and very enjoyable. Travis held me close the whole time, very protectively. I could tell that he was feeling more vulnerable than usual since he was out of uniform.

The quayside was a dangerous, dirty place. Here, the seawater wasn't like the fresh surf along the beach, but carried a swampy smell. Cigarette butts and other trash was scattered everywhere, and every bit of iron — whether a set of stairs or a wagon — was rusting. Rats, in both rodent form and human, trolled the area, constantly on the lookout for things to take.

We wended our way across to the storage shed, while I did my best to keep the massive volume of skirts and petticoats out of the street muck.

At last, I discovered a great use for my poofy skirts: they provided excellent cover. Even though I was standing next to an old barrel and off the main walkway, it felt better to be able to shield Travis as he worked. I glanced back to see him pry the metal from its frame at ground level, just enough to cut a neat opening just large enough for him to enter. With a nod and a wink, he folded back the little doorway he'd made with the shears and crawled into the big black void.

While waiting, I read my map, which mainly served as a prop to use in case someone approached me, but also offered a nice little distraction while my man traipsed somewhere we knew full well he should not be.

An hour passed — okay, so maybe it was really five minutes, but it felt like at least ten times longer that that — before Travis finally emerged. He gave me a quick thumbs-up, and inched the metal doorway back into place while I dropped the map and his tools into my purse.

After quickly dusting himself off, my mister took my arm and we walked off toward the west, where the sun was filling the sky with orange and red. Optimistic after our success, I decided that was a sign, telling us there would be a more peaceful tomorrow.

൞ ൞ ൞

Later that evening, I wrote a second short note:

Stolen quarry dynamite stored in SW corner of Storage 6, Lombard Street Wharf

Even though fingerprinting was a still-nascent science, I decided to wear gloves when penning the letter. It hasn't mattered with Walt's note, but since this was going to the cops, it just seemed safer — especially since the paper might end up in an evidence file kept for decades.

Well after the moon had risen, Travis put on his gloves and nipped out for a few moments — just long enough to deliver the message to one of his informant boys. For a pocket change payment, the lad promised that he would immediately take the letter to the police station nearest the docks.

And then we waited.

51: Why ask why?

The tulip buds were just starting to show the slightest hint of pinks and reds, and the gentle April breeze was doing its best to encourage them skyward.

As we walked down the winding paths between the trees and the grass of the park, I explained to Travis how the historic newspapers of the Now had offered no useful information — that is, no reports of any dynamite being recovered — but Travis assured me that was only to be expected. Even in the olden golden days of journalism, people still preferred a healthy dose of schadenfreude over a happy ending.

"Surely they got the message and it was found, then probably returned to the quarry — with the strong suggestion that they manage their explosives a little more carefully."

"Still, I'm wondering if we should have done more to implicate Walt in all of this," I said, nervously twisting the slowly-growing sprouts of hair at the front of my head.

"I thought we agreed we couldn't do that, in order to avoid getting ourselves in trouble."

"I know — and I do agree. I just wish there was a workaround. Have our cake and eat it too, I guess." I sighed. "I guess that's not my mission."

"Speaking of such things," Travis said, pulling me a little closer as the breeze picked up a little, "It's something we haven't really talked about. What *is* your mission, do you think? What is your goal in this time?"

"I have no idea... and the more I think about it, the crazier it makes me." At least I could still laugh about it. "I am pretty sure it can't be random. That wouldn't be... logical. I just can't believe that me coming back here like this is without a specific purpose," I said. "I don't think I was dropped here just to have a free bonus life."

Already, I had tried to imagine every possible scenario that could possibly explain any of this. All I had established in my own mind was that I was here for a reason. I *had* to be. Since I first became aware this wasn't a dream,

I had been looking for patterns in anything and everything, just hoping for a hint of what I was supposed to do. I watched for coincidences and repetitive numbers, attempted meditation, and tried to listen to my intuition. And for all my efforts, I got an equal and opposite response: lots and lots of nothing.

"Perhaps you're here now as Jennie to make things better for yourself as Robin."

"I don't think so," I said. "Nothing here so far lines up with that. Plus, it really makes no sense to think I'm here to create financial gain for my other self more than a hundred years from now. That would be way too much effort for something that could just as easily be solved by sending me back a week so I could buy a winning Lotto ticket."

"Good point, that," he nodded, and with a sly little grin quickly added, "I presume that also means you already tried."

That made me laugh — a big ol' from-the-belly guffaw. He seriously had me figured out. "Well, yeah, I thought I'd at least *try* to make a quick buck! That's human nature, right?"

I told him that I started collecting some coins, and how, during my very first week here, I'd looked into scoring a jackpot. "Then I found out the California state lottery wasn't going to start up until 1985, and the only one around now was down in Mexico..."

" The Lottery of the *Beneficencia Publica*."

"That was it! Anyhow, I didn't know how to get a ticket, whether or not it was legit, how and when it paid out, so decided to forget that idea. Went through a similar thought process on betting on sports — how would I do it, and was it even legal — and then thought about trying my luck on the stock market. I could have probably figured how to do that, but at the time, I only had seven bucks, and had really no clue if there was a bank account out there with my name on it."

"So what did you eventually do?"

With a sigh, I admitted defeat. "I just gave up on the concept. I figured if there were this many obstacles in my way, that was not the direction I was supposed to be headed."

Another couple out for a stroll came up behind us, and I nudged Travis to the side of the path so they could pass. After they had walked out of earshot, I continued. "I think I do have a goal here — a purpose. Unfortunately, 'they' are being coy about making what that is clear. Even though being here is not my choice, I'm not going to try to screw things up... too much. After all, it's allowed me to meet you," I said, fluttering my eyelids and mimicking the demure look of so many women in this era.

"Do you worry about changing the future — well, your past — in the wrong way?"

"You mean like causing a highly-localized distortion of the space-time continuum, that sort of thing?"

"I... suppose?" He asked it as a question, which for some reason amused me endlessly.

"At first I didn't — I was angry at being dumped here without any explanation," I said. "But since I got somewhat settled here, I have been feeling a little different about all of that."

"So you don't plan to do anything illegal?" I think he was only half joking.

"Nothing *too* illegal, at least," I laughed. "I haven't figured out any restrictions on what I can or can't do... though I suppose that has less to do with me, and far more to do with the fact that this time seems to be fairly well childproofed. That is, I can't really hurt anything — much." We nodded hello to a couple who passed us from the opposite direction, then I continued in a whisper. "Even if I did change something, from what I have seen, I think the universe or whatever would straighten things back out."

For the next hundred yards or so, all was quiet except for the crunch of the gravel pathway beneath our feet. We were both lost in thought.

Suddenly, Travis took a deep breath. "Here's a question: Why you?"

Yeah — why me? I was glad Travis actually had the chutzpah to ask.

"I honestly have no clue," I said. "There's probably a very obscure set of variables I happened to match — the perfect little storm. Things like experience. Proximity. Curiosity maybe. Ability to do whatever I am supposed to do back here."

He nodded.

"But if I'm experiencing this, I am all but certain someone else out there — likely several someone elses — are doing the same thing. Probably not everyone living in the past is as aware of it, though, just like I was at first," I said. "I think we live these things so much like dreams, many people just take them to be the mind wandering and musing at night."

"You are one of a chosen few," he smiled. "I like the sound of that."

That made me laugh, because I have gone through life as Robin being the one who was pretty much never chosen — not for the dodgeball team, not for the science fair, not for any contest I ever entered.

"I don't know about that, but I can't imagine it's entirely random," I said while giving his arm a little squeeze. "But I am sure that whoever is coordinating this little adventure could be a little more helpful. It's frustrating not having even a basic outline of what I'm supposed to be achieving, or how." With that last statement, I started to feel the contractions of a baby headache being born. "Because right now, I honestly don't know — and I am starting to doubt that I will ever know. Still, though, I refuse to believe there's not a purpose."

"Maybe that purpose is a person."

"If you're my reason for being here, hey — that's plenty for me," I said, and paused for a full minute to give him a kiss. "But even though I love you to pieces, but just don't buy that you're my *raison d'etre* here, either, babe. That would be a ridiculously inefficient process — much too far to go to find my soul mate." (No need to mention the depressing idea that I must be a really tough person to couple up if Cupid had to send me back more than a hundred years to find my main man.)

"On top of all that," I said, "my kids are in the other time zone, and, well, that's just wrong. How can I be all happy if the people I love best aren't even in the same reality?"

"Oh, Jen, if I had a nickel every time I heard that..."

"Yeah, yeah — you would be five cents short of a dime right about now."

We had finally reached Stow Lake, a pretty little pond in the middle of Golden Gate Park. We sat on a nearby log and watched the light reflect off the water.

I explained that I believed what I was experiencing was unique — special, even. And, in my mind, that meant that I had a job to accomplish. Maybe it was one task or maybe there a series of things to do, but I definitely believed there was a purpose.

What didn't make sense, though, was how muddy the concept got from there. "If I was here to achieve something, wouldn't it stand to reason that I'd be able to simply figure out what it was?"

"I'm a bit surprised to hear this concerns you. I rather thought you had a, shall we say, *laissez-faire* approach to such things."

I shrugged.

"How much effort have you put into it?"

"Since I've been with you, I'd have the mark the checkbox for 'little to none.'"

There was a long silence, then finally Travis asked, "Am I standing in your way?"

"Oh, jeez, — not at all!" I had to get this straight in my mind to explain. "I think..." I said. "I *worry* that if I get my job done here — then what? Do I die? Stop traveling to this time?"

"Try not to think of that, love," he said, trying to soothe me. "You don't know that you will cease to be here."

"Exactly — I don't know how this works, so I don't know that I will stay, either. It just seems like a really big risk to take," I said, starting to get a little weepy.

He held me close. "I can help you navigate these waters if you want — but only if you want. It's entirely up to you. I will abide by your wishes, even if it means you want to just..." he searched for some words.

"Wing it?"

"Use your intuition, follow your heart, seek signs — whatever way you choose to define that."

"I appreciate that. I do. But I don't know what I want to do yet," I said, then another tangent came to mind. "You know, maybe we shouldn't assume those are two entirely separate paths. See, right now, my intuition tells me to let you help me. So maybe what I think of as free will is really just fate playing itself out. What do you think about that, big guy?"

Travis made a show of fake-mopping his brow. "I think..." he said, then leaned over and gave my nose a little tweak, "you think too much."

52: Can't touch this

It was a wonderful drizzly, gray morning — thinking weather, I called it. I'd spent all morning browsing bookshops, and planned to visit them again soon with Travis in tow so he could carry home some treasures for me. Nearly every book was published in hardback, and the publishers apparently weren't worried about not fitting on store shelves. The "collected works" volumes in particular were nearly the size of the encyclopedias I had in school.

Still, I picked up two books — all that I could carry — and both were based on recommendations from the shop owner. The first was some historical fiction, "Janice Meredith: A Story Of The American Revolution," and the second was a strange one: an adventure/horror story set in ancient Egypt, titled "Pharos the Egyptian." Both were very trendy topics in the Then.

The smell of fresh bread wafted down the street and tempted everyone who walked by. Even me. In fact, it reminded me that I still had to grab some food to make for tonight and tomorrow.

Food shopping was so quick and simple in the Then. You want coffee? You picked up the only kind of coffee available. Ditto pretty much every food product you could imagine, save for dairy products — because those were delivered to your door by the milkman.

This body needed very few calories, and had the tiny appetite to match. Though I'd only been here for a few months, I would have to say the food I'd tried so far was a real mixed bag. Some of the menu items and flavor combinations popular here were not at all appealing to my palate. They seemed to actually like using things like turtle (or their cousin terrapin), oxtail, chestnuts, suet, Lima beans, citron (like a lemon with an inch-thick peel) and lots and lots of pickled everything.

There was a lot to love, though. I found myself enamored of several treats — there's just something amazing about cream-filled pastries made with unbleached flour, sweet butter, farm-fresh eggs, real sugar and all kinds of other ingredients that are reserved for the organic and specialty supermarket aisles in the Now.

Likewise, the beef, pork and chicken I'd tried were amazing — full-bodied and had an aroma that matched their taste. The apples and berries were altogether exquisite. Every type of bread was beyond delicious.

At the same time, some other things, particularly soups and sauces, seemed somewhat disappointing. I don't know if that was just because tastes have changed over time, or if I had (sadly) grown accustomed to synthetic flavor enhancers and foods that had been engineered to have the perfect taste and texture.

Ten minutes later, I left the store with a single shopping bag, containing enough food for the next two days. Now, though, I had to juggle my handbag with these two bulky books on my left arm, the bag with the groceries in my right, and hold my umbrella in whatever hand worked best as I navigated my way around the puddles and other sidewalk obstacles.

In front, behind and on both sides, there was only a sea of black umbrellas, shimmering under the downpour.

I was so focused on the forest of dark brollies that I didn't even notice a man had stepped in front of me until I had almost walked right into him. My apology was already forming on my lips when I looked up at the guy's face. It was Walter, and he had a look that was an unsettling combination of ogling and anger.

My immediate instinct was — quite naturally — to get as far away from him as possible, as quickly as possible. Alas, instinct provides the what, but can be kind of lousy on the how. I found myself stumbling into reverse, nearly tipping over in the process.

He kept coming toward me, so I kept backing up. Back, back, back... until I realized I was surrounded by brick walls on two sides, and a tall wooden fence on another. Blocking my only exit was Walt.

"Hello, Genevieve," he said. I had a lump in my throat and couldn't even reply. "I hear you have been busy lately." Then he leaned toward me, put his hand on my shoulder, and whispered very clearly, "So have I." I could smell beer and onions on his breath, and tried not to gag.

Then in a flash, my mind went somewhere else. It's like someone hit the pause button on a DVR, and I had a moment to discuss the situation with my alter ego.

So, seriously — you're just going to let this loser intimidate you? Push you into a corner? You're a twenty-first century woman. You don't need to put up with his crap.

I knew what I needed to do. It was the sort of idea I'd normally get only after I had time to stew, and the benefit of hindsight.

With a sharp intake of breath, I drew myself up to my full height. (Granted, that wasn't much, but I had the feeling that at that moment, I looked a lot taller than I really was.) I narrowed my eyes and lowered my head, then, with my nails bared, I grabbed his hand and threw it off my body.

"Don't touch me. Got that, Wally?" I said, with a smile that, when I felt it on my face, realized had come out more like a sneer. I may have also said a naughty word... or three.

I watched his expression melt from one of power and rage to a look of fear. Interestingly, Walter didn't seem scared *of* me, I think, so much as scared *by* me. I didn't care, as long as there was some fear there.

Holding my head up high, I adjusted my bags and umbrella, then walked down the alley and into the street and didn't take a single look back.

☙ ☙ ☙

Of all the days for Travis to not be around, it turned out to be this one. After arriving home, I found a note from him on the table, saying that there was going to be some big city meeting about an impending blackout, and he needed to attend. He was apparently going to be late, because the message ended, "Don't wait up. xxx"

I was fuming — not at him, but because of the hassle with Walt... and because of the crappy timing. The situation called for a good long venting session, and the only person here I could talk to was myself. I couldn't even partake in some good ol' vaguebooking from this side.

So I talked about it out loud. And yelled. And wept. Plus I stabbed a potato so many times, I ended up having hash browns for dinner instead of wedges. That all helped, and then a glass of wine buffed the edges off the rest of my frayed temper.

When I finally went to bed, I had let go of most of the anger, and was ready to channel my energy into finding exactly what Walter had meant when he told me that he'd been "busy."

☙ ☙ ☙

The next day in the Now, I spent every minute from the time I dropped off the girls at school until they got home on the web — and then put in another three hours later that evening. It wasn't fun, but I had to do my due diligence so I could at least give Travis a little good news with the bad.

My searches for all the various name keyword combinations came up dry — first name and last name, last name and initials, etc. Finding the correct terminology for criminal activity was also a bit hit-and-miss — think things like *robbery, holdup, theft, stickup* and other similar terms.

I found the description of what was essentially a home burglary. While that didn't seem relevant to my search, there was a nearby article that hadn't come up in results due to a crappy scan of the original newspaper. No, that wasn't the crucial evidence I needed, but it underlined the fact that I couldn't rely on the optical character recognition engine to necessarily point me in the right direction. I was going to have to go manual.

Without a doubt, reading — or even skimming — every old article was tedious. Journalists didn't use like the inverted pyramid common in news reporting nowadays, and they frequently proffered personal commentary along with the facts. They also tended to repeat themselves, and were often redundant. It made for painful reading.

What did I get for all the time invested? Eyestrain, headache, and the knowledge that whatever Walt had going on, he either did it elsewhere, used an alias, or — most hopefully — none of his efforts had managed to make a ripple in history.

So far, anyhow.

I'd already witnessed more than enough to know that the past was plastic, not at all set in stone the way everyone else believed. And that is why the more I learned, it seemed like the less I actually knew.

53: Time Scene Investigation

Still in the Now, I'd been trying to sleep for hours. My mind was too restless to let me drop off. It was creeping up on two in the morning, and at this rate, didn't know if I'd manage to drop off at all before daybreak. If I didn't, what then? Would I skip a day in 1900?

I decided that if I was still awake in half an hour, I'd have to get up and do some work. With the threat to my laziness set, I adjusted the pillow and closed my eyes... and merciful heavens, the next thing I knew, I was back enveloped in Travis's arms. Before I'd taken two breaths, all the stress disappeared and I was overwhelmed by sleep. Somehow I knew I could close my eyes again now, and I'd stay right there and then.

Some time after sunrise, I awoke to kisses on my shoulder, then my neck, my ear, my cheek, and finally my lips. Between the hours spent in both of my time zones, I'd gone far too long without seeing him. Very quickly, I got the impression he'd missed me, too.

◊ ◊ ◊

I waited until breakfast to tell him about my run-in with Wally. I thought a spoonful of fried egg might help the medicine go down.

His reaction was pretty much as I expected: Shock, anger, talons out... then eventually turned into an overall concern for my safety.

"It really wasn't too big of a deal," I said, trying to calm him down. "He didn't hurt me, didn't threaten me — just invaded my personal space and creeped me out, but that stuff's not illegal in this time or mine."

"I'm still considering pummeling him to a jelly."

"Well, you're not going to." To underline that point, I moved the pot of strawberry jam to the far side of the table.

"Convince me."

"Anything short of killing Walter is going to only antagonize him, and you're not a murderer."

He thought about that for a moment while he buttered his toast before deciding, "I could make an exception in his case." Then he took a vicious-looking bite of the bread.

"Yeah, and then I'd be here, and you'd be on death row. No thanks."

"Is that what your intuition is telling you — not to beat him to a pulp?"

"That, yes, but also that Walt seems to be our cross to bear. I don't know why, but it's pretty obvious. We need to keep him from hurting anyone — including us."

Travis sighed, and I continued. "Back in my time, I tried to figure out what he might have been talking about when he said he has been 'busy,' but I couldn't find anything useful yet."

"With all due respect toward your webs and such," he said, "mayhap we consider some of the investigative methods I know? I think we're going to need to do our own research if we want to get ahead of this."

I was absolutely on board for that idea.

"When the police are trying to discover who committed a crime — or, in this case, how someone might — they need to ascertain certain key elements. First, what was this person's motive? Second, who had the ability to carry out this action? For instance, was special knowledge or a certain talent required?"

"'Means, motive, opportunity' — is that what you mean? I've heard that lots of times on TV."

"I like that. Succinct. So now we have to apply those sort of concepts to your situation. Let's start with motive, and think about this in the most basic way — no specifics."

I watched him — admired him actually — as he walked over to the mahogany secretary desk/bookcase. (That piece was gorgeous, and even though it was practically brand new, I kept thinking of it as an antique.) He took a piece of paper from one of the cubbyholes, and then started searching for something else.

"Don't you have any pens?"

"Nope," I told him. "I can't get the hang of the fountain pen things. They're messy and they make an icky scratching sound if I don't make the stroke the right way. So I bought a dozen pencils instead."

He laughed, shook his head, and grabbed a pencil before making his way back to the table.

"As I said before, let's apply some logic." Then he started to make some notes with my help.

∽ ∽ ∽

By noon, we had a plan — one involving actual legwork. With a hearty "Why wait?" vote from me, just after dark, we headed across the city to start the first phase: covert reconnaissance.

Going out after nightfall was a little scary, as the after-hours world of Then was almost devoid of light.

Though I had never intentionally ventured out past twilight, I regularly found myself drawn outside to admire the nearly-silent nights. When it was clear, the sky was an inky black — much darker than the charcoal gray color of Now that I usually would see, courtesy of smog and light pollution. On foggy nights in the Then, there was an eerie but strangely romantic glow from that would wend its way through the avenues. It was really quite bewitching.

There was man-made light, of course, but not much. The gas street-lamps, though, lit only the immediate vicinity, and scarcely a handful of people left candles or lamps burning until morning. Even though it was hundreds of thousands of miles away, the moon was the brightest midnight light in the year 1900.

Not until I saw blackness like this did I realize how much we have banished darkness in the Now. You can't go out in the city or suburbs without seeing lots of headlights, powerful streetlights, porch lights, lights in store windows and entryways, and brightly-lit billboards and signs.

Travis's presence made the journey possible — not only did I feel safe with him by my side, he could walk these city streets with his eyes closed, and knew every intersection, side street, alleyway and trouble spot.

Wally and his gal-pal lived downtown, and, despite its proximity to the waterfront, their place was actually pretty nice. As a fringe benefit, it was also close to some cute little shops and a restaurant.

The two were shacking up together in a flat in a narrow row house that was pretty similar to my place, but not quite as quaint, and in the center of the block instead of my sweet corner lot. I guess crime *did* pay a fairly decent wage, since they had no visible means of support.

"They're probably doing small-time stuff — shoplifting, picking pockets, maybe a little burglary," Travis said. "Nothing to really get noticed, but enough to provide them with a bit of cash."

I was all into the idea of dressing like a ninja, climbing up onto the roof under the dark of night, and sneaking into their room via one of the windows. But Travis quickly dashed that notion.

"There are more people at home at night than at any other time."

"Okay, then — how about we use the darkness to spy on them from outside?"

The homes on this street were separated only by a couple feet, and I hoped that might work to our advantage. We could quite easily eavesdrop on them from the relative comfort of the alleyway on the right side of their house.

Or so we thought.

After we spent two hours of that night spent huddled behind a tree and below a small side window, straining to hear their voices over the noise of the trains running nearby, horse hooves, fog horns and the various other sounds of the city, we called it quits. It took but one loud flush to tell us our super-secret listening post was located not off the parlor, but was instead adjacent to the toilet. Travis tried to console me by saying it would have been an excellent idea if the two spent a lot of time talking aloud, planning their nefarious deeds, while sitting in their bathroom.

Clearly, we needed to find a better way to figure out what those two were planning.

༄ ༄ ༄

Early the next morning, we tried again — this time, our ruse required costumes. Travis was out of his police uniform, and instead was dressed in the kind of cap and overalls you would usually see on a construction laborer. (Strangely enough, it was actually a really attractive look on him.) I wore a housedress made of plain blue chambray, along with a simple cotton cap, which was similar to the ones I had seen some kitchen maids wearing.

It was garbage pickup day, and our plan was to get to the bins before they got picked up. As disgusting as it was going to be, Travis and I were going to rifle through their trash to see if there was anything we could figure out about what our good buddies were doing — or what they were considering.

The narrow service lane behind the row of houses was empty, apart from several dozen metal trash cans — several so full they were disgorging chicken carcasses, broken glass and greasy newspapers onto the pavement.

Once we found the dregs of Walt and Maggie's life, I started searching and Travis stood watch. Just before digging in, I slipped on some cotton gloves, which was the best hand protection I could manage. I hoped they'd at least help keep the oogy stuff from getting under my fingernails.

"You can learn a lot about a person by looking through their garbage," I told him my *Burn Notice* wisdom as I separated a moldy apple from the crumpled little paper to which it was attempting to mate.

"Look! Here we have... well, it's a receipt." I flattened it out and read the smeared ink. "It's for Oscar's Butchery. A pound of liver — that sounds disgusting. But see? Now we know where they shop!"

Travis gently took my arm and turned me around. Standing behind me, he pointed over my shoulder, down to the end of the alley. There I could see the red and white awning over a storefront no more than fifty yards away. "That's Oscar's, right there," he said. "I love you, but I don't think the contents of the rubbish bin will exactly crack this case."

I stuck out my tongue at him and turned back to the garbage can. "I'm not done yet, buddy. Just you wait."

A layer below the food and newspaper waste was something slightly more interesting: three empty booze bottles, all of which had contained gin.

This got Travis to nod and to start rubbing his chin — his thinking pose.

Toward the bottom of the can was a pair of worn-out black leather shoes. They were caked with dirt and stained with grease. I said to Travis, "Hand me an evidence bag, will you? I want to get these back to the lab for analysis."

"Pardon?"

"Just kidding. Think you can find a box?"

He disappeared down an the alley in the direction of the butcher's, and returned with a wooden fruit crate, complete with the kind of vintage paper label that would likely fetch a fortune in my day.

∽ ∽ ∽

Back home, we cleaned up and started to review our anemic haul.

"Please tell me again while you brought home those revolting old shoes?"

"They might tell us something," I told him, then removed one of them from the box. I looked at it closely, turning it over, looking in the crevices, trying to distinguish between everyday dirt and... well, anything else. I put the shoes upside down, then side-by-side, and let them speak to me.

Verdict: Walter walked through lots of muck on a daily basis, and dragged his left heel slightly.

"What does that tell us? Does it help?"

"The meaning of every piece of evidence isn't always immediately clear," I said. "You never know."

"So, nothing then."

"Nothing yet," I said, punctuating my sentence by waving a shoe.

That's what I noticed Travis was watching me — his eyes shining, arms crossed, and with one hand up by his face.

I pointed at him. "I know you're smiling behind there, boy."

"Sorry," he said. "Trying not to." And then he smiled even more. Then he really laughed. After finally stopping just before he hyperventilated, he said, "I was expecting this marvelous futuristic revelation, such as you being able to look at the soles and see a map of where he'd taken his last thousand steps or some such."

"Not yet," I said to the cheeky little monkey. "But, as I said, you never know."

∽ ∽ ∽

Tomorrow, we were going to try, try again.

Despite my suggestion that he sweet-talk the landlady into letting us inside the house — or to pretend we were prospective renters — Travis assured me that simply walking in the front door to the landing would be much simpler. He was amused I assumed the shared entrance door would be locked. "People who live in the flats don't want to go out to the front door for everything," he said. "Not during the day, anyhow. It would make it much too difficult for the mailman, the ice man, the delivery boys — not to mention the neighbors."

He did agree, however, that I might be a better person to enter the enemy fortress. For one thing, I wasn't a cop who could lose his job and face charges for breaking and entering. I also *wanted* to do it. Despite the shoes being a useless prize, I somehow still felt confident I had the mad observational skills needed — honed by years of watching shows like *Psych* and *Sherlock*.

But the first order of business was learning how to gain access.

Since he was a cop, Travis was well-versed in lock picking, and was able to teach me the basics. I was just happy I wouldn't need to have things like "how to pick a lock" in my web browser's search history in the Now. (For what it's worth, the locks we were talking about used skeleton keys — those big-ass keys that slide into the stereotypical keyholes.)

First, I practiced picking the lock on my own front door. Fortunately, it was keyed on both sides, so I didn't have to stand on my porch in full view of everyone while I figured it out.

Travis explained the concepts, drew me a picture of the lock mechanism, and then demonstrated — twice — the simplest method to spring it open.

I did it exactly as he had shown me, and... nothing. I attempted it probably another fifty times before it finally worked, but I couldn't figure out what I'd done differently that time compared to the forty-nine previous attempts. Finally, I got the process down to fifteen minutes, then eleven, then four... but that still wasn't good enough. I needed to be able to consistently tease the lock open in less than a minute.

After we took a break for lunch (Travis insisted, saying I was getting "dyspeptic") I tried some more. After about an hour, my best time was down to 27 seconds.

"Brilliant!" Travis said, and I reminded him how to fist-bump. Then he spoiled the moment by adding, "Now, let's try it on a different sort of door lock."

It was getting dark by the time I graduated to picker extraordinaire, having foiled four different locks in less than 31 seconds each.

With gritted teeth, I told my handsome teacher, "If this doesn't work on Walt and Maggie's door, just warning you now — I'm going to use a sledgehammer."

Training out of the way, we enjoyed a noisy evening at home, with me playing piano DJ with a mix of classic tunes from my sixties, seventies and eighties. I tried to play and sing a variety of different songs, based on my love for and knowledge of the tunes.

As entertaining as it (hopefully) was for him, it was positively therapeutic for me. Every single day in this era, I missed music as a sort of soundtrack to life. I loved nearly all of it — from classical to alternative, opera to emo, oldies to hip hop.

Making it all the more entertaining was that Jennie's singing voice was nothing like my own. Hers had a totally different resonance, and it was much easier for her body to hit the notes I was thinking. Every now and then, when everything fell in place just perfectly, it felt was like I was outside myself — just a spectator, listening to her clear voice, and watching her long, slender hands playing the notes.

To close out the night, I introduced Travis to one of my favorite songs: John Lennon's "Imagine." By the time I got to the last chorus, I was playing through tears — because of both the lyrics, and the understanding that unless my boy lived to be at least 95 years old, he would never hear the beauty and passion of the original.

54: On the inside

While Travis had been fast asleep in the Then, I'd gone back to the Now and spent the day making plans.

Just from reading the news and watching TV — and understanding how to separate fact from fiction — I probably knew more techniques for evaluate a crime scene than did the entire San Francisco police force of 1900.

My big idea was to take everything I learned, and create a profile of sorts. From that, I could compare to crimes and other incidents reported in the future. (Clearly, I had an acute case of optimism.)

Once I had my objective in mind, I set about devising an awesome cover story and a system of hand signals to use in case of emergency.

I'd read more than once that the best way to construct a lie that will stand up to scrutiny is to put as much truth into it as you can. Therefore, if I got caught, I was a head trauma patient who was totally off her rocker. Officer Donovan, on the other hand, was searching for the crazy lady who was last seen somewhere in the vicinity.

"If you need to get my attention when I'm inside, throw a rock at the window, or do a bird call," I said. "Then give me a signal."

We decided on two simple hand gestures Travis could use while I was inside. The first was a closed fist, meaning that everything was okay. A flattened hand, in contrast, was a warning: Get out through another exit, or hide. Both signals could be held in any position so as not to attract undue attention from passersby.

"And then, if you do this," I said as I did a quick little Safety Dance, "it means, 'You're screwed, and I'll try to bail you out of jail, but make no promises.'"

Mr Grumpy was not amused.

"I know you're having fun with this, Jen, but it really could be dangerous. Quite honestly, I am having second thoughts about doing this at all. I don't know if what we will find will be worth the risk."

I took both of his hands in mind. "I realize you think this is a continuation of the silly shoe evidence thing, and that's fair enough. But everything so far was really done with the hope of avoiding this step if at all possible... but it's *not* possible," I said. "History's not giving me answers, either."

"So why are we even doing this? I hope it's not a vendetta. I'd be terribly disappointed if that's all this was."

"Not at all — no chance. The guy's an ass, but it's not worth putting either one of us in harm's way just because of that."

I guided him over to the sofa, then sat on his lap with my arm curled around his neck. "The only guidance I have right now is my gut," I said. "If you asked me six months ago how reliable I thought my intuition was — or anyone's was — I would have probably laughed out loud."

"But now?"

"But now, well, it's an entirely different story, because my own story — or *stories* — have changed. And that's how I know if I can just find my path and follow it, without forcing it or trying to ignore the lines drawn, I can fix things."

"Fix history."

"Before you disregard that possibility, remember: You're talking to a time traveler. Why else would I be here?"

He reminded me that just a few days ago, I had been iffy on the point of this all. In exchange, I reminded him that time had passed, and my perspective had evolved.

"So," he said, "if you're to make an alteration to an event that is supposed to occur — or, in your time, has already occurred — there are two probable paths: creating an action, or stopping an action... or perhaps some of both."

I nodded, because that's the best explanation I had been able to come up with, too. Bottom line was that this wasn't a vacation, this was a mission. I had to change history, damn it. And things were just getting fun, too.

Just thinking about the weight of that concept got my heart rate up. I did a little Lamaze breathing to calm myself back down.

"It's okay, Jen," Travis said, pulling me even closer and looking right into my eyes. "I will be behind you. Or in front of you. Or wherever you tell me to be. This is your party."

෴෴෴

Travis had hired two boys to watch the house, starting at dawn. They didn't know about each other, but when both accounts agreed — the woman had left at about eight, the man a half hour later — we made our move. At that point, the house had been empty for nearly forty minutes.

Down at the end of the block, I put on my gloves and gave Travis a thumbs up. Then I walked off, knowing he would follow a minute later.

With a slightly wilted bouquet in hand, a happy dumpster discovery from behind the florist's shop, I held my head high and walked up to the outside entrance to Walt and Maggie's duplex.

I took the steps one at a time, listening after each. When I reached the landing, I knocked on the door — just in case. When there was no answer, I put my ear to the door and listened. I could hear a clock ticking inside, but otherwise, not a creature was stirring.

Setting the flowers on the floor in front of the door, I checked out my opponent. The lock was a piddly little thing — something that even in this body I could probably kick in without a problem. Of course, leaving evidence like that would be too far off-script, so I set about working my magic.

I slipped one of the tools out of my sleeve, and tried to slide it into the lock... but it was too big to fit.

I'd have to MacGyver it. After removing my gloves, I pulled out one of my hat pins. After a quick bend near the top, I could use that as my pick. It wasn't pretty, though, and it wasn't fast. With every second that passed, my hands got sweatier, and my heart seemed louder.

Finally, after a ridiculous minute and ten seconds, I heard a pretty little click, and the tumbler turned. I was in. I slipped back into my gloves, and with just the slightest touch, I opened the door as gently as possible, but the hinges still screamed their indignation. Ignoring their protests as much as I could, I closed the door and quietly stepped into the parlor.

Once inside, it was impossible not to notice a lingering odor of stale cigarettes, coupled with an undertone of rotten food.

Every vertical surface was littered with clothing, books, papers, and just plain garbage. In my day, I imagined this kind of place would have fast food wrappers strewn everywhere. Overflowing ashtrays, along with mostly empty bottles of booze and beer completed the charming ensemble.

As tough as it would make it to find anything, an upside to the squalor was that it would certainly mask any trace that I'd been in the house.

Before starting my search, I stepped softly over to the window. Travis was nonchalantly walking his beat across the street, both hands closed in fists behind his back.

On the ottoman alongside the sofa, there was a hodgepodge of printed paper — instruction manuals for a three kinds of locking safes, bank brochures. At the bottom, I found some press clippings with the semi-annual statements banks were required to publish, listing the bank's assets, including cash and bonds. On my notepad, I scribbled down the safe brands and bank names.

The worst of the stench seemed to be emanating from the kitchen. When I took a quick look in there, and instantly spotted a wide, seething trail of ants, I decided to make that the last room on my tour.

Stepping carefully between piles of cigarette ash, I moved over to the dining area. Three different newspapers were crowding the table, all open to the classifieds. Several "help wanted" ads were circled in pencil. From what I could tell, most of their interest was in governess positions, housekeeping jobs and work driving carriages. I remembered that we had seen several issues of *The Call* in their trash yesterday, but I hadn't thought to look if they had been marked or if pages had been ripped out.

There was also a city directory, with the corners turned down on at least a dozen pages. I noted the dog-eared page numbers so I could refer to them in Travis's copy of the guide, and even remembered to write down the guide year, too.

The bathroom smelled worse than the kitchen — a nauseating combination of musk and mildew. Holding my sleeve over my face, I took a cursory look around before deciding that nothing in the damp little room was going to be worth the price of discovery.

The bedroom was just around the corner, and it, at least, smelled okay. It was no surprise to see it was as messy as the rest of the house. The brass bed's sheets and blankets were a tangled heap — half on the bed and half on the floor, and the two pillows were stacked near the headboard.

I stepped over to the dresser, and looked closely for a string or strand of hair that might have stuck near the edge — a low-tech trick to tell if a drawer or door had been opened. I couldn't see anything, so I pulled out the drawers one by one, starting at the top. The first appeared to be filled with bloomers and stockings (which presumably belonged to Maggie, but who knew). I hoped the icky feeling of being a perverted snooper wouldn't cling to me for very long.

Shaking off the icky intruder feeling, I ran my hand around the bottom and sides of the drawer, then repeated the process with the next three drawers. Finally, in the bottom of the dresser, tucked under some gloves and scarves, I found a few rings, a jeweled bracelet, and a necklace with a golden locket, upon which a the letters GD had been engraved. I couldn't think of a reason why a girl named Maggie Gallagher would have something with my initials on it. After hesitating, I decided to leave it behind, only because I didn't want them to know that someone had been snooping around.

Twice, while rifling through the bureau, I heard an owl hooting, and ignored it. It called again, and something about the "who who" sounded urgent. I shut the drawer, then peeked out the window. There, I saw Travis on my side of the road, facing out to the street, nodding and smiling... all the while waving the "get out" signal.

How long had he been signaling me — and how much time did I have? I tiptoed over to the other window and couldn't see anything. Then I heard the front door open. Whoever just arrived was already coming in the front door, which was just one wall and about twenty feet away from where I was standing.

The bed was high and didn't have a skirt, so I couldn't slip under there. There was no closet or anywhere else to hide, and I didn't have time to get to another room.

My only option: A window. I had two from which to choose. One exited directly to the alley — a drop of about fifteen feet, I guessed. The other led to a tiny patch of roof that covered the back door, which, at least, would bring my fall down to a more manageable ten feet or so.

I ripped off my gloves, realizing I was still holding one of Maggie's scarves from the drawer I was searching when I heard the hoots. I couldn't spare even a few seconds to put it back. The dress had no pockets, so I shoved the scarf and my gloves down the front of my dress and hoisted up the window sash.

Leaning out the window, gaping at that angled four foot by four foot patch of roof — the only thing saving me from a long slide earthward — I seriously considered how bad it would be to get caught instead.

Some emboldened part of me didn't bother answering, but just threw my legs over the ledge. My feet slipped and scraped, trying to find a grip on the shingles. When finally I had steadied myself, I pulled down the window with all the quiet grace I could manage, then crouched down out of sight. Little rocks and bits of sand rolled past my head and off the ledge, and I couldn't even hear them land.

I felt my body sliding closer to the edge, but there was little I could do to stop. There was nothing to hold on to. I tried to stretch my arms and legs as wide as they would go, but couldn't reach from side to side to save myself.

Inch by inch, I was slipping off the roof. I didn't think that "they" — whoever was responsible for my time travel — would let me die from something as stupid as this. But any parent knows... sometimes your kids have to get hurt a little in order to learn a valuable lesson. A lesson like, oh, let's think — don't break and enter, maybe?

I tried to remember the rules for falling. *Roll as you hit the pavement. Don't try to break your fall with your arms. Don't land on your head.*

Major Jen to ground control... Ready or not, here I come.

55: Gossip girl

As my fingers relinquished the last of their grip and I fell from the little sliver of roof, I flung myself sideways so I could hit the ground in a roll. In the heat of the moment, the idea to spin was so firmly planted in my head that I kept trying to turn, even after my body had stopped moving.

"It's okay, Jen — stop kicking!" Travis said as I nearly tipped us both over.

The concept took a little bit of time to knock through my adrenalin rush, but he had caught me. Swooped me up in his arms like I was six years old again.

"How did you get here?" I whispered, but all he'd say was "Hush now!" as he hurried down the service lane, still holding me aloft. Down at the street corner — well out of sight from the house — he finally put me down.

"That was fun! I haven't been carried like that since I was a kid." I was still out of breath. "Can you do a piggyback the rest of the way home?"

"Perhaps later," he said, then pulled me in for a bear hug. "Now, promise me: We will never ever do something like that again."

I gave him a smile and a hug and a kiss. But I didn't promise.

෴ ෴ ෴

The ride home on the streetcar took an achingly long fifty minutes, and even though I tried to keep busy reviewing and expanding upon my notes, my mind was in too much of a whirl to focus. (It didn't help that I kept wiggling around, trying to keep things from poking me in all the wrong places.)

Travis was somewhere else, too — lost in thought, and not at all interested in making idle conversation. We would talk about the morning's escapades later, I knew. But not in public.

As soon as we got inside, Travis picked up an envelope addressed to him which had been slid under the front door. While he read the message, I started unloading my dress. It was a huge relief to pull the lock pick and modified hairpin from my sleeve, where they'd been threatening to pierce a vein for the last hour. Next, I stuck my hand down my dress to unpack my bosom "pocket." First out was my notepad, then a tiny pencil, my gloves, and finally Maggie's silken scarf.

Now ignoring the letter in his hand, Travis watched me with wide eyes. Finally he asked, "Hiding anything else in there?" I nodded no. "You certain? I'd be delighted to check."

Stepping close to him, I slipped my arms around his neck and leaned back. "You go right ahead."

He groaned — a long, sad sound that reminded me of Chewbacca. "Regrettably, I need to go to work."

"I thought your shift wasn't until tonight?"

"It wasn't," he waved the envelope, "but that's changed."

The message had relayed that not only did he have to head to the station pronto, the boy had a very long day and night ahead. The blackout threatened a couple days ago was now in effect. Most annoyingly, the outage wasn't due to an inadequate power supply, but, much like the rolling blackouts California experienced in my lifetime as Robin, came courtesy of politics and greed.

Travis showed me the news as reported in *The Call's* morning edition:

At 12 o'clock last night, the street lights went out and San Francisco was enveloped in darkness. With the exception of five nights each month; during the next four months, San Francisco will be enveloped in darkness on account of the mania of economy that has seized the present Board of Supervisors.

The editors had also written:

All the old excuses for not going home will now be revived by wary husbands who fear to brave a walk on unlighted streets and remain downtown till morning.

For most people, this was not such a big deal. But for the police, this would mean a lot more hours on the job, because everyone from the 10-year-old hooligans to the much older criminals loved to exploit the city under cover of night.

For the next few weeks, he said, the mornings would start with calls to the cops, reporting things like bricks having been thrown through glass, store burglaries, and several opportunistic muggings of both tourists and city residents.

As much as I wanted to tell him what I'd found at Walt and Maggie's, now was not the time.

"Later," he said, and kissed me in the middle of my forehead.

෴෴෴

After he was gone, I cuddled up in bed to review my findings, which were essentially three pages of scribbles. Grabbing a freshly-sharpened pencil, I transcribed each one of them onto fresh sheets of paper — one element per page.

I made a little patchwork out of the notes on Travis's side of the bed, trying various groupings to make sense of them. Propped up on one elbow, I took in the view, trying to see if and how these disparate bits of information tied together. Then I decided to close my eyes.

Already, I knew that naps didn't send me forward or back — they were just plain old mini snooze-fests. The reprieve was appreciated, because I didn't always want to just hop from one situation to another. Sometimes, like right now, I just wanted to doze off without an agenda.

But in the Then as in the Now, the surest way to make the doorbell ring is by trying to get some sleep.

During the past month, you see, I had become a society darling. One of the girls. A regular part of the neighborhood. The ladies nearby had held off to a large degree when I first got home, but shortly after Travis and I started to go out together for evening strolls, that all changed. I had four or five visitors each day of the first week.

It wasn't necessarily a bad thing... just took a lot of getting used to. But the constant barrage of questions and general nosiness? I don't know if I'd ever get comfortable with that.

On the other hand, it was kind of fun to be somewhere I could use every cliche in the book, from cheesy film references to expressions that had long ago jumped the shark.

One of the first to prevail upon me to play hostess had been my neighbor Mrs McAllister, who offered some walnut-studded fudge as a social lubricant.

"It's so interesting," she said just a few minutes into our conversation, "how clever a girl you are. Obviously you don't remember a lot of things, and that's understandable with your injury and all, but — and don't take this the wrong way — but you seem so much more intelligent than I remembered."

Wow. With the backhand on that compliment, she could give Venus and Serena a run for their money.

"...Thank you?" I couldn't help but to offer any gratitude as a question.

"From what I understand, you can even *read* now, is that right?"

"Read — yes, I can read. Are you sure I didn't before?"

"Well, unless you are quite the actress, you couldn't read two words last time we spoke."

"I have no memory of that," I said, which was absolutely the truth.

"Perhaps that knock on your head did you more good than harm," she suggested. "Did you ever figure out how it all happened? That unpleasantness, I mean."

Unpleasantness? I somehow resisted the urge to snort at her use of the term. I responded with the pure vanilla version of the story: "I think I just fell down the stairs somehow. I really don't remember anything."

She kept prodding. "Strange how you could forget that, and so much of your life before, but know so many other things, like how to read and write."

"Isn't it, though?" I said, looking her straight in the eyes, trying to convey so much without saying a word. She glanced around the room, momentarily flustered, then let the subject drop.

Amusingly, Mrs McAllister was just the vanguard. After she left — and apparently told everyone else that I hadn't turned into a werewolf or tried to promote prostitution — my neighbors started to show up non-stop.

The best part of it all was that everyone brought food. There were peach puddings and loganberry muffins, Charlotte russe and lemon cream cakes, fish stews and chicken casseroles, rice croquettes and Scotch eggs, and even creamed cabbage with cheese sauce (which actually tasted slightly better than it sounded — or looked). Come to think of it, they might have been on a mission to fatten me up. In this age, a few extra pounds was a sign of good health.

∽∽∽

Rousing me from my nap the day of the blackout was my neighbor Zelda, who smiled as she proffered a covered dish she apparently intended to trade for gossip. Tempted by the aromatic basil and tomato, I decided she might just get what she came for.

Gesturing to the white porcelain pan she was holding, she explained, "My sister visited the continent last year, and this is a new dish she tried in Italy," she said, beaming with pride.

"I'm sure it's fantastic," I assured her as I ushered her inside. "It smells like pizza, actually."

She couldn't hide her surprise. "Why, that's exactly it!" she said. "I guess you would know because you're Italian. I hope I made it right."

"I'm sure you did, and I am so excited to try it! I haven't had any for a long time." (A "long time" without pizza for me meant a couple weeks, so that was certainly true.)

Zelda followed me into the kitchen, and I put the pan down on top of the stove. With obvious pride, she removed the lid, and inside was something that loosely resembled a rectangular deep-dish pizza. It was covered from side-to-side with cheese, and basil leaves had been carefully positioned on top to spell out ITALIA.

"Thank you," I said. "It's beautiful. Really."

And this was her cue. "So, dear, I have noticed that young man, the police officer, here quite often," she said, at last starting her fishing expedition.

I adopted the rule I'd been taught when my former boss had been involved in a frivolous lawsuit: Keep your answers as short as possible, and don't volunteer any information.

"Yes, he is," I said. "Would you like some water to drink?"

"No, thank you," she said, then rolled that train right back on to the track. "So is he a boarder?"

"I'm sorry — is who a boarder?" When it came to playing dumb, I was a master.

"Your gentleman friend."

Finally. Travis told me early on to be prepared for this line of questioning. Sure, women had beaten around the bush, but nobody had been willing to come right out and ask.

As he told me, "If I'm to stay here with you — particularly overnight, obviously without the benefit of marriage — we must expect people to nose into our business as a matter of course."

I suggested everyone so inclined should attempt to procreate with themselves. (Those weren't my exact words, but I think my meaning was clear.)

My guy treated me incredibly well, but still, it was hard to defeat a lifetime of misogynistic programming. He had a very hard time accepting that my so-called reputation was of no concern to me here. (What was this — high school?)

But although I didn't hold typical Victorian values in high regard, Travis policed the community, and needed to accord respect. So for his sake, I went along with the ruse, and told people he was just renting a room from me.

"What kind of idiot is going to believe that after they see you and me out together all the time, arm in arm?" I asked him.

"Propriety states your assurance is guarantee enough," he told me. "For anyone to suggest otherwise in public would reflect poorly on them, not you, so it will be avoided."

"So we can just tell people you're just innocently renting a room, and even though this ploy is totally transparent, these women are going to buy it?"

He nodded.

I pressed on. "But if one chick tries to read between the lines and create a scandal out of it, other people are going to think she's just a freak with a dirty mind?"

After taking a few beats to process my blather, he nodded. "Yes, that's about the sum of it."

"Wow. Sucks to be them."

"But remember — what is said behind closed doors is entirely different. People will have their concerns and suspicions, and might try to avoid you," he said, sounding apologetic.

"Well, you already know what I think about that."

"Yes, yes," he said, holding up his hands. "No need to repeat, thank you very much."

Fortunately, having been appeased by Italian food, the notion of saying anything untoward to sweet Zelda was the furthest thing from my mind.

With a smile, I took my first bite of the pizza. It was actually pretty good — especially for a first-timer — though could do with a little more tomato and a little less dough.

"So which room does he rent?"

"The one upstairs, at the end of the hall," I answered from off the top of my head after I finished my first bite. "It's great pizza. Nice job!"

Please drop the subject. Despite my twenty-first century values, I was starting to feel a little embarrassed.

"I'm glad you are enjoying it," she said, but still didn't touch the slice in front of her. "Are you going to be renting out your other rooms?"

"You know, I hadn't really thought about it. Maybe!"

"How did the policeman come to board here, then?" Man, this lady was persistent.

"He needed a place to live, and I had this big house with just me rattling around in it, so it just made sense," I said.

Her hands were folded primly in her lap. "How ever did you find him? I didn't see a sign."

I chewed my little bite twice as long as I needed to. "Right after I got home from the hospital, I went downtown and then got lost." I took another little nibble of pizza before adding, "I found my way to the police station and he helped me home."

We continued in a similar exchange for another couple minutes until she finally ran out of steam.

Funny how people weren't nearly as chatty when they didn't score any new goods on the gossip front.

∽ ∽ ∽

I suppose part of the problem I had being buddy-buddy with the locals boiled down to the fact that I liked the people here better when I could just watch them from afar.

Often when I was by myself, I used some quiet moments to observe my fellow citizens. In particular, I loved to spend the evening sitting in the window of the upstairs bedroom, which had bay windows overlooking the street.

I'd keep the room dark, and curtains mostly closed, so I could quietly observe folks strolling down the street, some solo and others arm-in-arm, during the late afternoon and evening. With the sun's golden glow on their gorgeous gowns and the gents' natty attire, it almost felt like it was an elegant and entrancing parade just for my benefit.

Then as dusk ebbed into night, silence fell along with the darkness.

Here was a time and a place where there were no little blue lights from computers and TV sets on standby, no red numbers on alarm clocks, no microwave oven LEDs waiting for commands, no light switches with just a little hint of a glow so you could find them in the dark, and if your telephone could do double duty as a doorstop, but provided not even the tiniest hint of illumination.

At first, the depth of the darkness here had been unsettling. Eventually, though, I got used to it, and even came to appreciate it. The world of the Then was one in which tomorrow would wait.

※ ※ ※

I'd been struggling to stay lucid, but was a few breaths away from deep sleep when I felt footsteps shake the bedroom floor a little. Before my brain even had time to switch to 'it's a scary earthquake!' mode, I realized all the movement was from Travis finally getting home. Only the tiniest pinpricks of moonlight illuminated the room.

Through half-closed eyes, I watched him walk to the window, push back the curtains, and start to slide up the sash.

"Where are you going?" I asked, my voice a hoarse whisper.

"Where am I *going*?" he repeated back to me. "I'm not leaving through the window, if that's what you were wondering." He locked the sash open, and I could feel cool night air drift up the bed.

"Sorry — so tired. Not thinking. Glad you're staying."

"Go to sleep, you silly person," Travis said, and crawled into bed. I savored the feeling of him nuzzling against my neck for as long as I could... but before I knew it, I was waking up, all alone and far away.

56: The Now – Summer begins

From the crown of my head to the tips of my toes, I was covered in muck — dirt and potting soil and compost and mulch. It was smelly and sticky and for the first time in my life, I actually enjoyed the experience.

The girls and I were all outside with our little trowels and metal stakes creating not just wasn't any garden, but a little experiment in upcycling and growing our own food, inspired by my jaunts to the past. Now that school was over, this garden would be our summer project.

There, everyone grows something and shares the bounty with friends, family and neighbors. Canning and pickling were both popular, and they seemed to make jam and jelly out of every kind of fruit imaginable. I wanted to grow my own produce, too, but needed to wait. It was three months earlier in the calendar there, and weather was still too harsh for new plants.

In lieu of that, a few weeks ago, the girls and I started to sprout our own potatoes, sweet potatoes and ginger. At the same time, we took cuttings from a bunch of other veggies and herbs — including green onions, celery, rosemary, cilantro and garlic — and started to "re-grow" them. Now that they had little roots of their own, we were nestling them into the dirt in a rooftop planter box. At the end of each section, we pushed a skewer into the ground, upon which we hung a plastic bread tie with the name of that row's crop.

"Where does mud come from?" Iris asked as she used a white plastic watering can to flood the spot where we'd just planted twenty-two garlic cloves.

My daughters, particularly the youngest, never took a break from learning — usually through a nonstop barrage of questions. I loved them for it and did my best to explain what I knew, resisting the urge to hand over my phone with the words, "Search engines are your friends."

"Well, mud is wet dirt," I said, "and dirt is made from lots and lots of things. It's mostly something like sand or clay, but there are also bits of old plants, and tiny little pieces of all kinds of other things."

"Like food?"

I told her that, after several months, many different kinds of food would break down and turn into dirt, then made a mental note to teach her about composting.

"So what about dogs? Would they turn into dirt?"

Oh, where was she going with this? "Yes, I guess dogs that have been dead a very long time break down like that, too."

"And people?"

"Sometimes, yeah. After a really long time."

"Like a hundred years." This wasn't a question — she was just defining "a really long time" for both of us. Then she asked, "So will I turn into mud one day, too?"

I wasn't going to lie to the kid... and I had a feeling she already knew the answer, anyway. "Well, probably. You'd be part of it, mixed in with everything else."

She was quiet for a little while. I watched her rub the mud between her fingers, evaluating its consistency and color. Finally she said, "Cool."

༄ ༄ ༄

The rest of our day was spent in the pool — or, in my case, in a chaise poolside after a quick dip. The girls chased around with the other kids who lived in the complex, and they wore themselves out swimming and diving, snorkeling and somersaulting, racing and playing.

After a full day outdoors, home — with its air conditioning, butter-soft padded chenille sofas and an automatic refrigerator well-stocked with groceries from around the world — felt like the ultimate in luxury. As I curled my toes into the thick pile of the living room rug, I decided the only thing that could make this day better would be if Travis was here with us.

It wasn't until after dinner that I finally went online — and it was only out of a feeling of obligation that I even did so. I had to check. I had to make sure that the next morning, I wasn't going to wake up in a world bent or broken by a disaster I could have prevented.

My standard searches came up empty, and my newspaper previews returned nothing more eventful than an awesome sale on Easter hats — I could get my very own flowery monstrosity for the bargain price of just $9.50.

As for using the bits of information I'd gleaned when I was snooping around the Houlihan/Gallagher abode, I would have to wait. Most of my notes were in reference to help wanted ads, and I couldn't remember any of the specifics now. The sole bank name I could recall was the German Savings & Loan Company, and it took all of two minutes to determine they had done a pretty good job staying out of the news around the turn of the century, and no news was usually good news.

In record time on that fine June night, I'd done all I needed to do, and could go back to my regularly scheduled life. Right?

Not so fast. Messing with my head was the fact that I was relieved to have a break from all of the searching and finding, learning and sharing. It felt like a dereliction of duty or something.

It required a hot bath and a bit of meditation to remind myself that it was okay to take a break every now and then.

There's no denying that my life — or, rather, my *lives* — were wonderful, and I was unbelievably fortunate. But the dual existences were also overwhelming and exhausting. I was essentially jamming two days of living between every page that I flipped on my desk calendar.

I didn't have a "real" life anymore. I had two.

And now that the kids were off school for the next two and a half months? The struggle to juggle family with work and the ever-present past was going to be more intense than ever.

Could I do it? Of course, because I had no choice. It wasn't a question of *if* — only a matter of *how*.

57: Beside the seaside

I knew I was back the moment I felt my temples pounding. How sweet. I'd gone to bed with a headache on my last night in the Then, and here it was again, waiting for me like a faithful little puppy.

It was always so nice to go home to the Now, where, if I had cramps or body aches, I could just pop a couple ibuprofen and know I would soon feel human again. Because of the easy availability of such quickie remedies, I suppose I felt a little bit cocky about the advances of my time zone.

"I tell you what: Over-the-counter painkillers that you can take anytime you need are some of the greatest things ever," were the first words out of my mouth that morning — apropos of nothing, as far as Travis knew. "I mean, seriously, what do you guys have that even compares. Headache powder? Tastes awful and only works for certain things... and not always even then, in my experience."

"We have whiskey."

"Oh, yeah. Touché."

᭥ ᭥ ᭥

"These are the job listings for women they had circled," I said as I handed him a pile of nine papers, each of which said something like "Nursery governess - 1783 Larkin" or "Cooking/housework & childcare - 1241 Leavenworth."

I also had a separate set of notes, which I figured pertained to Wally's job search. For men, people were looking to fill different positions — for instance, a driver was desired for the residents of 1905 Washington, and the property at 1178 Sacramento Street needed a groundskeeper.

Travis shuffled through the two piles of paper once, then again. I could almost hear the gears whirring. Finally, he spoke.

"These homes — on Leavenworth, Washington, Sacramento, Larkin, Pacific and so forth — every single one of these addresses is in the Nob Hill area."

Nob Hill was San Francisco's ritzy area. We're not just talking "the nice part of town" fancy, though. Along with the standard expensive homes, owned by businessmen and bankers were some of the most palatial residences outside of New York City. Prominent mansions had been built on top of the hill by the "Big 4" railroad tycoons (one of whom was a former California governor).

"I suppose that makes sense — fancy neighborhood, lots of money. Get hired there because they probably pay well."

"But the thing is, they don't. Not usually. People want to work there, thinking it's all so dead posh, but the wages are often very low. Easily lower than you might get elsewhere."

"I take it that you have had some experience with them."

"Some of the families, yes. They seem to believe that the entire San Francisco police force, in fact, works for them," he said with a little huff. "But no matter. I am a sworn officer, and will always do my duty."

"'To Protect and to Serve,'" I said, quoting the old LAPD motto.

"I quite like that."

"Well, I can't take credit."

"Suspected as much, but like it anyway."

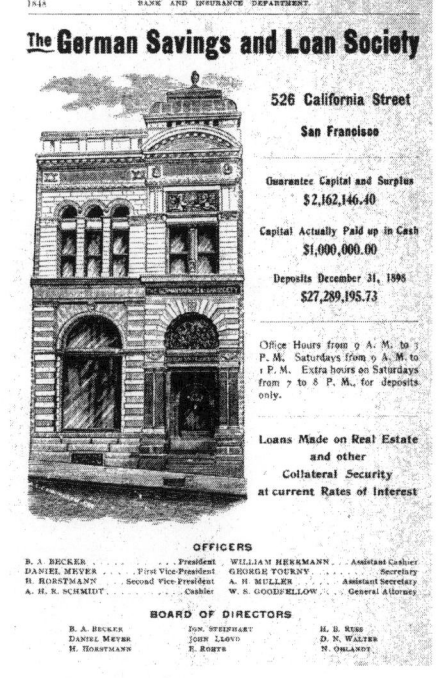

Travis's main career goal was to become a detective one day. He didn't want to be police chief or a captain — he wanted not to lead others, but to have the freedom to follow his own hunches and make sense of the seemingly senseless. I knew, from my recent peek ahead, that he was going to make it. By watching him get into investigative mode today, it was sort of like getting a sneak preview.

I told him there were a few other things to check out — pages in the Crocker-Langley San Francisco directory for 1899. It was the phone book of its day, and Travis knew exactly where there was a copy.

"Bottom drawer of the desk, far right side. Before you ask: I know because

I put it there." I gave his nose a little tweak and he ran off to get it.

"Page 1842," I said, and he read off the ad on the corresponding page.

"Bank of California."

"1848?"

"That would be the German Savings & Loan."

"Yeah — I remembered that one," I laughed. "And the last page is 1851."

"The Continental Building & Loan Association."

I added the names to the leaves of paper, then told him, "Finally, we need to find out what was on page eight of Tuesday's paper, in the lower left corner. On the copy they had inside, it had been torn off," I said. I held up my hands so Travis wouldn't burst my bubble quite yet. "I know, I know — they might have used it just to spit out a piece of gum or something, but I think it would be easy enough to check."

He nodded his agreement and took the last little paper from me. "Fair enough love," he told me. "We have heaps of newspapers down at the station. When I'm there, I will also look up these addresses, and see if I can put names to them. Check each of them for reports of burglaries or any other disturbances in our records."

"Sounds perfect. I can't wait."

He checked his watch. "I'm afraid you might have to. Need a bit of extra time to sort this out, so will be home late. You'll be all right?"

I gripped my hands together and looked skyward before saying breathlessly, "I think I will be able to manage."

"Speaking of late nights, there's one more thing I need to ask." He took my hand, and, in a show of mock sincerity, asked, "Do you have plans for dinner this Thursday, Miss?"

᭜ ᭜ ᭜

This morning, when I packed a lunch for Travis, I had also made one for myself. That was fortunate, because my plans for the day had changed. I wouldn't be shopping or researching. Instead, I was finally going somewhere I'd been avoiding ever since I arrived in this version of San Francisco.

Today, I would journey to the westernmost part of the city with my own eyes. What I sought lay along the ocean, on the north end of the beach, right where the land started to turn into the opening of the bay… otherwise known as the Golden Gate. There I would visit two places that were merely relics in my day — shadows of their former selves: The Cliff House and Sutro Baths.

The Baths in my time were just some water-filled ruins in the ground, visited mostly by seagulls and the occasional tourist. The whole complex had been ravaged by fire in the mid-1960s and never rebuilt. But in the Then? The huge and extravagant swimming pool establishment wasn't yet four years old, and still basked in all its glory on the very edge of the ocean.

I took the Sutro Electric Railroad as far as it would go, and disembarked near the entrance to the Baths, designed to look like a Greek temple.

Once I went inside, the scene was breathtaking, mind-boggling, and almost surreal. To think of that place as being only a place to go swimming is like saying the Empire State Building is just another high-rise with offices. Truth, yes, but not the whole truth.

Shortly after the facility opened, this portal into another sphere was described in an 1894 souvenir book "Sutro Baths, Cliff House, Sutro Heights"

From [the main entrance], by broad stairways, flanked with shrubs and flowers, the Museum gallery is reached. Here are placed the archaeological and other collections of Mr Sutro. Mummies and innumerable other curiosities from ancient Egypt, a goodly number of specimens of Aztec pottery and art that show a curious resemblance to the work from the land of the Nile, beautiful fans from various countries,

From the Museum gallery, the visitor can reach the Baths, either by stairways or by the elevator. Striking as is the first view, familiarity only makes it more striking. Its size seizes the imagination, yet it is not oppressive, owing to the lightness and airiness of the structure. Sitting on a rock, watching the waves of the Pacific, dreaming of a way to utilize the gigantic power of the sea, part of this whilom dream of Sutro's is here turned into reality.

Nearly three hours were spent — invested, really — in touring the Baths. I ate my lunch on a bench along the Main Promenade, and explored the galleries and exhibits. And while I didn't go in the water, but watched hundreds of others jump, dive, slide and swim in the various pools. The timeless delight that radiated from the children in particular was mesmerizing to behold.

After climbing staircase after staircase, I emerged into the blustery day and headed downhill.

Of everything in this city that had been lost over the years, I think the demise of the Cliff House broke my heart the most. That was one landmark that had so perfectly exemplified the city's style and grace.

The first Cliff House had been built in 1863, but the version that existed in 1900 had opened just four years before. Designed to honor the French chateau style, the building jutting out on the cliffs over the Pacific, and featured eight stories of grandeur, along with an observation tower that was 200 feet above the water. It survived a huge fire and then the great earthquake… only to be burned to the ground in 1907.

I lingered only a little as I passed its front doors, but didn't go inside. Stepping over the threshold was something so special, I wanted to do it with Travis at my side. I only had a couple days to wait — until Thursday night.

There was some sort of police function in one of the Cliff House's banquet rooms, and though Travis wasn't originally on the guest list, he wrangled an invitation because he knew how thrilled I would be about attending an event there.

I followed the path that led me closer and closer to sea level, then took the steps down to Ocean Beach. I covered half the distance from the wall to the surf before spreading out my scarf and settling myself in the sand.

That was pretty much the same spot I'd chosen the last time I was here — well over a century from now. From here, I could see the Cliff House and Seal Rocks, and, beyond, the wide horizon where blue waves briefly shimmied toward the sky, then melted back into the whole.

There's nothing like staring at the ocean and the sky above to make you feel like an infinitesimal speck of nothing.

In the 21st century, there was a building on the same spot with the same name… but where there used to be a lovingly-crafted castle, now only stood a much smaller, flat-topped white structure that, from a distance, I thought resembled a prison.

Truly, though, it was the juxtaposition that rubbed my nerves raw. The spectacle before me now exemplified everything beautiful and wonderful in this age. In comparison, the squat and safe, modern and minimalist version rebuilt in 2003 seemed depressingly emblematic of my era.

I was becoming quite the proper housewife, and had dinner all ready ten minutes before Travis got home. I was wearing an apron and everything.

He was about an hour later than usual, but he'd made good on his promise to get the names that went with each of the addresses.

Sitting side-by-side at the dining table, I dished up a Denver omelet, and we dished on the fragments of information he had found.

"This family — specifically, Mrs Dougall — has made several calls to the police, but it all seems to be for nothing. There was someone who rang her doorbell but disappeared. The Bluecoat dispatched found there had been a package delivery. She also reported a strange man 'hovering' around their carriage house, and that turned out to be a new gent her husband had just hired."

"It's a wonder that woman hasn't frightened herself to death," I said, and that got a sad nod.

"One family had a confirmed break-in, but otherwise, there's nothing else to report," Travis said. "One tiny detail, but it's probably nothing. One of the homes belongs to the president of a bank — a bank they marked in the book. It could be coincidence..."

"Or it could mean something."

"Precisely," he said, and popped a fallen bit of ham into his mouth. "I thought for the next step, you could take these names back to your time to check there as well. Does that sound good?"

It sounded perfect, and I told him so. The only problem with the plan was the second part: memorizing the list long enough to look all of those people up in the future.

"Well, how about we put an ad in the paper for you? You can just go look it up in your time, and go from there?"

"That's a great id..." I started, but then couldn't finish my sentence. My knees collapsed, and the world started to get fuzzy. I was so tired. I felt my head tip forward, chin to my chest, and I couldn't pull it back up. I felt Travis catch me before I dropped to the floor.

"Jen! Jen, what's wrong? What are you feeling?"

"Just... want to... sleep. So tired."

"No — not like this," he said, and I felt him patting my face. "This isn't right."

I was so close to falling off to sleep... and then, as quickly as it came on, I was okay again. I sat up and looked around. "That was truly bizarre."

Travis felt my forehead and checked my pulse.

"Maybe my blood sugar level dropped or something," I offered, then realized I really felt fine — didn't have any of the lingering spaciness I'd experienced from a few bouts of hypoglycemia in the past. What didn't make sense was that I had been snacking all day, and was right in the middle of dinner now.

Once he was sure I wasn't going to tip over, Travis rushed off to the kitchen and got me an apple. "Eat. It has sugar."

I'd finished my omelet and wasn't even hungry anymore, but I ate. For him. In between bites, I said, "You know, maybe I need some of that Pinkham's Vegetable Compound." I laughed. Travis rolled his eyes.

A lot of women here took these special "tonics," as they called them. They supposedly helped with pretty much whatever ails you — cramps, low-energy, sleeping problems and all the other stuff we're still dealing with today.

Once upon a time in the future, I looked up the ingredient list, and found out that — surprise, surprise — they're really mostly alcohol. I gathered that there is sort of an unspoken understanding these treatments for "female complaints" existed mostly to help get a little buzz on. (Some brands went even further, and laced their potions with cocaine or opium. It was all legal at the time.)

"So where were we?" I asked.

"Do you really want to talk about this now?" Travis said, and I could hear the worry in his voice. "Perhaps we wait until you're feeling better."

"I feel absolutely fine. Really. Plus, I just had an apple."

He sighed, so I began. "I was just about to say I thought the classified newspaper ad was..." and then I swooned again. Travis caught me before I started to crumple this time. Almost as a joke, I yelled a new ending to that sentence, "... was a really bad idea!"

And I felt less tired.

I spoke the next words slowly and deliberately. "No, we should absolutely not place an ad in the paper."

Then I was right back to pegging the meter at 100% normal.

There was a long silence. Finally Travis said, "Okay, what was that?"

I shook my head. "So strange! It felt like I was drugged or something — being knocked out. I was exhausted for a second there, but now I'm fine."

He cleared his throat and said, "I'm just wondering if there's a chance you have…" He shook his head in a "you know" gesture.

"Oh my God — what do you think I have? Smallpox? Scarlet fever? Something even worse?" My throat was choking on all the possibilities.

"No, no! Nothing like that," he said. Glancing over at him, I swear it looked like he was blushing. "I know — I've gone red. Just wondering if, well… if you could have fallen pregnant."

That idea — and the phrasing — instantly launched me into a giggle fit. "Did you really just use the words 'fallen pregnant'? That has to be one of the worst expressions ever!" When I finally caught my breath, I expanded on the topic, "And no. Not possible. I just received crimson confirmation of that fact."

There was more blushing, some sputtering, and eventually he looked away. He was, though, still smiling a little.

Something was spinning through my head, but I didn't know quite how to explain it. Eventually I said, "I think I know what it was." Breathe, breathe. "First let me say I realize that outside of the context of being a time traveler, this would sound crazy." Travis nodded, and I continued. "I think those little episodes were me being told not to do something, by some part of myself, or by whatever sent me back here."

When I thought about it, I realized that I had experienced a few much more minor bouts with fatigue that came on suddenly and inexplicably. It had mostly happened in the Now, and usually, it was enough to get me off the computer and into bed for the night.

"That is quite vexing," Travis said, and started rubbing the back of his neck.

"Yes but no," I said, and leaned up to give him a kiss. "Maybe it's part of the price I pay for getting to be here with you. Totally worth it." He kissed me back, and then held me close. I knew his hand was in the middle of my back so he could feel my heartbeat — making sure that I was still alive, and that I was still here with him.

I started to sway my hips, dancing in time to my heart, but without any music. We had done this several times before, and I knew he found it soothing when we would step and swing. "Also," I said quietly, "it could be keeping us from veering off track or making a bad decision. Let's think positive."

I gave him the beat, and he followed my lead while I turned and twirled, out into the room, then back into his arms. A gentle lilting melody filled my head, and I hoped that in some way, he could hear it, too.

58: Fairy godmothers

I planned to wear my nicest dress to the Cliff House — the taffeta one that had last been in play at the player-piano party. When I pulled it out of the closet on Wednesday morning, I found a stain the size of my hand on the side of the skirt.

Since the lighting inside my house was relatively dim, I brought the dress outside, which was the only place I could get a good enough look to assess the extent of the damage.

In the daylight, the spot looked suspiciously like a where a splash of punch had landed. I, um, think I might know how that happened.

While I'd pretty much figured out how to do my own laundry, this gown was made of silk — and I was at a loss when it came to do-it-yourself dry cleaning.

Enter Mrs Fletcher, she of the famous fudge. The sparkle of the few sequins on the aqua bodice had sparkled and caught her eye from across the street, she told me as she walked up.

"Lovely dress, my dear," she said, and started to examine the reddish blotch. "Terrible stain, though. Is it fresh?" She visibly cringed when I told her it was more than a month old.

She ran her fingers over the fabric and asked, "I suppose you hoped to wear this soon?"

"Tomorrow night. There's a thing at the Cliff House." Party? Gala? I didn't even know what to call it.

"Oh my goodness," she gasped. "Do you mean the police benefit?"

I nodded — surprised she knew about it at all.

"Yes, yes, I read about that. They say the mayor's even going to be there. A rare privilege!" She looked back at the dress and frowned. "I'm afraid you're not going to be able to get this stain tended to in time, if such a thing is even possible."

"That's what I was afraid of. I'm going to need another dress, when it was a total fluke that I found one that fit so well in the first place!"

Mrs Fletcher sized me up, looked back at the dress, then back to me. "A new dress? Hmm," she said. "Not necessarily." And those turned out to be the magic words.

∽ ∽ ∽

She called on two of our neighbors, and by that afternoon, the three ladies had a plan. One of the women, whose name I forgot as soon as I heard it, was "in the family way" for the second time in two years. The kind woman didn't think she would ever fit back into her old formalwear... particularly not a certain black taffeta gown, so contributed it to the cause. The dress was far too big for me on top, but the skirt portion... well, that could be tailored to fit.

That is where the third lady came in — Mrs Woods — who had spent years working as a seamstress. In her words, it would be "easy as pie" to connect the top half of my aqua dress to the black bottom portion of the other. "Plus," she whispered to me, "if you get a stain on it, it's not likely to show."

Under the direction of the sewing expert, Mrs Fletcher and I set about separating the top and bottom portions of the two dresses. Once she had done a brief fitting, Mrs Woods took them back to her house to stitch them together on her Singer machine.

While we waited for her return to perform any final alterations, I helped my new friend in the kitchen. Today, though, there was no chocolate on the menu, but she was preparing food for the next several days.

She used one hand to quickly crack two eggs into a small bowl, and the other started whisking them as they fell. Then she beat in a cup of milk.

"You are quite the chef," I said doing my best to make appropriate conversation. "Is that your favorite hobby?"

"Hobby?" she said, and then there was a pause. "I suppose I think of it more like my job."

"Because it feels like work?"

"No, dear. Because it is my role. What I do. How I contribute," she laughed. "It's the way I can keep my family healthy and strong, you see. I want them to enjoy their food, so I make every effort to make things that are palatable to each one."

I watched as she eyeballed a cup of flour and poured it into a larger bowl, then did the same with a cup of cornmeal. Next, she tipped spoonfuls of salt, sugar and baking soda and started to blend the dry mixture.

"With your talent, you could open your own restaurant — or at least a candy shop," I told her. "I'm serious. Yours was the most amazing fudge I have ever had."

"Oh, I wouldn't want a job like that," she said, but beamed at the suggestion. "I already believe that my job here is already the most important of all."

With the ease of a seasoned pro, she gently folded in the egg and milk into the dry ingredients.

"Haven't you ever wanted to go out into the world? Make a difference to people?"

"Well, of course, child — that is precisely what I am doing," she said, with a smile on top of an expression of confusion. I think she thought I was trying to bait her, when I was only trying to encourage any entrepreneurial spark. (I figured that any progress for women in this time would be a good thing.)

She pulled out a darkened metal baking pan from a cabinet and started to slather the inside surfaces with butter.

"Home is the essence of life," Mrs Fletcher said as she worked. "It must be cared for and tended to properly for a family to flourish. Don't you agree?"

"Yes, of course," I answered, because how couldn't I agree? I was a mom, too — not that I could tell her so.

"I realize you are too young to have had children, but know this: When it comes down to it, your home holds your heart. It's where you can be yourself. Where you can be with your family. Where you entertain friends and neighbors," she said, nodding to me. "It is the foundation of everything else. There is not one thing in this lifetime that does not depend on a healthy home."

While she poured the cornbread mixture into the pan, she continued her counsel. "As we well know from our neighbors up there on Nob Hill, you can have all the money in the world, and the biggest house, and yet not a very nice home life. Do you know what I mean?"

I nodded, and she looked pleased.

"That's because you can't build a home out of money. You build a home with love, care, time and effort." She slid the pan into the oven and shut the door firmly. "So if you do not do these things — you know, cooking and cleaning and everything else required to make a good home — for the people you love and care about the most, what's the point?"

Before I could even think of a response to her thoughtful words, Mrs Woods slipped in the door, cradling my new dress in her arms.

I slipped it on right then and there, and after they expertly fastened and adjusted it just so, both women pronounced the fit to be "like a glove."

"It you wear it with a black beaded necklace and a black hat," said Mrs Fletcher, beaming once again, "you, dear girl, will be the fairest of them all."

59: The Now & the Then – Of fairy tales

On my first day of Mission: Memorization, I recalled only three of the five names. I did get a hit, though — one of the women at the second address on my list killed herself in 1903 by turning on the gas in their guest cottage and going to sleep. The newspaper said that she had "recently been despondent over some financial matters," but didn't elaborate. I couldn't locate any other seemingly relevant information on the family before or after that point.

After my second trip back from the Then, I tried a different technique, and remembered all five of the families on my list. Again, there was one hit, a guy named Elliot Cooper who was interesting to me in two ways. First, he was the president of a bank (though apparently not one Walt & Maggie highlighted). Second, the poor guy was booked to have a fatal heart attack next month.

On their own, those clues meant nothing much — but I felt sure that, in time, and combined with other research, we might start to discover a pattern. I wasn't just being optimistic, either. At some deep level, I simply knew that the frightening and borderline insane search the other day was going to turn out to being key to something big, something important... and something I needed to change.

                                       ᔆ ᔆ ᔆ

Summer vacation meant a lot of free time for the kids... and as young 'uns are wont to do, they hoped I would fill it for them with non-stop fun and frivolity.

While they were smart enough to understand I wasn't going to be putting on daily puppet shows or letting them veg all day in front of the TV, we would need a couple weeks to come up with a new schedule. (What we'd done last summer wouldn't necessarily work, as the girls were now a year older and ever so much more mature... according to Lily, anyhow.)

The most effective tool in my arsenal was, like last summer, our neighbor Aggie. Her grandkids lived in another state, so my kiddos were sort of her grandchildren by proxy. So I could work, she offered to take the girls to the pool and up to the rooftop gardens. They would also just hang out next door, where, if things were anything like last year, they would cook and draw, and she'd teach them card games, including cribbage and pinochle.

Still, that didn't mean I wouldn't have plenty of time with my progeny. For one thing, I was still the only one who would tell them about the latest adventures of the Rainbow Princess.

"Last night," I told the girls, "Rainbow took a very special carriage ride over roads and up hills and down hills, and right to the very edge of the ocean."

"Oh!" Iris said, her intake of breath accompanied by wide eyes. "Was the carriage made out of a pumpkin, like in *Cinderella*?"

"Actually, It was made of something called ebony, which is a beautiful wood they use to make the black keys on a piano. It was so shiny and polished, though, it reflected everything just like a mirror."

༄ ༄ ༄

Travis had hired a gleaming black Hansom cab to deliver us directly to the door of the Cliff House. It was my first time being in an enclosed coach, complete with red velvet seats and curtains on the windows. The thing was gorgeous.

Used to the rowdy bunches on public transit, it was so remarkable to see the city slip by so quietly. I snuggled up to Travis, who looked perfect and polished in his dress uniform. Ensconced in our own warm and comfortable little chamber, that ride ranked as one of the most romantic experiences I had ever known.

Alas, as is true for everything wonderful, the time passed too quickly. Before I knew it, our destination filled the view.

While it was very much a part of San Francisco, the way the Cliff House stood tall at the end of the earth set it apart from the city. It almost felt like a doorway to another realm.

༄ ༄ ༄

"Do you know what was right there, where the land met the sea?"

"A castle!" they said in unison. These girls knew their fairy tales.

Then Iris asked, "Was the castle big and huge like that place we went?"

I blinked a few times and quickly searched my memory for any castle I'd visited with the kiddos. No surprise that I couldn't remember a single one. "Which place was that, sweets?" (Have I mentioned how much I love the way a five-year-old's mind works?)

"You know — the place that was tall and big and brown and had the big pointy windows with all the colors." She paused, and I thought some more.

"Like in *Hunchback*!" Lily added when she figured it out.

"Oh — you mean Grace Cathedral? The big church in San Francisco we went to a couple months ago?" That building had, in fact, been modeled after Paris' Notre Dame.

They both nodded vigorously.

"Well, I guess the castle wasn't *quite* that big or fancy, but it was close, and they had a lot of different things there. For instance, there were more than ten different dining rooms, and many beautiful ballrooms where people could dance."

We drove up to the entrance, and the moment we stopped, a young man in a uniform opened the cab and offered me his hand. I pretended I'd done this a hundred times before and said a silent prayer that I wouldn't miss the tiny step and wind up dragging the poor boy down to the ground with me.

Travis took my arm, and we walked through one of the Gothic archways, a few steps across the porch, and then inside.

From the outside, the building looked sizeable... but in reality, the place felt *enormous* — probably in no small part due to the high ceilings that still impressed this girl who had only known rooms to be just eight feet high. (The surreal effect was exacerbated by the fact that I was looking at everything from about eight inches lower than normal.)

We were immediately escorted through the stately center hallway, and out to the balcony overlooking the ocean and Seal Rocks.

Every window offered the kind of breathtakingly beautiful view that forced you to stop mid-step and just stare. Watching the sunset light up the world — shades of pink and orange set against the still-blue sky — then seeing it melt down beyond the horizon was practically a religious experience.

Now that I was here, I was so glad I'd waited and not peeked inside before. The first impression is nearly always the most indelible, and now those beautiful first moments were etched in my mind.

෴෴෴

"Why was Rainbow at the castle?"

I leaned toward them and whispered, "Because she was going to a wonderful ball."

Lily clutched my wrist and asked, "Did she have a beautiful ball gown, like Belle in *Beauty and the Beast*?"

"She did!"

Iris wanted to know, "Did her fairy godmother make it for her?"

"Not just one, but *three* fairy godmothers."

"Like in *Sleeping Beauty*!" she squealed as I wondered how many more Disney movie titles we would work into this conversation.

෴෴෴

The building had three main floors, three more of what they called "attic floors," then two tower floors. There was no shortage of amenities — not with the wealth of elegant dining rooms, bars, kitchens, ballrooms, reception rooms, parlors, private lunchrooms, exhibition halls, and even art and photo galleries. The whole place seemed to just go on and on.

Throughout, the attention to detail was breathtaking. I can only imagine how many trees gave their lives to be glossy paneled doors and intricately-carved picture rails and all manner of other wooden moldings, but each bit of that forest was truly celebrated in death. Many of the floors I saw were also made of wood — parquet-style inlaid wood and highly-polished dark hardwood.

In the grander rooms and several public areas, there seemed to be a mountain's worth of stone flooring — marble and granite — along with detailed mosaic tile masterpieces. I peeked in a door to one of the other banquet rooms, and saw it was lushly carpeted with a huge expanse of navy blue and golden tufted wool in some regal motif.

Nothing was left plain. If there was a passageway, it was arched. If there was lighting, it was via a stunning chandelier or a row of elegant sconces that bathed the area in a warm glow. Nearly every wall was wallpapered or wood-clad, but also featured something more, whether a painting or a mirror or a sculpture or a clock.

Strangely enough — to me, in any case — the Cliff House was not a hotel in the sense that you could get a room for a night or three. Instead, it might be best described as more of a public country club, or perhaps a top-tier hotel without sleeping accommodations. They had an abundance of rooms available for daytime rentals, where you could host anything from a cozy luncheon for four to a huge and lavish wedding for four hundred.

The space for our banquet was somewhere in the middle. To me, the scene seemed very Victorian — that is, gloriously over-the-top.

The newspaper the next day described the fête as so: "The dining room on the upper floor was handsomely decorated in honor of the mayor and distinguished guests. Bunting, flags, flowers, palms and ferns literally covered the walls, and the table, which was arranged in horseshoe shape, presented a superb spectacle."

భ భ భ

Since she was going through a growth spurt, Lily seemed to be perpetually hungry, which meant her next question was no surprise: "Was there good food?"

"Yes, they had a lot of great food… and, I guess, some icky stuff, too."

"Like what? The icky stuff, I mean."

Of *course* my girls would want to hear about the gross foods first. "How about... turtle soup."

There was a rare moment of silence as they contemplated that. Then Iris asked, "Like turtles *swimming* in soup?"

"Not so much... More like chicken soup, except made with turtle instead of chicken."

"That sounds horrible," Lily said, and I had to agree. In fact, when the man behind the ladle told me what he was going to scoop into a bowl for me, I had to work hard to hide my look of horror.

Iris was still thinking. "Was it turtle *noodle* soup?"

"I don't think there were noodles in it. But Rainbow didn't actually try it, because she thought it sounded terrible."

"You know, she should have tried it — just one bite," Lily told me, parroting official parent-speak.

"Well, unfortunately, you weren't there to remind her of that."

"I think Rainbow was okay, mom. It was a bad idea to have that there. I bet nobody else wanted it, either," she said in her most reassuring tone. "What other food did they have?"

"Well, there were several kinds of fish, and also oysters. There was chicken, along with squab, which is sort of like chicken. Duck and goose. Stuff called sweetbreads, which is really some animal parts — but it's not sweet, and there's no bread. Cream of lettuce soup, which tasted better than it sounded. Let's see," I reviewed the buffet table in my head for the most interesting stuff. "Oh yeah — there was steamed pickled pig's feet and pickled lamb's tongue — and no, she didn't try those, either."

But Lily was done hearing me talk about stuff she'd never dream of eating. "Okay, okay — was there anything yummy? Stuff we'd like."

"How about mashed potatoes and roast beef?" She gave me the so-so hand gesture. "Lots of different cheeses? Crackers?" I got just a shrug for those.

"Raspberry ice cream?" Her eyes lit up. Dessert — of course. That had been my favorite part of the spread, too. "They also had apple pie and peach tarts, plus little tiny cakes with flowers made out of frosting, and custard pie. There were also cookies and chocolate eclairs, steamed plum pudding and blueberry pie, along with lemon sorbet and hazelnut ice cream," I told them. "Believe me — Rainbow thought there was plenty of good stuff at the dessert table."

After all that, Iris, who'd been listening quietly for the past couple minutes, had just one question for me. "What did they do with the turtle shells?"

⇜ ⇜ ⇜

Aside from the scenic locale and unique buffet foods, the remainder of the gala was a blur of names and faces. For the sake of my escort, I kept my behavior in check... which was made a little simpler because before we even entered the banquet room, I'd made the decision to drink only water.

I do remember receiving many compliments on my dress — one woman even described it as "most daring" and "exceptionally beautiful" in one breath.

Travis had showed me around the room, and before I knew it, we were in a receiving line to meet Mayor Phelan, the wealthy son of a prominent family who had made their fortune during the Gold Rush. His was one name that didn't escape my attention, because it was one I knew from my own time, thanks to a prominent flatiron-style building downtown. Both the ladies and the gents were all fawning over the rather unremarkable-looking man.

Finally we were at the head of the queue. After he informally greeted "Officer Donovan" by name, it was my turn to meet the man. I wanted to shake hands properly, but Travis gave me The Look, so instead I offered my hand in the demure and wimpy style of gals in this era. The future California senator held it for just a moment as I was introduced. Then he blew my mind by saying, "Ahh, Miss diMedici. I've heard about you."

"You have?" I asked, and tried to overcome being totally flustered with the old standard, "Nothing too bad, I hope."

He laughed by way of response, then took Travis's hand and shook it firmly. After some small talk, the mayor moved on to glad-hand the next people in line.

Once we were out of earshot, I leaned into Travis and whispered, "You never told me you knew him!"

He shrugged like it was no big deal. "As a city policeman, I have been on security duty for the mayor's office several times," he said. "And then you know that situation with the runaway horses? The people in the carriage were friends of his. He signed my commendation."

I was impressed, but still I wondered, "So how the hell did he know about *me*?"

"I truly have no idea," Travis said, and looked completely baffled. "I suppose people talk."

※ ※ ※

"When the ball was over," Iris asked, "did her carriage turn back into a piano?"

I didn't have the heart to correct her. "As soon as it dropped her off at home, yes it did. So now, whenever you see a big, shiny, black piano, you can wonder if maybe that was the one that Princess Rainbow rode in!"

Lily wasn't buying that, and instead had a couple questions of her own. "What was the Prince's name?"

"He was the kind and great Prince Travis."

"Did Rainbow have to kiss him?"

"She didn't *have* to. But she wanted to," I said, then leaned forward and mirrored the look of disgust on her face. "And she did."

※ ※ ※

Every night, just before we drifted off to sleep, Travis had a sweet little ritual: he kissed the center of my forehead, kissed each closed eyelid, the tip of my nose, and finally my lips. I always called them my five bonus kisses, and he'd always respond by saying that every kiss he got was a bonus.

Tonight was no exception. After we said goodnight, I heard the clock downstairs start to toll. It was now midnight, and right in tempo with the twelfth chime, I found myself transported back to the place where fairy tales are just stories... although even there, true love abounds.

60: The view from here

During my time in the Now over the next two weeks, I chased leads down, trying to see a pattern where I knew one should be. But, as I told Travis, it was a lot like trying to figure out four different puzzles at once, when you only had a jumble of a tenth of the pieces from each.

I seriously thought about getting a big bulletin board and tacking up photos and notes, then connecting various parts together with bits of red thread, because that seemed to look so clever in the movies. Alas, I couldn't think of a point to it. (I also knew that the girls would want to play with the it, and we'd likely wind up with red thread going from a doorknob to the refrigerator handle to my computer mouse.)

I had to organize my thoughts somehow, though, and hit on the idea of creating a spreadsheet.

I put all the names in column A, and their addresses in column B. Then going across the top, I wrote down every type of clue I had — largely obtained courtesy of the census records that would be compiled in a couple months. The fields included address, occupation, birth year, birthplace, length of marriage, number of kids and how many servants lived on-site. (One category I didn't need was for race, because the families were all Whitey McWhitersons.) Other records and news articles — past and present — helped me figure out religion, political affiliation, employer, and, when possible, their net worth. Finally, I added any hits on those addresses found in the help wanted ads during any time in the year 1900.

Every day, I found something to add to the picture. I used the type of jobs Maggie & Wally had been researching to track ads for Nob Hill and the vicinity as they appeared (or would appear) during the next couple months.

The end result was kind of like Picasso's famous work, *Grand Nature morte au guéridon* — fascinatingly complex... but I couldn't really tell what I was looking at.

When I mentioned (whined) my difficulty (annoyance) to Travis about the lack of order for the chaos, he said, "Seek things that fall outside of their normal patterns."

"Like what?"

"Really, any exceptions to the standards," he said. "Perhaps they're replacing several members of household staff at once. Job changes for the men in the family. Moving house. A spate of anything happening in the neighborhood, in line with the types of things I'm looking for — reports of petty theft, insurance claims, any disturbances in the area."

As he said those words, I felt my heart sink. I honestly didn't know how much more I could take on.

"I will do my best," I said, trying not to let on just how much I wanted to cry. "It's not easy to get all this done, but I'm trying really hard, Travis."

He hugged me close while rocking me from side to side, and didn't mind a few tears. We stood like that, in silence, until the clouds in my mind started to part and I could see the blue sky again.

"I have been meaning to ask — how are you finding the time to figure this all out? You have the children and your job, and I know your life is far more hectic than here."

Everything had been taking a hit, but I was managing to roughly keep it together... even if I was clinging on by my fingernails. (My day job seemed duller than ever, but I'd imagine that any job would have a hard time competing with the experience of flitting back and forth in history.)

"I have been really slacking on work — you know, goofing off, of however you say it — and Aggie has been watching the kids during the day."

"Eggy?"

"Not *Eggy* — her name is Aggie, short for Agapanthus — which, as you might know, is a flower," I said. "I think I mentioned her before."

"She's a relative of yours?"

"We're not family, biologically — and if you saw her with my girls, you'd figure that out pretty quickly." I laughed, "My girls are these skinny, pale little things, and Aggie is a big, beautiful black woman. She lives next door, and she's really sweet and just great with the girls — probably because she has about ten grandchildren of her own."

"Black?" he thought for a moment. "Oh, you mean *colored*?"

"The correct term now is 'African-American,' actually. 'Negro' and 'colored' are pretty much off the table when it comes to acceptable language."

He nodded then asked, "You find she's capable enough to care for them both?"

"Of course, Travis — why are you asking?"

"Simply because I read that colored folk have smaller brains than Caucasians."

"What? No. That's ridiculous."

"The newspaper has stated this as scientific fact." That blew me away. I knew that racism was still rampant in this age, but didn't really comprehend the extent to which propaganda had been created to serve the bias.

Anyone who thinks that the Internet started the flood of misinformation should get a load of the journalism of yesteryear. As just one example, in the early 1900s, people were pretty much convinced there was life on other planets in our solar system. (As recently as 1920, the *New York Tribune* published a full-page article under the headline, "Scientists, agreeing Martians are super-race, believe that planet may be signaling to us.")

I sighed loudly. "Let me assure you: that is completely wrong, and though I'm sure you don't mean to be, it's racist, too. People make stuff like that up to justify subjugating others."

"I didn't realize..."

"I know, I know," I said, trying to calm myself down. I took a few breaths. "Just remember, love: we are all the same species. Researchers now know that people from sunnier climates adapted to their environment, which included more sun, by increasing the amount of melanin — the dark coloring that also makes freckles — in their skin and eyes. It has no bearing on intelligence."

Travis nodded, and I could see he was confused and a little contrite.

"So is this well known in your time, and bias a thing of the past in your time?"

I couldn't answer that one without a sigh, either. "Not really, no, but we're making strides."

"Well, thank you for telling me. I don't like being taken for a fool," he said. "I hope you understand that I do my best to treat all citizens fairly, as part of my duty, of course."

"I would expect nothing less from you, no matter what you were told was true."

∽∽∽

All the time I'd been lecturing Travis about racism, I'd been thinking about how I also fell into the trap of occasionally painting too many people with the same broad brush. I'd allowed myself to become biased against Victorian society... particularly the women.

Sure, there were the gossips... but there were a lot more people who really were just fascinated by what other folks were up to. Meddlesome? It seemed that way to me at first... but when I finally took the time to look closer, I found that those women were trying to help the only way they knew how.

Then there were people who seemed irritable about so many things in life, but somehow had the patience of saints when it came to their family and friends... and even their oddball neighbors. Once I'd warmed up to them — something that had been greatly aided by the women who helped me with my dress for the recent gala — they took every opportunity to include me on their social calendars.

I was invited to play whist with a few other women from the neighborhood. I was flattered, and a little panicked. Travis had to explain what the game even was, and when I returned to the Now, I did some mind-numbingly boring research on the game. It's easiest described as sort of a variant of Bridge... which I don't know how to play either. I did, however, learn to ascribe new meanings to the words *rubber, dummy, trump* and *trick*.

Back in the Then, we practiced until I was somewhere between terrible and mediocre. But worry not, Travis told me: the point of the this sort of womens' gathering wasn't about winning or losing, but was all about how you played the socializing game.

The game was being hosted by my neighbor Myrna, a San Francisco born-and-bred mother of twin toddlers. Also in attendance was Karoline, who spoke perfect English but was German by way of New York; and Elizabeth, the first of her family to be born outside of Sussex, in the south of England.

When I first got there, the women offered me tea and four kinds of sandwiches. But these sarnies weren't like subs or hoagies – they were "delicate" finger sandwiches, and each type was cut into a different shape with a cookie cutter.

Apparently, when entertaining, it was all-important to dream up all kinds of novel sandwich fillings – and women scoured the land to find the finest and most unique blends of stuff to spread between a couple pieces of crustless bread.

Here are the treats we were served:
- Trefoil shape: Nasturtium flowers and leaves with butter

- Diamonds: Lettuce dipped in mayo on Boston brown bread
- Long rectangles: Minced celery, grated cheese and a little cream cheese
- Circles: Thin shavings of candied ginger and orange peel, mixed with whipped cream

From the accolades my hostess earned for these little munchies, you'd think she had discovered a cure for typhoid.

I tried them all. Varieties one and two were bland, and left me feeling like the main ingredient had been forgotten. The third one was not bad — pretty decent, actually, and the only one I took seconds on. But the fourth? I bit into that bad boy and just about gagged. At that moment, I was so very disappointed to discover that I was holding a cloth napkin, and not the paper kind. That meant I couldn't spit that candied vileness into anything that I could stash in my purse or slip into the trash. With the help of tea, I managed to choke down that one bite, and then smiled and pronounced myself full.

That is, full until my dessert stomach was called into service.

As relieved as I was that the lunch portion of the affair was over, the minute Myrna brought out some truly gorgeous petits four, my appetite roared back. The chocolate ones, in particular, were amazing – the cake was moist, and the frosting was pure fudge. At her insistence, I had three. I think the women were all amazed I could down so many of those treats, but I could also tell how pleased Myrna was by how much I enjoyed them.

The most surprising thing about the whole afternoon was the fact that the food wasn't the most interesting aspect of it all. It was the women themselves. They actively engaged me in conversation, but shared their own stories as well. They all seemed to know just how much to talk, how much to listen – as well as when to prompt for more information, and when to drop a topic and move on.

They told me about the other women on our street and the ones adjacent, but did it in such a way that it didn't seem like gossip. In fact, they seemed very proud of their friends' interests and achievements. One neighbor, for example, was very artistically-inclined, and whiled away much of the day creating beauty from canvas and oil paints. Another was an inventive and prodigious baker, and regularly offered an assortment of muffins, cookies and breads to everyone she knew.

They mentioned a woman one block over had nine children. What was remarkable about that? Turns out that she was the only person they knew whose kids had all survived past age five. (None of her kids had died – the youngest just happened to have recently celebrated her fifth birthday.) The infant mortality rate in 1900 was between 15 and 20 percent – and older kids were lost to all kinds of accidents and illnesses like diphtheria, measles and pertussis – so keeping a brood that big safe for so long was a considerable achievement.

I was also told about a couple talented musicians, an animal-lover who took in stray dogs and cats, several women who cultivated gorgeous gardens, and even a resident witch. "But she's a *good* witch," Elizabeth assured me.

Another surprise was the fact that all the women seemed pretty handy around their own homes. This went way beyond cooking and cleaning – these gals were often the ones painting the walls and sanding the floors, unblocking the drains and fixing the loose doorknobs. As Karoline put it, "If we waited for our husbands to do all the work that needed to be done, we would be old and shriveled and the work would still not be finished!"

That can-do attitude was one that continued to this day. I found out the neighbors were the ones who had helped Jennie stay sane and safe after her father died. They brought her food, invited her to their homes, and even helped her with her day-to-day chores. These same ladies also kept up the house every week or so while she (the one who was now me) was cooped up in the hospital.

It was hard to piece together because not one of them wanted to come out and say it, but I realized now they had been helping Jennie since long before her accident. Why were they so tight-lipped about it all? I think it had less to do with being humble, and more to do with the fact they shrugged it off as being just all in a day's work.

While I didn't realize it at the time, getting to know the locals provided me with two keys that were essential to complete my tasks in the Then.

First, as I came to understand more and more about the people of this time — inclinations, motivations, goals — I could add new dimensions to the data I'd collected. The greater my knowledge, the more likely I would be to spot anything outside the norm.

The second was something I didn't know how much I needed it until it was there: Inspiration. As I got to know the men, women and children of this era, I started to feel protective of them, and mentally invested in their futures. It stopped mattering to me that in my time, their names were only to be found etched into weather-worn tombstones.

When they were mattered no more than *where* they were. The only important thing was for me to believe I could help them.

61: A world of changes

It started so simply.

Based on Travis's suggestions, I looked into everything — as many times as I could stand — until something changed, or a new thought occurred to me.

Nob Hill (nicknamed "Snob Hill" in my day) was a posh neighborhood located on top of one of San Francisco's original seven hills, just adjacent to downtown. With the amazing views and such a central location, it was the golden area where tycoons — millionaire railroad developers, stockbrokers, bank owners — mingled with the riff-raff: doctors, lawyers, bankers and your garden variety wealthy folk.

Most of the area would be destroyed by the disaster in six years, so it was a particular privilege to see this area in its heyday. Travis called the homes "stately," but to me, the term "magnificent" better suited them... though some definitely erred slightly on the side of flamboyance.

The first notable information I found seemed completely unrelated to anything, but it was new and it was strange: The residents of Nob Hill were putting their homes on the market in record numbers. Normally, two or three houses might be available at any given time, and they might take months to move. But within the next two months, there would be seven luxury addresses up for sale.

"But I don't know what it all means," I told him. "There was nothing I could find — like a bad smell or murder in the vicinity or anything else — that might explain the sudden spike."

Travis tapped his fingers on his chest, deep in thought. Then, "What would make *you* move house? I've never owned one, so would appreciate the perspective."

"Getting a good new job, losing a job — something that totally changes your financial situation. Divorce. Maybe not feeling safe — like if something happened in the neighborhood or someone broke into my house."

"Considering we have seen no significant changes in the lives of anyone on that home sale list, such as hiring or firings, perhaps we would be well served to look at the safety option?" Travis said. "Many times, though, residential burglaries aren't reported in the media, so you won't be able to find any of that on your web. We aren't going to know if we're on the right track until someone calls the police."

༄ ༄ ༄

When Travis got home that night, he hung up his coat and hat, then his first words were, "You were right. Something has changed."

"What did you hear?"

"It's what I *saw*. I walked by Walter and Maggie's house today, and it's vacant. There's even a 'To Let' sign in the window, so they must have cleared out a few days ago."

"Maybe you can check with her parents?"

"I did. As far as they know, she has been living with a lady friend for the past few months, and nothing's changed. I asked for the address, but she said she wanted to check with Maggie before she gave it to me."

By the time we went to bed that night, we still didn't have any new theories. It was frustrating, but somehow I was able to continually convince myself that, tomorrow, I would discover news we could use.

Even Travis had started to drink my Kool Aid, I thought. Every morning, he would eagerly wait for me to wake up to deliver the latest updates. And while he waited for me to open my eyes, other sweet thoughts fluttered through his mind.

"I watch you a lot, you know. I look at you and think about where you really are, years and years and years away. That is still amazing to me," he said. "I can lie here and hold you, feel your heart beating against my hand, and know that you are living another life at that very moment."

༄ ༄ ༄

This time at least, the anticipation wasn't misplaced. By the time I got back to the now, things were really rockin' and a-rollin'. I don't know what sparked it, but starting early next year, the tawdry twosome were back on track.

While my spreadsheet eventually turned out to be helpful, what really kick-started the whole investigation was a little light bathroom reading.

Upon waking up in the Now the next morning, I hit the head, and grabbed off the dresser the first reading material I found. It turned out to be that "Greatest Grifters" book I'd randomly picked up recently in San Francisco. (Randomly. As if.)

Whereas before, the narrative was notable only for a passing reference to a certain cop I knew, things had changed.

I discovered the bastard had a full page dedicated to his exploits in a book about the so-called "Greatest Grifters" from the first decades of the twentieth century. Published in 1978, it mentioned several of Walt's earliest crimes — for which he'd never been caught — but also gave me a sneak preview of coming events: Armed robbery, kidnapping, extortion, and about fifty counts of fraud.

Although utterly disgusted by the fact that he had merited such attention, at the same time, I was grudgingly grateful. Hey, I couldn't deny that even the inclusion of a few meager passages about the guy made my job easier... even if reading said passages felt so skeevy that I wanted to take a shower afterward.

Walter Houlihan was a dashing, handsome young man, looking to make his mark in a spectacular way. He wanted to do something daring, memorable and, most of all, profitable.

Walter wasn't a bad looking guy — kind of nondescript in my opinion — but what he was lacking in the handsome department, he'd apparently made up for in spades in terms of charisma and style. Forgettable but slick: exactly what every great con man needs to be. Personally, I didn't see it, but that probably was because I had already pulled back his veil and seen the low-life scum hiding under there. Still, proof of this was apparent from some of the scams he had run.

What was most disturbing was how some people apparently held him up like some sort of outlaw hero, all because he never actually shot a man. Sure, he caused death and fear and destruction... but that was somehow not as vile. Why? Because through the rose-colored veil of time, there is a certain quaintness and an aura of intrigue around mayhem and murder during the Victorian and Edwardian eras. Want proof? Look no further than today's cult-like fascination with Jack the Ripper and Lizzie Borden.

It made me laugh to read about Maggie's involvement. She came across as being somewhat conniving, and they even said she was "a well-bred girl who changed her ways and oft sought lowbrow amusement." (I took that to mean that she was kind of slutty, but that might just have been me reading between the lines a little too enthusiastically.)

Even though I kept seeing demonstrations of the fact that history was fluid, every time I witnessed a major example of this law in action, it amazed me — awed me.

Think of seeing the green glow of the Aurora Borealis filling the sky, or watching a trio of humpback whales breaching the water to catch a few moments of sun. It was sort of on par with that, although the magic of change had a very different kind of beauty.

The morning's musings were interrupted by a quick triple knock at the door once, then again. Someone was impatient.

Opening the door, I found Mrs Fletcher standing on the porch, her mouth pulled taut. "We need you. Over at Priscilla Graham's house."

Priscilla was the pregnant neighbor who had been one of my fairy godmothers, contributing the skirt to my "ball gown" not too long ago.

"What's going on?"

"It's little Peter. He's..." she looked around, struggling to find the right word. "He's passed on."

The phrasing reminded me of a polite rejection in the business world, so it took me about two seconds longer than it should have to figure out what she was saying. Then I felt faint.

"Oh my god, no!," I finally managed to say. "Are you saying that gorgeous little baby boy died?"

"Yes, dear," she said, choking up at the words. "We're all taking turns sitting with Prissy."

I turned to Travis, who said, "You go. We can talk more later."

After shoving my feet into my boots, I left the laces undone and rushed to follow Mrs Fletcher to the house just a few doors down. My chaperone was walking so quickly, I didn't have a chance to ask any questions. I was in such shock, the tears hadn't even found their way out yet.

Several women were already assembled in the Graham's small sitting room, talking in hushed tones. A neighbor I'd met just a couple times gave me a somber nod and said, "Priscilla has taken to bed upstairs."

"What can I do?"

"In a few moments, we will start to arrange their meals and care."

"Sounds good," I said. "May I ask what happened to Peter?"

After a long, slow blink, she answered, "This morning, the baby suffocated in his sleep."

"Suffocated? Like on a blanket or something?"

"There was nothing. She went in this morning to feed him, and he was already cold and blue."

Sounded a lot like SIDS. "Did they try to resuscitate? Did a doctor check him over to see..."

With a slightly raised hand, she cut me off. "We asked you here to help the family. The coroner has the situation with the infant well in hand."

The reality check made me cringe, but I got the point. "Of course. Whatever I can do to help."

"Wait a few moments, until everyone has arrived, then we will begin," she said, then moved on to brief the lady who had just walked in.

Ten minutes later, the Most Organized Woman in 1900 had plotted out the next week — meals, shopping, companions — and started to work on planning the funeral and burial. I had never known anything involving a committee to be handled so thoroughly, quickly and elegantly.

I was enlisted to both bring over three meals, and to sit by her side tomorrow... with the caveat that I might be called back for more if needed. (I got the vibe there was some concern over Priscilla's mental health, particularly since she was seven months pregnant and awash in hormones.) Several other women were doing the same, while others pledged to clean and do other household chores. There was even one dear soul who promised to ensure that Mr Graham's uniforms were washed and ironed, ready for each morning.

Along with a half dozen women, I spent the rest of the day downstairs in the family's parlor. We cooked, coordinated, and let other people know what happened. Of course, tongues also wagged, and more of the story came out.

As soon as her baby boy's death had been confirmed by the local physician, apparently Prissy had rushed to the window, pushed it up and made an attempt to leap into the roadway below. Only the reality of her huge belly not fitting through the rectangular opening kept her first reaction from being her last.

"She's in the poppies now," one lady told me. That, I'd learned, was a reference to the opium poppy... meaning the doc had dosed her up with heroin or something to chill her out. As much as I was disturbed by the idea of a massively pregnant woman being doped up, the thought of said woman becoming sidewalk splatter was worse.

By the time I got back home, it was eight o'clock, and this morning's fire about the situation with the Tricky Twosome was now a tiny ember. I was exhausted in every possible way.

On nights like these, I loved the little shivers my arm or leg or hand would make as my body turned itself off. They served as confirmation that I was almost enveloped in sleep. That I was almost in my other world. That another day was dawning, and news of something important might just await.

62: The heart of the matter

Fortunately, once I woke up back in the Now, I was raring to go. Once I got used to the strange dream cycles, I discovered an unanticipated fringe benefit: I felt more rested than I had in years.

Now that I knew what to look for, other chunks seemed to fall into place. The text in the "Greatest Grifters" now spilled over on to three pages, and the newspapers were suddenly speckled with clues and tidbits of information.

Every night now, after I got ready for bed but before I let myself go to sleep, I had a new task to tackle: major memorization. Since notes wouldn't travel to the future or the past, it was necessary to carry everything I needed in my mind.

To certain people, this may be easy. But for someone like me – who needs ten minutes to locate her car keys every morning, and too often forgets to check her bank balance before running her debit card through the handy little machine at the grocery store — it was about as fun as math class.

The first few times I tried a deliberate approach, I read my list to myself a half dozen times just before bedtime. Results came in first thing in the morning, and they weren't exceptionally promising. I was batting .500 for a set of ten items.

After a little more experimentation, I finally figured out that the act of writing something down by hand fixed the ideas in my mind better than anything else. Whenever possible, I needed to keep the list to six or seven points per day. Beyond that, they tended to get jumbled — or just plain forgotten.

∽ ∽ ∽

The instant my eyes fluttered open, Travis wanted to know everything I'd found out.

"I can't — too much," I said, scrambling to search the bedside table for what I needed. "Paper. Pencil. Shh — don't talk, so I don't forget."

Ten minutes later, I was finally ready for the debrief.

After a big intake of breath, I began. "Okay, well... it seems like these two have set up some kidnapping business," I explained. "They seemed to have a really... I guess you could say 'innovative' technique, and got away with the crimes for years. They were successful largely because they blackmailed the families to stay quiet, during and — most importantly — after the kids were taken."

I explained that from what I could tell, they threatened the families with violence if they went to the cops — but allegedly promised no harm would come if they paid the ransom and never told a living soul. "I guess it's worth mentioning that, as far as I can tell, they lived up to that — no reports that anyone was physically hurt."

When the mister and missus were away, the baddies would play — entering the house when the owners were out. "That's when they would overpower any babysitters or butlers or whatever, and kidnap one of the family's children. Then they would kidnap one of the family's children, and make a handprint of the kid as proof they had him or her. By the time mom and dad got home, all that was left to do was complete the financial transaction."

"I think the fact they demanded relatively low ransom amounts — affordable, I guess you could say — helped them stay under the radar."

"Radar?"

"Radar is a thingy that uses radio waves to locate objects — sort of like how bats see."

He shrugged and looked confused.

"Sorry — bad example," I said, waving the thought away. "I just mean they escaped detection. Stayed away from where people were looking."

"Okay, I understand. Enough so, anyhow. Standard English is appreciated."

I gave him a little kiss and laughed. "Sorry — I get a little carried away sometimes."

"Sometimes?" he said with a wink. "So how did they find the families with kids? Mere observation?"

"Apparently, Wally and Mags went for job interviews at the homes in question, and then used that time to case the places."

"Ah — that would explain the purpose of the classified newspaper sections in their flat," Travis said before adding with a snort, "It only makes sense that there was some motive other than seeking out actual labor."

I got up out of bed and started pacing. I needed it to help keep myself focused... and using language that made sense to Travis.

"Then here is where they were clever — actually lots smarter than I would ever have given Walt credit for," I said. "First, their demands were based on the money and valuables the people had on hand — the reason why the ransom amounts were usually on the low end."

It appeared they would choose a time to strike based upon when when a family had an unusual amount of cash in the safe at home, the wife had just gotten her jewelry out of the bank vault to wear for an event of some sort — things like that. This way, there was very little time needed to pay up and get out. From first demand to their departure, it took fifteen minutes or less in most of the cases.

I flipped through my notes, which were all out of sequence — the way the details had come back to me on this side of the timeline.

"Oh, right. If that was smart, this part is brilliant: they never actually removed the child from the property. The would bind and gag the poor kid, and stash him in the basement or attic or garage or something."

Travis let out a low, slow breath. "So the parents had no idea their son or daughter was nearby."

Of course, the family had no idea he was so close. All they knew was that Junior was not where he was supposed to be, and these two masked people — who had guns — were demanding something for his return.

"So they would collect their ransom, and then tie up the parents with a few simple knots that could be undone in ten minutes or so. The entire object there was to keep the adults occupied just long enough for Walt and Maggie to get away clean."

The theory went that they didn't want the adults out of the picture so long that others would start to notice their absence — probably because that didn't fit in with their concept of keeping things as hush-hush as possible.

"Once the parents worked themselves free, they would immediately look at the piece of paper that had been left for them — a handwritten note sealed in an envelope — which told them where their son or daughter was hidden."

Travis was listening intently, taking in every word, but saying nothing.

"They used wording like, 'Alexander is playing hide and seek in the attic today' — the theory was that this minimized any evidence that could be used against them. And also on the conviction front: If the kid never left the property, might be impossible to allege kidnapping, too."

"Of course, before they left the parents, they made it very clear they would be back and would cause real harm if the situation ever reported to anyone — authorities, newspapers, friends, etc. They insinuated that they had compromised the home's security in numerous places — never quite revealed, of course — but basically saying, 'We can get to you.' Maybe it was a bluff... but maybe not. I don't think anyone ever tested them. But they definitely believed them."

To keep the fear fresh, a day or two after the kidnap, an anonymous package would be delivered to the home. Inside would be a lock of their child's hair, taped to a printed condolence card. "Those packages, together with the threats made at the time of the abductions, apparently worked like a charm."

For all I knew, there had been dozens of cases that never came to light. It was only thanks to some serious good luck that three of the kidnappings were reported... albeit several years later, after the two were behind bars.

"Two of the families who came forward in the later years said they moved to new homes immediately after their kidnappings — and once I figured that out, I found a couple other wealthy families that suddenly decided to up and leave the area, or to relocate to a different part of the city. I assume they did that in an attempt to avoid any traps or soft spots that had been left... but they all seemed to stay quiet in any case."

During the entire time I had been presenting my information, Travis has been sitting up in bed, listening intently, with his arms crossed. When he was sure I'd finished recounting the tale, he finally spoke.

"Firstly, I don't know that I'd characterize them as particularly intelligent or creative," Travis said.

"So you think I'm giving them too much credit?"

"Well, yes — at least in terms of the sanctity of their motives," he said. "Don't mistake their lack of aggression for anything other than a part of their technique. Dealing with a wounded person can get messy and unpredictable. Furthermore, the penalties for injury or death are far greater."

Shrugging, I supposed I could understand that. I slipped back under the blankets.

"I see their ploy as being only slightly clever," he continued. "Mostly, it's extremely convenient, allowing them to completely avoid the issue of escaping with the victim," he said, as his fingers traced the edges of his badge. "It's sort of a lazy man's guide to criminal activity, is it not? Kidnap, but not really. Steal, but just what's on hand. Bind, but only minimally. Then, coerce the victims to keep it secret so you can keep using the same methods again and again."

He thought for another moment, then put his hand on his forehead and laughed. "Now that I've framed it like that, I suppose their scheme *is* rather slick."

"Yeah," I said, tossing the last of my notes on to the bedside table. "Sucks, doesn't it? None of these things even happen until next year. What are we supposed to do with this information — just *wait*? I can't stop a kidnapping that isn't going to happen for ten months or so."

Travis shrugged.

"The whole thing feels really anti-climatic," I sighed. The kind of scenario I expected — and anticipated being able to thwart — had ended up being such a letdown. It was I'd just seen someone slip a box of raisins into my trick or treat bag.

"Maybe it's not over yet," Travis offered. "Perhaps this is just the beginning of the tale. In any case, don't devalue what you have already learned. It offers great insight into their motives and technique — how much they are willing to work, and how much they are willing to risk."

༄ ༄ ༄

That afternoon, the second since the Graham's son died, I returned at two in the afternoon for my shift at Priscilla's bedside. I had no idea what to expect, or what exactly my role would be other than to offer support and make sure she stayed safe.

As I entered the room, I overheard a well-meaning neighbor trying to enforce calm. "Just put it out of your mind, petal. He was a good boy, to be sure, but you're a grown woman and must see clear to care for the new babe. He's the one who needs you now, dear."

The lady, who I didn't recognize, nodded to me as she started to gather her belongings. "I'll be taking my leave now, Prissy. Keep a stiff upper lip, and all will be back to usual before you know it."

The mourning mother did nothing to acknowledge any of the woman's words, and just continued to stare into space.

After lowering myself into the leather chair, I pulled it close to the bed so I could talk quietly. "It's Jennie, and I'm here to keep you company for a bit."

Priscilla was propped up on a mound of pillows, and had a blanket tucked firmly around her. If she heard me, she gave no sign. The only movement came from her right hand, which tightened slightly around a white and blue handkerchief as I spoke.

"I am so sorry, Prissy. This is a horrible thing you're going through." I leaned to the side to try to get in her field of view, but she still looked out vacantly into nothingness. "I don't think you need to 'keep a stiff upper lip' and bottle up your feelings, though. He was an amazing, wonderful boy! You have every right to grieve."

For just a half second, she glanced at me, and I registered a look of surprise. Just as quickly, her gaze returned to the blank space between here and infinity.

Not wanting to push her, I was content to just sit and listen to the breeze softly rattling the shutters. Finally, after about fifteen minutes, she took a deep breath and asked in a soft voice, "Have you lost anyone?"

I tried to keep my tone calm and warm, even if my words weren't free from all the rough edges. "Only my grandparents — never a child. I can only imagine," I said, and felt a little shiver. "There are two little girls I am very close to, and if something happened to them... well, I don't know how I could survive."

She looked at me, surprised. "That's how I feel right now."

"I know — and I can understand that. I think it's only natural for a mother."

Another ten minutes of silence passed before her thoughts built up enough pressure to make it worth the effort to speak the words.

"Everyone tells me, 'Just think about the new baby — think about the new baby.' As if that ought to stop me from thinking about my old one." Tears started to well up in her eyes again. "When I hear those words, I just despise this world." She wiped her face with the soggy handkerchief. "I hate that people assume this child could replace the one I lost," she said, using fists as she gestured to her belly. "That is a disgusting thought."

"I agree — this baby is his or her own person, not another Peter," I said. "Although this new sweet little life will be wonderful, but it won't take away all the pain you feel."

Obviously showing great restraint, she began to weep in near silence.

"It's okay to cry — and to be upset, heartbroken... yes, even angry. I think you should feel all those things. Get them out and deal with those emotions, so you can move on."

"I don't think I will *ever* be able to move on."

"You will — trust me. The human race is a species of survivors. You will get through this."

"I can't imagine a time when I won't mourn my Peter."

"You will always miss your son. That's a given. There will always be a sadness. But you have to remember that this little one will need you, too. The new baby is an innocent."

As her tears rolled ever faster down her cheeks, she pulled and twisted the handkerchief so tightly, I expected it to fall to shreds at any moment.

"But, Pris — it will get better. A little easier by the week. It won't hurt as much. I have known a lot of people who have dealt with loss, and I know this to be true."

The floodgates then opened, and I held her, until the wracking sobs peaked then finally ebbed.

Wiping her face on the bed sheet, she looked at me through swollen, red eyes and asked, "When? *When* will it get better?"

I took a deep breath and tried to find my zen again. "The timing is different for everyone, but believe me when I tell you that it will happen," I said. "You need to let yourself feel his loss to get past it, though. Otherwise, the pain will just stay there, front and center. You can't heal if it's always blocking your way."

"It hurts. So much."

"I know, and it's so awful. There's no way around that, I'm afraid. But Prissy?" I waited until she looked at me. "I will tell you what my mom told me when my grandmother died. She said that although I'd never forget and would always miss her, I needed to have faith there would be a day when all the good memories would come to mind before any sadness," I said, and took Priscilla's hand. "Mom said I'd know that time had finally come when I would think about Gram and find myself smiling."

I leaned in close and clasped her hand a little tighter. "And you know what? It happened, and then it lasts and lasts."

Finally, the girl's eyes showed a little sparkle. She was hearing me... and perhaps starting to understand the truth. "Even now, I can just think about her — the cookies she made, the kind of hats she wore, what holidays were like at her house — and I feel this sense of joy," I said. "I can't help it, because the happy memories far outnumber the sad."

63: The Now – Bad mommy

To those moms who handle a career and the kids and still manage to eke out a life for yourselves, I sincerely applaud you.

Before I went travelin' through time, I held it together about half the time. And now? I'm one percent adequate, 99 percent disaster. I forget to take showers, miss the kids' bedtimes, forget about almost every permission slip sent home, my nails look like I just clawed my way out of a coffin, and if the girls ask me what's for dinner, far too often I want to respond with, "I don't know. What?"

One of the things throwing a wrench in the works was the staggered continuity. With one day here, one day there, one day here, one day there... well, I was constantly forgetting my place in both lives. Most of the time, I could handle it — but sometimes (especially recently), I just completely lost my groove.

Really, I'm not complaining — but I sure do wish I could explain to people why I was forgetting all kinds of stuff, and how come I have a hard time remembering what day of the week it is. Sometimes, I'm so tired, it takes some truly intense effort to even get out of bed.

Lately, Roseanne Barr's (in)famous quote about motherhood has applied to me pretty well — minus the husband part: "I figure by the time my husband comes home at night, if those kids are still alive, I've done my job."

I knew it wasn't enough... not really. But I thought I was at least getting a passing grade.

Then I got a reality check, courtesy of Miss Minnie's Produce Patch.

That was the name of the play that Iris's summer school class was putting on this month. The first performance was on a Tuesday night, and I had been so distracted by tracking down crime patterns and the other things part and parcel of living in the past that I completely forgot.

The biggest problem was that my baby girl was supposed to be *in* the play. When the production was short one very precious carrot, and I got one very frantic phone call from her father, justifiably worried that something had happened that made her miss the show.

Even though I felt terrible, I think Iris felt worse — and Lily felt like she had to console us both.

"It's okay, mom. She really wanted to be an apple, anyway."

The next day, I was able to take a step back, and realized how much I had been phoning it in at home lately. In particular, every time the action ramped up in the Then, my life in the Now suffered. Our dear neighbor Aggie had saved me too many times to count, swooping in with half a lasagna or some fried chicken, and sometimes babysitting the kids an hour longer than usual. (Aggie was the kind of grandma I hoped to be one day.)

Making matters worse, when the kids went to their dad's house for the past few weekends, I felt both relieved and guilty — a really lousy combination. I was happy to have some time to myself, and quiet moments to think and muse and wonder and plan... but felt lousy that I wasn't clicking my heels in happiness to be on mom duty every minute of every day.

I thought I had been making things work well enough at least, but that was clearly not the case. Something in their mother's life had to give... but I didn't know what.

Lily and Iris were the two halves of my heart. I had grown them, I had given birth to them, was raising them, and thoroughly adored them. We had never been apart for more than four days at a time, and even that only happened once. In trade, those two loved me back and kept me grounded, which was more vital now than ever.

So the stinging irony was that although I was deeply devoted to my girls, I couldn't gather the energy and brainpower to show it.

Over the course of just a few months, my experiences in 1900 had seriously altered my world view. Now, all this stuff with Priscilla had tweaked it to an uncomfortable degree.

From the very start of my dream travels, I knew I'd never really get over the heartbreak of the fact that all the people I saw — even the newborn babes — were, from my modern-day perspective, decades gone from this earth.

When it came to contemplating the Then, my emotions were in a constant tug of war. One part of me despaired the fact that everyone around me in the Then was dead, but they just didn't know it. Another part of me believed that because I could see and hear and interact with those people, they remained very much alive. In a sense, their essence had been brought back into being.

So while the first thought chilled my heart, the second warmed it.

And then there was Travis. Like my kids, the man was love, personified. Wrap the boy up in a big red bow. He provided the heat that tipped the balance. Because of him, I couldn't ever lament visiting the past, except in one way: for the sake of my daughters.

As much as I hoped for a nice, neat solution to my parenting dilemma, I knew I wasn't going to get it. In fact, I was pretty sure that I wouldn't have a reprieve from this "burning the candle at both ends" thing in the near future. Such a notion came courtesy of a tiny little feeling that wriggled and wiggled and tickled inside. It oh-so-quietly whispered to me that everything I'd experienced so far in the Then was really no more than a dress rehearsal. The big show — the point of sending me back all those years — was coming soon... and I was going to be in the spotlight.

If that proved to be true, I'd just have to wish, hope and pray that I wouldn't be forced to take my final bow after it was done.

64: The chessboard

I figured it out... or maybe it just wrote to the future and I just found it — but no matter: I'm pretty sure I've pegged what we're supposed to stop from happening.

It had been a long time coming.

Despite how much Walt's inclusion rankled me, my dusty old "Greatest Grifters" book was turning out to be an incredibly valuable resource, mostly because it kept changing. Shortly after events were altered, my printed volume would reflect the new version of history.

While I'd been aware of some of the events that winked into and out of existence, I was truly awed to witness the past catching up to the present.

I actually had to blink at least ten times before I understood what I was seeing. The words — black ink on paper — were changing right before my eyes. They shifted into new forms from the top of the page down, and the switch between past and present was subtle and graceful. It was sort of like watching a blind slowly being closed... but kind of magical and enchanting beyond the scope of most window coverings.

During the next few days, I discovered something even wilder: the number of pages dedicated to Wally ranged from zero to twenty, presumably depending on how much we all had had been influencing the timeline. While the book didn't cough up all the details — and, sometimes, offered information that seemed contrary to published reports — I mainly used it to decide where to focus my own research. As such, it was much simpler than trying to scrounge every iota of ever-changing data from the antique newspapers.

Reading and researching consumed much of the day and even the night on my side of the timeline. It had taken me hours to dig up the whole story, and hours more to comprehend it all. I hadn't even finished when I suddenly felt chilled to the bone. I'd slipped into the past.

Sleep hadn't even waited for my surrender, but just took me right there at my desk, like an enthusiastic — if slightly off-kilter — lover. I was mildly annoyed to know that the next time I woke, I'd regain consciousness on a drool-soaked keyboard in front of a page with about fifty thousand letter Bs typed by my cheek.

The cold permeated the house thanks to the fog, which was so thick this morning, I could probably take a stick and wind it like cotton candy.

Just because I had been thrown back to this side of the time wall, I wasn't going to rush my process. Travis offered to make brekkie while I jotted down my notes, and allowed myself a few extra minutes to mull it all over.

Over toast and eggs, I explained what I'd read, what I knew, what I deduced, and how I could see the little bits created a sad, strange criminal mosaic.

"Before I go too much further, you need to understand that most of this book is based upon the author's own investigations in the 1930s," I said. "Mr Houlihan and Miss Gallagher were never convicted for any of these crimes... at least not as far as history has revealed."

While its ratio of truth to fiction was not fully known, the book provided me with a lead... and the instant I followed it up, my spidey sense told me I was on the right track.

I saw his furrowed brow make another appearance. "How reliable is the evidence? You know for certain it's them?"

"As certain as I can be," I said while I carefully scraped the soft top layer off the butter. "All the indicators are there — physical descriptions, timing, MO," I continued. "But there were no names attached in any official reports. As far as the cops were concerned, the suspects were never positively identified."

"Otherwise, though, the information you read in the book matched up with newspaper articles?"

"Pretty much, yeah — but there's nothing I have yet found that ties it firmly to our duo," I said. "But f or the sake of this scenario, let's just assume it's them. Because if it's not, there's not really anything we can do."

I took his little halfhearted chuckle as a signal of agreement.

There probably wouldn't be anything like laughter for the next few minutes while I told him how, after a few months of success, t he two had decided to up the ante this summer.

"They keep with the same general concept of the fake kidnaps, but start to go for a bigger reward. They begin to target bank managers and bank presidents. With a kid as a hostage, the poor schmuck is forced to access the bank vault."

"Tried and true, I suppose," he said as he mopped up egg yolk with a bit of toast.

"They did the whole thing once, and it went fine. Of course, it didn't stay under the..." I had to stop myself from saying 'radar' again. "It didn't stay undetected, because, of course, you can't really cover up a bank heist — not when there are shareholders and a board of directors and so forth. But the part of the scheme with the kid stashed away in the house remained the same."

"Unfortunately, that tidbit didn't come out until years later. But when I found that information, it was the link that really made all the pieces fall into place." Then I added a bit of my own analysis. "If the bit about the child staying on the premises had been public knowledge back then... well, maybe things would have ended differently."

Now, in my history, I'd patched together the lurid tale of the city bank that was held up in broad daylight. The head honcho had helped make it happen — under duress, because his daughter had been stolen.

"I probably should ask: Who is the family in question?"

"Judging by the media coverage, they're pretty heavy hitters. The Coopers on Nob Hill."

The look on his face made it clear that this was not good news.

"It's not just the who, though, Travis — it's the how." I explained that what set this robbery apart was how there were several innocents involved — tellers and customers who were unfortunate enough to be at the wrong place at the very wrong time.

When the bank president was brought into the bank, the other folks on site became bonus hostages. As soon as the thieves had taken as much as they could carry, the witnesses were forced into the vault. The strongroom dedicated to warehousing the valuables was about the size of a handicapped restroom stall, and the installed shelves took up about eighteen inches of space on three of the walls.

Just before they made their exit, Walt and Maggie did the whole "tie up the guy with something he can get out of in 10 minutes" thing, and made their getaway. It had been working brilliantly for them, so why not?

Why not? Because, as everyone knows, all good things must come to an end.

They probably couldn't have known that the bank president — a gent who was was about fifty years old — had a heart condition. And the stress? Too much for the man.

After they made their exit, the poor guy struggled to get out of the rope.

Whether that was too strenuous an activity, he was intensely worried about his kid, or otherwise just stressed out to the max... he had a heart attack right there on the bank's highly-polished Italian marble floor.

The Call laid out some of the details in their typical frothy style:

Death's Hand Laid First Upon Bank President
Weakened by a Previous Illness, Succumbs to an Attack of Heart Failure, Disallowing Rescue
During the course of a daring heist, San Francisco banker Elliot Ray Cooper suffered an attack of the heart. Due to the most lamentable circumstances, the cessation of his life could not have been more poorly-timed.

"As atrocious as that was," I told Travis, "that wasn't the worst of it."

His head sunk face-first right down to the table. "Keep going," he said, his voice slightly muffled by the cloth napkin pressed against his mouth. I think he knew where this was going: With the boss out of commission, there was nobody around to release the captives.

"Nine people jammed into a pretty much airtight bank vault — it was standing room only," I said. "It wasn't until around eight o'clock that night that the alarm was raised. By the time the hostages and Cooper were discovered, they were all long dead."

As soon as I told him that, Travis raised his head, and swore for the first time since I'd known him.

The newspaper report attempting to chronicle the time in the vault was haunting, and as I envisioned the scene, my throat tightened and I couldn't get a full breath.

Clearly, the poor souls had tried everything they could to escape. All four walls of the small room had been battered with all available might, and bloody claw marks were only part of the proof. Shoes were littered throughout the space, and scuffs on the walls showed that they had been used to bang on the walls, presumably to call for help.

When they examined the bodies, they were surprised to discover a wide range of injuries — including shattered shoulders and knees. The doctors theorized that the breaks had occurred when the men had kicked and thrown themselves at the steel-reinforced door in an attempt to force it open.

"The fire marshals said that the people in the vault had probably survived a little over an hour — two at most, but every last one of them had suffocated."

And that, boys and girls, is how on June tenth, 1900, Walter and Maggie killed ten people... without even being there. That's the way I imagined their defense would have gone, anyhow.

"How are we going to be able to stop that? Do we simply bide our time?"

Travis started to massage his forehead, as if to coax the solutions out of his mind. After a lengthy pause, he said, "We can't forget that they're terrorizing people with these kidnappings until then — and who knows what else? For all we know, they're doing that more often, just in other places around the Bay. Or, conceivably, they're doing something else. We know they have to be up to no good."

"I'm afraid if we just wait until next month to do anything about it, too many of the wheels will be in motion to stop — well, not unless we want to risk making everything worse."

"Is there any more information you can find? Corroboration, perchance?" Travis scanned my notes. "I wonder if you could possibly seek out some evidence you haven't considered, such as other books or reference materials that might not be on the computers."

"Sure, absolutely," I said, secure in the knowledge that my boy had some some first-rate brains behind those bright blue eyes. "When I go back, I will find out more. See if I can get some other sources, find out more — make sure we're chasing this up intelligently."

Travis nodded and wordlessly finished the last of his four pieces of toast. Then it was quiet. And even quieter. Just when I was about to break the silence by belting out the first '80s hit song that popped into my head, he finally spoke.

"I'm loathe to say this, Jen, but you know I can't involve the police without proof. Not when it involves such a well-known family, and not... not after last time."

Pushing away my plate, I twisted around to face him. "Last time with the bank and the dynamite was a fluke. Or, hey — maybe we were just very effective. But you know that things change in unpredictable ways sometimes."

"I know," he said, and there was a deep sigh, like he was letting off steam. "Of course I know that. But whole incident jeopardized my career."

I hated hearing this. It was the truth, and I knew it, but every word stung. "I'm sorry," I answered after taking a pause to get a grip. "Not sure what I could have done differently, but I apologize."

Travis reached out and caressed my cheek. His hand was warm, and I could feel the callouses earned through years of holding a horse's reins.

"Jennie, know that I believe in you, and all your discoveries. I think they're positively remarkable," he said, smoothing my skin. "But it's only as reliable as the information available. Records can be lost, incomplete, incorrect — and that doesn't even take into account... what's that you call it? The phrase that always makes you laugh."

"'Temporal flux.'"

"Right — that. Clearly, all things are perpetually in motion, and you have told me several times that alterations in time are not immediately apparent," he said. "So no matter what we learn of the future, your notes aren't evidence that can be put in front of a judge. We need something more."

"Shh, shh, shh," I whispered, and put my finger on his lips. "As it stands right now, we have time. More than a month," I said. "You can relax. We'll figure it out."

Even though I knew damn well how fickle time could be, I somehow ignored the possibility there might be way more to this story than I could ever predict. Then again, maybe that was just life's way of not letting me see too far ahead, lest I decide to run screaming in the other direction.

65: *Pies and surprise*

During the regular school year, all the kids in my daughter's kindergarten class had little calendars. Every afternoon, just before the final bell, they would draw a little picture with the mood of the day. Most times, Iris would color a blue sky with a sun peeking out of the corner, which meant "happy." The very best days would get a rainbow. The bad days usually got a green "ugh" face that very much resembled Mr Yuk.

After calendar pages of mostly all rainbows and sunshine, the last dozen days I lived — the past six or so in each time — would definitely all have earned icky faces. I was lucky enough to have someone in my life who knew it, too.

Travis surprised me by walking in the door — long before he was scheduled to be off work — right at the very moment I was easing the last of three freshly-baked tangy-sweet strawberry rhubarb pies on to the kitchen windowsill. One was for us, the second for Priscilla and her hubby, and the third I planned to offer to another neighbor. I heard a little scuffing sound, and, glancing to my right, I saw the shape of a man filling the frame of the kitchen door.

By the time I realized it was just Travis — who wasn't scheduled to be home for a couple hours — my body had already twitched with a "fight or flight" response, and the last pie slipped out of my potholders and went flying out the window. The wet splat it made when it landed even produced a little echo.

"Oh my godddd — what are you doing here?" I said in a voice about three octaves higher than my usual.

"I... I thought I'd surprise you," he said, gaping as he looked from me to the pies to the open window and back again.

"Well, I'd say your mission has succeeded, commander." Up on my tiptoes, I peeked out the window, and saw the pie steaming on the concrete of the side alley below — just over the property line. "I think the pie is dead, sir."

Travis looked over my shoulder and confirmed the loss. "Well, you mentioned you were making one for a neighbor, right?"

"Yeah — instant delivery."

"Speaking of..." and that's when he brought out a bouquet of flowers from behind his back. "Plus, we are going out to dinner tonight."

I started to grab him for a huge bear hug, forgetting about the gooey fruity ooze decorating my shirt until the last millisecond.

"Whew — that was close. I almost got strawberry and rhubarb all over you."

He leaned over, and licked a little bead of pie filling off my sleeve. "Very nice," he said, and started to unbutton my shirt. "Now let me help you get cleaned up."

༄ ༄ ༄

An hour later, were dressed and ready to go. I looked at the clock then asked, "Isn't it a little early for dinner?"

"We have another errand to run first."

"Ah," I said, my head filled with visions of dropping stuff off at the cleaners or grabbing a loaf of bread.

I should have known better.

With all stressful and depressing events of late, I had blanked out the upcoming anniversary of Jennie's birth — otherwise known in this timeline as "my birthday." Travis, though, hadn't forgotten.

Our first errand related to an early birthday present. For the occasion, he decided to offer me the kind of gift that, for centuries, husbands have bestowed upon wives, and wives have presented to husbands: something the *giver* actually wanted in the first place.

In this case, it wasn't the Victorian equivalent of NASCAR tickets, but something honestly romantic, sweet and that I wouldn't have bought for myself: a professional portrait photo sitting. He explained that he wanted a picture of me to always remember how I looked the year we met. It was so a-dork-able, how could I possibly say no to that?

"Besides," he said, "it will be fun, and you need some fun. All work and no play..."

"... makes Jen a dull girl. I hear ya, mister," I said as I fixed Travis's collar and straightened his tie.

"My dear," he began, and I had to interrupt him again.

"Try 'Sugar Bear,'" I said while reaching over his head, crossing my wrists behind his neck. "You know how I just *love* to hear that in your accent."

Smiling, he shook his head in resignation, and started over. "Sugar Bear — you could not be dull if you tried. I daresay you wouldn't even know *how* to try."

∽ ∽ ∽

The session itself was scheduled for early next week — on the day this body would turn twenty-one years old. Tonight, before we went to the restaurant, we were going to meet the photographer for sort of a pre-sitting consult.

You have to realize that in 1900, portraits were a Big Deal, and not simply the result of trundling down to the local mall's studio, where you can show up without an appointment and leave with prints of six different poses an hour later.

Portraits in this day were reserved for the privileged. Unless you wanted to get really spendy, photographers took only one picture per person. They used large glass plates for the job, and those babies were expensive, very fragile and had to be handled delicately. But as you would hope from something so costly and time-consuming, the result was nearly always something classic and unforgettable.

The photographer Travis had chosen was a dyed-in-the-wool San Francisco legend: Isaiah Taber. Though he was now seventy years old, the man still had a brilliant eye, along with an impressive legacy of having captured magnificent images of both places as well as people. (The literature in his studio noted that he had photographed seven American presidents, along with British royals Queen Victoria and Edward VII. Pretty nice company to keep.)

As I was helped into the waiting carriage, my excitement runneth over. "I have to decide how to style my hair, what makeup to use, as well as plan the most 'becoming' dress and jewelry to wear," I told Travis, who sat down beside me, looking more bemused than befuddled. "My goal should be something flattering, yet representative of this era," I said before explaining how I felt it was really important to get it right, because my choices could very likely be looked upon for hundreds of years.

"You can worry about all of that tomorrow," he said, taking my hand. "Tonight is for you and me — and Perini's. I've been told it is the most elegant

Italian restaurant in all the city."

And elegant it was — along with romantic and unbelievably impressive. Over more than three leisurely hours, we ate our way through nine amazing courses, from *aperitivo* to *secondo* to the *digestivo*.

By the time we headed back home, I was very full, a little tipsy, and so deliciously happy, I almost thought my heart would burst out of my chest.

༄ ༄ ༄

Figuring out what to wear was a blast. After research in both the Then and Now, I decided to buy a simple cream-colored silken dress with short sleeves and a squared neckline, which I paired with a forest-green tulle shawl, draped over my shoulders. For my birthday, Travis had also given me a pair of drop earrings, which I decided would be the only jewelry I'd wear.

My hair was my biggest concern, given my grossly unconventional hairstyle at the moment. My mullet had been growing out nicely over the past few months, but I still lacked the length in front to pull off many of the looks I liked. Then, too, there was the issue of camouflaging the nasty jagged scar that sat near my left temple.

I pored over photos for hours in the Now — examining hundreds of portraits from museums as well as family collections that had been posted online. I also looked through the US newspaper archive — all in the pursuit of something that just felt right.

Thanks to the advice from hairdresser Miss Minnie Meyers (whose salon was next door to the portrait studio) I was able to decide on a combination of styles, for which Miss Meyers' technical expertise would be required on portrait day.

The long hair in back would be augmented with hair pads to create extra volume, then waved, loosely twisted into ropes, then bundled. Next, we would take a dark blue silk scarf — six to eight inches wide — and wrap it around the problem area on my head, artistically disguising the unfashionably short hair and effectively bridging the gap between the two different lengths.

Travis and I even discussed my facial expression beforehand, too. I didn't want to smile widely, because that wasn't correct for this period in history, and, quite honestly, the teeth I'd been gifted with weren't something I wanted to show off. At the same time, I most definitely did not want to wear the constipated expression so many Victorians wore in their portraits.

Clever Taber had a simple but effective strategy for dealing with my scar — he changed the composition of the shot so the old wound would be hidden from the camera's view. Instead of a full-face portrait, or even a three-quarters view, he had me angled to the left of the studio.

After I was sitting up straight enough to satisfy him, Mr Taber gently moved my head a tiny bit down and to the right, then nudged my chin ever so slightly closer to the camera. From a huge collection of props, the expert chose two big silken rose blossoms for me to hold loosely to my chest.

The pose felt so unnatural, I had my doubts — but Travis, standing back by the camera, gave me a big smile and a double thumbs up (an expression I had taught him). If my awkward head tilt and the bunch of flowers looked good enough for him, it was good enough for me.

The photographer watched our exchange, then walked about five feet to the right of the camera and called Travis over. "Stand here, please," Taber said, tapping a point on the floor. The photographer's assistant dutifully made a small X out of tape on that very spot. "Now look back at her," he said, and with a little smile and shake of his finger, added, "but don't make her laugh!"

Contrary to popular belief, by 1900, the exposure time needed for a picture was often less than a second.

In the past, headrests were commonly used to help hold people immobile for portrait sessions which required them to hold still for lengthy periods. The assistant asked if I wanted to use one to help maintain my precise position, and, given that my neck was already starting to droop a bit, I agreed immediately. The young man assisting me said that I should be mindful not to lean hard on the headrest, but simply to use it as a guide — a reminder of the desired pose.

After checking his view through the lens, adjusting the reflectors and the lights, and once more verifying that everything was pretty much as good as it was going to get, Mr Taber carefully repositioned me just so. His assistant followed him a half a second later, reminding me to stay in position, and reassuring me that I'd only have to hold on for another minute.

Travis and I looked at each other while we waited for the telltale click — and before we knew it, the camera's shutter opened and closed.

In just one moment, my soul in these eyes had been permanently written to history, and my life as Jennie became a little less ephemeral.

66: The Now: Pearl's legacy

After searching an offline newspaper archive and hitting the San Francisco Public Library in the Now, I still had little more to go on other than some random fragments. They served only to enlighten me a little bit about the family's financial status (that which a forensic accountant discovered in the course of confirming that the family was not part of the conspiracy), and Mr Cooper's health (in the form of an autopsy summary).

Finally, I got lucky with a genealogical database, where I found that the little girl had gone on to have a daughter... who, in turn had a daughter of her own. Pearl's granddaughter, in fact, lived in San Francisco.

Under the auspices of writing a book about the whole terrible affair, I made an appointment to interview Mrs Beatrice Cooper Hudson, the great-granddaughter of Elliot Cooper. ("Book research" was most assuredly easier to explain than my real motive.)

The widowed Mrs Hudson lived in a standard-issue house that had been built in the late forties — a modest but well-kept home out in The Avenues, west of downtown.

When I rang the doorbell, I was greeted with barks and wails from within from what sounded like about ten Chihuahuas. For a long minute, I waited for someone to answer. Just as I was about to ring again, the door was opened by a white-haired woman who was nearly as wide as she was tall. She was wearing a red flannel bathrobe, and there was a cockatoo perched placidly on her shoulder.

"Mrs Hudson?"

She looked at me blankly for a moment, then realization dawned. "Oh. You're the author who wanted to interview me."

"Yes, that's right!" I answered with the best smile I could muster for someone who gave off the vibe that I was interrupting her favorite infomercial. "I'm Robin."

"Come on in, then," she said, and took a few shuffling steps over to a walker that was parked a few feet away. I followed as she slid into the living room, a smallish dark room that was stuffed with furniture and trinkets and her various collections. I had never before seen anyone painstakingly decorate an entire wall with empty potato chip bags — and who knew that they made dill pickle and ketchup-flavored chips?

She pointed me toward a recliner with an enormous 49ers football jersey stretched around the entire back of the chair. It felt like I was going to sit in a linebacker's lap. Beatrice settled herself on the sofa, propping up her left leg on several pillows.

"So," she said, before I had a chance to ask, "you want to know about my great grandpa?"

"Yes, please."

"Well, I don't really know much about him, other than that he was some big mucky-muck for a bank, and he had a bum ticker."

I nodded, hopefully encouragingly — meanwhile wondering if I slipped her a twenty, she might be prompted to remember more.

"Now if you really want a story," she said while gesturing to me with one of those yellow back scratchers with a little molded hand on the end, "you want to know about my grandma."

"I do?"

"Oh yeah. I can tell you one thing right off the bat: the lady was certifiable. Completely off her goddamn rocker, to hear my mother tell it," she said.

Against my better judgment, I nodded for her to continue.

"Now, my mom didn't talk too much about what it was like for her growing up, but I know it wasn't great. She didn't ever have real parents."

"I'm not sure what you mean." The parrot looked at me suspiciously with one eye, then turned to surveil me with the other.

"See, Pearl never wanted to have a child — she made that clear many times to my mother. But when she was fifteen or sixteen, she was 'taken advantage of' by an orderly at the mental hospital," she said, and lit a cigarette. "We'd call it rape now, but then it was just one of many complaints, and I'm sure people were paid off to look the other way."

"That is horrible! I didn't realize." That ugly bit of history certainly hadn't been included in any book I'd seen.

"Well, that all started with the kidnapping and robbery."

"Yes — that is my focus — the events of the year 1900."

"Yeah, when the kid was just eleven years old. The funny thing is they hid her in her own attic. But the cops didn't know that 'til much later. Not until after her father — my great-grandfather — was found."

"I read that he died trying to rescue her. A terrible story."

Beatrice's eyes were misting up, and I was humbled by the notion that she, too, felt real emotion about the lives lost so many decades ago. "He was just one of several people who died that day. My grandmother always said they died because of her," she said, a tear escaping each eye. "No, not because of the lousy people who committed the crime, but because of *her*. She really believed it was her fault, and couldn't cope with such a burden."

Maybe this information would be helpful after all, I decided.

She dabbed her face with a tissue. "Anyway, that's why she ended up in the loony bin. They actually called it the insane asylum or the lunatic hospital — can you believe that? They'd never get away with that today."

For a the length of an entire commercial break, Beatrice just stared at the smoky ribbons flowing from her cigarette. I let her have her moment, then prompted her for more.

"Did Pearl ever talk much about the experience itself — not just what happened at the end? For instance, how did they enter the home?"

"Oh goodness, yes, she talked about it a lot — constantly, even. Such a waste of her life. The old girl couldn't stop replaying what happened in her head, as if she could go back and change it if she just figured out the key to the puzzle."

I felt a little tingle to think that maybe I could be the key that would spare little Miss Cooper a lifetime of pain.

"Please tell me more about what she was like. I'd love to hear what you know."

"Well, she was a violinist — a truly wonderful player, I was told. But it wasn't all a natural gift, you see. She had lessons every afternoon, then practiced another three, four hours a day. Her parents hired a governess just to make sure she got her practice in and her homework done."

Beatrice took a sip of water from a football-shaped mug on the table, and then continued, "Her parents were too busy to supervise all of that. Her dad had a bank to run, and from what I understand, but was never quite said out loud, her mother was far more interested in her own standing in 'society' than with dealing with the day-to- day care of a daughter — especially a precocious one." Although there wasn't anyone else in the room, Beatrice leaned in and whispered, "I think the girl was a lot smarter than her own mother, to tell the truth."

"And her father?"

"My great-grandfather was an older gentleman. Pearl was his third child, and only one with his current wife. So he was in his fifties, rather portly, as they said in the day, rarely got any exercise, and worked in a very high-stress position. A heart attack waiting to happen, but they didn't know much about that stuff then."

I made a few notes and nodded for her to continue.

"Her mother happened to be home that afternoon, because a few friends were in from out of town. Pearl's beloved Papa had gotten home from work a couple hours early so he could visit with them," she said while plucking another smoke from the pack.

"So they were all drinking tea and having biscuits or something all proper like that when the governess came into the dining room, screaming. She was being held at gunpoint by a man with some sort of scarf or bandanna over his face."

"The man with the gun said that his partner had just kidnapped little Pearl and they were holding her for ransom. The women were all terrified by this news, but my great-grandfather stayed strong. The bad guy told them that if they ever wanted to see their daughter again, they had to get into the bank's vault," she said. "See, it was a Thursday afternoon, and that is when they usually had the most cash on hand — just before the Friday morning pickup."

That was new information to me, so I scribbled it down.

"The kidnapper promised to reveal the girl's location if the family did exactly as ordered. So George, the kidnapper and the governess took a carriage down to the bank... and I think you know the rest of the story."

"I have read some newspaper articles about it," I said, "but I'd really like to hear it in your own words."

She nodded, but I could see her hands shaking a little when she went to take a long drag from the cigarette.

"Most of this part is just guesswork, since there were no living witnesses, but they got their loot, herded everyone but George into the vault, and locked them up. Then they tied up poor Papa, and left an envelope with the girl's whereabouts written inside."

She recited, "'On this pretty summer's day, with a ribbon pink and gay, a young girl went upstairs to play.' At first, the cops didn't make anything of it, and just thought it was some bad poetry a customer left behind. Then one of the policemen got the wild hair that the note actually meant something, and that led to Pearl finally getting rescued. Still, they didn't find the girl for almost two days. *Two. Days.*"

The child's hands had been bound, then she was tucked inside a steamer trunk. Once the lid was closed, a pink ribbon was tied to one of the handles.

"Funny thing is, Pearl didn't even make a fuss. In those days, children were supposed to be seen and not heard, and if a grown-up told you to do something, you did it — not like kids today," she said, gesturing vaguely to the world outside the window.

"Basically, they came to realize later that the governess was in on it all — and probably had been right from the very start," she finally said. I shivered to know we were very likely talking about Maggie.

"My grandmother couldn't speak a word for weeks, she was so traumatized by everything. That damn governess. See, the two of them had been buddies. If it really had been just a couple men with guns, I think it would have been easier on the little girl. But someone she'd come to trust bound her up with rope and gagged her and put her in a box that she said was like a coffin, up in the dark attic space. Then when the kid got the news about her dad, well..." She made a 'kablooey' gesture around her head.

"I can imagine." I was desperate to hear more, but was having a hard time focusing with two of the dogs competing to see who could lick my shoe the most.

"The lady had only been there a couple months, but since Pearl didn't see much of her parents, and was allowed little to no time for friends, she unfortunately came to love her governess," Beatrice sighed. "She used to let my grandmother brush her hair, which was a big thrill for the kid, because she had this beautiful long, straight, blonde hair, while Pearl had what my mother always called a 'mop top' of dark curls."

Long blonde hair. That sounded familiar. "Do you happen to remember the nanny's name?"

"Jenny something." She shut her eyes to think. "Jenny... Donovan? Something like that. But who really knows if that was her real name, anyway? I don't think that the police ever figured out exactly who she was."

When I heard that name, the blood started to pound so loudly in my years, I could hardly hear the rest of what she said.

Jennie Donovan. Was that an attempt to somehow implicate me, or merely an enormous screw you? The former made no sense — but the latter... yeah, that was right in line with what I knew of Walt and Maggie.

"Are you okay, honey?" my hostess asked me.

Before I passed out, I needed to force myself to keep it together. I took a big breath and managed a smile. "I'm fine — sorry. Just felt a little sick there for a moment. Please continue."

Though she looked a little unsure, she resumed her story while I tried to bring my blood pressure down.

"Even if they had figured it all out, it wouldn't have mattered to the family. My grandmother's mind was already melted at that point. She lost her father and confidant in one fell swoop, plus felt the weight of the world on her little shoulders because of all the other people who died," she said as she added one more butt to the already-full ashtray. "Now, we'd medicate her and have her talk to a shrink… but back then, institutionalization was the only answer."

"You said the family kept it all quiet for years. Why?"

"You see," she sighed, "there was a rule: If they called the police or anyone else, they would never see Pearl again. The man also said that if they told anyone about what happened — not just that night, but never ever — they would come back in the night and kill them all." Fidgety Beatrice opened a little plastic tub, fished out some sunflower seeds, and set them on the table. The parrot walked down her arm to the table and started chowing down, scattering bits of seed shell all around. The lady of the house ignored the mess.

"Then," she said, "there was the letter."

She seemed to be waiting for me to request elaboration.

My pulse sped up about twenty beats per minute. "The letter?"

Beatrice pointed to a brass dresser over by the window. "Second drawer, on the left side."

Making sure I didn't step on any of the members of her menagerie, I walked to the prescribed location, and opened the drawer. She told me to look in the cigar box, and I did.

Inside was a yellowed envelope, the flap already open. Gingerly, I pulled a card from within. "With deepest sympathy" was printed on the front, alongside a drawing of an angel. Inside was only a curl of dark brown hair, fastened with a tiny scrap of pink ribbon.

"My great-grandmother received that right after her daughter was found. She and Pearl moved out of the city immediately." She shrugged, "Didn't matter. The damage was done, then o nce the family moved away, I think the case was pretty much dropped."

"Just one more question, if you don't mind," I said, "and then I'll be on my way."

She nodded, as she put her hand out to the bird, who was still on the table. He waddled back up to her shoulder, and they both looked at me expectantly.

"What became of Pearl?"

"What became of her is exactly what you would expect. She took her own life," Beatrice said. "Mom woke up on the morning of her eighteenth birthday to get the news that her own mother had hung herself shortly after midnight. Pearl left behind a note. I have that, too. Want to see it?"

"Sure," I answered. What else could I say?

Slowly, painstakingly, the granddaughter of a very broken woman handed me a photo album — the kind with sticky pages and thin plastic cover sheets. She turned to the back of the book, and there I saw the second yellowed letter that had survived all these years.

The printing was tiny but legible, and the message itself was tragically brief:

Congratulations, you're an adult now. I have to go. You don't need me anymore and life will be better that way. Sorry and goodbye. - P

⸻ ⸻ ⸻

As she opened the door for me to leave, Beatrice said, "Good luck with your book. It's a big job, I'm sure."

"Thank you," I said. "I really appreciate your help, and I'm sorry if this was difficult to revisit." She smiled and shrugged, but didn't speak. Then there was an awkward silence I felt compelled to fill.

"Would you like me to send you a copy when — and I guess if — it's published?"

Beatrice chuckled and then shook her head. "No thank you, dear. I've lived with it for eighty odd years already, and I'd say that's more than enough for a lifetime... or even two lifetimes."

I knew the feeling.

67: Intent

As soon as I drove away from Beatrice's house, the tears began, and continued to blur my vision all the way across the city and back over the Bay Bridge.

The idea of Maggie using a potential future version of my name seemed so petty and vindictive — but what I'd later learned about Pearl's fate effectively knocked some perspective back into me.

The bottom line was that my wounded ego didn't matter — and even the duo's actual goal was irrelevant. The fact remained that through their greed, many lives were lost... and I didn't just mean the people who died.

As terrible as I felt now, my field trip had served its intended purpose: There was now no question that we were on the right track. Several key data points had been confirmed, and the mention of a blonde woman who went by the name "Jenny Donovan" left not even the tiniest shred of doubt in my mind.

I stewed the rest of the day, and as soon as I got back to the Then, I explained the whole situation to Travis. Then I told him in no uncertain terms that we needed to make something happen, and we needed to do it now.

"Just waiting for this shoe to drop makes me nervous. I don't want to wait — I just want to end this."

"If that's what you need to do, I'll back you. Whatever you need."

I asked him to come sit with me on the sofa, because this was going to take a lot of explaining.

"I have a plan," I told him. "It's a strange one, but it might work."

He sat up straight and visibly braced himself. "What do you want to do?"

"Well, that's the beauty of it. We might not have to do anything."

Travis returned to his normal posture, and I started to explain my theory: When events occur in the past, they ripple throughout time, changing history in their wake. Even small changes can have great impact, depending on how the dominoes are stacked.

"Right now, I could go running out into the street, waving my arms and yelling. That could make a horse decide to bolt. Or it could cause just enough chaos to make a man one minute later to arrive somewhere — and that could have been the exact time he was supposed to meet his future wife... and he misses the moment."

"That sounds paralyzing," Travis said. "I'm a bit scared to move, actually."

"We can't worry about everything. I learned that early on in my days here," I said. "But my idea is that maybe, if I turned toward the street, started to put my arms up... at that moment, the rest of my path — my intent — would be already set in motion."

"I'm not following."

"Think of it like this. Imagine the timeline for that scenario is paced out on a yardstick. Me running into the street and creating a scene happens at the two inch mark. The horse bolting is at the three inch mark. The man's missed meeting is at the four inch mark, and so on."

He bobbed his head from side to side. "Okay, sure. And?"

"What's at one inch? For that matter, what's at zero inches?"

"Your idea," he said finally. "Then at zero, you recognized the need to take action."

"Exactly."

He started to do the whole rubbing the front of his neck while looking into space as he pondered all this. (Or maybe he was just really bored and had sore throat. I didn't ask.)

"If I'm understanding you correctly, you're proposing that we needn't complete an action in order for it to have an impact on the future?"

"In a broad sense, yes. For it to have an actual effect, we would eventually have to follow through. But my hunch — and it's just a hunch, remember — is that we can model different scenarios without doing anything more than coming up with a plan. Create a concept, see how it plays out in the future. Lather, rinse, repeat."

"Experiment, you mean."

"Exactly."

"Hate to say so, Jen, but this sounds like some sort of ridiculous attempt at witchcraft."

"I was thinking it was really like *wish*-craft. Think it and make it happen."

Travis looked down, and I could tell he was trying not to laugh.

"Yes, yes, I know it sounds stupid," I said. "But worth a try, right?"

While Travis was off at work, I multitasked: cooking while sketching out a concept I'd started the night before.

Every time I cooked dinner or dessert this past week, I made a double or triple portion so I could share with the neighbors. All of my menu ideas came from the preschool cookbook I had helped put together a few years ago. I would knock their socks off with early twenty-first century fare, including a few taste treats they probably never have imagined: chocolate chunk cookies, caramel popcorn, brownies, seven-layer bars, kettle-style potato chips, mini pizzas and hamburgers.

Tonight's entree was macaroni and cheese. The macaroni noodles here were quite similar to the ones I was used to — except they were straight, and came in foot-long lengths. I broke them up into pieces of a more familiar size before cooking, and made a cheese sauce from scratch.

By the time Travis got home, I was ready to surprise him with both my culinary mastery and my cunning scheme.

He, though, had a surprise of his own: He'd brought a friend home from work.

"This is Kieran Quinn, one of the city's finest," Travis said before we exchanged pleasantries, then waited for the rest of the story. (I really didn't want to ask, but my curiosity needed to be assuaged.)

"My wife is heavy with child, and the house is right now overrun with midwives and cousins and the like," Kieran explained.

"She's having the baby today?"

"Today, tomorrow — who knows. I can sleep there, but that's all."

I felt terrible that the poor guy had been kicked out of his own home so the ladies could deal with all that messy birth stuff. In this age, that was strictly girlie business. But as happy as I was to host the displaced policeman, it put a damper on any discussion of our little situation until he was gone.

Two long but pleasant hours later, Officer Quinn was on his way home. That was good timing, because my patience level had dipped down to about four percent.

As soon as the door was closed behind our guest, I began to tell Travis my cunning scheme.

I outlined my plan, which started with me faking my way into the mansion by pretending to be a maid. There, I would steal certain items of Mrs C's jewelry — ones she wouldn't notice missing for a few days (like ones from deep inside her drawers). Next, I would plant the necklaces and rings and things somewhere inside Walt and Maggie's house. After that was done, we would drop a hint to the Coopers, and make sure they tipped off the police.

"So, what do you think?" I asked, mentally preparing myself for a round of applause.

"Well, it's certainly ambitious..."

"I know, right? It accomplishes a couple things at once — gets her fired, and the cops will be on to them."

Travis was quiet. *Too* quiet. The stalling kind of quiet.

"But...?" I prompted.

"But, well," then a long pause. "I think it's maybe a little too complicated."

"Are you serious? This is the *simple* version of my plan." I told him, probably with a little bit of a huff. "You should hear what I had in mind originally."

He took my hand and gave me a sympathetic little smile. "It's certainly a clever notion, but the more variables we introduce, and the further we stretch to make it all work, we are that many more times likely to fail," he said. "Believe me — I see it every day. Nearly every time we catch a swindler or a thief, it's because they gave their scheme too many ways to break down."

I was antsy, annoyed, and wanted a solution pronto. "Okay, then, Mr Genius — what do you suggest? Do you have an idea or are you just anti-mine?"

"I am not anti-anything — and certainly not against anything you'd come up with." He kissed me on the nose and ignored my bitchiness. "I am merely pro-success. Your plan, however, has given me some other ideas. To start, what do you think is the number one reason behind nearly all criminal activity?"

"I don't know the number one, but I'd guess the top reasons are sex — or love and sex — then probably money and power."

"If you pare those all down to the absolute minimum, what they all have in common, you get *greed*. Greed for love, money, power — wanting to have what one does not have."

I decided that made sense.

"By this self same token, fear of losing what one desires also elicits a very strong response," he said. "So how can one provoke such a response from another person without truly taking anything from them?"

"Um... faking them out?"

"Exactly — threaten them in some way with the loss of that which they hold most dear," Travis said. "For a woman like Mrs Cooper, what does she care about most deeply? Probably her family, then her home and her social standing. Those all also have one thing in common, too: Mr Cooper. If she were to lose her husband, that would mean the loss of all the other things she values."

"You cannot *possibly* be suggesting that we kill the old guy?"

"No — of course not," he said, looking appropriately alarmed. "No, no. We merely need to make her feel as if there is a threat to her way of life. In that, we could implicate the governess."

I had to think for a bit before the light bulb went on. Finally I got it: He wanted to make the missus think that the pretty young this was after her man.

"A couple suggestions, insinuations, hints dropped to the right people, *et voilà*! The governess will be fired *tout de suite,* eliminating all need for you dressing as a chambermaid... well, at least in this particular instance," he added with a wink.

And that's how Frenchy and I decided we could send an anonymous letter to Mrs C, advising her that the governess was a known husband-stealer — and Jenny wasn't even her real name.

"This is all we need to do, you think — make the plan?" Travis asked. "We don't need to commit it to paper or etch it in stone? Sacrifice a fatted cat?"

"It's a fatted *calf,* you dork."

"This is San Francisco. Far more cats than cattle."

"Let's just see what happens with what we've done so far, silly boy." I would have some good news to share tomorrow, hopefully — though understood that what we were attempting was quite different, and already was preparing myself to wait two or three days for results.

"Agreed. And now that we're done with all of this for the time being, I have another idea." Travis slipped off his shirt, tossed it over his shoulder, and reached out to me with his long, strong arms. "I believe there was some mention earlier of you in a chambermaid's dress?"

68: Predictions

When woke up on the next bright summer morning of the Now, the first thing I did was to pull my tablet from the bedside table and looked to see the result of our plan... and found no change at all. Same thing that afternoon. And night. And ditto throughout the next day.

While I waited for history to reflect our work — and I just knew it would happen — I kept busy.

"What are you working on?" my sleepyhead asked when he woke up to find me making notes on the ever-present pad of paper by my side of the bed.

What, indeed.

As terribly schmaltzy as it sounds, I was becoming more aware by the day that I really needed to make my time here matter. Would I be able to fix this situation with Walt and Maggie? My confidence was faltering slightly — but that didn't mean there wasn't anything to be done.

Based on my belief that Murphy's Law rises up to greet the unprepared, I decided that over the next few weeks, I would work to cross things off my to-do list. Leaving too much unsaid and undone felt too much like tempting fate.

It should be no surprise to anyone that Travis was Priority One. On his behalf, I created a little cheat sheet.

I wanted to give him the inside track on a some key details that could save his life. I also added a few major world events unlikely to impact him directly, but would help him keep faith in my predictions (and yes, maybe even win him some bets).

"I was going to tell you about this as soon as I finished, and," I added one last line to my list, "now I'm done."

He looked confused, but didn't peek at the paper.

"There has been something on my mind. A worry that I might leave this place just as suddenly as I came. I might not live long... or maybe one day, you will wake up alongside this person here," I said, gesturing to the body I was currently using, "and I won't be the one inside anymore. You need to realize that." I took his hand, gave it a kiss, and then held it to my heart. "There are some things you really should know, in case I'm not here."

"Don't say that..." Never before had I seen the glint of tears in his eyes.

I waved him off. "Trav, let me just tell you a few things — and if I'm still around for all of them, great — no harm done, right?"

"Fine, fine," he said, pulling me close so my cheek settled on his chest. "I will play along." He softly raked his fingers through my hair before whispering in my ear, "But you, young lady, are not to leave this party early."

༄ ༄ ༄

Travis told me he could not possibly hear what I had to tell him about the future on an empty stomach... and as soon as we'd eaten, he tried to convince me that he couldn't possibly hear the news on a *full* stomach, either.

"If you get a cramp, you won't drown — I promise."

Handing him his own notepad and the pen thing he somehow liked, I explained the safety rules I had dreamed up, so to speak.

"Please be careful with what you write down," I said. "I don't want you to forget, but also don't want someone to stumble on your notes and decide you're a psychic or psychotic or something."

He laughed.

"It sounds ridiculous, but I'm serious, too. Think about what it would be like if some group like the mafia got hold of some of these predictions, or the government found out you knew about presidential assassinations."

As a policeman, he understood that point very well.

Together, we created a way to code the list — translating the details into what looked vaguely like a series of ordinary dinner recipes.

I had worked up a list of up with ten events to share:

I took him through these ten, one at a time, and gave him some backstory on the 1906 disaster, which I'd already mentioned to him more than once.

"I don't want to be all doom and gloom, but you have to promise me — seriously, you need to *swear* — that you will get yourself and your loved ones the hell out of San Francisco before mid-April of 1906."

"The earthquake?"

"A huge earthquake. It's bad enough on its own, but the fires afterward are even worse."

He nodded, and I could see the gears turning and grinding.

"Death toll?"

"About 3,000. Crazy. Enormous," I said, then told him that formally, fewer than 400 deaths were reported. Some said the discrepancy existed because officials didn't want the real count to scare people off and keep the city from being rebuilt. I also told him that estimates in my era say that 80 percent of the city was severely damaged or destroyed — another figure that was downplayed at the time. I wanted him to know both sets of numbers, in case he thought he changed something... or did, in fact, change it.

"Staggering."

He looked pained, and I know he was envisioning the scenario.

"Why was it so deadly? That seems impossibly destructive."

"The fires raged for three days, over something like four square miles of the city. Pretty much every wooden structure in its path was burned down."

"Where could people go to be safe?"

"Away from San Francisco is the big thing — the farther outside of the Bay Area is better. Downtown Santa Rosa was demolished, too, and that's fifty miles north. If you're at all in the area, avoid brick structures that might be knocked down, and be prepared to battle fires."

"Do you know the time and date?"

"Almost everyone knows the date by heart," I told him, and then immediately realized I'd forgotten the specifics. "Um — April... somethingth. 1906. I gasped, "Wow. I am totally drawing a blank."

"Your memory 'gremlins' again?"

"I guess," I sighed. The little critters were a somewhat recent development.

For the first few months of my travels, I had a pretty much rock-solid recollection of one place in the other. But starting around the beginning of April, I noticed ideas and information were not making it into the other timeline. For example, I would work really hard to memorize five things in the Now, and when I arrived in the Then, I could only recall two or three of them. The others had just faded into the ether, like memories of an everyday dream.

But then it started getting worse. I would make a point to something specific commit to memory — such as Walt and Maggie's address as of June — but when I got to 1900, I completely forgot the entire topic. I had no recollection of even trying to bring back data at all. Stranger still, when I woke up in my original time, it was all fresh in my mind again.

It was frustrating, but I took it in stride, figuring it was a byproduct of trying to jam double the pleasure and double the fun into my little brain.

By breaking up lists of things to recall over a few days, I tried to work around the flawed system. I thought of it like carry-on memories: I couldn't check so much mental luggage anymore, so had to bring what I needed back in smaller bits.

We could think of only one explanation: Whoever or whatever was sending me through time had decided that when I started going off-mission, impediments were going to rain down on me. This strange brand of forgetfulness pretty effectively got the point across, and, at the very least, was not nearly as unpleasant as the fainting thing.

"Ha — I think so, yeah. I guess even the universe considers it a big deal."

He looked very solemn as he considered this information. "I won't forget," he said, then he added it to his list.

When we were done, I gave him a little disclaimer. "Now, remember — I'm not a historian. Nothing I say is guaranteed." Then I added something else that had been consuming my thoughts lately. "And, if history can be changed by someone like me, you have to consider that there's probably someone else out there doing it, too."

He didn't say anything, but gave me a big hug, like he was saying thank you. Or maybe it was more of a goodbye.

Then we both stood by the fireplace and burned my original note.

∽ ∽ ∽

Although Priscilla Graham was hanging in there — and had made no more attempts to fly — the circumstances had taken a real toll on the neighborhood. Despite the fact that the April showers were slowing, and the May flowers blooming, morale was at a real low.

The next day, I broached the subject tentatively. "I think I'd like to have a party, and invite everyone who lives around here — sort of an open house."

Travis answered without even looking up from his newspaper, "Sure you do."

"No, I really do, Trav." Using one finger, I gently pulled the newspaper down so he could see my Serious Face. "They've all been so helpful and nice, and I know they were just as good to Jennie before as they have been to me since. I'd like to give back a little."

"You," he said, then pointed to me, "want to have a party? You realize that means inviting a lot of people — many of whom you don't know well — into our home?"

I could give as good as I got.

"Yes. I, *Jennie*," I said, gesturing to myself with an exaggerated motion, "want to have a *party*," (hands wiggling in the air as if confetti was falling) "with a lot of *people*," (here, I let my fingers do the walking) "at our *house*," (pointing up, down, and all around).

"Okay, okay," he laughed. "If that's what you want, let's do it."

"Awesome! When do you think would be good?"

"Not to cast any doubt whatsoever on your entertaining ability, but particularly given the limitations of this era, I might suggest that you take a couple months to plan and prepare for something as major as an open house."

"What kind of limitations?"

"The storage of food, for one thing," he said. "I haven't forgotten how sad you were to discover that we didn't have electric iceboxes. Then we will need to borrow some tables, arrange for musical entertainment, prepare a menu, find out who could help."

"It sounds like we're planning a wedding! It doesn't have to be that fancy."

"This isn't fancy, Jen — I already discarded all thought of a formal dinner party, because I can't imagine you want to provide five-course meals for a hundred people."

He also reminded me that many evening parties stretched on until the wee hours of the morning — in fact, it wasn't unusual for the last guest to leave just in time to catch the sunrise.

After much discussion, it was decided: we would have a lunch party — otherwise known by the hoity-toity name, "luncheon." It would be an open house, meaning all the neighbors would be invited.

I gave myself one month to make it happen, which I figured was plenty, considering most parties in the Now took me only a week to set up.

Of course, if I'd had any clue about the kind of crazy days waiting for me just over the horizon, I might have been wise enough to a little wiggle room to my schedule.

69: The Now – Being there

Three seconds after I opened my eyes in the morning, I turned over and checked the pages of history. No changes as far as I could see. What that meant, and what to do about it? I didn't know, but I'd work on that tomorrow in the Then.

After the school play catastrophe, I started to keep myself on a tighter leash. The biggest change was to try to keep what happened in the past in the past. To that end, I tried to confine my research to the hours after the kids went to bed, and the planning and musing to the times when I was actually back in 1900.

The irony was not lost on me that no sooner had I made a commitment to be more available to my girls that the action ratcheted up.

I decided to allow the process of figuring what to do with Walt and Maggie to be a top priority... in the Then. Back in 1900, I could brainstorm, plan, hunt for clues — whatever I needed or wanted to do.

While I was here in the Now, though, the kiddos were at the top of my list — followed by my day job. Historic research, therefore, was relegated to third place. That meant I still ran searches and checked the news daily... but made every effort to minimize all that, and to keep it out of my head the rest of the day.

For that, distraction was key. I need to keep busy, and the most sensible way to do that was to do something productive with the kiddos.

In addition to the usual diversions — swimming, playing, reading, cooking — I decided to capitalize on the fact that the girls loved doing anything crafty (a passion they probably got from me).

Together, we decided to create our own little business. We'd make jewelry and fridge magnets, sell our wares locally and online, then give one hundred percent of the profits to charity.

"Maybe we can donate the money to our teachers?" Lily suggested.

Their school happened to be located with an enclave of very expensive homes, and needed an influx of cash like a morbidly obese person needed a six-pack of deep-fried Twinkies.

Instead of specifically drawing attention to that fact, I told them about schools not ten miles away facing library closures and sports program cuts. "How about we help those schools instead?" My daughter, who had wanted for precious little in her eight years, agreed immediately.

Within days, our dining room was overrun with beads and string, glass blobs and rare earth magnets, hole punches and scissors, magazine pages and scrapbook papers. We were industrious while building up our inventory, producing about twenty pieces on day one, and thirty per day thereafter.

ᔕ ᔕ ᔕ

Travis asked me why I kept working so hard when, by placing a simple bet, I could have enough money to make it rain — all day, every day — at Target, the crafts store, and the local coffee shops. Oh yeah.

But no. "I'm pretty sure if I tried it, something would go wrong. I'd forget the details, pass out, or just attract the wrong kind of attention."

"But what if you weren't disruptive — didn't take it from elsewhere, just left it to yourself? Make a little bank account."

I shook my head no. "I just don't see it working."

"You think it seems like cheating, don't you?"

"Well, yeah, but that's not the only reason."

"Please, do explain," Travis said. "I'm not arguing with you — but am very curious."

Honestly, I didn't know how much he would understand. Women here rarely had careers... and even when they were successful, respect more the exception than the rule.

"I can't give up my work," I said after several moments. "More to the point — I don't *want* to. I've put so much into building my own company. It's small, but it's mine, and it has sustained me. I like what I do, and get a lot of satisfaction from a job well done."

"It's unusual, but I can relate to that," Travis said. "With police work, the hours are long, the work hard, and the pay average... but I can't imagine going into selling stocks or practicing law."

"Exactly, Trav."

"I've been nearly broke, and I've been pretty wealthy, too, but I can tell you this: Though it's handy and greases a lot of wheels, money doesn't kiss back."

∽ ∽ ∽

Had reprioritizing my schedule helped? Yes — I felt a little less torn, and could fall asleep at night without first stressing over the top 100 things on my to-do list.

Don't think for a minute, though, that I was all organized and had this dual life thing down pat. The problem could be identified with simple math. For me, 5 + 5 = 5... or, in layman's terms, I jammed ten days of fun on to a five day calendar:

Now: Work through the morning while kids swam, spend afternoon doing crafty things

Then: Plotting and planning, cooking... and even cleaning

Now: Take girls to the park, meet with a client for work, an hour of craftiness, go out to dinner

Then: Run errands, visit neighbors, have time with Travis

Now: Drive up with the girls to visit my parents in Sonoma; swim and play and hang out

Then: Spend the day traipsing around San Francisco with Travis and learning how to play whist

Now: Wake up (still in Sonoma), take the kids to the beach, then browse antiques with my mom

Then: Conduct covert surveillance by day; Go to neighbor's for whist party (and realize I have forgotten all but the absolute basics of the game)

Now: Leave my parents' house in the morning, drop the girls off at their dad's, try to focus on work

Then: Spend half the day washing laundry, and the other half cooking and trying to figure out the crime puzzles

There was no getting around the fact that if my life had a gauge, I'd spend most of my time right on the redline.

70: The letter

Three strikes for my "think positive" method for revising history, and now I was out — or, at least, ready to try something different.

"I didn't want to say as much before," Travis began, and I tried not to clench my fists, "however, I believe that simply stating our intention was not enough. I believe it might be necessary for us to actually make strides to truly embark upon the path."

My hands loosened on their own, because I had reached pretty much the same conclusion: If planning alone didn't make things happen, we needed to start making physical steps toward our goal.

To that end, Travis and I drafted the note together. Later in the afternoon, I bought the paper and envelope, and then, wearing my white gloves, wrote down those maddening words in a variant of my handwriting.

The goal was to plant the suggestion that the governess had some lascivious intentions. Playing on someone's fears wasn't nice and it wasn't kind... but it was easy, direct and served a purpose. We decided to keep the phrasing as simple as possible — with few details and no signature. There was no need to muddy the water with facts or examples, because what red-blooded woman's claws wouldn't come out after getting a letter like that?

Travis assured me that in this time and place, a letter — even one as libelous as this — wasn't likely to be considered fishy. Even if it did somehow arouse suspicion, there was little that could be done to investigate something so anonymous.

If there was no change in Maggie's employment situation, we'd move on to subtly alerting the household staff and perhaps one or two of Mrs C's friends.

While there were the devious exceptions, in general, folks in the early 1900s were quite trusting. This vulnerability was something we could exploit — but I had to believe it was all for the greater good. And I could.

◁◁◁

"I want to do this now — today. Let's just get this moving and drop off the letter at their house," I said. "Slip it into their mailbox."

"Slow down, Jen. Take a breath," Travis started to massage my shoulders. "Things don't need to work at such a hurried pace. Mailing the letter though the post will only add a day, and will give us distance from the situation. We can't have anyone suspect a connection, especially given that I know Maggie."

Eventually it was decided that he would mail the letter on his way to work in the morning. I slipped on some gloves before I sealed the envelope, wrote out their address, then used a damp sponge to adhere the stamp. (What can I say: Fingerprints and DNA were always on my mind.)

Travis slipped it into the pocket of his jacket, which was hanging on a hook by the front door.

Then we waited.

☙ ☙ ☙

I spent the whole next day in the Now second-guessing everything. Did we plant the suggestion strongly enough? Did the message not get delivered... or was Mrs Cooper made of strong enough stuff to just cast any such concerns aside with a laugh and a head shake?

By the time evening rolled around, I had pretty well come to grips to the fact that this situation was just a symptom of what I feared the most — that I couldn't effect actual change. Sure, I could alter little inconsequential stuff — the pencil marks along the margins of the book of life... but when it came to saving lives, some things were apparently written in permanent marker.

Of course, an hour after I decided to acquiesce to fate... there finally was a change. In fact, the whole thing with the Coopers? Never happened. Bank vault deaths? No such tragedy ever occurred.

A huge shiver ran down my arms. *I could change the past. I could change the future.* I wanted to don a red cape and tights and proclaim this from the rooftops (or, at least, from my little balcony).

☙ ☙ ☙

After I woke up Travis to share the delightful news, he seemed even more jazzed about it than I had been.

"To be honest," he said, "and this isn't a knock on you, but I was starting to think we were going to be well and truly stuck with whatever destiny had commanded."

"To be honest," I said, "I was starting to think the same thing."

"No matter," he said, and wrapped me in a hug. "Tonight, we will celebrate!"

Sometime during the long afternoon hours, the doorbell rang, interrupting me in the middle of attempting to clean the oven. After rushing around to make my *hausfrau* self presentable enough to be seen by whomever might be calling, I finally opened the door... and there stood Travis with a huge grin on his face.

I stared at him, then finally sputtered, "You said *tonight*!"

He looked so delighted, I couldn't help but to smile back. "Yes," he said, "because I wanted this to be a surprise."

And it was. My sweetheart cradled two plain brown cardboard containers that looked like small shoe boxes.

"Let's go inside, shall we?" he said, "and then I will show you what I brought."

We sat down on the sofa in the living room, and he handed me one of the packages. "Consider it an early birthday present. Open it!" he urged — but I didn't need any encouragement. I folded back the top, and inside, wrapped in tissue, were two gynecological stirrups with wheels. Or maybe it was a pair of old-fashioned metal roller skates. When I thought about it, I decided the second option was more likely.

"Oh, these are awesome! I haven't been roller skating in years," I said, and jumped into his lap to give him a hug.

"Nor have I," he said, "and I was never very good at it."

For weeks now, Travis had taken it upon himself to get me outside as much as possible. My natural tendency to stay indoors baffled him. "I grew up in England, remember. I have seen many snowfalls as high as my head, and endured rain for months on end," he told me. "So this I know to be true: When one has the privilege of living in a place such as San Francisco, one must enjoy the weather."

He reminded me how important it was for me to continue to exercise, plus insisted that the fresh air warded off disease.

"All this kind of activity is healthy, of course. But the air in my house is just fine. And if people here really cared about health, they wouldn't wear these damn long sleeves all the time. That's what causes rickets and other problems — when you don't get enough sunlight on your skin to produce Vitamin D."

"Really? I have not heard that."

"Of course, too much sun will give you skin cancer."

His brow furrowed as he compared one health tip to the other, then finally said, "Advice of your era is extremely contradictory."

"True that."

∽ ∽ ∽

The skates were made to hold a shoe, and the heel-to-toe size was adjusted with the use of a matching metal key. The things were heavy, and were made entirely of steel, apart from the leather straps.

"Shall we?" he asked. How bizarrely blissful it was to just go off and do something so recreational on a whim, with no planning, rearranging or postponing my entire schedule. I wasn't used to such freedom.

"Let me just grab a hat!" Let me say unequivocally that I was not bowing to societal pressure. I just finally understood why women loved their head adornments: those babies hide a multitude of sins. No time to shampoo? Bad hair day? Slap on a hat and you're all set. (The only lousy part is, of course, when you're required to take the hat off and it looks like you have been hiding a poorly-groomed possum under there. But whatever.)

Sitting on the bottom porch step, Travis helped me into my skates, and then fastened his own. Holding hands, we stood up, and we were off, slip slidin' away.

The ride was as rough as I expected, but having been mentally prepared for that made all the difference. We were running metal wheels over concrete sidewalks, and the way those two interacted was a far cry from the smooth ride offered by the much softer urethane wheels of today's skates. When we tried to cross on the rough and often rocky streets, the experience became a little more hazardous and a lot more bumpy, but I was having a grand old time anyway.

Skating in a big poofy skirt, of course, offered its own challenges. For one thing, I'd never realized how much I relied on being able to see where my feet were — even just out of the periphery of my vision.

Once I got into the groove, and we found a few long stretches of smooth surfaces, it was fun. Fantastic, in fact. All the thirst for speed I'd been denied in the Then was quenched in just an hour of noodling about on these quaint quad skates.

If you must know, I spent much of that time totally rockin' the moves from *Xanadu*. I thought the Olivia Newton John/Gene Kelly was greatest thing in the world... when I was six. If only I had a shorter skirt and some leg warmers, I would have totally nailed it.

We ended the evening by racing down a hill, hootin' and hollerin' all the way down. Who won? Yours truly — by about two seconds. Travis congratulated me by sliding into me at full-tilt, the power of which pushed us about ten feet along, and landed us in a foot-deep fountain filled by little peeing cupids.

In the Now, any sudden dunking would produce major anxiety due to cell phones being ruined, purses getting waterlogged, and contact lenses washing away. But at this moment in my existence, I hadn't a worry in the world. I was able to simply delight in the fact that I was resting in a cascade of sparkling water, nestled amongst the wishes made on pennies, and loving it all so much that I couldn't help but to just laugh and laugh and laugh.

71: Reverse

The gift of a lovely day in the Then meant even more to me once I woke up. That's because the present greeted me with such a sore throat and stuffy nose, I wanted to staple myself into bed for the remainder of the day so nothing and no one could drag me out.

When I finally ventured out into the world beyond my blankets, I was, per usual, compelled to check the status of history. Why didn't I just let myself remain blissful to the machinations of time until that evening? I really should have.

The results were in, and they were unambiguous: The whole nasty mess was right back on track. Except now it all happened two weeks sooner, and the heist was pulled before opening hours instead of in the late afternoon.

The timing tweaked the outcome. For whatever reason, there were more employees at work in the morning. Consequently, there were three more people to entomb in the vault. That meant the death toll at the bank was now thirteen.

All of that was horrendous news, but what ripped at my soul the most was what happened up at the Cooper's house. Walt and Maggie had nabbed Pearl right from her bed, but instead of hiding her in the attic — the way the story went before — they stashed her in the basement. She was eventually found, in the words of a newspaper reporter, "tucked away in the bottom of a wardrobe at the east side of the cellar."

There was one minor saving grace of the new scenario: the girl would never have to worry about coping with survivor's guilt. By the time the police reached her, she was already dead.

༄ ༄ ༄

The instant I smelled 1900 — a quirky little blend of manure, wood varnish and Travis's soap — I sat up bolt upright and started talking. "Did you mail that letter? The one to the Coopers?"

"What? Why?" He rolled over to face me and struggled to open his eyes.

"Just tell me: Did you put it in the mailbox?"

"Sorry," he started. "I didn't mail it yet. I thought I might hold off a day or two. I didn't want to tell you, lest that upset the process."

"Oh, thank god," I said, and fell back onto the pillows. Don't send that letter — it won't work. In fact, it's going to make it worse."

"How much worse?"

"They move the whole thing up half a month, and end up with four more dead... including the little girl."

My best guess was that Maggie either figured out she was going to be fired, or someone had tipped her off. There were obviously a lot of loose lips at that house, which is something we'd counted on... we just hadn't thought about anyone sharing that information with Miss Gallagher so quickly.

It was a little shocking to realize that the dangerous duo were so committed — and so well-prepared — they could weather the changes we had forced on them. But how come they revised the plan, and why the rush? It seemed the changes were important to identify, because they exposed their scheme's pivot points.

For now, though, we needed a completely different strategy.

"Well, there is the idea I considered before..." Travis started to say.

I gave him the (impatient) rolling hand gesture to suggest he continue.

"I might know people who would appreciate their belongings, and might be willing to remove their property from their current residence."

Not the worst idea in the world. "What do you think that will get them to do?"

"Ideally, it will encourage them to leave town. Especially if it happens more than once."

"How much of their stuff might an interested individual — and definitely not you — be taking?"

"Everything, I would imagine. Dump it all on the bed and take it all. Leave the furniture itself, after carefully checking it for any hidden items, of course."

I was still confused. "How do you see this working as a deterrent?"

He explained that if the thieves were lucky, they would find weapons and money — both of which are tough to replace. "We know that stealth is important to their method, so that's something we can interfere with."

But another goal would be to make them feel uncomfortable and unwelcome, so they would hopefully decide it might be time to move on to greener pastures.

"We don't have to stop them per se, but maybe we can figure out a way to make it not worth their while," Travis said. "Obstruct the process?"

"That," I said, "I think we can do."

⸲ ⸲ ⸲

While Travis got dressed for another day at work, I mulled this all over. Assuming he could find the right people for the job, the only problem I could see was that we didn't know where Walt and Maggie lived anymore.

I wrote down the first two ideas that came to mind, along with their rather significant downsides.

- Get info from Maggie's mom. Cons: She knows Travis, and can connect us to anything that happens; Might not be willing to share info.
- Ask the landlord of previous flat for forwarding address. Con: Might not have the information; Could be traced back to us.

While I pondered other options, I doodled on my notes.

Travis peered over my shoulder as he fastened his jacket buttons. "You forgot one: Follow Maggie from her job."

I started to say we didn't know where she worked — then realized my error with a big "Duh." (For some reason, my transtemporally-addled mind had filed her employment information in the "hasn't happened yet" category.)

With the last foreseeable barrier removed, we could start cobbling together our new agenda.

My job would be to trail Maggie to find out where she lived now. Meanwhile, Travis would get in touch with certain individuals who, *hypothetically*, might be willing to help clear out a home for people who were moving... or something along those lines.

As we were setting the wheels in motion, I also had a foot on the brake — and there it would stay until I looked ahead to find out where this new approach would take us.

⸲ ⸲ ⸲

Here and there, around all the ridiculousness involving the tragic twosome, I was still working on my party plans, which was a nice counterpoint to the other stuff on my mind. Honestly, I got a little kick out of the fact that my agenda here lately was twofold: on one hand, I was figuring out how to prevent several deaths; on the other, I was prepping for one of the most awesome and memorable parties this neighborhood had ever seen.

That said, I was making every effort to keep the gala very simple, and not so hectic that I wouldn't have a free moment to enjoy my guests. I'd already thrown too many parties where I was constantly running around like a chicken without a head, and consequently have few memories of the event other than the constant stress.

While I intended this open house to be a thank you to everyone we knew for their support and acceptance , I also decided it would be wise to graciously accept the non-stop offers to bring food and drink and to otherwise help out. Without question, I could do with the assistance. After creating utter chaos — not once but twice — on the preschool playgroup party circuit, I had come to understand my limits. In my modern life, I didn't mind being "that mom" for whom every event was a debacle. Here, though, I wanted to set my standards a little higher.

To that end, I'd originally hoped to hire a singer and a couple musicians, then to teach them a few songs. I had visions of the guys playing Sinatra and Elvis showstoppers and wowing the crowd.

But a vision is where it started and where it ended, because I didn't have enough time to find the talent, write out all the music, and spare hours for all the rehearsing required.

In lieu of that, Travis made arrangements to borrow the player piano that had so fascinated me months before. He assured me that the next time we entertained, I'd just have to allow an extra few weeks for the planning phase, and I'd be able to entertain my guests with all the futuristic music my little heart desired.

As silly as a little party might have seemed in the grand scheme of things, I look back and am so glad I devoted so much energy and enthusiasm to planning it while I could, because — unbeknownst to me — life was just about to get crazy.

༄ ༄ ༄

It wasn't until a month later that I finally looked at what the local society maven had written about our gala. I was so glad I hadn't previewed the news, because I would have been paralyzed with fear to discover that nearly *five hundred* well-dressed folks found their way to our address that day.

What would have softened the fear then still turns my heart to mush today. The newspaper presented the usual list of the most prominent names in attendance, a recitation of the foods served, and noted a few other details. But what makes me tear up every time was what the writer added at the very end of the article. That's where she described our shindig as having been "beautiful, memorable and joyful."

Even if our little party didn't turn out at all how I expected, I knew it had been perfect in its own way.

72: Surveillance

A few hours later, I found myself in the bushes. Not near some bushes, but actually inside a wall of shrubbery so thick it effectively served as a divider between the Cooper's house and their neighbor's.

The ragged, empty branches at the center of the mass caught on my clothes and slashed at my skin, but from my vantage point, I could see right into the house, and watch Pearl playing the violin. They had even done me the courtesy of leaving the window open, so I could hear the music as well as the words spoken.

I arrived shortly before four in the afternoon, thinking that most of the hired help would probably depart at some point during the next hour or two.

Maggie was in the shadows, so I couldn't see her directly, but she occasionally offered some direction to the little girl. I was really surprised, because the things she said actually seemed rather intelligent — as if Mags truly had a skilled perspective. I wasn't simply being catty, but really thought she'd taken the job only to get close to the family, and not because she had any talent.

Pearl coaxed smooth melodies from the strings, putting them together to form classical tunes that seemed familiar but I couldn't actually name.

While I was admiring the marble wall paneling and crystal sconces, something descended into my field of view. It was a spider on a delicate thread, close enough that I could see its eyes, and it took every last milliliter of my strength not to scream and run away. Instead, I swatted it away with my white housemaid's cap and did my best to regain my composure.

Right then, the song ended, and I froze while imagining my silent but panicked waving around had been spotted. Fortunately, it only seemed like the lesson was over. Maggie stepped out into the room and stood in front of a mahogany grand piano and... I saw it wasn't Maggie at all.

"Very nice, Miss Cooper. You have made considerable progress in this past week. I shall inform your mother of that fact," I heard the mystery woman say in a nasal tone. "Now, you have no doubt noticed your bow grip is worsening, and I noticed some sliding, I will suggest a rehair soon. I will leave a note for your tutor, Miss..."

"It's Miss Donovan, ma'am," Pearl said.

"A note for Miss Donovan, then. Tell her I expect it to be done before our next lesson. Do you understand?" The lady's voice came floating out the window, crystal clear.

"Yes, ma'am," the little girl replied obediently.

"Now I understand you and your parents are going on holiday to Oakland through next Tuesday, is that correct?"

Pearl nodded, and the teacher bit back with an immediate, "I cannot hear you, Miss Cooper."

"Yes, Mrs Durham, that is correct."

"Very well. In that case, I will see you next Wednesday, Miss Cooper. Three o'clock sharp," the teacher said. With a finger waggle she added, "Be certain to complete your practice work each day. I will know if you haven't."

The girl replied politely, walked the woman to the door, and then all was quiet.

With the family heading out of town — ooh! all the way across the Bay to the exotic land of Oakland — apparently I'd have to come back next week to stalk Maggie.

∽ ∽ ∽

Even though I didn't get the information we needed, at least I had a handle on when and where I would be able to get it. I hoped the fact that I had a specific plan — combined with Travis's success at reaching out to the "movers," shall we say — would be enough to make history change.

It seemed somehow wrong to celebrate Travis's success at booking a burglary, but he was relieved to report that the associates of acquaintances he contacted agreed to take the job. We just needed to tell them the date and place, and slip them a twenty dollar bill.

"They are going to take everything they find in Walt and Maggie's flat, get away with it, and we have to pay them, too?"

Travis nodded. "I think you would say, 'Nice work if you can get it.'"

You need to remember that, compared to modern-day America, the year 1900 wasn't far removed from the days of gunfighters and cattle rustlers. It was hard to believe, but Buffalo Bill Cody had put on the first "Wild West" show only seventeen years earlier, in 1883.

Right in line with that, the term sometimes used to describe law enforcement of the era was "frontier justice." Although San Francisco was a big city, vigilantism was still common. Though people (especially the police) weren't supposed to play judge and jury... it happened a lot. Men were beaten, broken, run out of town — and on rare occasions, yes, even killed. It was all off-book. Hard evidence was hard to come by, and witnesses could be paid off.

I didn't agree with the way some things worked here, but I understood it, and wasn't afraid to let things happen if it was for the greater good.

What right did I have to decide? I ask myself that, too.

If this situation was happening today, I probably wouldn't be making the same moves. While I think that the our country's legal system is bloated and ego-driven, I'd do my best to work within it. (The exception would be anything to do with my kids. If someone harmed one of my babies, the gloves — and all bets — were off.)

In the Then, though, I'd adopted a sort of "When in Rome" attitude — for better and for worse. By the power vested in me by the timelords who sent me here, I had to make judgment calls — but if I made the wrong one, I knew it would be my cross to bear.

☙ ☙ ☙

The roller skating days before had put me in mind of thrills, so the next day in the Now, the wee ones and I headed down to Santa Clara to visit the only big amusement park in the area.

After a long, wonderful and very hot day, all three of us were exhausted when we finally got home after dark, with sunburns, 150 new photos on my camera, and a couple lollipops nearly as big as the girls' heads.

Once the girls were all tucked into bed, it was time to check the state of the world. With a few clicks, I pulled up the link I'd bookmarked before... and the story was gone. To make sure it hadn't just moved, I looked back through every one of the ten pages of the evening edition of the newspaper, and still nothing. Back a day, ahead a day — still nada.

Just to make sure there was nothing there, I ran a couple keyword searches — *bank, banking, robbery, heist, vault* — to cover the entire year.

Still zip. In fact, I didn't find any more weird or otherwise suspicious bank robberies at *any* point during 1900 — nor were there any in the Bay Area that fit their pattern in either 1901 or 1902.

If I was reading this right, all we needed to do was follow through with our plan, and this nightmarish element in my dream life would be over. Finally.

Travis was giddy when I told him the news, and didn't even mind that I interrupted him mid-snore to do so. The fact that we could fix the situation without any violence was a big, sweet cherry on top.

Nearly a week would have to pass before I could track Maggie from her job. I appreciated that history had faith in our actions, but I wouldn't be able to stop holding my breath until I'd finished my part and the whole scheme had been completed.

While the Cooper family would only be out of town until Tuesday, it appeared Maggie didn't work Wednesdays, so I would need to wait until the following Thursday.

I needed to remind myself to see the big picture here, because every time I thought about it, I got annoyed that two days before my party, I'd be hanging out in the bushes again instead of putting in time getting everything ready.

∽∽∽

I learned that when planning a social gathering in the Now, one thing you rely on is preparing as much food ahead of time as possible, so in the hours before the guests start arriving, you can concentrate on everything else you need to do.

That is not the way things work when you live in a time without electric refrigerators and freezers in every household. We were going to have to assemble the perishables at the last minute, and to keep them cool we planned to bring in huge blocks of ice.

Apart from apples, which kept well in cold storage, I could really only use seasonal fruit and vegetables. In the Now, I could get a banana at the grocery store any time of year — ditto almost all fruits and vegetables. I had to constantly be mindful of the differences because there were no huge commercial hothouses, refrigerated train cars or planes to fly in produce from far-flung continents.

There was also a whole lot of bakin' goin' on. Cookies and cakes, mainly, which were perennial favorites.

It's lucky I didn't have a particular hatred for insects, because they were constantly all over the place here. Flies were the worst, especially because of all the horses everywhere. Bugs, though, were are not the only pests — there were also all kinds of mice and rats and who knows what other kind of rodents.

It was very much a part of life here — a really disgusting part. People took it in stride, and dealt with it as needed. For example, when I suggested merely dumping the flour in a bowl when making a cake, my neighbor Mrs Fletcher "reminded" me that part of the reason you sifted the dry ingredients when baking was to filter out the (mostly) dead insects.

The same neighbor also told me that the reason we frosted cakes was to keep the "sponge" soft and fresh, so they could last for days. I just thought it was fantastic to have yet another reason to make buttercream icing.

In all other aspects, too, party prep was going along swimmingly. My foyer and living room were both full of sofas and loveseats, borrowed from ten different neighbors. They weren't yet in position, but I had floor plans drawn up. I had decided to try to recreate a cushy, cozy coffee shop-style atmosphere for the guests (although there would be plenty of standing room available, too). It was something new for me — and I thought would be new to our guests, too.

And since no festivities in this era would be complete without it, I was working to perfect a recipe for a sparkling red drink. In my day, it was easy — tropical punch plus lemon-lime soda. Recreating a sweet and sour punch with a fizzy kick, using only ingredients available in the Then, was a considerable challenge.

I hoped everyone would like the stuff, because by the time my countless beverage experiments were over, I was pretty sure that I'd never again crave a nice Hawaiian Punch.

73: A silver dollar

We were in the home stretch of party planning, and my nerves — in both time zones — were showing the strain. Still, great progress was being made. Some of the neighbor children had cut hundreds of leaf and flower shapes, colored them, and shaped them into garlands and other types of whimsical decorations. Doilies were laid out on every surface, and vases set out in various positions for the florist to fill Saturday morning.

The piano delivery was tomorrow, and I was going to need to usher the men inside and show them where to place the ragtime music box. That's because Travis had something to pick up downtown. The boy was getting my portrait matted and framed, and I would get to see it for the first time — along with all my guests — at some point during the festivities, during its grand unveiling.

Normally, I'd balk at doing anything so ostentatious. But in this time and place — and with such a sweet man behind the gesture — I didn't even consider saying no.

∽ ∽ ∽

Mid-morning on Thursday, Mrs Fletcher came to my door to tell me the good news: Priscilla had delivered a healthy baby boy the night before. I was invited to come meet the newborn, and didn't hesitate a second.

The midwife told me that Prissy had managed delivery "admirably," and little Andrew emerged weighing eight pounds, and, as they proudly told me and the other neighbors, he apparently had a rugged appetite.

Little though he may have been, he filled my Jennie-sized arms. I swayed back and forth with the little pumpkin, which brought *oohs* and *ahhs* from the other women. "You were made to be a mother," they said. "You and your gentleman there need to have wedding soon so you can have your own babies."

I nodded and smiled. "I know I'll be a mom one day. It might be a while, but it will happen. I'm sure of it."

◆ ◆ ◆

Around four o'clock, I worked my way into the bushes again — but this time I was a little more prepared. I was wearing long gloves, and wore a deep green head scarf to protect me from the creepy crawlies, thorns and brambles — and double as camouflage.

The violin was still being played, but there was no instruction being offered. It looked like Pearl was just following the lesson on her own, while Maggie sat nearby, reading a book and scarcely noticing the girl.

When the clock gonged five times, Mags reluctantly put down "The Cat in the Hat" — or whatever had been entertaining her for the past hour — and told the girl she could be done for the day.

I took this as my cue to make my way toward the front of the property, snaking along the outside of the bushes on the neighbor's property. When I reached the street, I moseyed up and down the block until I saw Maggie finally emerge from the Cooper's house.

She crossed the road and started walking with her head in the clouds — ignoring everyone she passed, and scarcely glancing around her. (If I didn't know better, I'd have guessed she was wearing earbuds and blasting country music.)

I started tailing her, always staying at least a hundred yards behind, and walking on the opposite side of the street.

◆ ◆ ◆

Ever heard the expression life turns on a dime? Well, in my case, it was a dollar.

Who hasn't driven down the road and seen a car accident up ahead? I'd bet most people would look at it and do a little quick calculation: "If I hadn't taken that phone call, I might have left the house two minutes earlier, and then that could have been me in that crash."

Life is a series of choices — of chances, even — leading to specific events happening at specific moments in time. It's rare we put real thought into the complex circumstances moving us toward any given conclusion.

For example: You're grocery shopping, and all of the registers have lines of about equal length. But instead of choosing the line closest to you, you pick another, because a certain magazine in the rack there caught your eye. A minute later, someone else pushes their cart up behind you — and hey, wow! It's Karen from high school, who you haven't seen for years (and, frankly, had forgotten about).

Since you're both in a rush, you swap email addresses and reconnect online. Through your friends list, she gets in touch with some other long-lost pals... including a former neighbor of hers. Six months later, after a whirlwind romance, she ends up marrying the neighbor. A year after that, the couple welcomes a healthy baby girl... then that little kid grows up to invent a cure for some horrible disease.

And so, three decades from now, thousands of lives will be saved each year... all because you just *had* to take a peek at a gossip rag for photos of the worst celebrity stretch marks.

Usually, you never know what *didn't* happen because of the path you took. But, when you get to mess with time, sometimes you can spot a single action that changed the course of your destiny, and forever after.

⌒ ⌒ ⌒

The agonizingly steep Nob Hill was a tough enough hike when I was on my own, but it was even worse when I was trying to keep up with someone who apparently had been smart enough to at least wear flats for the walk.

I dearly hoped Maggie would not be taking the trolley anywhere, as it would be really hard to follow her if that was the case. I would really have only two options: Get on and stand as far out of the way as possible or just run after hers. (That would be a challenge, but not an impossibility. Don't forget these things went only 10 or 15 miles an hour, and stopped rather frequently both for passengers and because of traffic.)

She just kept walking, and about a mile in, I really wished she had considered taking the streetcar, because my feet were getting really achy.

Every time she slowed or stopped, I would slip into a doorway or alley to get out of her direct line of sight. After the third time I had to hide, I took off my scarf and swapped it out for a pink shoulder shawl to change my look a little.

On the outskirts of downtown, she entered some kind of store, so I waited impatiently across the street, between a produce vendor's cart and a homeless guy. "Obediah the beggar man," as he said, introduced himself, and immediately launched into an explanation of how he came from Ohio to California in 1850, hoping to make his fortune. "That didn't pan out," he said, then gave a big toothless grin, laughing at his own gold mining joke.

Before I had a chance to ask for details, Maggie emerged into the sunlight. Pulling a five dollar bill out of my bag, I handed it to the man behind the fruit and vegetable cart, and told him to give the "beggar man" food for as long as the cash would last. With a nod of agreement, I dashed off in pursuit.

My Good Samaritan bit nearly left me with a cold trail, I managed to catch sight of her skirt a quarter second before she disappeared off the street and around the corner. I did my best to follow a safe distance behind as she navigated her shortcut, zigging and zagging through alleys, side streets, and even the tiny space between two homes. We wound our way through beggars and dogs and cats and towering piles of horribly smelly garbage and somewhat smelly people loading things out of wagons. (Long before, I'd become accustomed to the manure smell, and hardly noticed it anymore.)

I was out of breath by the time I finally emerged onto a main drag, and jolted myself into a bit of a panic to realize I had almost gotten too close to Maggie. I made myself comfortable near a wall, pretending to look at a map, to give her time to get ahead of me. When she ran across the street and up the steps to the entrance of a simple four-story apartment building clad with whitewashed brick, I was relieved the chase was over.

Even though I was 95 percent positive that's where she lived — wasn't as likely she would have an obscure shortcut for some random spot in the city — I hovered out of the way and waited to see if she was going to come back out.

After about five minutes passed, I decided she would be staying put for a while. I made a note of the address in my book. It would be too risky to seek the apartment number now, I thought, so we could work on that aspect later.

The whole time I'd been standing, a bright light kept flickering and shining into my eyes. Initially, I thought it was some Morse code transmission.... but I eventually realized there was something reflective on the ground in the street, and I was at the perfect angle and distance to catch the bounce of the sun's rays whenever wagons and carriages weren't rolling by.

Curiosity got the best of me, and I walked to the edge of the sidewalk to see exactly what had been winking at me so impertinently. I was surprised to see a shiny dollar coin, stuck in the gap between two cobblestones, the way a piece of parsley will wedge itself between your front teeth. It didn't look like anyone else had noticed it.

I stepped closer to it, and it threw a steady, welcoming beam of light at me. A silver Siren's call. I reached out to grab it, and the moment my fingers clutched the coin's grooved edge, I felt a hand grab my dress and yank me backward.

Scarcely a breath later, a wagon came barreling around the corner, thick steel wheels rolling over right where the coin had been. While I was out of its direct path, I was still close enough to see the wood grain on the slats of the cart as it passed, and the hoofbeats from two horses pounded in my ears.

I spun around to heap praise and thanks upon my rescuer, a businessman who brushed off my gratitude and congratulations from other passersby and tried to remain stoic and manly. After only a minute, a small crowd had gathered around me and my savior, and I totally felt like shouting, "No autographs, please."

Some people admonished me for being careless, while others expressed their version of relief I had not become roadkill. Once I explained, though, that I'd seen a dollar in the road — and showed them my glittering prize — they all understood and exclaimed over my good fortune.

One guy (because there's always that one guy) asked me if I needed to have someone fetch my husband. After I told him I wasn't married, he gave me his business card and held my hand just a little too long.

Finally, the herd thinned out enough for me to escape. I looked once more at our target location, then turned around to orient myself so I could head home. As I turned, I noticed a person in my direct path, and jumped back a little, startled. Standing directly in front of me was the one and only Walter Houlihan. He didn't say anything, but just stared at me.

"What — what..." I said, stumbling on the single word. After my brain caught up, I could complete the sentence. "What are you doing here?"

"I meant to ask you the same thing." His breath reeked of cigarettes and whiskey, and he looked at me with beady lizard eyes.

I blinked a few times, trying to think of a reply — any reply. Finally a question occurred to me: *How much did he know?*

"What do you mean?"

He looked at me up and down — very slowly — before replying. It was actually less a lascivious look, and more like an examination.

"I saw you looking over there," he pointed to the brick building across the street. "Why?"

I think it would be true to say the speed with which an average person can think is inversely proportional to the amount of pressure on which said person. Have tons of time? Ideas flow freely and excitedly, like rafters on a white water river. Have one second to compose a brilliant excuse? Please wait here. Mr Sloth would like to have a word.

A few random words had punctured my haze, and I was eventually able to string them together somewhat coherently. "Just here. Walking around. Have to get exercise."

Aimlessly roaming the city really was a common pastime for me... but that wasn't why I was here today. I was still so shocked by Wally's sudden presence, I'm sure my cover story sounded pretty flimsy.

Finally I asked, "What about you?"

"Same — just walking around," he said, with some lame bravado I found amusing. "The hubbub caught my eye. I was surprised to see you in the midst of it all."

"Yeah, well," I said, and opened my palm to show him my coin, "some people will do crazy things for a buck."

"I wouldn't know," he sniffed, as if the very model of nobility.

At that moment, a couple kids ran by, almost bumping into Walter. He responded by moving a foot closer to me. Reflexively, I moved a foot back.

"You don't have to be scared of me," he said — which, as most women come to know, usually means the opposite. "Perhaps we could even be friends again."

My mind roared into play, showing me a montage of images — the way I imagined Jennie's tumble down the stairs, the angry scars still visible on my forehead, his off-the-cuff remark about not having pushed me "hard enough," how he'd accosted me on the street months before, the trail of disasters I'd prevented — and, most of all, I recalled the frightful details in my book at home. Those pages told the tale of the man Walt once had become — a person who was no longer afraid to kill.

How do you respond to a psychopath? I figured a lie was better than pissing him off.

"Sure, maybe," I finally answered, and tried to force a smile onto my lips. "But I need to be getting home now."

"Donovan waiting for you?" I couldn't read the accompanying expression. Frustration? Jealousy? Gas?

"Yes, he's expecting me at any minute."

Walt nodded, making me uncomfortable with how steadily he tried to hold my gaze. "Yes, and Miss Maggie is certainly wondering where I've gotten off to," he said, and couldn't stop my eyes from automatically flickering over to steal a glance at his apartment building. Had he noticed? I couldn't tell.

"Good evening, then," he said, and with a little nod, walked past me. Just to get away from him, I scuttled off down the alley that brought me to this point, and hoped I could find my way back through the maze. From there, I'd find a ride home, then slide into a got bath to wash off the grime of this hectic day.

As I said before, life sometimes turns on a dime — or on a dollar. Funny thing is, sometimes you don't know you've gotten all turned around until later. Until it's too late. Until the last thing you *want* to do becomes the only thing you *can* do.

74: The Now – The new picture

The next morning in the Now welcomed me to the lowest point of my cold, complete with sniffles, coughing, and an unfortunate loss of the sound that normally accompanies the letters N and M.

From the relative comfort of my bed, I set my laptop on the pillow next to me and hit the web. The first thing I did today was the same as the first thing I had been doing for several days now: scan the old papers for Walt and Maggie's names, and still nothing showed up.

Today, though, it finally occurred to me that something might be amiss. Maybe it was just a lucky guess, or possibly a result of my general edginess after another run-in with the target of my investigation.

If you have ever taken care of a toddler, you know there's a difference between quiet and *too* quiet. This was suspicious. By this time, there should have been some activity showing up — either in the newspaper or my grifter's book (which now didn't include Walt at all).

I decided to look for kidnapping- and bank-related crimes farther ahead, and further afield. I extended my fishing expedition to cover through the year 1905, and to include the entire United States.

With a tap of the "enter" button, thousands of archived newspaper pages displayed. I brought the limit back to California and Washington state only — since Maggie apparently had family there — and scavenged for *any* insight at all. I felt positive that if those two dirty, rotten scoundrels were still alive, they would definitely be up to their old tricks.

Two hours in, I wanted to cry not just because I hadn't turned up much pertinent to our case, but because I had read so many tales of heartlessness and despair, it made me want to run away with my girls to some remote island.

A thought occurred to me, and I pushed it aside, only for it to pop right back into my mind even more forcefully. It wasn't so much an idea as an uneasy bit of intuition — one that asked me to circumvent my own rules: I needed to run a search to see what the papers said about Travis's future.

Several results popped up at the top of the list, the first was one I'd never seen. Instantly, I regretted peeking and didn't want to look, because I knew in my heart it wouldn't be good news.

When I clicked through to the page, the headlines confirmed my suspicion:

SOCIETY LEADER PERISHES IN FIRE
Shocking Accident at Nob Hill
MRS. COOPER RECEIVES FATAL BURNS
Home Destroyed and a Neighbor's Attempt to Save Woman From Death Proves Unavailing.

At least five souls were lost to-day in a fire that destroyed the Nob Hill mansion of Elliot Cooper early this morning. The cause of the fire is not yet known.

T. J. Schaefer, a neighbor, heard the explosion and saw flames issuing from the doors and windows of the Cooper residence. Schaefer hurried to the scene and met Mrs. Cooper coming out of the front door with her clothing ablaze. Schaefer had the woman lie down and roll near a hydrant, where the ground was wet. In this way, the flames enveloping her were extinguished. Mrs. Cooper later walked to Schaefer's house, a block away, where she died an hour after.

Upon arriving at the scene, Police Officer Louis Connolly discovered a household servant crawling out of the flaming wreckage of the home. The young lady was pulling the nearly-lifeless body of a young girl from the fire. Their victory was short-lived, as the two succumbed to death almost immediately thereafter.

No other persons are known to have survived. Mr. Cooper and his daughter Pearl are thought to have surely perished.

～～～

Rolling over quickly, I only just managed to grab the garbage can by my beside before losing what was left of last night's dinner. Pulling a tissue from the box on the nightstand, I dabbed my mouth before slumping back on to my pillow.

I wish I could say I was surprised, but I wasn't — but seeing it on the printed page was more disturbing than I expected.

"This is too much," I moaned. "I've had enough, and am calling in sick today." The bobble-eyed fuzzy someone attached to my headboard just stared at me, but I felt better for having said it. The girls were at their dad's all day, so there was nobody else to hear. But that also meant there was nobody else I had to please, so the past got my full attention.

When all my search ideas were exhausted, I pulled the sheet over my head and went back to sleep.

Hours later, I woke up — disoriented at first (where was Travis?), but actually feeling like I'd made a bit of progress toward recovery.

Before the afternoon ebbed, I re-ran my searches. True to form, new facets of this strange, sad story had echoed through the decades to come to light in the Now. Goosebumps appeared on both my arms when I saw there were easily two dozen stories about the event, from a front-page column to the purple prose that filled the Cooper family's obituary.

The first "new" article I read was on page one of *The Call*, and featured the kind of multi-tier headline reserved for bigger news:

DOZEN DEAD IN FIRE
Prominent Family Killed on Nob Hill
Police Officer, Servants Also Among the Perished
Coal Gas Stove Exploded
Neighbors Shocked, Devastated

Several sections down the page, I saw this:

San Francisco policeman Louis Connolly found Miss Jennie diMedici, savagely burned and bleeding, crawling out of the flaming wreckage of the basement level of the home. The lady had heroically rescued the battered young Pearl Cooper.

In previous reports, Miss diMedici was incorrectly identified as a servant who worked at the Cooper home.

As I was taking in those few sentences, I swear it looked like some of the letters a couple lines below shimmered ever so slightly. I don't know if new words were being written, if my attention was being drawn to that part of the text, or if I was simply imagining things. All I know is when I read the entirety of the next passage, what had been written gave me hope, a headache, and a bad case of the heebie-jeebies.

The paragraphs that caught my eye had been published beneath the headline, "Bizarre Testimony From Injured Woman Before Succumbing to Death."

Miss diMedici, who had previously suffered a brain injury, was hopelessly traumatized by the night's events. The policeman said she was behaving aggressively, screaming the same two sentences until her death mere minutes later.

"She kept shouting, 'Tell them to get there earlier. The shots hit the pipes,' over and over again. She didn't stop repeating it until she died right there in my arms. That's what she said with her last breath, 'Get there earlier.'"

No explanation or further information was revealed by the horrifically injured victim, who was one of three souls to survive the explosion and fire, only to expire within the hour.

I didn't need an explanation, because I understood it the moment my eyes slid across the text: *That was me in the Then sending a message to the me of the Now.* I had arranged for that information to be delivered the only way I knew: via my favorite courier service, the newspaper.

My freakish insistence to be heard at all costs had served its purpose, and now I just prayed I wouldn't have to do the same thing all over again. The idea of being broiled nearly to death scared the hell out of me... even if I did have another life to occupy me after my turkey timer popped in the year 1900.

75: The Now: No options

Showers are magical things: they can wake you up when you're tired, refresh you after you travel, and make you feel more human when you're sick. Today, that — along with some food — was just what I needed to realize that I was on the clock.

It was six in the evening now. I figured I would be lucid until midnight — and maybe, with enough coffee, could squeeze out another two or three hours after that if I had to.

When I considered everything, from the various scenario changes over the last several months to how critical the current situation had become, one the only things that seemed clear was that my back was now to the wall.

The other point that was crystal clear: I had completely and utterly screwed it all up. My involvement in the past had been making every situation *worse*, not better — and that in particular was a tough pill to swallow.

This wasn't a "Groundhog Day" scenario, meaning I'd have endless loops of time to perfect a solution, and there wouldn't be enough time to plan anything with Travis.

It was solely up to me to figure this one out... and I had until I fell asleep tonight to do it.

᭧ ᭧ ᭧

The next hours were spent reviewing every last scrap of information I could find in this century, considering what I already knew, and taking into account everything and anything available to me in the other time zone.

Then I thought about the long, rocky road that had brought us — me and Travis, Wally and Maggie — to this point. And that's when it dawned on me: The reason all of these crazy, terrible situations involving Walter and Maggie kept cropping up was because I wasn't solving the problem, and just treating the symptoms.

Why hadn't I seen this before? Looking back, it was only too clear. Jennie had survived to take care of this problem, and, most importantly, to keep everyone else out if it.

I reached the only logical conclusion: The only way to end this was to cut off the snake's head.

⸂ ⸂ ⸂

A few months before, Travis had given me a brief pistol primer... although in this case, he told me proudly that the weapon in question was actually a Colt New Police .32 revolver with a four-inch barrel, made in 1898.

"Have you ever fired a gun?" he asked.

"Actually, I don't think I've ever even *touched* a gun."

"I don't know many — truthfully, any — women who have. Thirty years ago, sure, but not today."

He emptied all the bullets, then pushed the revolver across the table to me. "Pick it up. Get a feel for it a bit."

It felt cold and solid, and had a unique odor. It was lighter than I expected, especially given how much damage the thing could do.

A week later, we went out to the beach for a little target practice. (He said that he had learned to shoot deep in the forest upstate, but felt safer with the rocks and water for a backdrop than any wooded area the city could offer.)

By the end of the day's lesson, I had the basics down. Of course, I wasn't going to be winning any shooting contests, but I could handle the gun somewhat competently, and wasn't afraid to fire it if I had to.

⸂ ⸂ ⸂

So, in my mind, it was decided: I would catch the terrible twosome at home. If they weren't there, I would meet them outside the Cooper's home, before they went in — or, worst case scenario, after. And I would shoot them, as quickly and humanely as possible.

Let me be clear: I loathed everything about this plan, and hated that it had come to this. I felt like a terrorist's hostage, strapped with a bomb that would detonate now if I tried to take it off, and detonate only a little bit later if I didn't.

Besides, in the immortal words of Spock, "the needs of the many outweigh the needs of the few." Jennie was the few, and history held the many.

Travis could not be involved in this. It was all on me, so I needed to wake up early and get it done. I would have to take his backup revolver from the lockbox in the second dresser drawer, then ditch it at sea when I was done.

Although it wouldn't be until 1920 that ballistic evidence would be used to convict someone in court, bullets can easily survive for decades, even in lousy storage conditions. Therefore, if I used his service weapon, there was a chance that Travis could eventually be tied to these shootings — even two decades hence.

◈ ◈ ◈

Although I had been drop-dead tired since sundown, the moment I crawled into bed, my eyes didn't want to close. For hours, it seemed, I stared up at the ceiling and agonized about what I was going to have to do. Violence was completely contrary to my nature — I'd never even witnessed a fist fight, let alone been in one.

The only salve for my soul came from the knowledge that I would never make a choice like this in my lifetime as Robin — not only because of the girls, but also since I didn't have the benefit of future sight for events in the Now.

Eventually, exhaustion dragged me off for a fitful rest. When I woke, I could feel where the tracks of my tears had dried on my cheeks. A half second later, I realized I was alone in bed... and noticed my pillow was foam, not feather. Turning my head, I saw the dawn light streaming in through the blinds... not the curtains.

My sleep had started in the twenty first century, and that's exactly where I found myself the next morning. For the first time since all this began so many months ago, I hadn't returned to 1900.

I felt my mouth forming words, but didn't know what I'd said until I heard the whisper, "I'm not going back."

76: The Now: Live in the present

My first feeling was one of panic. *What am I still doing here?* More to the point: *Was I ever going to go back?*

Breathe, breathe. Maybe I had just been too tired — too sick — too stressed — to cope with traveling back just yet.

It was just a fluke, right?

Then the same thing happened the next night. And then the night after that.

I got myself all wound up, not only heartsick that I might ever return, but also wondering if time would march on in the past with or without me.

༺༺༺

One question was soon answered: After I fully recovered from my cold, it was apparent that my return to the land of the past had not been delayed due to illness. Unsurprisingly, that didn't make me feel any better.

By the time I'd been grounded for four days, it had become a constant struggle to stay focused and keep busy. I tried — really, really tried. Some hours were easier than others, and the more I could focus on the present, the better I felt.

At a loss for what to do with myself, I ended up calling an old friend. One thing turned into another, and a few hours later, five women who I'd known since seventh grade were taking me out for a night on the town.

We had so much fun, I could even laugh off their well-meaning comments like, "We haven't seen you for *sooo* long," and "I can't believe how busy you have been since the divorce."

I had completely forgotten how much fun a good old-fashioned girls' night out could be — and was thrilled by how well it helped me take my mind off the Then.

The best part of those days, though, came when I finally got to meet the new miniature human Vivian and her wife Samantha had just welcomed. My first thought was that their adorable little boy was adorable — with wide eyes and a shock of brown hair, styled by nature into a sort of faux-hawk. (I didn't mention that my first impression had been surprise at how remarkably alert he seemed for someone whose head was still squished into a cone shape.)

"What's his name?" I asked.

Vivian took a deep breath and answered, "Mozart Confucius Ebeneezer Kendall-Lee."

I stood there and stared at them, and they stared back at me. The women seemed completely serious.

"Oh," was all I could think to say. Half a second later, Samantha broke into a fit of giggles. "Joking — totally joking."

Cue an enormous sigh of relief.

"His name is really Jason Takei Kendall-Lee," she told me. Vivian nodded her direction and added, "She was worried that people might have a hissy fit about the name Takei. But when we tell everyone the name *this* way, they're so relieved, people don't even hassle us about being total geeks."

"Takei, huh?" I said, because I took her explanation as a challenge to provide a small measure of hassle. "Why be coy? Why not just name him Sulu and be done with it?"

"Ha," Vivian said. "Ha. Want to hold him?"

Of course I did. They handed me the little bundle, and I admired him from his perfect little nose to his tiny little toes. I touched his cheek, and he reflexively turned toward my finger, which instantly made me fall in love. "He's beautiful," I told his moms. "If I hadn't already met my quota on children, I'd totally want to take him home."

I started to rock him back and forth, and they told me that their new little man weighed eight pounds, two ounces — almost exactly the same as Priscilla's newborn. That baby had seemed so huge in Jennie's arms, but this guy was dinky in my Robin-sized snuggle.

Then I had to go ruin my happy by letting my thoughts slip into overdrive. Chubby-faced little Andrew had probably been dead for fifty years before — a thought that bypassed "sobering" and went straight to the core of "depressing."

The joyful new parents saw the tear in my eye and smiled. "You miss those days?" Samantha asked.

I knew they meant my past days of rocking chairs and baby swings, diapers and feeding times — and yes, I very much missed those days. But now

I was back to thinking about the *other* days tugging on my heart, and trying not to ask myself when and if I was ever going to get them back.

༒ ༒ ༒

After too many long days of alternating between crying over my keyboard or my pillow, I gave up on trying to figure out why I was stuck. I decided that I'd just pretend I was on a time vacation, and focus on work and the kids. Anything to keep my mind off turn-of-the-century life.

Iris and Lily were the unwitting benefactors of my surge of energy — because, let me tell you, it took a lot of power to punch through my melancholy. We attended our first baseball game together, drove down for an overnight trip down to Monterey, and hiked deep into the Oakland hills and rewarded ourselves with a picnic lunch.

The hills are where I discovered that my daughter's handheld video games were surprisingly good at keeping my mind occupied... even if I played a lousy game.

"Just go! Stupid thing," I muttered within earshot of my firstborn when I tried to bypass a particularly frustrating part of the fun.

"Mom — you can't get to the next level unless you finish this one first," she said with an embarrassed groan. "It won't let you skip it."

"What?"

She pulled the console out of my hands, and her fingers started flying over the controls. "See, you have to get through all of the obstacles here before you can go to the next world. If you don't do it the right way, you just have to start over and over and over again."

Lily was enjoying her teaching moment very, very much. I tried not to let on that I thought she was being positively, scrumptiously adorable.

I watched as she fiddled with the thing, then turned to me triumphantly when she got the musical reward for completing the level. "See, mom? You just have to be patient and keep trying. If you keep trying something and it doesn't work, you're probably doing it wrong, and you will be stuck."

Stuck. Yeah, I knew the feeling. I was probably doing it wrong.

Wait... what if I really *was*? It suddenly dawned on me the plan I'd worked up must be completely the wrong track. If that was the case, maybe I would be sitting here on my bum — eating chips and online shoe shopping and jumping virtual banana peels — until I figured out the *right* way.

Who said video games were simply mindless entertainment?

∽ ∽ ∽

Assuming my earlier plan was a total no-go, I grabbed the paper with my nighttime notes. I tore it up by hand into tiny pieces — a very satisfying and therapeutic process. Grabbing a fresh sheet, I sat for a few moments with my pen hovering over the page.

Mentally, too, I stepped back from what I'd decided before. I needed to think this through like Travis would — in a logical, commonsense way.

While it was true that if I shot and killed the terrible twosome, we'd stop the assault against the Cooper family. Mission accomplished.

Okay, and what else? What would be a normal consequence?

I supposed I'd be arrested for their murders... or would try to dodge the law before being arrested — and, most likely, convicted — for murder. Travis would almost certainly be treated as a suspect or co-conspirator, and if he didn't end up in jail, he could almost certainly kiss his career goodbye.

Yes, I believe I spotted a very major potential flaw. I needed a whole new strategy.

∽ ∽ ∽

I decided to move ahead under the assumption I would return to 1900 the morning after I left. Apart from being the only scenario for which I could plan, it also felt the most plausible.

This time, too, I would include Travis. My head was much clearer now — literally and figuratively — and now it seemed perfectly rational to seek his help. I also knew his level head would steer us the right way... and keep us both out of jail.

So where to begin? I followed my old motto: When in doubt, research it out.

To that end, the next hours were devoted to tracing reports of this whole tragedy through the years, seeking out every possible mention I could find. Compared to what I'd seen before, there wasn't a lot more out there... but after bowing and thanking the computer gods for the wonder of the Internet, I re-read everything and started compiling a timeline.

Neighbors said the explosion came just before seven in the morning, and the first responders hit the scene within about five minutes.

Along with the timeline, then, let's draft a to-do list. First item:

To-do: Tell them to completely turn off the gas

My other self had made such a point of reporting the shots had hit the pipes — which I took to mean the gas supply — it only seemed fitting to write that in the number one slot.

Several days had been required for the authorities to tally the final death toll, due to the fact the entire house had collapsed. The explosion had come from the basement, and ignited the first fire. That fire, in turn, burned into the kitchen directly above. The blaze then apparently caused the boiler and stove in the kitchen to burst, which led to the home being further engulfed in flames. Eventually, the whole structure fell in on itself, and the basement become a tomb.

All told, seventeen lives had now been lost on that relatively balmy San Francisco morning.

Six bodies, those of four women and two men, had been burned beyond recognition. Another eight people were identified, including Mr Cooper, the butler and four other members of the household staff — kitchen help, maids and stable hands. The badge in Travis's pocket helped to ID his body, and I was grateful to at least have that.

Mrs Cooper, Pearl and I were the only ones to be rescued from the fiery wreckage, and none of us escaped death for very long.

The newspaper said my sweet, sweet boy had been located in the ruins of the home, near where my historic/futuristic self had managed to escape. I knew as soon as I read those words that Travis had pushed me ahead of him, and he was the only reason the little girl and I made it out at all.

To-do: If we go inside, tell Coopers to call for the police, fire department and emergency medical

From what the coroner could tell, everyone had died from burns and smoke inhalation — except me and the little girl. I had a bullet in my thigh and a stab wound in the neck, along with my injuries from the fire.

Part of another news story was very revealing — not about my own demise, but that of sweet little Pearl. When she was first seen by the police officer on the scene, she was wheezing, and her face had "mottled skin and bloated lips." Those clearly weren't gun, knife or fire-related injuries. If I had to guess (and I did), I'd say they seemed more in line with anaphylaxis — a severe, life-threatening allergic reaction. Given the timeline, I was thinking we were dealing with an insect bite or bee sting, or that the idiots had shot her up with something to keep her quiet.

I knew myself. Though I was a mom, and was predisposed to be caring and compassionate, I wasn't in love with this girl. The poor kid was already mostly dead. If I had gripped her tight and raised her from Perdition — ahead of Travis, no less — there was a reason.

As I said, I knew myself. Just like the incoherent ranting Jennie had delivered forcefully enough to merit a few lines in the newspaper, this, too, was a message. Something had happened to this girl... and in the here and now, I was supposed to figure out how she could be saved.

Though I figured allergies had been around about as long as there had been humans, I decided to cross my A's and dot my J's, and check a little bit of medical history. (While it was no shock that epinephrine autoinjectors wouldn't be around for about seventy years, I was surprised to learn the term "allergy" wouldn't even be coined until 1906.)

Fortunately, there was a treatment out there: adrenaline (another name for epinephrine). It was still somewhat rare, and very expensive, but it was out there. It would be great if she could have an antihistamine, too, but those wouldn't be available until the fifties, so we were out of luck on that front.

I needed to distill the essence of my message — short enough to remember, direct enough that I could pass on the information. Given the warm weather of late, my best guess was she had angered some bees or wasps, so I would cross my fingers and just go with that.

To-do: Tell first responders Pearl's not breathing — bee sting. Needs adrenaline.

While in the Now, this whole thing was just considered an insignificant little bit of history, I was irritated to find out nobody ever figured out *why* this all happened. They didn't know there had been a kidnap in progress. They didn't understand a bank robbery was at the core of the scheme.

༄ ༄ ༄

Once I had my timeline and to-do list, it was time to come up with a solution. If we weren't able to physically stop Walt and Maggie before, during or after the kidnap or heist, maybe the best approach was to remove what they were after: the girl.

Everything hinged on her. Without Pearl as collateral, the creepy couple would be left trying to force Mr Cooper over to the bank with a gun and harsh words. For a man committed to his bank and career as much as he was, and minus the part with his kid being held hostage, he had little reason to cooperate.

The key to it all was to *get there quickly*. This wasn't only because of the message I'd sent myself, but was also so we could truly nip this thing in the bud — as much as possible, anyway. I also recognized that no matter what we chose to do, we'd have only minutes to prepare.

With every one those points in mind, I sketched out the basics of my plan.

಄ ಄ ಄

Assuming this worked, would it end everything? Would Walter and Maggie end up behind bars — or might they sneak off to somewhere their luck might be a little better.

This girl from the future had evidently reached her quota on predictions, because even though I was ready to put a rescue into action, I couldn't find even a hint of a "corrected" timeline.

The riddle that remained was the one and only thing to which I could trace the changes: My run-in with Walt. What could he have possibly taken from that encounter to make him go all-in, and to move the timetable all the way up?

Even as I asked myself the question, I accepted that I'd never find out the answer. After we fixed this piece of the past, the point would become moot — and any desire Wally might have had to rationalize the circumstances would disappear.

An odd feeling settled over me, and it took me all the time I spent getting the kids in bed and doing my own nighttime routine to recognize the unusual sensation. It was *calm*. I wasn't worried about whether or not I'd wake up in the Now or the Then. It seemed only sensible to assume that since Fate had already taken me this far, whatever timetable he/she/it deemed best, I would just go with the flow.

While slipping into bed, something else occurred to me. Tonight — in contrast to every other night this past week — I was actually excited for the possibilities ahead, rather than being anxious about the difficulties we might face.

Simply put: I was finally ready.

77: Rise and shine

When I next opened my eyes, I was thrilled to feel my body cozy and curled up in bed in the year 1900 — exactly where I hoped to land. Strangely, though, it was still dark outside, which was unusual and completely disorienting.

Tiptoeing around the bed, I opened Travis's pocket watch and checked the time using a tiny shard of light from the street lamps. It was obscenely early — a quarter past five in the morning.

Not once in the past few months had I woken up before six, but — assuming I had the date right — we had been given the time necessary to make things happen the *right* way.

"Rise and shine, sweetheart," I cooed, tousling my boy's hair.

He mumbled something incoherent. I pulled the sheet back and gave him a big raspberry on his stomach. That's a trick I sometimes used on my sleepyheaded girls, and what do you know — it was just as irritating to people of this era.

He opened his eyes for a second, and I leaned in close. "Babe — is it Friday? June fifteenth?" So close to his eyes, his lips, I was unable to resist peppering his face with kisses.

After reveling in the attention, he finally nodded. "Aye — yes."

"I've been back in my time for a whole week, so need to be sure."

"A week? You were gone a *week*?"

"Seven miserable days," I said, and held Travis as close as skin and bone would allow. Every part of me — brain and body — was rejoicing to be back by his side.

"I found out a lot in that time, though. Something happened. But it's a go... for today. This morning. We have to get going." Not wanting to give up a single minute with him, I nestled deeply into his embrace as I explained that the kidnap and robbery had been moved up to today. This morning. Not even two hours from now. But, never fear, I had a plan to fix it.

He didn't ask what prompted the change, what sort of evidence I'd found, or even the outcome. He had just one question: "Do we come out of it okay?"

"You..." My lips were moving, but no sound was coming out. I felt like there was an iron fist grabbing my throat. "We need to be careful, let's just put it that way."

I knew we didn't have time to go by the station house to try to convince his captain or even one of the other officers to provide backup, and Travis was concerned that if he even tried, they might delay the process, or refuse to allow him to follow his nebulous lead. Time being of the essence, and given all the oddball circumstances, he agreed with my idea to try to handle this ourselves -- at least until we decided to call for assistance.

"Which reminds me," I said before slipping out of bed, "Don't get dressed yet. We need to get some protective gear."

I threw a robe around myself and hurried downstairs to the perpetually frigid kitchen. My idea was to see if there was any way I could remove an iron door from my massive stove/oven unit so Travis could wear it as a bulletproof vest. (Yes, I got this idea from "Back to the Future III." Don't judge.) Unfortunately, the hinges were welded and still quite new, so I wasn't going to be able to remove it with anything sort of a sledgehammer... and I didn't have one handy.

Protection Plan B was *layers*. Mr Interwebs told me that in the 1860s and 1870s, the Korean military discovered thirteen layers of plain cotton fabric could provide some degree of protection against bullets. How much guns and ammo had improved in the thirty-something years since that point, I didn't know, but it was my last best practical hope.

"You need to put on every undershirt you have. The sleeveless ones. And if you don't have at least a dozen of those, you'll need to put on other shirts. We will cut off the sleeves to keep them from binding."

"What are you talking about?"

"It's a method of bulletproofing — keep any bullets from breaking the skin. Not a great solution, but it's all we have at this point."

I sat down on the edge of the bed, took a long, deep breath, and tapped the spot beside me for him to sit, too. He did so without question.

"Look. I know I seem a little crazy this morning."

"*This* morning?" he said, because with me, mornings full of crazy were nothing new. "Just tell me what's going on."

I took both of his hands in mine. "If we don't change things up, it's going to be a very bad day for a lot of people. But especially for us."

"How bad?"

There would be no sugarcoating. "The dead kind of bad."

"What's the toll?"

"Seventeen."

He closed his eyes and bowed his head for a moment, then leaned over and gave me a big hug and a long, sweet kiss.

With his face just inches from mine, he looked deeply into my eyes and said, "So, a dozen shirts you say?"

I laughed, having expected to hear something profound. "At least thirteen, actually. The more the better, I'd imagine."

"Will see what I can find," he said, jumping to his feet. "Now you go do the same."

"No — it's just for you."

"No, it's just for you *and* me. What's sauce for the goose is sauce for the gander, and all that sort of thing," he told me with a wink before shooing me out the door. "Go on — get moving! We don't have a lot of time."

He didn't need to tell me twice. I started by dumping out my handbag, and started to fill it with things from various drawers. I'm sure it looked like a completely random hodgepodge of junk, but each piece had purpose.

"What's all that?"

"I'll explain everything on the way over. Which reminds me — think you can get a cab here in ten minutes?"

While he dealt with the phone, I scrounged around for every top I thought would work for this purpose, but I didn't have enough pieces offering adequate flexibility. Instead, I sandwiched cloth napkins between the layers on my front half. The only thing that could fit over all of this was my grubby maid's outfit, which, I decided, would be just fine.

When I was all dressed, I could barely move my torso, and had a tough time getting a deep breath. I could imagine this was probably what wearing a straitjacket felt like.

There was a quick rap at the door. "Cab's here," Travis said, struggling to get his police jacket to fit over the two inches of extra girth he now sported. "Don't bother, love — just bring your badge."

"One more thing," he said, and handed me his extra gun... just in case. I tucked it into the top of my boot, then hoisted the bag of odds and ends over my shoulder.

"Okay, then," I said, smoothing down my outermost shirt and taking a steadying breath. "Let's do this."

78: *Looking for a Pearl*

As much because I missed him as I feared losing him, I held Travis so tightly on the ride over that someone glancing into the carriage might have assumed there sat a two-headed creature.

As we headed across town, the sun still lingered below the horizon, forcing more and more of an orange glow on the night sky. Though I would have welcomed more time to prepare, our schedule was set -- and like Lucy Ricardo, I got some 'splainin' to do.

What I had in mind was less of a to-do list and more of a strategy. It wasn't pretty, it wasn't nice, and it certainly wasn't like anything I'd done before... so I had a lot of hope it would be effective.

I was humbled that Travis liked my plan, dubbing it "logical" and "cunning." From a cop in this day (and him in particular), that was high praise. Still, he managed to apply his unique perspective, streamlining our mission — and, true to form, taking on more of the risk.

So that's how we found ourselves on the front porch of the Cooper home, ringing the doorbell in the wee morning hours. Travis was in his uniform pants and hat, and otherwise channeling the Incredible Hulk. I, on the other hand, looked like a poor and portly housemaid.

"I hope we're done with this by ten or so," Travis said, checking his watch. "The man delivering the piano for the party is coming over just before noon."

In that moment, I felt a flush of love and pride at how much he and I were on the same track.

While we waited for someone to answer the door, I checked out the house itself. It was definitely a beautiful building, but the term "ostentatious" was far too weak a word to describe what they had going on here. It was so ridiculously pompous and pretentious, it seemed like a theater set.

The front doors were guarded by a portico, held up with six columns. There was a little stone balcony above — clearly decorative, as the railing was only about eighteen inches high. The front of the house had a flat facade, punctuated by windows, and on either side were three-story turrets, each probably about twenty feet wide.

Before I had the chance to look more, an actual butler answered the door. It was surprising to me that he was fully dressed even at this hour. He said nothing, but just stood there, waiting for us to announce ourselves.

"I'm with the San Francisco City Police," Travis said, holding up his badge. "We received a tip that their child is possibly the subject of a kidnap plot, taking place early this morning."

Not even that news could ruffle the butler. He merely opened the door wider, waved with his hand to show us in, and then closed the door. Once we were standing in the grand foyer, he said, "I will return momentarily." I hoped he was going up to wake the mister and missus, and not call security on us.

If the outside of the house had been ostentatious, the inside was absolutely dripping in flamboyance. There were statues — full-on naked Romanesque sculptures — on either side of the entrance, and the walls were clad in a yellow marble and some sort of carved wood, dappled with gold leaf. Richly-detailed archways led at four points off the foyer, itself the floor of which had been finished with a glossy mosaic tile.

No more than two minutes later, a portly red-faced man wearing an embroidered satin bathrobe came flying down the stairs. "What is this about?" he demanded before he'd even reached the tiled floor.

It was interesting to see this man I'd read so much about. The drawings in the newspaper had represented him quite well, although couldn't quite convey the pinched expression and sweaty brow.

Travis repeated what he'd told the butler, adding, "We believe the conspirators are already on the property. I'd like to take a look in your daughter's room if I may, and move her, and the rest of the family, to a place of safety."

Mr Cooper paused, thinking of how to deal with this crisis. Finally he asked, "Are you absolutely certain this threat is legitimate?"

"I wouldn't be here if I didn't believe it, sir," Travis said, his firm request buffered with compassion for the man who we knew was supposed to die this day. "I'd be happy to tell you all that we have learned, once we ensure that Pearl is out of harm's way."

With a stiff upper lip, Mr Cooper agreed, and took us over to the grandiose curved staircase with gray-veined marble stairs and a polished copper balustrade. He led us up the stairs, gestured down the a long hallway leading off to the right, and whispered, "The night nursery is the second room on the right." ("Nursery" was the universal term for kids' bedrooms and playrooms, and didn't have the baby-only connotation of today.)

Travis walked in front, and I trailed slightly behind, treading gently on the carpeted floors. We both used the "fox walk" — one of the quietest ways to get from A to B on foot. He had showed me the method months before, but I already knew how to do it, having learned years before as a "be-quiet-the-baby's-sleeping" walk. We reached the little girl's bedroom almost silently. I glanced back down the hall to see Mr Cooper and the butler looking back at us, fear etched on both their faces.

The nursery door was, of course, closed. With a steady hand, Travis quietly unholstered his revolver, and gripped the weapon in his right hand. With his left, he gently turned the knob, and the door swung inward on silent hinges.

From his post in the doorway, I watched his eyes swish from side to side as he carefully looked around the room. After a few seconds, he stepped inside and continued his survey — opening the closet, looking under the bed and behind the curtains. Once he was sure that the room was clear, he shook his head and gestured with his hand to let me know he couldn't see anyone.

That was a good news/bad news scenario: Good that Walt and Maggie weren't lurking there; Bad that the bedroom was empty. It wasn't supposed to be. The little girl was already gone.

The idea that we were too late was not a surprise, but more the kind of bad luck I'd almost expected for this day. With the information I had available, I really hadn't been able to tell how early they started their process. We did our best.

One thing I had gleaned from the papers, though, was that both of them were probably still on site — laying in wait before they came forward with their demands. The way that Walter had seemingly appeared out of nowhere was just one of many things that truly rattled their victims.

If we were at this stage of the game already, there was only one thing to do.

"Downstairs?" I asked, and Travis nodded.

Leaving the door open behind us, and I followed him as he rushed back down to the hall. In a hushed voice, he asked the men still waiting at the top of the stairway how to get to the basement. Mr Cooper offered to show us the fastest route. I arrived a few steps behind, and reciting from my notes first written in the Now, gave a couple directions to the butler. "We need you to do two things, please. Turn off the gas supply to the house immediately. After you have done that, we need you to call the police and tell them Pearl's been kidnapped." The man nodded and shuffled off.

After we navigated three switchback staircases, Mr Cooper pointed us to a wooden door off the kitchen that led to the below-ground level of the home.

It was at this point that Travis made a difficult request of the girl's father: he asked him to go no further. "We don't know the situation below, and I don't want there to be any more people down there than need to be," he whispered. Mr Cooper reluctantly agreed. "Just point us in the right direction, then you get your wife and anyone else out of the house and far away from here until this is over."

Just as we were about to part, I remembered something else from my to-do list.

"Mr Cooper? One more thing," I said. "Do your family a favor and get a doctor to check out your heart." Of course, he looked doubtful and generally weirded out. Really didn't have time for explanations, but... "My father was a doctor, I know some signs, and can tell by your, uh, pallor that you might have a problem."

After Travis gave one more terse reminder to make sure someone shut off the gas, we rushed back down the hall to reach the back steps by the servants' quarters. One story down, we made a U-turn and opened the thick planked door leading to the basement.

Then, with my favorite policeman leading the way, we silently descended into the cool, damp darkness of the home's lowest level.

With every footfall, though, I knew we were aligning ourselves more and more completely with the version of events that had turned the foundation of this house into a man-made hell.

79: *Here there be dragons*

Maybe because it hadn't been me in this body when he nearly pushed Jennie down the stairs so many months before, I still couldn't see Walter as a credible threat. He was a grade-A pain in the ass, sure, but more Severus Snape than Freddy Krueger.

Likewise, because Maggie and Walt had never actually killed anyone — even in the most atrocious scenarios attributed to the duo, the resultant deaths had been accidental — Travis didn't consider the two of them to be especially dangerous, either.

When making these assumptions, however, we had neglected to consider two new variables — ones that were so obvious, but perhaps too close for us to recognize. Only in retrospect did I realize that when Travis and I walked on to the playing field, we completely switched up the game once again.

And when the game changes, the rules do, too.

As we reached the bottom of the stairs, Travis and I surveyed the scene, seeking out anything at all that might be helpful.

I saw a panel of push-button light switches, which was the first electric lighting system I'd seen inside a residence in this era. Instantly I realized I'd caught a lucky break: If the home still had gas lights, my request to the butler would have forced us into total darkness.

With Travis's nod of approval, I hit every button, illuminating the huge room to about the degree I'd expect from ten 40-watt bulbs in my time — things were visible, but it wasn't especially bright. But more than just making it easier for us to see, we were announcing our presence.

Now that we had light, I could confirm what I'd expected: This wasn't going to be easy. Since the four-story home's footprint was probably at least fifteen hundred square feet, there were countless places to hide. The basement housed an enormous maze of dusty pipework and support beams for the floors above, along with chimneys, sheet-covered furniture, and about a hundred boxes of varying shapes and sizes, set about in haphazard stacks.

Straggly old spiderwebs and shimmering new gossamer threads adorned almost every joist and metal pipe running along the ceiling, and drooped to face height in many places. The whole area smelled distinctly musty and earthy, with a mild, top note of mothballs.

Travis leaned over and whispered in my ear, "Do you remember where the reports mentioned she was found?"

"It wasn't very specific," I said, using my quietest voice. "It said near the east wall, in something called a wardrobe. I'm hoping you know what that is, because I forgot to look it up."

"I do," he said distractedly, then he pulled a compass out of his pocket, and oriented himself to the cardinal directions. After a moment, he gestured to the right. "That's east." Of course, it had to be — that was the side of the room furthest away from where we were.

Time was of the essence, because we didn't know when Pearl had suffered the sting or bite — or if, even, it would happen the same way today. The best course of action was to rescue the kid as quickly as possible, but there was a method to our madness. A reckless, kick-down-the-door approach would put every one of the lives down here in danger (not to mention the potential for harm to the folks topside).

This morning, we were each going to play to our strengths. While I rocked the future knowledge and the "screw with their heads" angle, when it came to actual crime-fighting, I was just the trusty sidekick. You know — the Robin to Travis's Batman, but subtract the tights and the capes.

"What would you normally do now?" I asked my Bruce Wayne.

"We'd probably split up, so we can cover more ground."

"Okay, in that case, I think we should stay together instead." My working theory was that whatever we'd done last time had such craptastic results, we should try to mix things up a bit.

Travis nodded, then gestured for me to get my gun out. The weapon felt icy cold and unfriendly in my hand, but I made sure to hold it steadily with my finger alongside the trigger, even as it pushed a little shiver up my arm.

Though my goal was to remove guns from the equation as much as possible, we had agreed that we both needed to be armed — just in case. I was incredibly nervous, of course, mainly because of the words seared into my brain... even though I had not yet spoken them: "*The shots hit the pipes.*"

From what I had been able to tell from the earlier scenario, bullets had ruptured some metal pipework, causing the basement to flood with combustible gas. Once that had happened, any number of things could have ignited it and caused the explosion — including another gunshot, the action of a light switch, or an open flame in the kitchen above. I crossed my fingers that the guy had shut off the fuel supply as requested.

Travis tapped me on the shoulder, then pointed me to the spot between two piles of boxes — the starting point for our slightly circuitous approach to the eastern side. He would follow close behind.

We both moved as stealthily as possible through the area — but that didn't mean we were silent. Only small portions of the basement were dirt and concrete, but most of it was covered with rough plank boards, which would offered soft squeaks and groans under our feet. The only benefit, I decided, was that if the floorboards weren't silent for us, they wouldn't stay quiet for Walt and Maggie, either.

Out of the corner of my eye, I saw some movement. I spun around and started to level my gun in the direction of the disturbance, and came close to wasting a bullet on a tiny gray mouse. Before I even had chance to start breathing again, a ginger tabby cat went barreling across the same path, in hot pursuit.

I laughed. Laughed with relief, with amusement.

The moment I did, though, I heard a telltale squeak from somewhere up ahead. Immediately, I oriented myself to the direction of the sound. From about ten feet away, I saw a man move out of the shadows about a quarter of a second before Travis did — or maybe it was my wide eyes that alerted him to the new presence. He turned, and that's when we noticed it wasn't a he but a she — Maggie dressed in men's clothes: grubby gray pants, a work shirt, and a sooty hat. She was brandishing some nasty piece of metal that looked like an iron fire poker.

As Travis had reminded me after I explained my plan: *Don't be surprised by anything that happens, anything they say, or anything I say. Take it in stride.*

Before either of us had a chance to respond, she swung the metal stick at Travis. It was a solid hit to the chest, and accompanied by a dulled 'thwack' sound. I knew the protective gear he had on had dulled the impact, but still — that had to hurt.

If so, he wasn't acting like it. Maggie was so shocked by how fast he moved after she struck him that she didn't even have time to react when he rushed over to her. With a swiftness that seemed almost magical, had his weapon pressed into her side. "Nice try, Mags. Now lay it down," he said, and a look of wide-eyed bewilderment muddled any expression of guilt or fear.

Slowly, she knelt down and put the heavy metal stick on the ground, then held her hands up. Travis re-holstered his weapon and grabbed his handcuffs. I watched as he kicked the bar away, then slipped Maggie's wrists into the steel bracelets. Meanwhile, I patted her down, and in her right pants pocket — surprise surprise — found she was packing some firepower.

I handed Travis her revolver, and he immediately checked the cylinder. "Six bullets." He dumped the ammo into his hand and handed the empty weapon back to her. "You promised you weren't going to have your gun loaded, Maggie. Did you forget?"

"Forget?" So dumbfounded by the staggering turn of events in the last fifteen seconds, all she could do was echo back the last word she heard.

Her confusion was only natural — after all, we were making this all up.

From my bag, I grabbed a cloth napkin — one from my prodigious collection — and held it up so Travis could see it. He nodded. With a few twists of the wrist, I quickly spun it into a rope shape. Stepping around behind Maggie, I loosely gagged her with the cloth, tying it around the back of her head. (Well, the plan was to make the gag loose... but I might have tied a little too tight. Purely by accident. And, also completely inadvertently, I may have entwined some of her hair in the knot.) Even though I had never gagged anyone before, I was proud to have accomplished it so neatly... though was simultaneously a little creeped out by my competence in that department.

Travis pulled her up, and led her over to a more central part of the room just a couple yards away — a space that was fairly well-lit, and looked like it would be visible from multiple angles.

We had our prisoner sit on the ground in the open area in the center, while the two of us stood on opposite sides, allowing tall pieces of furniture to shield us from any sudden encroachment.

Cue the curtain and the orchestra, for the performance is now beginning.

"You said you were going to get Mrs Cooper's jewelry," Travis said, projecting his voice to ensure the audience could hear. "Do you have it yet?"

Unable to speak, Maggie nodded no, and her eyes registered utter confusion.

As I said before, my strategy wasn't pretty, and it wasn't nice. But because it was so out of character for both me and Travis, I hoped it would deliver healthier results than it had in the other timeline.

The spectacle had been inspired by the "Greatest Grifters" biographer, who noted that Maggie was, in many ways, Walt's Achilles heel. Turns out he really loved the girl. Who knew? But that love was his weak spot, and he lived in fear that she might regrow a conscience and eventually betray him.

Our goal this morning was to save the day by drawing the two out and playing them against each other so we could take them without a struggle. "Pretty please" wasn't going to work. Keeping them occupied — and off-balance — until we could capture them or assistance arrived was primary on our agenda.

Walking over to where we'd just nabbed her, I tucked my gun back into my boot and leaned down to the ground, and made a show of picking up Maggie's own scarf, which had been wrapped around a lumpy bundle.

In truth, I had dropped it there during the kerfuffle just before Travis handcuffed her — it was one of the treasures I'd loaded into my handbag that morning.

I had tied her silk scarf — the one I accidentally took from her dresser drawer the day I poked around her flat — around a stash of shiny silver and golden baubles from my own collection. I figured we could definitely convince Walter it was stuff a socialite like Mrs C would wear, because it really *was* stuff a socialite (Jennie's mother) had worn. All told, it was probably worth about five hundred bucks, but looked far more impressive than that at first glance.

"She got it already. It's here, Trav," I said, holding up a big handful of jewel-studded necklaces and bracelets so they would twinkle in the light.

"Bring it over here," he said, gesturing with his head to the right.

I handed him the bag, and he examined the loot briefly before shooting her a look that would have wilted an entire field of daisies. "Have to say, I'm disappointed in you, Maggie."

Travis played an impressive good cop. "We did everything you asked. We fixed it so he couldn't go through with the hotel robbery. We put a stop to that bank heist the other day, and never let anyone know that you were helping us out," he said. "We had your back, Mags."

"And this is how you repay us? Seriously?" I said, taking my turn as bad cop and adding a touch of whiny melancholy. "When we met week at Oscar's Butchery, you said that this job wasn't going to be going down until *next* Thursday."

As though it had been elegantly scripted, Travis had the next line. "We only realized that you moved it up to today because I happened to be at the police station late last night, and saw the note you left. You thought we wouldn't be able to guess who gave up Walter?"

"We knew you were planning to stay here with the kid, play the victim and all that, Maggie... but you were going to cut us out of the deal?" The words had taken on a life of their own, and were tumbling out of my mouth with a Tony Soprano-style accent. I calmed myself with the reminder that Jennie was, at least, Italian. "I know we never would've been able to do any of this without you — but come on. You're killin' me here! I thought we are all partners on this. One hand washes the other and all that stuff. *Capisce*?"

My boy didn't even blink.

Even as I got a little carried away, I was aware that the little girl might be listening, and hoped she was too innocent to understand what was being said. Although we spoke these words only as part of our cover, I worried that she would believe it and become even more fearful.

All the newspaper accounts I'd found suggested that Pearl spent very little time with the kidnappers — she had been in her bedroom, then was chloroformed, and woke up bound, gagged and stuffed into a dark drawer. Only later did the sweet child find out who had been involved, and how much she had been betrayed.

For now, it was too risky to grab the girl. With these two loose cannons, it was probably safer for her to stay tucked out of the way.

I moved to the left, trying to get a view of the back of the room, and got my head caught in an old spider web. I flailed a little bit to get the fly carcasses out of my hair.

We've all heard the expression, "I didn't know what hit me" — but, until the next moment, I thought it was just some cliché. No longer. Someone swooped in on me so quickly, I truly didn't even realize I'd been attacked until there was a vise grip across my chest, and the tip of a knife was stretched against the soft skin on my neck.

My first thought? No, it wasn't something intelligent or heroic or protective. What I remember popping in my head was, "I'm wearing fourteen damn layers today, and you go for my *neck*?!" The blade was so sharp and so thin, it was instantly warmed through by my skin. I was afraid to move.

Travis turned toward me and started in my direction. The second he saw the blade, he stopped mid-step.

From there, everything slid into slow motion. I watched as clear expressions of shock and horror, fear and sadness, anger and determination cycled across his face in rapid succession as he looked at me and then the huge armoire, behind which Walter had apparently been laying in wait.

From what little I could see of my captor, he was wearing a suit. Given the fact that we were standing in a basement at six in the morning, the dude seemed to be unusually well-groomed — right down to the 1900s equivalent of splashing on too much Aqua Velva.

"I have truly had enough of you two," Walt finally said, pressing his head to mine. I felt his hot breath ooze into my ear. "I wasn't entirely sure before, but as you're here today, it's clear that you were responsible for the 'mishaps' I've experienced as of late. The banks. The dynamite. And right here, now."

"*Of course* we were responsible," Travis said, somehow mustering a semi-smile. "We had help. A friend of yours. Someone you trusted. Confided in. But someone I know *very* well."

I felt Walter's head turn ever-so slightly in Maggie's direction.

"That's right, Wally. We're only here because Maggie invited us to the party."

The pain in my throat had dulled enough that I could throw in my two cents. "Don't you understand? She's been telling us things in secret. Showing us your maps, your calendars, the newspaper ads you've found. Whispering where you'd be and when you would be there."

Maggie tried to yell some words of protest, but what came out through her gag sounded more like a concerned moan.

After a long pause, Walter said, "Never. She wouldn't do that. She's too loyal to me."

"She *would*, and she *did*," the smooth talker continued. "Maggie's been playing you, mate. She had you all wrapped around her little finger, and you never even knew it."

"How would you know?"

"I know, 'cause Maggie still loves me. She's my girl — just like it was, and just like it's always been. You," I heard Travis say. "You were just a means to an end."

Pressed against Walter so tightly, I could feel his pulse quicken. He might just be buying this.

"But you and Jennie…?" Walt asked, and for a moment, he looked like a little lost puppy. "I thought you were nearly betrothed."

"Jennie?" Travis scoffed. "Jennie is my *cousin*! Surely you noticed the family resemblance."

If time is short and the situation stressful, you can imply connections where none exist, and they will probably be accepted as truth.

There was only silence — thick and uneasy.

"Why did Maggie turn on you? Because you're *out of control*. You are proving her point right now." He was creeping ever-so-slightly closer as he talked. "Mags knew what you did to Jennie, and she didn't want to end up at the bottom of a staircase like that. Especially not now. Not with the baby."

Travis turned to Maggie and asked, "Does Wally here know that you're in the family way?" She looked shocked — beyond shocked — that we knew she was pregnant.

Hitting that nerve had been a stroke of luck. During one short-lived view of an alternate timeline — what I called a shimmer in history — I had read that a little baby Houlihan had arrived in October of 1900. The story was gone an hour after I noticed it, as the ever-changing past caught up with the future, but my memory of it remained. I couldn't be sure it was still true... but it was a play Travis said he would make if it felt right.

"Dear God — did you tell Walter it was *his* baby?" I asked, my voice just a squeak. The girl was apparently still so thrown by the initial revelation that she couldn't even answer.

With every second spent talking, convincing, I was losing steam, and getting more and more overwhelmed by the buzz of pain that was only growing in intensity and radiating up my face. My ear now felt like someone had jammed an ice pick in it.

Dropping my right hand to in front of my stomach, I steadied my gaze on Travis, and tried to signal that I was going to do the only thing I had strength for. I pointed to myself, then to the floor, and started a count — three fingers, two, one, and on the fourth beat, I collapsed my legs. With the slippery blood aiding my escape, my body slid from Walt's grip and on to the dusty rough-hewn boards.

As I scrambled away, Travis closed the distance in the blink of an eye.

"Stay right there," Travis said to Walter, but the fool kept inching toward him. "I'm serious. Stop and put down your weapon. Don't make me shoot you." I saw Travis's thumb move up and smoothly pull back the revolver's hammer.

"Don't — don't shoot!" I yelled as I scrambled for cover behind Maggie. I was still completely paranoid that even if the gas had been turned off, there was still enough in the pipes to cause a pretty good bang. I turned to Walter, pleading. "Please put down your knife. Don't make him fire his gun. If he does, everything likely to end really badly. I don't want anyone else to get hurt."

Walt stared at me, his expression equal parts sadness and intensity. I didn't know him well enough to understand what that meant. Finally, he released his grip on the knife and it clattered to the ground, though looking straight at me the entire time.

"That's good," Travis said, and I nodded my approval. "Now get down on the ground."

"Put your hands on your head," I added, and Wally squinted at me, probably because this was still "hands in the air" territory.

The man with the gun barked, "Do as the lady says."

After Walt complied, Travis held his gun in front of him, took a few steps, and kicked the knife away. It skittered off, out of sight and out of reach.

Whether out of passion or frustration or to purposely provide a distraction, I'll never know, but Maggie chose that moment to try to escape — rising to her feet and lurching toward her partner.

Though I grabbed her immediately and yanked her back to the ground, the damage had been done: she'd interrupted Travis's concentration just long enough for Walt to take advantage.

It only took two seconds, but I turned back to discover that Walter had Travis in a sort of choke hold — which was bad enough — but he had also pulled a snub-nosed revolver out of somewhere, and was now pressing it into the soft space under his hostage's jaw. His fingers looked awkward and gnarled as they rested on the trigger.

A red mist of anger came over me, and was so overwhelming, I immediately discarded all of my concerns and went for my gun. With my own weapon in hand, I summoned a mysterious reserve of strength, swung my arm around Maggie until I had her in the same type of grip, and held the gun barrel against her head.

"I think we have a stalemate, Wally," I said, almost panting. "Let Travis go, and you can have her."

Somewhere in those last couple seconds, I'd decided that stopping Walter and Maggie had become optional. The only really important thing was to get Pearl, and get at least me and Travis out of here alive. By doing that, we'd also stop the bank holdup, and save all those other lives. *Yeah*, I told myself. *Let these two losers walk — we'll deal with them later.*

The cop in the room, though, had no intention of letting them off so easily. "There is no way out of this, Houlihan. More police are already on their way," he said, his voice expressing absolute authority. "Thus far, you haven't committed any hanging offense. I suggest keeping it so."

Maggie shivered in my grasp, and I felt bad for putting her in this position, but she was my shield as well — as my only bargaining chip.

I repeated my demand. "Walt — please. I'll give you Maggie if you just let Travis go."

It's often been said that there's no such thing as too rich or too thin... and it stands to reason the same logic would apply to success. Seriously — who ever heard of someone being too successful?

Um, yeah, over here. My sweetheart and I had apparently given award-worthy performances, working together so well to drive a wedge between the terrible twosome that one of the parties had become so thoroughly persuaded of his accomplice's guilt that he snapped.

In a flash, Walt turned his gun on his girl. After a bone-chilling roar, he yelled, "You can keep the whore!"

I heard a loud bang — and then another — but everything happened so fast, I couldn't tell if that was the sound of something exploding or the noise of a gun. That question was answered a half second later, when I realized I'd just felt a spray of blood. Then Maggie's full weight fell on me, sending me to the floor. I heard a high-pitched scream, but I only knew it wasn't mine because I could still hear my own breaths, coming ragged and wet.

Feeling seriously loopy, my brain immediately likened the sensation to how the Wicked Witch of the East felt when Dorothy landed the house on her head.

No sooner did I think I thunk that thought when the mass of evil was shoved off me, and just as quickly replaced with the face of an angel. Travis's face.

A gentle rain of dust and dirt sifted through the basement air, creating a lingering brown haze.

"Stay still, my love," Travis said, slipping his hand on the side of my neck. "You've been shot."

"Not me," I whispered. "Maggie."

"She was shot, too, darling, but the bullet went through her," he said. He was looking down at me, and I could see he looked pained, the vein pulsing in the center of his forehead. "It went out of her and into you. Right here," he said, pressing my neck. I winced. Yeah, that hurt. "I am going to try to stem the bleeding. Relax, my love." He plucked one of those blessed cloth napkins out of my bag and put pressure on my wound.

"What," I coughed, and blood spattered from my lips. "What about Walter?"

Travis looked over his shoulder, then back to me. "Pretty sure he's dead."

I tried to nod, but was fading. Even in the dim room, I could tell the blood soaking into the napkin was bright red, and there was way more of it than I'd ever seen come out of a person before. "Carotid artery," I guessed out loud.

Travis nodded. "Probably." My vision was blurring, but I could still see well enough to see tears falling from his eyes, each one reflecting tiny pinpoints of light.

"Is this the real life?" I asked.

"Say again, sweetheart?"

"Is this just fantasy?" I thought it was fascinating and beyond bizarre that significant blood loss apparently led me to channel Freddie Mercury. I felt drunk or stoned or something... but I didn't care. It was an easy, breezy, pleasy feeling.

Then I gasped as I suddenly remembered something that seemed of immense importance at that moment. "The piano," I said with the tail end of a breath. "Delivering it. Soon."

"Oh, Jen, Jen," he said, and I heard a little laugh. "Don't worry about that right now, you silly lass."

He pulled me up into his lap, and cradled my head with his free hand. He started to rock me ever so slightly, and I felt the end beginning. My spirit began to surrender to the pull of elsewhere. It was a pleasant sensation at first, but then brought sorrow, as the man who I'd so easily come to adore — the competent, strong, intelligent, sweet and kind soul who had made every day here a joy — started to fade from my view.

Travis was still front and center — in fact, all I could see. He was talking, I knew, because his mouth moved, but I could hardly hear anything more than a mild whoosh that kindled a memory of a rushing ocean wave meeting a distant shore. I'd never seen him look so lost.

"Thank you. I love you," I said to him over and over — as many times as I could.

Now my energy was at about ten percent and falling, but it was, at least, taking much of the pain along with it. Still, I needed to reassure my sweetie that everything would be fine — no matter what. With what I understood was likely my last bit of strength, I tried to smile... but I couldn't be sure if the thought reached all the way to my lips. It was so strange — I could hardly feel my body anymore.

As the seconds ticked past, I found that I lost the ability to focus my eyes, then my throat collected one last wheezy breath before it stopped and could do no more. I felt my lungs slowly release the last bit of air, but, somehow, I wasn't worried. It didn't hurt — in fact, I felt pretty good overall. Floaty.

No sooner had the sound of my breath faded did I notice that my view of the room was going dim. As I let my eyes close, there was a gentle warmth on my forehead — a kiss. I felt Travis then kiss each closed eyelid, the tip of my nose, and finally my lips.

In the tempo of one blink, everything faded away — softly, smoothly and sweetly swept away by time's gentle tide.

And that's what it felt like to die.

80: Lost

What hadn't seemed so bad — rather peaceful — in the Then hit me like a flaming pile of bricks the second I woke up here and Now. The moment I looked around my bedroom, full of modern comforts and conveniences I'd so happily give up, sobs began to replace every breath.

No, no, no. This couldn't be the end.

Maybe, I told myself, *maybe Jennie had only been badly injured, and rendered unconscious.*

Instantly, I was overwhelmed by the urge to curl up into a ball and go back to sleep. Deeply desperate to return, I needed to know how this turned out — I needed to get back.

I tried, but knew there was no point. It was finished. It was done. I wasn't going back. Jennie was dead.

But Robin was alive — and that meant I still had to get up and go about my day, because the girls and had a fully-booked few hours ahead. While I didn't usually hide all vestiges of sadness from them, I didn't want them see me as a weeping, quivering mess. Slapping on a happy face, I told myself that I'd just have to put my dream-turned-nightmare aside until this afternoon, when I could have some time alone.

Two seconds after I decided to suck it up and hold it in, I threw back the covers and thought, "This is the first time I have gotten out of bed since I died."

Oh, yeah. This was going to be a very, very, very long day.

The harder I tried to avoid thinking about Jennie's life, the more fiercely it pushed itself into my mind. Everything reminded me of what I'd lost.

For example, at the grocery store, there was a woman wearing a blue flower-patterned blouse that totally reminded me of a dress I had back in 1900. Then we drove by a couple Victorian homes in Alameda, and I immediately pined for my old neighborhood.

Then, of all places we could have gone for a birthday party, we ended up at a park with a little area called "Western Town," featuring a play-friendly stagecoach and storefronts.

When we all sang "Happy Birthday" to the twins who were celebrating, I remembered: My party! What had become of all the planning — the food — the damn player piano?

The thought of a canceled celebration almost too much for me. I had to pretend to be on the phone and go sneak off behind a tree to regain my composure.

◆ ◆ ◆

Once the kids had been deposited at their father's, I allowed myself to resume my previously-interrupted period of depression and self-indulgent whining. I started crying in the car, and as soon as I walked in the door after dropping the kids off, I threw my purse on the sofa and sprinted over to the computer.

The little "page loading" icon swirled and swirled, and I was feeling pretty sure that time was playing one of its nasty little tricks on me again... but then the front page of Saturday's newspaper appeared.

I was shocked — and a little impressed — to see that we actually earned about eight column inches on the first page of the paper, and the headline appeared exactly where the inferno story had appeared in the alternate version of history.

An excerpt:

KIDNAP PLOT FOILED: TWO DEAD

Prominent society member Elliot Cooper, President of a city bank, alerted San Francisco Police to the nefarious doings of his governess and her fiancee, and foiled his plot to kidnap his daughter Pearl, whose mother is Mrs Patricia Cooper (nee Warner).

After a shootout, two were dead, including perpetrator Walter Houlihan. Miss Genevieve diMedici of Clayton Street was killed by a gunshot wound to the throat, having been mortally wounded by the man to whom she was once betrothed.

Accomplice Maggie Gallagher was injured, and, after treatment at a hospital, was arrested and charged with murder, armed robbery of citizens and state banks, kidnapping and extortion.

Officer Travis Donovan, slightly wounded by a gunshot during the incident, is credited with saving the life of the Cooper child, for which the Chief of Police says he will receive a commendation.

If I hadn't already been bawling before I read the last line, that one would have done me in.

༄ ༄ ༄

After those words sunk in, I couldn't sit still or think for more than a couple seconds — my mind was completely reeling.

As glad as I was that the little girl had been saved, I had to ask myself: Was it worth it? I couldn't say for sure it was. Now, if it had been my kid in danger — no question — I'd throw myself in front of a bullet for one of my girls in a New York second. And I'd smile while I did it.

I knew that I changed things on some level, but had those changes actually mattered? Had anyone's life improved? I needed some sort of answer. I had to know that what I had done was right — that my sacrifice had been worthwhile. Or, heaven forbid, had I continued my cycle of swapping one misery out for another?

I tried to imagine how Travis would approach this problem. He would force me to clarify my thoughts with the most fundamental answers.

What was my specific question?

Did I make a difference?

Make a difference to whom?

Pearl and her family.

What resources did I have available?

I could do a web search, and try to trace Pearl's life story. No — too complicated. Simplify.

Again: What resources did I have available?

I had Beatrice Hudson, Pearl's granddaughter, who I had interviewed not long ago. I could ask for a quick a follow-up on her story, and see if and how her life had changed from my perspective.

Right from my phone, I sent Mrs Hudson a brief text, asking if we could meet again. Within seconds, I received an error message saying there was no such email address. I tried once more, double-checking the address that auto-completed in the TO line... and got the same error again.

You know the cold, panicky sensation that overwhelms you the instant you realize you've monumentally screwed something up? Oh, yeah. I was feeling that.

I may have said a bad word at this point.

After sliding into my chair, I tossed all the used tissues off my desk and keyboard and hit the keys to start a new search.

First things first. I ran the same web search I'd tried a week before for "Beatrice Cooper Hudson." It was still in my browser history.

Zero results. There had been at least ten links last time.

I took out the quotes — no longer forcing the search to be limited to those three exact words in that precise order — and got 59 million completely unhelpful results.

Inside my head, I heard Travis telling me to take it back a step. The shin bone's connected to the thigh bone, and Beatrice was connected to Pearl.

I typed in "Pearl Cooper" and braced myself for the results. This time, though, instead of just a few mentions of her sad story, those notes were absent, and in their place there was so much more.

The first to catch my eye was a wedding picture from 1921, showing philharmonic orchestra violinist extraordinaire Miss Pearl Cooper — soon to be Mrs Clarence Gartrell — and father exiting a Rolls-Royce Silver Ghost limousine in front of a church. Pearl was shown beaming as she clutched a bouquet of tulip buds, her chestnut curls peeking out from the sides of a lacy bridal veil.

It was clearly the person I had met in 1900... but she was very different. She was no longer a haunted little girl who, in another lifetime, had her picture published alongside newspaper stories about a most tragic tale.

Paging through more of Pearl's history, I found that she had enjoyed a successful career, married well, she and her husband even had three boys. A trio of handsome sons... but no daughters.

∽ ∽ ∽

If I was reading this right, I had un-made an entire person... and her daughter, too. In fact, the latter was the most disturbing to me, because I was grappling with the nauseating contempt that someone I had met with a week ago no longer existed — or, from the perspective of the rest of the universe — had *never* existed. Was this tantamount to murder? There was nobody I could ask, and I knew my answer would be yes, anyhow.

I barely made it to the bathroom in time to return my breakfast and lunch. Then my head started pounding so hard, I thought my brain might explode. I turned the cold water on high and stepped into the shower, clothes and all, before my blood pressure could go any higher. The water was freezing, but was somehow just what I needed. It even washed away the tears and the sound of my sobs.

Fifteen minutes later, my mind was in a better place. Wrapped in the softest, cushiest spa towel I owned, I poured myself a glass of Syrah, and brought it — along with the rest of the bottle of wine — over with me to the computer.

To the cat we were babysitting for the weekend, I said, "Let's try this again, shall we?" He snored his agreement.

Pearl's story was a happy one, by all accounts. She had become a professional musician, and one of the first women to play in a very notable orchestra. Little Miss Cooper had never been institutionalized, which, of course, explained why she hadn't been raped, which is why she never had a baby girl, which is why *that* girl never went on to have a child named Beatrice.

That got me thinking. I went over to where I'd thrown my purse, and scrounged around inside until I found my journal. Leafing through the pages, I found something that apparently transcended time: handwritten notes from my interview with a person who didn't exist. They all read exactly the way I remembered writing them, and I could actually visualize her expressions from when she told me some of her story.

Who else mourned her loss?

After tipping another cup of red nectar into my glass, I decided to put an end to this maddening cycle of circular thought, and move on to something more rewarding but equally cosmic... like pondering what good was possibly served by the invention of mosquitoes, or why there were so few blue fruits.

81: Messages

Saturday, I woke and saw that I had done something I hadn't managed since college: I'd slept in until two in the afternoon. After such a promising start, I stayed in bed, staring at the ceiling, trying not to think.

It didn't take, because almost immediately, it occurred to me how strange it was going to be to go to bed in one place and wake up again in precisely the same location every day again. The notion of my return to normalcy sent me off on a crying jag, interspersed with choking laughter at the sheer absurdity of it all.

I didn't want to be in the house — and definitely didn't want to be in front of a computer — so headed down to the nearest coffee shop, where I could be by myself without being alone.

When I got there, my brain was fuzzy and muddled and exhausted. Two lattes later, I could think much more clearly — and didn't even have to indulge in more tears.

That's when it dawned on me: There's no way Travis had just moved on with his life without a look back. He would have tried to reach me. Sent me a message.

Finally, and for the first time since Jennie bid *adieu*, I felt hopeful.

The pages were too big and tough to browse on my phone, so I started for home, walking as fast as I could... without actually breaking into a run. Once I reached my building, I took the steps two at a time, and almost ran right into Aggie and another neighbor walking together down the stairs.

"Woah — where's the fire?" Aggie said, followed by her usual big and warm laugh.

"Sorry," I said breathlessly. "I have this... thing... I have to do really quickly. So hi and bye!"

"Hi and bye, little songbird, and tell your girls we'll be making cookies tomorrow!"

᠀ ᠀ ᠀

There was no search key I could use — I'd have to browse the classifieds section ad by ad... which meant skimming through hundreds of notices that were all so unique to the era, I was instantly nostalgic.

And then I saw it, under the heading "Lost and Found" was a little ditty that appeared three days after Jennie died:

J-R, Your last words were heard. I love you and am desperately sorry I couldn't protect you. Thank you for being in my life. You have changed me forever, miss you terribly. Revisit this paper one year from good-bye. Will find a way to tell you more. - T

On June 8, 1901, the following was published:

J-R, You are not forgotten. Still heartbroken for your loss; hope you are faring better. - Much love, T

And a year later, in 1902:

J-R, Think of you each day. Have a plan in motion. Check this date in many years hence. I will find a way to reach you. Love forever, T

After that... there was nothing. I looked and looked — forward and back a day, even read all the ads that appeared around that time.

Then I searched the entire archive, year by year, from that point on until copyright laws came into effect at the end of 1922 — twenty one years after our last communication — and couldn't find anything more for me.

A reality check — replete with black, pointy quills and a weight off the charts — came and stomped on my heart: Perhaps there was no more to be found because there was no more that existed.

The rest of the evening was spent playing music of every shape and color at a volume so loud that it almost drowned out all other thought.

၅ ၅ ၅

I had a hell of a time waking up the next morning. I felt like I'd had just the saddest, most stressful nightmare, when all I wanted to do was go back to sleep and have *normal* dreams. Happy ones. Dreams with stupid non sequiturs and people I knew in fifth grade and maybe a sexy celebrity or two.

But there was one thought that drifted into my mind repeatedly through the night: I gave up too easily.

It was all in how nearly every human deals with a deadline: crams the work into a short space before it's due... especially if your boss or teacher doesn't need to know when you did the required tasks — just that they were done.

Travis didn't need to go to the trouble and expense of updating me each year, because from my perspective, no matter when he contacted me via the newspaper, I'd receive all of the messages at the same time. (That was only logical, you see — and logic was certainly one of my boy's strong suits.)

Fueled by the possibility of discovery, I splurged on a paid membership to a different digital archive that served up fresh, hot newspaper pages from throughout the entire twentieth century. Then, I checked the San Francisco newspapers for every June eighth, year by year — an exhausting task.

I almost gave up after World War II ended, and nearly quit again at the end of the fifties, but faith kept me going. Finally, I out of the corner of my eye, I caught a cryptic little note in the *San Francisco News-Call Bulletin* from 1961:

J-R: Find your resting spot in Oakland. From the center of the base, look 7 inches out and 7 inches down. Love always, - T

Hey, I'm all for being interesting and enigmatic when appropriate... but my resting spot? What was that — my bed? My sofa? Park bench? What the hell, boy.

Okay, let's think this through calmly and rationally , I told myself while taking a deep breath. WWTD? Where *did* I go for rest?

The coffee shop came immediately to mind, and was dismissed just as quickly because it presented too many unknowns. Next up: My house, which truly was my most restful spot of all. But my place was on the second level, so I couldn't see what was seven inches down — and, besides, had never actually showed Travis where I lived.

Returning to the original newspaper copy, I checked for possible printing errors. I thought maybe "testing" had come out looking like "resting"... even though that made less sense than resting. I next examined the word "base." What if there was a typo? Bale, bake, babe. Stupid, stupider, stupidest.

I knew Travis, and therefore knew that he would not make this a puzzle that I couldn't solve. It had to make sense. I was just over-thinking it.

I took a shower. I went for a drive. I went shopping, where I perked up every time someone used the word rest.

Finally, I gave up and went home to watch TV. An hour later, I flipped past an ad selling Halloween decorations (already?!) and they panned by some plastic headstones, most reading RIP. And the answer popped into my head — simple as that.

Travis didn't know me as *me* — he knew me as Jennie. And where was Jennie now? I didn't know, but I'd sure like to find out where she had been *laid to rest*.

⁓⁓⁓

I had avoided checking out my own obituary because it was just too morbid, and this whole thing was just too new. But now? There was an actual purpose behind finding it, beyond salting my wound.

With almost no effort at all, I found it in the paper from Sunday, June 10, 1900. The column on the second-to-last page carried the oh-so-delicate title, "The Day's Dead."

DIMEDICI - In this city, June 8, 1900, Genevieve diMedici, beloved daughter of the late Gianni and Luciana, sister to Giovanna diMedici of Berkeley, and fiancée of San Francisco Police Department Officer Travis Donovan. Jennie passed into the next world at age 21 years, while heroically saving a child. Friends and acquaintances are respectfully invited to attend the funeral to-morrow (Monday), at 4 o'clock at her former residence, 333 Clayton Street in San Francisco. Interment at Lake Meadow Cemetery in Oakland.

Well, that certainly supported my theory — Jennie was buried in Oakland. Cool, awesome, just what I needed to know. Lake Meadow was actually just up the road — not far at all. I could easily go to check it out in the morning (since I wasn't really hot on the idea of wandering a cemetery alone at night).

But first... Back the truck up! *Fiancée?* Travis and I weren't engaged... although, had our lives kept moving the same direction, I had no doubt we eventually would have married. It would have been one of the trickiest relationships ever, but if anyone could make it work, we could have.

Seeing his name in print — next to such a beautifully-loaded word, no less — made me so melancholy, I had to let loose about a thousand tears.

೨ ೨ ೨

Has there ever been a scientific study on why so many good ideas come to mind when you're in the shower? That's where I was when I got to thinking about the timing of his last note. Travis would have been about 85 by the time that notice appeared.

Why *that* year, more than sixty years after he had last seen me? And, too: Would an octogenarian really be hanging out in a cemetery with a shovel?

As ghoulish as it seemed, I'd searched for Travis's death notice before, but never found anything. But this time, somehow I *knew* it would be there.

Wrapped in a towel, but with my hair still sending streams of water down my back, I tapped the keys that would tell me what I should know — but didn't really want to see.

I was right. My sweetheart's obituary appeared on September 12, and the notice with the clue for me had shown up in the same paper a week later, on September 19. I had to force myself to read every word.

Travis James Donovan
Age 85 and a longtime resident of San Francisco, Travis J. Donovan, a businessman, philanthropist and former San Francisco Police Department detective, passed away on Sunday, September 10, 1961 at Pacific Presbyterian Hospital. Travis had been born in Horsham, England on July 4, 1876. He was a loving father, grandfather, son and friend whom will be missed dearly.

He leaves behind his wife of 53 years, Marguerite, four children and ten grandchildren. His many friends and family will miss the sunshine of his mischievous smile and quick wit. In lieu of flowers, it was Travis's wish that you please instead surprise three strangers with a random act of kindness.

A celebration of life will be held at 1:00 pm Saturday, September 16, 1961, at the Gersitz Funeral Home.

It was beautiful.

Yes, there was an immediate stab of jealousy when I read about his wife...

but just as quickly, there was happiness. My boy deserved a lifetime of love, and I know he returned it well. Proof of that was in the "pay it forward" line in his obit — a concept I'd taught him, and one that he was only too willing to embrace.

⇆ ⇆ ⇆

Although I was the one who had experienced death so recently, it was Travis I mourned. It was nearly impossible to believe I wept for a man who had been returned to the ether more than fifteen years before I sprang from it.

I think what made this all particularly unbearable was that to everyone in the world of here and now, nothing at all had changed. Misery loves company, true... but what it really *needs* is a sympathetic ear.

82: Can you dig it?

Does digging in a cemetery constitute grave robbery, even if you don't touch the coffin? After hours of pondering on my own — more than once bemoaning the fact that I couldn't ask anyone else for feedback — I figured out how I could do it.

Later that morning, I dropped the girls off at their dad's house. He was going to take them to the country club pool for a friends' birthday party, and I was absolutely thrilled that I didn't have to chaperone such an event again. Most of the parents at the club really weren't my kind of people — they had too much money, too much silicone, and made too many snotty jibes to put up with the likes of me... and vice versa.

Oliver would drop t hem off at my place after the Hello Kitty fiesta, probably around noon. So I had three hours, which should be more than enough time for me to find my buried treasure.

↩ ↩ ↩

After swooping in and making a few purchases at the closest home and garden store, I drove into Lake Meadow cemetery, and parked my car in the grave l lot adjacent to the area where I was buried. No, I decided right then: That's just too creepy to say. I parked near where *Jennie* was buried. There were two other cars in the small lot, but I couldn't see any other living people anywhere.

With a bang, the jitters hit me — and I hadn't even had any coffee, so it wasn't about caffeine. My hands were sweating and shaking so much, twice I nearly let the plastic-potted live daisy plant I'd just bought slip through my fingers as I was getting it from the trunk.

Once I had a firm grip on my alibi, I hoisted into my biggest purse onto my other shoulder. This bag was so huge, it could probably hold a toddler comfortably, and still have room left over for snacks. Along with my usual complement of everything a mother could ever need, I'd just tucked in a set of six metal skewers, a small trowel, a ruler, and a couple of plastic bags.

I checked the map on my phone, and moseying as calmly as one should in such a place, made my way toward Jennie's grave.

The cemetery was small, and actually pretty pleasant for a dead person storage facility. Gently rolling hills were dotted with trees and flowers along with the headstones, and cast-iron benches with wooden slats invited friends and family to sit back and spend some time with the dearly departed. The lawn had just been mowed, and the sweet smell of freshly-cut grass was soothing — helpful in this case because my nerves were pretty fried at this point.

The grave markers got progressively older as I walked — obvious from their distinct shape, engraving, and wear. Some faced into the sun most of the day were almost illegible, and looked slumped and sad. Jennie's headstone was hard to miss, because it was the only modern-looking one in the bunch. The original had obviously been replaced — probably thirty or forty years ago — which made it a sprightly thing here.

Her stone was lit by the mid-morning sun, and I could see the crystals in the otherwise dark granite flare and twinkle as I drew closer. It was actually really pretty... you know, as far as headstones go. It almost looked happy.

The engraved letters were crisp:

Genevieve diMedici
1878-1900
Believe you more every day

As if that wasn't enough to make me start tearing up, right at the top of the stone, etched inside a star, was one word: *dream*.

༄ ༄ ༄

Moving around to the side with the coffin six feet below, I knelt down in the shade of the stone — the spot that also best blocked the view of this plot from most of the cemetery.

Beneath me lay the bones I'd worn... and to say that didn't crack me to the core would have been a lie. For the first time in this whole process, I hesitated. Then I decided: If I wasn't meant to be here, I wouldn't be. By virtue of the fact that history had aligned in countless ways to lead me to this spot... well, it had to be right.

Under the guise of pulling weeds, I plucked a few blades of grass and a lopsided dandelion. Then I quietly withdrew the ruler from my bag, and counted off out seven inches from the center of the headstone's base. I marked that spot with a skewer, which melted into the ground all the way to its hilt. It was kind of like playing *Battleship*.

From the center of the base, look 7 inches out and 7 inches down.

At this point, I half expected someone to come over to ask me what I was doing, but nobody was looking at me. In fact, there were only two other people I could see, both in much newer sections of the cemetery, and they were clearly focused on their own losses.

I surreptitiously took a second skewer, and pushed it down about one inch to the right, and did the same with a third. They metal pokers were all going down the full 12 inches of their length without hitting anything. The plot thickened... perhaps literally.

With another quick glance around to make sure the coast was still clear, I pressed the fourth skewer into the dirt one inch further away from the headstone. This time, there was a *tink tink* sound as I stabbed something embedded in the ground.

Leaving the marker with a hit, I pulled out the other skewers, shoved them into the plastic bag, and set the daisy plant down on the ground in front of me. After quadruple-checking that nobody was watching, I withdrew my new little trowel, and quickly carved a hole in the grass, about four inches in diameter. I popped off the little bit of lawn like it was a toupee, and set it next to the daisy.

"Excuse me," came a voice from behind me. I think I peed a little from the shock. Recovering quickly, I put on my melancholy face, and slowly turned to see who had caught me dirt-handed. My flower-planting explanation was already forming on my lips.

There stood an older man looking down at me. He was wearing big mirrored sunglasses, and I could see my wide, panicked eyes reflected right back at me. It was tough to look at anything else.

"Is that your car over there?" he asked, pointing to my beloved auburn-colored horseless carriage.

"Yeah, that's mine," I tentatively replied, waiting for the other shoe to drop.

"Ah, well," he smiled, "you left your driver's side door wide open. I was going to close it for you, but didn't want to in case the car would lock you out."

"Oh! Thank you," I said, and so relieved it hadn't been something bad,

I found myself laughing way more than any normal person would in such a situation. Through giggles, I told him, "I was so intent on bringing these flowers, I guess I just forgot."

"Happens to me all the time," he said with a smile, and gave me the okay sign as he started to shuffle away.

I dashed back to the car and closed the door, somehow summoning just enough brainpower to confirm that I did, indeed, have my keys with me before doing so. My mind had been spinning so fast, I was getting all tangled up in half-considered ideas and random notions. So I stopped myself right there in the parking lot, and forced myself to close my eyes and take a few breaths. I needed to calm the hell down. As the last sixty seconds had demonstrated, I was absolutely not ready to deal with even the slightest degree of subterfuge.

With some semblance of normalcy achieved, I returned to where my story had left off — back at Jennie's graveside. Kneeling on the ground, I used the trowel to remove small shovelfuls of dirt under the patch I had removed. I put everything I took out in a separate plastic bag, so I could easily fill in the spot later.

Seven inches came and went, and then eight. Just about nine inches down, I felt it — a smooth, capped pipe of some sort. It was pointed down into the ground, so I didn't need to do any sideways digging to remove it. With one more nonchalant glance around, I pulled it out of the ground and took a quick look at my treasure. It was a metallic tube, about seven or eight inches long, with what looked like red sealing wax around the screw top.

I'd open it up and peek inside... later. For now, I just wanted to get the hell out of dodge. I slipped the tube into my purse's side pocket and carefully zipped it closed.

With the dirt I'd set aside, I filled the hole back in and stuck the grass rug on top. I thought about bringing the daisy plant home, but decided it should stay with Jennie — and besides, it would camouflage my little graveside surgery until the grass grew back.

After making sure the plot looked at least as as pristine as it had before, I got down on bended knee, and said a little prayer of sorts to the woman lying six feet below. I spoke not to the form I had animated, but sent a thanks to the soul who had been there before me, and who had given me the opportunity to understand, "It's better to have loved and lost, than to never have loved at all" from the inside out.

83: Curiouser and curiouser

My girls and their dad were waiting outside the door from me when I got home.

"I didn't think you'd be this early — sorry," I said as I scrambled to unlock the door with my dirt-stained fingers.

"We wouldn't have been, but they had to close the pool."

I must have looked a little freaked out, because he jumped in with, "Not because of one of our kids. Someone else's."

Taking the cue, and with some decidedly unladylike excitement, Lily asked, "Guess what, mom?" She didn't even wait for me to ask. "They had to make everyone get out of the pool because someone *pooped* in there!" Then she started giggling uncontrollably, and couldn't even squeak out another word.

Iris filled in the blanks. "It was a baby and he had diarrhea and it was brown and it went all over the place and it floated and it was *so gross*!" With her little kindergarten lisp, the last words came out like "thow growth," making Lily laugh all the harder.

༄ ༄ ༄

The girls were too old for naps, but since I wasn't ready to give up those still moments I'd grown to need and love, I enforced an hour of "quiet time" each day. They could read, draw or play in their room quietly. I didn't really mind what they did for that time, as long as they didn't make any noise. For them, it was a refreshing little pause during the day. For me, it was a plain old sanity saver for these last few days of summer vacation.

Once the girls had settled down with their books of choice, I had no more excuses. Why did I need excuses? Because I was afraid of what I would — or, perhaps, what I *wouldn't* — find. Maybe I just didn't want the mystery (and my final connection to Travis) to be over.

After plucking the tube out of my purse, I used a paper towel to wipe off as much of the dirt as possible. The end with the opening had red wax dripped all over it, presumably to make the thing waterproof. I hoped it had done its job.

With as gentle a touch as I could manage, I chipped off the wax seal, then with gentle turns, unscrewed the top of the silvery container.

 Peering into the darkness inside, I could see there was a paper within, rolled up like a scroll. When I went to shake it out, I gasped aloud to see my favorite stick pin from 1900 — which had been a gift from Travis — fall into my lap.

It was a pretty little piece, featuring a faux emerald set in silver, with amethyst accent stones at seven points around the central gem. I'd last worn it a couple weeks ago (DST, or Dream Standard Time), and seeing it again brought on a rush of memories — all beautiful, but each with a bite.

With a little more work, I was able to extract the paper from the little time capsule. Yellowed by age and stubbornly curled, I used both hands to smooth out the note on the table. The handwriting I recognized, but there was an unmistakable shakiness to the pen strokes. These words had been written by hands that were perhaps arthritic, or suffering from the tremors common to the elderly.

There were three brief — and curious — lines of text on the paper:

J-R: Ask your good friend whose name starts with A for a message from me. My love forever & always, T

84: *A is for answer*

My friend whose name started with A? There was Ashley, Arden and Angeline — and those three were just off the top of my head. The first two I knew from college, and the last I had worked with about five years ago. I hadn't been in touch with any of them since exchanging Christmas cards last year. More to the point, I don't think I had mentioned any of them to Travis. It only stood to reason that he would only write such a thing about someone he was sure I knew well.

It reminded me of those times when you're walking along the street when a car drives by, and the people inside wave at you as they speed by. You wave back, all the while trying to figure out which of your friends that could have been... because when a car drives by you going 35mph at night, you're not going to get a very good look inside.

I was drawing blanks, so did the only logical thing I could think of: I went over to Facebook and browsed through my connections. When I saw there were more than thirty results for the first letter A, I knew I needed more to go on.

Travis had written "good friend." A *good* friend is probably going to be someone I talk to regularly. Probably someone I'd even trust the kids with. Then, given that the ad that led me to the cemetery had been placed in 1961, there was a pretty good chance it would also be someone who was alive back then, too... so that cut out about ninety percent of my social network.

In that case, the only person who fit that bill was my neighbor, Aggie, which made no sense. The idea that Travis pointed me to the lady next door was possible, I suppose, but just didn't seem remotely likely. There just wasn't enough mystery about her.

She was A is for Awesome, though, and took care of the girls a lot. While she was even older than my parents, we had hit it off right after I moved in. Aggie had always been very friendly to us all, and seemed to be on a mission to fatten us up by always baking cookies and other treats.

In her favor was just one thing: I remembered mentioning her to Travis at least once, as the lady with the flower name who babysat Iris and Lily.

In the absence of any other viable leads, I decided to risk looking like an idiot, because the answer I needed could be just a few doors down the hall.

After holding off on opening the tube for so long, I was fresh out of patience.

"Hey girls!" I called to my reading beauties. "Want to go say hi to Aggie?"

Since visiting her always meant something to appease a sweet tooth, the kids were totally up for that idea. And if Aggie wasn't the person whose name started with A that I was looking for — hey, no harm done.

With my hand poised over the nickel door knocker, the adrenaline suddenly hit me. I took a breath and reminded myself that I saw the lady practically every day. If she didn't know what I was talking about, that was fine. I'd figure it out soon enough.

I got my zen back just in time, because Iris was tired of waiting, and rang the doorbell before I even had a chance to knock.

About twenty seconds later, Aggie opened the door, smiling a megawatt grin when she saw the three of us. "How are my favorite girls?" The kids bounded in the door and went to play with her cats or watch TV or eat Play-Doh, or however they usually whiled away the hours. They were safe and I didn't have to worry, which allowed me to focus on the one thing that I was now absolutely dying to know.

"I feel really stupid asking you this," I said, getting off to a great start, "but did you by any chance know someone named Travis Donovan?"

For several long moments, Aggie just stood there, smiling. I didn't know what that meant, and given that the lady was pushing 70, I was a little worried she hadn't heard me.

"Travis Donovan, from San Francisco."

Finally Aggie spoke the words I had, in a way, waited a century to hear. "As a matter of fact, I did know Travis. I knew him very well."

Goosebumps riddled the flesh on my arms and down my back. "Really? Are you serious?"

She nodded and smiled and was clearly delighting in this all. "He was my grandfather."

Aggie was Travis's *granddaughter*? That seemed impossible. She obviously misunderstood what I said... or was getting a little senile.

"Sorry — but just to clarify: I'm talking about Travis Donovan, born in 1876."

"That's right," she replied, "Travis James Donovan, born in England on July the fourth, 1876, and later moved to San Francisco."

I think my jaw dropped — down to about a mile below sea level.

"Travis was your grandfather? Your biological grandfather... or adoptive, or in spirit?"

She broke into her deep, hearty laugh. "He was my flesh and blood, but he even said you might have a hard time putting that together at first."

Indeed I did, though my confusion was based largely on appearance — clearly an unreliable indicator. But to be fair, my boy had been a skinny white British boy, and Aggie was a full-bodied American woman, with skin colored a rich mahogany.

"Your Travis," she said, and I liked those words, "married a black woman — in those days, they called us colored or negro or worse — so my father was half and half. Then my daddy found the love of his life in a girl named Cleo, my mother, who was also black." With a magician's flourish, she added, "So here I am!"

Shock. Happiness. Amazement. Pride. Excitement. All these emotions and more were jumping up and down, vying for attention inside my head.

"Wow — I guess I'm a little surprised," I finally said. "Happy, of course — but surprised."

"You want to know something else?" Aggie said as she opened her front door wide and made a sweeping gesture to encourage me inside. "He told me stories about you, my dear — ever since I was a tiny girl." She clutched me up in a little hug as I went inside. "So I've been waiting for this day for a very, very long time."

85: Behind the curtain

Once I came inside, Aggie invited me to sit down, then handed me a framed photograph of a smiling older man and a giggling little girl.

I looked closer, and realized and both the subjects looked vaguely familiar. Could that be Travis forty or fifty years after I'd last seen him? I closed my eyes and envisioned his face, and then I knew it was him. And the cute kid had to be Aggie — still at an age where the pigtails she sported looked adorable.

Aggie asked, "You know who that is, don't you?" With a smile on her face and tears in her eyes, she said, "That's me and my grandfather. That picture was taken in 1948, when I was four years old. He was 72."

After my eyes had taken in every detail of Travis's new/old face, I set the picture down on the table, angled toward me so I could still look at it while we talked.

"Before I get too carried away here, Robin, let me say that I'm very sorry for what you have been through recently," Aggie said. "I know it must be so hard, and you have my deepest sympathy for your loss."

Words I never thought I'd hear.

For the first time since my life in 1900 had ended, I had someone who understood, and who I could talk to. The floodgates opened, and all the tears that had been held back for the past few days came rushing out. Aggie gave me a big hug and let me sob into her shoulder until the tide ebbed. While I was recovering, she disappeared into the kitchen for a moment, and came back with a box of tissues and a cool, wet facecloth, which she gently placed over my eyes.

"Just relax, sweetheart. The hardest part is over."

I nodded from beneath the soothing terrycloth eye mask.

"There were a few things Gramps — Travis, to you — wanted me to tell you right away after you found me. Things he knew were on your mind. First off: About your party."

I tensed up. Couldn't help it.

"The party went ahead mostly as planned — well, it turned out to be a lot bigger than anyone expected, but it went off without a hitch."

She paused. "The difference, of course, was that it served as your wake. 'A celebration of Jennie' they called it... and from what I hear, it was a wonderful, joyful memorial, with song and dance, food and drink," she said. "You would have been proud, Robin. Hundreds of people showed up to say goodbye to you — but also to thank you, and to thank Gramps. As you might suppose, Officer Donovan was a bit of a celebrity at that point."

Taking the towel off my eyes, I smiled to think of all the praise heaped upon my boy... and how much that probably made him blush.

"What you didn't know was that the party was not what Travis expected in another way," she said, then leaned in. "He was going to surprise you."

"Surprise me? He told me about the photo he was getting framed."

"No, it's something else," she said. From a wooden box on the bookshelf to her right, she delicately removed a round Sterling silver trinket box, which featured an antique floral *repoussé* design running around the top and sides.

"Oh," I said, absolutely awestruck. "It's beautiful!"

Aggie tried to stifle a laugh with her hand. "Sweetheart," she said, "that's just the wrapping. Look inside."

The top half of the box popped off, and inside, nestled against white velvet, was a diamond and sapphire engagement ring. The stones weren't huge, but they had a brilliant cut, and the setting of the ring was very much of a gorgeous Victorian style. I removed the band from its nest, and reveled at how tiny it was. Sized for skinny little Jennie, it only would go up to the knuckle on my pinkie finger. Maybe, I thought, I'd wear it on a necklace.

Aggie poured us both some coffee while I admired Travis's stellar taste in jewelry.

"Forgive me for being nosy, but I simply must ask," she said. "What would you have — "

I interrupted her. "Yes. I would have absolutely, definitely said yes."

There was her laugh again.

"I still can't get over the idea that Travis was your grandfather? That just completely blows my mind."

"Yes, yes — he was my father's father. And though he loved all of his grandkids, we had a very special bond."

"Which was...?" I sniffed.

She smiled and leaned toward me. "You."

This was just too weird. Good... but so strange.

"My mother was very spiritual, very fanciful. Believed in fairies and all that. They had a naming ceremony for me when I was five days old, and hadn't told anyone what they were going to call me," she said. "So Gramps was there at the party — having a drink, celebrating with friends. He'd had grandkids already, and he was happy, but I wouldn't exactly say he was all that excited about what boiled down to being a fancy baby shower."

I nodded, and thought I might have a vague notion of where this was going.

"Well, when they got to the actual naming bit, everyone was standing around my parents and me to watch, but Gramps? Oh, he was was across the room, taking advantage of the buffet."

This made me laugh out loud, remembering not too long ago when I'd expected that he'd do the exact same thing at our party. "Some things never change, huh?" I said.

"Well, as he told the story, he had a drink in one hand and a cheese cracker in the other, and he'd just shoved the whole cracker in the mouth when he heard them announce my name... which is, as you know, is Agapanthus. Let's face it — it's a lousy name for a kid. But it's also very, very unique."

"It is that," I laughed.

"So he hears them say Agapanthus, and remembers you — forty some-odd years before — mentioning that name. He's so shocked that he inhales in surprise, and chokes on the cracker."

"Oh no!"

"It's okay — he was fine," she said, "Well, after a few punches on the back, anyway. He just loved to tell that story!" she laughed. "And though he mentioned you as someone important from his past, I was the only one he ever told about who you really were. When you were really from."

"So you have known it was me all this time? You never said anything."

"Yes, I knew — from the minute you moved in. But, see, Gramps had made me promise that I'd wait until you came to me. He was concerned about messing up the timeline, I think. From the sounds of it, you didn't — or *don't*, rather — really understand how it all works.

"You've had no problem accepting all of this?"

She smiled as she ran her hand along the top of the picture frame, while her other hand went to her heart. "I have heard your story ever since I could understand words. I never judged it, because it just *was*."

I didn't know what to say. So much to process.

"There's so much more, of course — he and I had so very many adventures in your name," she laughed. "Not the least of which was burying something in a graveyard."

Picturing Aggie on her hands and knees, digging in the cemetery was an even more bizarre thought than imagining Travis doing the same.

"So it was you who hid the note for me to find, so I could come and find you?" I was still trying to get a handle on this... and failing.

"I had to wait until you found it — *if* you found it. Then we both would know it was real. We made the note purposely vague. It would have no real meaning to anyone else — it had to be you." She cocked her head and asked, "Tell me how you found out where to look?"

"The newspapers! The classified ads. He wrote me a message with the exact same code he used when he first tested me."

She nodded and smiled. "Just what we hoped," she said. "We were a little worried, actually, there might be some retroactive crossover of messages. We didn't want you to discovered the other set of personal ads when you did the search for the ads from 1900."

"It probably helped that the information about the cemetery wasn't published until much later," I explained. "I didn't search that far into the future at first."

"That's part of what he thought: the timeline accommodated change, and rippled outward from there."

Words did not exist to express my delight at hearing those words — and that crazy brand of logic — coming from another human being in this time zone.

"Now I don't want to put a damper on your happiness, little songbird, but there were another few things Travis wanted you to hear from me."

I nodded.

"He said you would want to know why things went the way they did that night, and what was really behind it getting to that point."

As my body gave a little involuntary shiver, I wasn't sure if this was information I really wanted to know. Then again, if my boy had wanted me to know..,

"Gramps talked to the lady Maggie several weeks after you, um, died... and confirmed what some version of you had already learned in another version of the timeline — that the man Walter had been jealous."

I sighed. "Not a big surprise."

"To hear her tell it, apparently, some discontent was stirred up when those two ran into you and Gramps walking on the street. That spurred the man's decision to risk everything on a big haul — the necklace from the Palace Hotel — so he could get out of town with a lot of loot. Story goes that he couldn't handle seeing you happy with someone else — healthy, strong, doing better than ever."

If Wally had only known it wasn't even Jennie in that body anymore, he might not have cared so much. Or, maybe, he would have been so freaked out, he might have run in the other direction. Either way, the outcome would probably have been better.

But when the insecure man's various plans failed, his frustration level apparently amped up. He kept looking for other scores, and all of those fizzled out before they even began. He couldn't figure out why.

And the day before I died, when I ran into Walt? He got paranoid because I was so close to his home. He didn't know what to make of that, and went back to his initial concept: Make a big score, then get the hell out of Dodge. Walter had hoped to prove to everyone how awesome he was... but really only proved that he had a textbook case of narcissistic personality disorder.

Aggie put her hand on mine. "Don't dwell on that, Robin. There are so many more good things to remember. Like these," she said, and produced another treasure from the seemingly bottomless black box — a stack of photographs I'd taken, none of which I'd ever seen printed.

As vibrantly as I remembered those days — only a month or two in the past, in terms of my experience — these pictures that I took with my own hands now look simply antique. I know that's all to do with film and processing techniques of the past, combined with the prints aging over the last century, but it just made my heart crumble a bit to see such a lively and colorful era captured forever as dreary, grainy black-and-white stills. I almost felt like my whole time in the Then has been misfiled.

"I have just a couple other things for you," she said, and disappeared into the room next door for a few moments, where I heard closet doors opening and closing. When Aggie returned, she set a large shoebox down on the table in front of me.

"My grandfather, you will soon see, was unapologetically sentimental."

Upon removing the lid from the box, I immediately smelled aged leather. I lifted back the yellowed tissue paper and laughed to see what lay within: my favorite black boots. And draped across the toes was one dried rose, which, despite its age, was still clearly hued a rich ruby red.

"Gramps told me there was a story about all of these. He wouldn't say exactly what it was, but said I could wait for you to tell me."

"The rose was part of a bouquet he brought to me on what I guess was our first official date," I said, smiling as I recalled the events of my not-too-distant past. "And as for the boots, well... I have always been a lousy housekeeper — leave stuff out everywhere," I said. "Like dropping my shoes right where I took them off... in this case, next to a chair in the living room."

"So these," I said, gingerly removing the tiny, pointy-toed boots from the box and setting them in my lap, "are what I tripped over one day when I happened to have Travis over for lunch. I was carrying a plate of cookies, and didn't see them on the floor, and fell straight into your grandfather's arms."

I looked over at Aggie, who looked a little amused... but also a little confused.

With blush starting to fill my cheeks — suddenly acutely aware that I was talking to his kid's kid — I added the most pertinent detail: "And, well, falling on him led to our first kiss."

Aggie laughed and winked. "Which, I suppose, eventually led to this," she said, and handed me a small leather-bound book with a buckle holding it closed. "This was his journal, but he kept it for you." She dabbed her eyes with a handkerchief that looked as old as Jennie's black boots. "He said for me to tell you to read it from the beginning, not — how did he say it? 'Not skip around like you usually do.'"

The words she said, together with the accent, was so spot on that I promptly demonstrated how tears mixed with laughter make a huge snotty mess. Aggie handed me three, four, then five tissues.

"Let me keep your sweet girls here for a little while — I'll give them dinner. You go back over to your place and read."

I nodded and clutched the journal to my chest with my left hand while swabbing my face with my right.

Today had held so much weirdness compressed into such a small amount of time, my heart and mind and soul were all reeling. Losing Travis so suddenly, then getting little bits and pieces of him back like this was a strange brew of pleasure and pain.

"Robin?" She snapped me out of my reverie. "Just so you know — my Gramps absolutely adored you. *Adored* you. He loved my grandmother deeply, and she knew it... but I think that diary will make it clear that you were forever in his heart."

86: *Messages from the past*

Before I had the strength to open it, I brought the journal to my face. Breathing in deeply, I let the scents interplay — leather and paper, sandalwood and cigars, dust and time.

I started at page one, per Travis's request. Before I realized it, two hours had passed. Although the book held scarcely more than a hundred pages, every passage deserved to be read more than once. Sometimes, too, I'd use my finger to trace the loops and points of his handwriting, and imagine him penning each word.

Several of the entries were personal, or related to little shared moments from our past which would have no meaning to anyone else. But more than a few offered his well-seasoned reflections on history as it happened, and those deserved to be shared. Below are some hand-picked passages from the pages of this treasure.

◞ ◞ ◞

August 8, 1900: My Dearest Jennie-Robin,

Two months gone and the moments surrounding your passing still echo in my mind constantly.

I never thought I'd lose you in such a sudden manner. You came into my life with such purpose, I thought we'd be together for years, not mere months. It was almost unfathomable to me you would be snatched back to your time so soon.

I understand now, I think. This was how it was meant to be. You are a martyr in the most loving, wonderful way. You gave yourself for the greater good.

I mourn your loss with feverish agony; which I tell you not to bring any pain or guilt, but only so you understand how very much your soul has been etched into my heart.

September 15, 1901: President McKinley died yesterday, in a terribly unpleasant manner, after having been shot last week. When he was not immediately killed, I thought perhaps history had been subverted; now I understand it was only delayed. I do not know why I find this fact (outside of the sad certainty of his death) to be disappointing.

March 12, 1903: Using the funds you bequeathed to me, I have purchased several properties throughout the city. They are of low to moderate value at present, but, I plan to reinforce these buildings to withstand shaking and combustion as much as practicable, using very modern materials and construction methods. The same process I am applying to our home on Clayton Street. Three years from now, I expect to find out how well I have accomplished this rather arduous task. But I do it gladly, and in your name.

April 18, 1906: The earthquake roared into the city early this morning. You were right — the devastation is simply shocking. Fires burn as far as the eyes can see, and those same eyes water from both sadness and the acrid smoke that fills every inch of air.

I know you told me to get out of town, but, with loving apologies to you, I did not. Will explain my reasoning later. For now, I'm grateful to have survived, and need to go to help those suffering.

April 20, 1906: I am one part awed at the most major of your predictions to have come true so far (despite expecting same); and nine parts dismayed at the extent of the destruction. A gent today described downtown as "damned," and it could almost be considered true.

April 25, 1906: The fires are out and our once fair city lies in shambles. I feel blessed to be secure in the knowledge that SF will rise like a Phoenix from the ashes, and go on to be stronger than ever.

As for my lack of departure, per your repeated request: I could not leave knowing so many lives and homes would not be spared. As the only one who had truly prepared for such an event, I felt certain I must make myself immediately available to those in need.

My properties "miraculously" survived, and throughout these locations, I had long been stockpiling food along with hundreds of bottles of water and other packaged beverages. Further, I assembled basic medical supplies, packing them into cloth bags so I would be able to distribute them as needed then the time came. Also on hand: Clothing, shoes, and even some toys for the little ones.

You might ask: Didn't people question the quick availability of such supplies? Turns out most people were grateful and elated than in the mood for much questioning. The few who inquired were told the items had been donated by an anonymous citizen. I thought of you as I said those words, and could well envision the smile you would have worn had you been there to hear.

July 18, 1906: Three months have passed since the quake, and our city has shaken off the embers well and is starting the rebuilding process. People are still in camps, but I have been able to house well over a hundred men, women and children in the dwellings I purchased.

And now, an admission.

How silly it is, with you so far away, that I have been putting off telling you something. But I will do so now: I have met someone. She is not you, but a wonderful woman in her own right. Her name is Marguerite, and I met her whilst helping people whose homes were destroyed in the earthquake and resulting fires. She's a widow, as her husband died in the fire. He had returned to their apartment to rescue his mother; sadly, they both perished.

As you are acutely aware, I held some misconceptions, shall we say, as to the intelligence of those you say are best termed African American. Without you setting me straight, I might never have made Margie's acquaintance.

I tell you this in the hope and belief that you wish me to find happiness in your permanent absence. I feel tremendously grateful for your ongoing influence in my life, and credit you directly for enabling me to have helped many folks, including Margie, and to have been open to a relationship with this woman.

Truly, Jennie-Robin, I think you would be pleased to have made her acquaintance. She is whip-smart and clever, has a marvelous laugh, and a mouth (like yours) she's not afraid to use, even if the words get her into trouble.

October 19, 1906: Tomorrow is my wedding day. It is bittersweet for me, as I fully intended to marry but once, and have you as my bride. But, having become well versed in destiny's stubbornness, things that are not to be will not be.

So, my sweet Jennie-Robin, while I know you would never expect otherwise, know my wife will not replace you any more than I will replace Marguerite's late husband.

If you have ever wondered if it is possible to wholly love two people at the same time, I can tell you it is. If you were both here together, that would not be a healthy circumstance, in my view. But as it is today, it proves life is intended to be joyous.

You have been, and will always remain, a true joy.

January 19, 1910: It's been ten years today since you and I first met, and I began one of the most thrilling and wonderful adventures of my life. Thank you for our time together, and the magnificence you left behind.

June 8, 1910: Ten years since I lost you. A decade. I can scarcely fathom such a thought. You are still very much in my heart, and your loss is always remembered. Know that I consider you my angel.

April 15, 1912: When I first read the news of the *Titanic* last week, all reports suggested casualties were minimal. I was a lone voice of reason against a tide of men who would not accept otherwise. I was unable to convince any party this was a disaster of epic proportions; and therefore did not in any way assist in minimizing the death count.

Abashedly, I admit that much of these past few days was spent mourning this gift of foreknowledge, and wondering its purpose if not to help.

Today, however, I shook off this anger and resumed preparations to help where and when I am able.

November 12, 1918: At long last, the Great War has officially ceased. The fighting — together with the toll of influenza — has turned our world into a grievous nightmare for far too long.

I remember some of what you had told me of the horror, but was unprepared for the fierce grip it took over humanity. The loss of life in France and Russia in particular is beyond anything I can conceive.

I mourn all of this destruction, and with a heavy heart know we will be facing a similarly egregious battle in little more than two decades hence.

It is most clear that a lesson was not learned.

November 20, 1922: Today, ran into a certain Mister Andrew Graham. You will remember him as Priscilla's baby boy. I happily report that he has turned into a fine young man, who is at University, training to become a physician. (He said he hoped to go into the burgeoning business of film, but bowed to his mother's wishes. I wondered what you would have said to him about that!)

February 2, 1930: I wish you to know this because you will appreciate it, and because you made it possible in a hundred different ways: I have been able to feed thousands of people over the past many months.

This has been done anonymously, because I am merely a trustee. You should know many folks, including hundreds of little children, have resisted starvation due to processes you began during your short time here. If that is not a remarkable legacy, I don't know what is.

May 27, 1937: At noon today, my family and I crossed the brand-new Golden Gate Bridge! For four years, we have watched this marvel being built, and the whole city is dancing with delight.

Years back, of course, there was great debate about whether or not the bridge should be built. I was always for its construction, as I knew from you it would come to be, and it would be one of the most recognizable symbols of American ingenuity.

January 28, 1944: My newest granddaughter was born last week. She's a beautiful little lady named Agapanthus. Unbeknownst to her parents, I think I shall make her a partner in all of this. You know why.

September 4, 1945: This war is now over, and I am grateful you spared me the worry of the details. I would not have been able to believe such things as Hitler, and Hiroshima. It's as if the devil has shown his face repeatedly.

I feel like now I can finally breathe again. Now, we wait for our country to get back on its feet. Enough time has been wasted, and far, far too many lives have been sacrificed.

Many times over these years, I have wondered why you did not have me eliminate Hitler. I have come to understand it is not something I could have done (particularly if it meant killing a then- innocent boy) and I further expect it is not something your "timelords" would have permitted.

If, however, you return to an era before he comes to power, I do suggest availing yourself of anyone who might be able to nip that bud. You now have a second opinion that says such action would be be worth nearly any risk.

September 5, 1945: I couldn't sleep, thinking you might consider my statements of yesterday to be in some way arrogant or otherwise as if I was not approving of your course of action. Nothing could be further from the truth. I recognize (as much as an observer can) the difficulty of your position, and the love and honor you bring to all you touch.

June 12, 1948: You did it again. Aggie watched with me from the stands as a bay colt named Citation took the Triple Crown. The hefty chunk of change we won will be donated to our foundation... except for the part we plan to use to buy my granddaughter her very own horse.

January 19, 1950: It's was fifty years ago today that I met you. Fifty years gone, yet you won't be born for twenty five. Yes, these thoughts sometimes make me feel as if my mind has already gone quite feeble.

December 25, 1952: I will say only of today: What a beautiful, joyful, unforgettable surprise.

March 6, 1954: Recently read a story by Ray Bradbury in Collier's called "A Sound of Thunder." It has prompted me to suggest: When time traveling, please be ever-mindful of your potential impact on the future. Cause and effect may not be clear. You are far too dear to me to risk being lost to time, particularly due to the merest of errors.

April 4, 1956: Not one hour ago, I saw Elvis Presley on Uncle Miltie, and thought he was ludicrously wonderful! My family all thinks I have lost some of my precious few remaining marbles. (Side note: I seem to have initially remembered his name as Evlis rather than Elvis, which brings my clan even greater amusement.)

July 4, 1956: Today is my 80th birthday. Positively remarkable. If you still think of me as that nimble young man, you should see me now! I hope it won't make you uncomfortable for me to tell you I still love you and think of you often. (My wife understands this, as she keeps her own first husband close at heart. Needless to say, she is a wonderful, kind, understanding soul. Given that you and I could not be together, I have been absolutely blessed with her presence.)

September 10, 1956: Elvis (or *Evlis*, to his friends) was on Ed Sullivan last night, and as you might say, my "mind was blown." I finally heard his rendition of "Love Me Tender," which I well remember from you. This old man's eyes got a little damp.

January 27, 1959: My granddaughter turned fifteen today, and she is a constant delight. Her character was born with her, and I fully understand how you came to appreciate her, and trust her with your most precious daughters.

You might be interested to know, Aggie well understands how unique the relationships are: of me to her, me to you, and you to her. She marvels at it all. (She also knows how to keep a secret.)

Agapanthus

September 1, 1961: Feeling weaker this day than any other, but then, I am a very old man, and such is to be expected.

Before it gets much later, you must know some things.

First: Please realize, my dear Jennie-Robin, that because of you, I have come to anticipate an afterlife. (If there is not a higher power, how else would you have possibly have been known to me?)

Additionally: Excepting for our Agapanthus, I have never told anyone you were from the future. It would serve no good. Further, their inevitable disbelief would only harm your memory, or make them think I was delusional.

Finally: Thank you, thank you, thank you — yesterday, today and forevermore.

September 9, 1961: Ridiculous as it might seem, I thought I'd have more time. I even selfishly prayed I might hang on long enough to see you arrive in this world; now I am certain it is not to be.

I expect that by this hour tomorrow, I will be flying among the wishes and the hopes and the dreams; where the rhythm of time carries a completely different beat. There, I hope, I will eventually find you again.

Until then, know in your heart you have been adored for more than sixty-one years. I remind myself of the same.

With great love always,

Travis

87: The Long Goodbye

Over the course of more than three months, I made steady — but slow — progress toward getting back to my old self.

After one month, I stopped crying randomly throughout the day.

After two months, I no longer cried daily. I created new tactics to cope with life in this singular world.

And three months after I lost my other life, I wasn't all better, but I could hold it together without constantly reminding myself how fortunate I was and how grateful I should be. (I was aware, too, that part of my problem had completely selfish roots: I missed being unique, along with the almost supernatural ability to tweak time.)

But then I discovered that returning to my previous starting point was not enough. After my time in the past, I had a new normal, with higher expectations — both for myself and the world itself. Of course that wasn't a *bad* thing, but meant my already exhausted soul still had a little further to climb.

Every day, I wondered if I'd ever feel joy again.

↜ ↜ ↜

As tortuous as that time was, looking back, I can see now that it was necessary. Without the reflection that was part of the long healing process, I think I would have missed the point, and maintained the self-centered assumption that this was all about me.

Every day, and with every person I met in the Then, I created tiny ripples in time that hadn't been there before. As those waves moved through the years, they repaired some breaks, smoothed some bumps, and balanced some injustices.

Had the changes I made completely altered this world I live in today? Probably not in any major way... but suppose that I'll never really know. Besides — who's to say that whatever changes I created have seen themselves through already? Just as easily as I could have re-aligned history to help save a guy who went on to help achieve the US victory in WWII, there's a chance

I helped turn the tide on something hugely important that won't happen for another hundred years.

But I do have a feeling — call it a hunch, hope or faith — that I did my job, and the world is better for it in some small way.

I felt pretty sure that stopping Walt and Maggie from wreaking havoc had been a goal, but was not the only one. In particular, I think I helped set Travis on his path — giving him the tools and the motivation to help soothe some of the hurts in this world.

That, more than anything else, gave purpose to my loss. But still, each day, I longed to feel joy.

∽ ∽ ∽

I made it through Christmas, which was a triumph in and of itself, and at that point, all I had left was to get through the rest of this year. As my time in the past had started on New Year's Eve of 1899, that holiday, more than any other, served as a wistful reminder of what I used to have.

Aggie, my brood and I had been invited up to Vivian and Samantha's hillside house to watch the show that night, since their backyard offered amazing views of the city below. If you didn't want to battle the crowds, you couldn't ask for a better ticket.

Though I was hardly in the mood to celebrate, the girls were all pumped up — especially for the chance to be awake at the midnight hour. I agreed to let them go with one caveat: They had to go to bed at the normal time, but I'd wake them up in time to get to see the show. Lily set her alarm and I set mine (in case my insomnia reversed itself just for fun), and the kids shuffled off to dreamland.

I, on the other hand, settled down with an espresso and a book. In fact, I was reading in bed when there was a quiet knock on the front door. I glanced at the clock — it was already after ten.

Peering through the door's peephole, I saw a profile of a face turned down the hall, and a bit of white hair. It looked like Jim, the guy with the maximum allotment of eight cats, who lived at the far end of the hall. After unlocking the various bolts and the chain, I opened the door, the question as to why he was here already primed and ready to go.

But it wasn't Jim. It wasn't anyone I'd ever seen through these eyes before, either. The words, just a moment ago on the tip of my tongue, evaporated as the face — aged, but with a noble profile — turned to me. I knew him in an instant, and he recognized me just as quickly. Despite the slight stoop and the years having written a thousand lines on his face, Travis's eyes were as blue as ever, and his smile just as sweet and mischievous as it had always been.

Without a word, I pulled him close for a hug. He felt solid under my arms. So warm and real and comforting. When I finally let him go, I just stared at this much, much older version of the man I once knew, and asked, "How?"

With a grin and a wink, he put his finger to my lips. I asked no questions — too scared to break the spell. Somehow, I knew that whatever events had coincided to allow him this time here, it was all as delicate as a soap bubble. At any instant, and with the slightest pressure, it could all be gone.

Slipping my hand in his, I welcomed him home.

The girls were sleeping, but I wasn't going to miss this chance. I brought Travis over to where my eldest was fast asleep, curled up with a book in one arm, her pillow in the other. We both admired her for a moment, then he gently traced her cheek with her finger. Across the room, my littlest was sleeping sprawled out on top of all the covers, looking perfectly angelic and content. When he touched her hand, it was adorable to see Iris's fingers curl for just a moment.

Then we danced the way we had once upon a time — swaying to the melody inside our heads. Travis spun me out, and when I returned to his arms, the person who caught me was the young man I had known just a few months ago... but also so many years ago. He pulled me close, and my head nestled perfectly into the little space between his neck and shoulder.

I knew that this was probably just a dream. But if a dream had given me such a magnificent adventure before, well... who cared?

For what seemed like hours, Travis and I played and danced, reminisced and reconnected. Finally, warm and exhausted, we fell asleep in each others' arms.

I hate alarm clocks was my very first thought when the annoying little klaxon went off at a little past eleven that night. After a moment of disorientation, I realized I was in bed, alone, in the Now — and it was time to get the kiddos up to see the fireworks.

I fought myself not to over-analyze my earlier adventure, and to accept it for whatever it was — dream, reality... or something in between.

Half an hour later, Aggie, the girls and I were high in the hills, walking out onto a deck that offered breathtaking views of Oakland, the Bay, and the stunning San Francisco skyline beyond.

As I sat down on one of the benches, my fingers traced over the delicate ring hanging around my neck, and I bit my lip to resist the tears that the little gold band always seemed to provoke. Aggie caught my eye, smiled then looked away, as if apologetic for interrupting my moment.

As the countdown from ten began, Lily and Iris came over and scooched next to me, one on either side, snuggling close against the chilly midnight air. A moment later, our entire world was filled with shimmering arcs of color, each bursting out of a backdrop of a velvety black. Holding tight to the people I'd brought into this world, I saw the dance of the fireworks reflected in their smiling eyes.

Right then — and without remembering to brace myself against the weepiness that always accompanied such a thought — I wished Travis could be here with us. A heartbeat later, the wind changed direction, and an odd little sensation burst into being, catching me by surprise.

It was joy.

About the author

Born with a super-sized "can do" attitude and a love for words, Nancy J Price started self-publishing music fanzines at age 14, and graduated to interviewing major-label rock bands at 16. Not quite a decade later, during a three-year-stint in the music industry, she moonlighted as a freelance writer, earning bylines in *Parents* and the *San Francisco Chronicle*, among other publications.

Together with her best friend, Nancy co-founded SheKnows.com in 1999, and helped turn it into a top lifestyle website for women, reaching more than 30 million readers per month. While serving as the site's Executive Editor for twelve years, Nancy also helped launch five national newsstand magazines, including *ePregnancy* and *Cooking Smart*.

A fourth-generation San Francisco Bay Area native, Nancy now lives in Arizona with her four kids, husband and their menagerie. *Dream of Time* is her first novel. See her portfolio and the latest from her online at **nancyjprice.com**.

Notes & thanks

This book really began while doing research on my own family's history. In fact, genealogy inspired me to create two projects — this book, and the ClickAmericana.com site, which features hundreds of articles and other fun stuff from throughout American history.

And by searching my ancestry, I found records showing that my great-grandmother, Genevieve Segarini Robinson (born in San Francisco in 1890 to Italian immigrants), went by "Jennie" during her younger years. I hope she would be happy to have her name memorialized in such a way.

I am incredibly grateful to the US Library of Congress, particularly their "Chronicling America" project, which allowed me to spend hundreds of hours reading newspapers of the era. (Thanks, too, to the University of California Riverside for providing the images of the *San Francisco Call* to the LOC.)

A hat tip also given for the wealth of historic resources on the Internet Archive (archive.org), including the many contributions of the San Francisco Public Library, the New York Public Library, and the Google Book Search. Finally, Berkeley California's Bancroft Library was very helpful, and I'm proud that their collection includes many items from my family's history.

Read Robin's journal, find bonus content & see more at DreamOfTime.com

∽ ∽ ∽

Text from the speech in Chapter 45 adapted from material published in the *The San Francisco Call* on May 31, 1896.

Text from the news story in Chapter 49 adapted from statements in *Proceedings of the Annual Convention of the American Bankers' Association, Volume 31* from 1905, courtesy Harvard University, via Google Books.

Kangaroo walk explanation from the *Montgomery Tribune* in Montgomery City, Missouri; November 9, 1900.

"Ready for tea" image on page 266 from *The San Francisco Call.*, September 16, 1900.

∽ ∽ ∽

Trademarks: This book identifies product names and services known to be trademarks, registered trademarks, or service marks of their respective holders. They are used throughout this book in an editorial style only. Use of a term in this book should not be regarded as affecting the validity of any trademark, registered trademark, or service mark. Unless noted, Synchronista LLC is not associated with any product or company mentioned in this book.

Disclaimer: Although every precaution has been taken in the preparation of this work, neither the author(s) nor publisher shall have any liability to any person or entity with respect to any loss or damage caused or alleged to be caused directly or indirectly by the information contained in this work. The information in this book is distributed on an "as is" basis, without warranty.

Made in the USA
San Bernardino, CA
13 September 2013